THE JESUS FACTOR

"I meant to take a whole week to read *The Jesus Factor*, and started at six in the evening. But once I got into it, I couldn't put the book down until seven the next morning.

"It's a brilliantly sustained sardonic novel with a double whammy of a big idea that keeps you reading to the last page. The twist at the end even convinced *me*. Edwin Corley is a fascinating storyteller."

—Mario Puzo, author of *The Godfather*

Edwin Corley

STEIN AND DAY / *Publishers* / New York

THE JESUS FACTOR

FIRST STEIN AND DAY PAPERBACK EDITION 1984
The Jesus Factor was first published in hardcover
by Stein and Day/*Publishers* in 1970.
Copyright © 1970 by Edwin Corley
All rights reserved, Stein and Day, Incorporated
Designed by David Miller
Printed in the United States of America
STEIN AND DAY/*Publishers*
Scarborough House
Briarcliff Manor, N.Y. 10510
ISBN 0-8128-8104-4

FOR

Sol and Renni,
who know why.

Contents

BOOK ONE

Tickling the Dragon's Tail

In the Utah desert, west of Salt Lake City, there was once an Army Air Corps base named Wendover Field, where the men of the 509th Composite Group practiced to drop the atomic bomb. As you drove out of the base, it was impossible to miss a sign that read:

> What you hear here
> What you see here
> When you leave here
> Let it
> Stay here!

"It's the Cuban Missile Crisis all over again," the President said. "With one important difference. This time *we're* the ones being told to get out."

I sat in the Oval Office at the White House, puffing uselessly on a pipe that had gone out long ago.

The President passed a packet of matches to me. They bore an advertisement for the International Correspondence School in Scranton, Pennsylvania. I shook my head, as discouraged about the chances of keeping my pipe lit as about this post-midnight conversation.

"Under the circumstances," President Howard Foster went on, "I think you ought to moderate your statements about the ABM program."

"I'm sorry, but I can't do that, sir," I said. "You know how strongly I'm opposed to escalating Safeguard. Those missiles are eating us out of house and home."

"Damn it, Hugh!" the President snapped. "Don't make wisecracks. This is serious."

"I know it is," I said. "That's why I want to see us get our ABMs out of Japan."

"You suggest we knuckle under to the North Koreans?"

"We never should have put missiles over there to begin with."

"The Japanese government requested them," said the President. "*Defensive* ABMs to protect Tokyo and—"

"Come on," I said. "Who the hell would be bombing Tokyo these days? Those ABMs are there to tighten the ring around China, and China isn't buying it."

"You don't know the whole story," Foster said, spreading both hands on the glass top of his desk, pressing hard with his fingertips. "Suppose I order you to cancel your trip?"

11

"That's one of the benefits of the system," I said. "You can't."

"All right," he said, looking at me as if I were very much the Junior Senator from New York. "We *are* tightening the ring around China. So is the Soviet Union."

"Contain seven hundred and fifty million people?" I said. "Good luck."

Now Foster's hands were nervous fists. "Hugh, it's almost three A.M. and I've got an important meeting at eight. Can't we wrap this up? I'm asking you to cancel this tour of yours. The last thing we need right now is a U.S. senator rocking the boat."

"Sir, I wish I could accommodate you. I mean that. But there's more to my trip than just the Safeguard program."

"Talk all you want about disarmament," he said. "But lay off the ABMs."

"Not unless you tell me why."

He stood up, his shoulders slumping wearily. I could not help feeling sorry for him. Seven years in office had aged Howard Foster tremendously. I wondered what it would do to me if my bid for the nomination succeeded and I got the job.

"All right," Foster said. "That's the way it is. Tomorrow morning I'm going to put out the word to slow you down. I hope your tax forms are in order."

"I wouldn't have it any other way," I said, anger tightening my voice.

The President looked away, stared out the window for a moment, then turned back to me. When he spoke his voice was quieter. "I'm sorry, Hugh. This thing's got me all disconnected. You know I wouldn't harass you. I'm just sorry you won't see things my way."

"I'm sorry I *can't* see them your way."

He walked with me to the door, one hand on my shoulder. I had always held the impression that Howard Foster was taller than I, but either I was wrong or this night had somehow shrunk him.

12

"Celia's outside," I said. "She's smart enough to know something's up."

"Tell her the truth," Foster said. "At least I can get back at you by keeping your wife up the rest of the night writing. I hope you like sleeping alone, you bald-headed bastard. Just tell Celia not to let a word get beyond her typewriter until six A.M."

"That's the time, then?"

The President sighed, easing me out the door.

"That's the time," he said.

I rode the elevator down to the White House garage. Celia was talking with a Secret Service man and making notes on the long fold of yellow copy paper she always carried in her purse.

"Thank you, Frank," she said as I joined them.

"Good morning, Senator McGavin," said the Secret Service man.

"Morning, Frank. How's the bowling game?"

"What?" he said, first surprised and then flattered that I remembered. It's a trick I picked up in my first political campaign, seizing on some minor detail about people I meet and filing it away for future use. "Well, I was on my way to three hundred last week. Then"— nodding his head toward the ceiling—"*He* decided to go for a walk. I tried to get off one more and guttered it."

"Too bad." I gave him a gentle punch on the arm and joined Celia in her blue Mercedes. I have neither the legs nor the hair for sportscar riding. The legs are too long, and I end up propped on my ankles. The hair is long-since gone, and I wear a cap to keep from windburning my scalp.

My wife, on the other hand, is a born sportscar accessory. The wind catches her tawny hair and tumbles it around. Her green eyes blaze away, and her gloved hand coaxes the stick shift through five forwards or whatever the hell goes on underneath the floorboards. The hand on the wheel usually holds the little microphone from her Sony casette recorder as she dictates half a dozen juicy items for her column, "Celia Down the Potomac."

This morning she left the microphone in its magnetic nest and, without a word, handed me my leather cap. She was Being Ethical. I knew wild horses would not drag a single question from her about my nocturnal meeting with the President.

"It's all right, Ceil," I said. "The lid's off. Except you can't release it until six A.M."

"You don't have to tell me, Mouse," she said, accompanying the remark with a violent downshift as we passed a limping Ford. "Mouse" is her private name for me that goes more with bed than with a sportscar rocketing down Pennsylvania Avenue, but it always gives me a little tingling thrill in the pit of the stomach no matter where I hear it.

"I think I'd better. For one thing, I need advice."

"For yourself, for us, or for the good of the country?"

"All three, unless I'm wrong. The word has leaked out about our Third Generation Safeguard ABMs being in Japan."

The little Mercedes lurched; then Celia got her eyes back on the road and slowed down.

"I guess I gave myself away there," she said sheepishly after a block of silent driving. "Us lowly fourth estaters aren't supposed to know about the Third Gens."

"Don't worry, Ceil. I know you haven't been ransacking my notes. In fact, I haven't been keeping any. But I had an idea you knew we'd sneaked that complement of Safeguard Threes into Japan."

"Are you telling me I talk in my sleep? After all these years?"

"No, but when you read Robert Kennedy's *Thirteen Days* and follow it with Tuttle's *Analysis of the Japanese Constitution*, it doesn't take a genius to realize you know what's happening and where."

"I didn't want to be right," she said. "I never thought I'd see the day when the Japanese allowed nuclear weapons on their territory. Japan seemed like one last bastion of sanity in this lousy world."

14

"Well, we tried to pull a Khrushchev," I told her. "We set up two squadrons of Safeguard Threes with, I'm inclined to believe, a certain amount of collusion from the Soviet Union."

"Did you know about it?"

"Not in advance. By the time I found out what we were up to, it had already been done."

"Why didn't you blow the whistle on them?"

"In a way, that's what I intended to do with this junket. I figured that if a potential Presidential candidate went all over the world speaking against the ABM system, Foster and his hawks might decide to sneak the Safeguards out again. They might have, too. But as of six A.M. the game is up."

"Who found out?"

"The North Koreans are fronting. But there's no doubt the Chinese are behind them. All Foster's got so far is an eyes-only flash from the Swiss Consulate General in Pyongyang. There's no indication yet what the official North Korean reaction will be."

"They'll run a bluff, of course."

"Maybe," I said. "But even with a bluff, this is a dangerous time for everybody concerned."

"Let me guess what our fearless leader said. Now is the time for us to form the wagons in a circle and forget partisan views as we rally against the common enemy."

I smiled. "That's pretty close."

She did not smile back. "There's only one big catch," she said.

"Well, I told him to climb a tree, if that's what you mean."

"It's not. Hugh, if we've really done this—and I guess we have—don't you realize that makes *us* the common enemy?"

When my head snapped toward her, the wind streamed over the windshield, caught the leather cap, and whipped it away before I could grab it. Celia started to hit the brake, but I waved her on. "The hell with it. It's going to be quite a while before I'm riding in this crate again."

We drove over the Rock Creek bridge into Georgetown, and neither of us said another word.

Celia and I had met at the Tokyo Press Club on Shinbun Alley, around the corner from the huge Dai Ichi building that housed SCAP. I was twenty-seven, and I had just been elected to Congress. A meeting with President-elect Eisenhower's military aide had led to my being sent on a secret mission— ostensibly to tour Far East Air Force bases, but actually to hand-deliver a message to General Matthew Ridgway, then Supreme Commander of Allied Powers in the Far East.

"You mean you're a *congressman?*" Celia had said. I didn't blame her. I was wearing a sweat-stained flight suit, reeking with cockpit odors from the twenty-three-hour flight in a stripped-down B-26. Since my multi-engine ticket was still good, I had wangled a co-pilot slot on a ferry run instead of flying commercial. The only trouble was, some clod had forgotten to put my suitcase aboard the bomber. Until the PX opened the next morning, the flight suit was all I owned.

"The most junior of the junior," I said, sipping my Nippon beer.

"What are you doing in the press club? Giving interviews?"

"God, I hope not," I said. Then, flustered, "I mean . . ."

She laughed. At twenty-three, her face was lovely enough, but it had not yet formed into the strong beauty it would acquire later. "Don't worry, Your Honor, or whatever it is one calls congressmen. I'm not offended. Besides, I'm on R and R. No interviews tonight for this girl."

"What are you resting and rehabilitating from?"

She jerked her head toward the west. "Frozen Chosen."

"Good Lord," I said. "You're *that* Celia Craig!" In less than six months of covering Korea, Celia Craig had raised official eyebrows and blood pressures even higher than Marguerite Higgins had the year before.

She fluffed her collar and smiled. "Didn't recognize me out of uniform, hey sport? Well, don't worry about it. I just got back from Pork Chop Hill. And I've had more than a little to drink. Jesus, Congressman, when are they going to stop this nonsense?"

"I wish I knew," I said. "Ike sent me out here with a message for Ridgway. Maybe . . ."

Her look stopped me. She stared a minute, and when her voice came it was sharp. "What kind of congressman are you, anyway? You sit in this dive surrounded by reporters and calmly disclose that you're on a secret mission to SCAP from the President?"

"Sorry," I said. "You're right. It was a fool thing to say. Forget it, if your news-hen's conscience will let you. I'm just bushed. I've been at the controls of that damned B-26 for the last twenty-three hours."

Her eyes softened. "It's forgotten, Congressman."

"Call me Hugh."

"How about Hey Hugh?"

I groaned. She patted my shoulder.

"You look frazzled all right," she said. "Where are you staying?"

"Who knows? I didn't want to go banging at the Embassy door at this hour. My jeep driver thought I could get a room here, but the manager says they're full up. Guess I'll just sit."

She frowned. "You can't do that. Let me see what I can do."

She slid off the bamboo stool and went out to the front desk. A tall, bronzed man got up from his table and stood beside me.

"You're Hugh McGavin," he said. "You probably don't remember me."

I studied his face, which was lined with weariness. That seemed to be the common denominator for those in this room.

"*Collier's* magazine," I said. "Charlie Kern. Tinian. You covered those last days of the 509th."

"That's me. What brings you to Tokyo?"

"Nothing special," I said. "Call it a junket."

He looked at my greasy flight suit. "Looks like a working junket to me."

"On my salary, how else can I get in any twin-engine time? I swipe it from the Air Force."

"How long do you think you'll be here?"

"I hadn't decided. Why?"

Kern waved for a drink. "As long as you've got the time, I think there's something you ought to see."

"What's that?"

"Hiroshima."

I put the beer down with a thump. "That isn't funny, Kern."

"I didn't mean it to be funny, *Congressman*. What's the matter? Afraid to look at what you did?"

"Afraid isn't the right word. Why should I?"

"You guys were fast enough to help it happen."

"That was war. They didn't give us any choice."

"It seems I remember the guards at Buchenwald saying the same thing."

I sighed. While I have never made any particular secret about my involvement in dropping the first atomic bomb on Japan, I do not refer to it if I can avoid the subject. Kern was drunk, but not so drunk that he didn't know what he was saying. I wondered why he was baiting me.

"Drop it, will you?" I turned away.

His hand gripped my shoulder and pulled me back. "You haven't answered my question, *Congressman*."

"I thought I had. And take your hand off my shoulder before I break your wrist."

"You probably would," he said. "What kind of a government are we getting, when a killer like you—"

That was all he had time to say before my fist sat him down with a heavy "Whoomph!" He gasped for air.

Feeling ashamed of myself, I held down my hand to help him up. He batted it aside and struggled to a kneeling position. Two other correspondents came over and pulled him to his feet. One led him from the bar. The other turned to me.

"Charlie's just back from two months in the line," he said. "While he was over there, he got word his son bought it in a troop carrier crash at Clark Field. The kid was only nineteen, and Charlie's all twisted up over it. I wish you hadn't hit him."

I looked down at my clenched hand. "So do I."

The correspondent left, and I sipped at my beer. It had gone flat. I waved for another. When it came, it tasted flat too.

Charlie Kern had peeled away the protective covering I'd worn for seven years. And I didn't like what was underneath any more than he did.

"I hear you clobbered poor old Kern," said Celia Craig, sliding onto the stool beside me.

"Don't talk about it," I said. "I feel like a shit."

"You *are* a shit," she said cheerfully. "But don't feel too bad. We all are, in one way or another. And Charlie's been asking for it ever since he got back from Korea. I know he's got problems, but dammit, a man doesn't bleed in public."

"You lay it out there hard and cold, don't you?" I said.

"If you grew up the only broad in the *St. Louis Times* city room, you'd be hard too, my friend."

I looked at my watch. Almost three A.M., Tokyo time. Before I could stop myself, I was yawning.

"Look, Congressman," Celia said, "see that door over there? Well, you go through it, up one flight of stairs, and down the hall to the very end." She handed me a key, one of the old-fashioned ones with a long, round stem.

"Thanks," I said. "I guess I just didn't know the right people."

"No, he wasn't lying. They're full up. You're using my room."

I looked at her.

"Don't worry," she said. "Martha Kinney's out here doing a photo series for *Life*. I'll bunk with her."

"Miss Craig, if I were less tired, I'd try to be more of a gentleman, but—"

"Buy me breakfast in the morning and we're even. Okay, Congressman?"

"Make it Hugh."

"Okay. Hey Hugh."

"Goodnight."

"Goodnight, Congressman."

Halfway up the stairs, I remembered I hadn't paid the bill. Celia Craig would have reason to remember me—first I'd poor-talked her out of her room, and now she was stuck with the bar tab. I considered going back down, but decided one more entrance and exit would wear out my welcome.

The key rattled around in the hole for a couple of minutes before I managed to get the door open. Inside, I stumbled around trying to find the light switch, then finally lit a match and discovered that the overhead bulb was controlled by a dangling chain. A paper lantern covering the light made everything rosy, cheerful. It was a large room. Near the window was a huge bed with a brass bedstead. Along one wall was a sofa, and against another, a desk with a typewriter. The floor was littered with crumpled balls of yellow paper. I went over and read the three lines typed on the sheet in the machine.

> Last week, a young marine shared his
> last canteen of water with me. Today,
> in Tokyo General Hospital, he

That was all there was. I wondered what had happened to the young marine.

I took a fast shower in the tiny bathroom, and then, tucking my passport wallet with its enclosed message for General Ridgway under my pillow, crawled into bed.

The light bulb glowed at me through the Japanese lantern. I groaned, got up, pulled the chain, and slid back between the sheets. For a while I lay there, my head buzzing with weariness, listening to the grinding wheels of streetcars on a nearby street. Then, without knowing it, I was asleep.

I woke with a frightened start, as if the bed had dropped out from under me. The room was dimly lit by light from the street lamps outside, seeping through the window.

Someone was in the room with me.

I sensed, rather than saw, a shadow moving toward the foot of the bed. Then a white, circular blob over me.

I swallowed hard and croaked, "Who's there?"

The shadowy figure stiffened. A voice whispered, "Me."

"Who's me?"

"*Me*, goddammit!" said Celia Craig. She sat on the edge of the bed where the light could hit her face. "I didn't want to wake you."

Still numbed with sleep, I asked her what she wanted.

"The bedspread, Congressman, nothing more. Go back to sleep."

"What are you going to do?"

"Curl up on the couch. Now, don't argue. It's a hell of a lot more comfortable than some of the places I've been recently. You just go back to sleep, we'll talk in the morning."

The spread rustled as she stripped it from the bed. I heard her shoes drop on the floor, and then a soft whisper of what I presumed to be clothing being removed. Drowsily, I sighed.

"Are you still awake?" she whispered.

"Yes."

"I don't want you to get any ideas," she said. "I honestly thought I could stay with Martha. But when I got up there, I heard them having a great old time."

"Heard who?"

"Martha and her boyfriend."

"Oh."

We lay in the silent darkness for a while, and then—I don't know why—I asked, "What happened to the young marine?" She did not answer, and I added, "The one you were writing about?"

After a while she said quietly, "He died."

"Oh," I said again. I heard her twisting under the bedspread, and then, "Goodnight, Hugh."

I don't remember answering.

It was six-thirty when I awoke. The city outside was still dark, but some windows showed yellow lights. I lay there, listening for something I knew I would hear again, something that had dragged me up from the depths of sleep.

Then I heard her, crying softly—trying to stifle the sound but gasping with some feeling that was too strong for her to contain. At first I pretended to be asleep, not wanting to intrude on her private grief, whatever it might be. But then I had to reach out to her. "Celia?"

The sobbing continued.

I slid out of bed and went over to the sofa. There was enough pale light in the room for me to see her slim body, wrapped in the thin bedspread. When she turned and saw me, her arms reached up and I bent down into them and hugged her to me. She was clammy with sweat.

Gradually, as the tears subsided, she began to feel warmer.

"Oh, Jesus H. Christ," she said, still crying a little. "I'm sorry, Hugh. It just comes over me sometimes. I can't help it. I'm sleeping off a drunk and I wake up so afraid I want to scream. My heart pounds until I'm sure it's going to burst. But the worst is the fear—waves and waves of fear that strip away everything you think you are and leave you out there all naked and alone."

I stroked her damp hair. "What are you afraid of?"

"Of everything," she said. "Of the war, of being killed, of being disfigured. And most of all, I'm afraid of me. I'm afraid I'll crack, freeze up on a patrol and get some poor kid killed trying to drag me out."

"You don't have to go back, you know. You've done your job."

"Oh, yes I do," she said, anger changing her voice. "I've got to keep going back until those rat bastards in St. Louis eat their own gall. They're not going to have the pleasure of watching Celia Craig run. I'm going to pull a Pulitzer out of this, you just watch me, buddy boy."

She snuffled and rubbed the bedspread against her eyes. I held her quietly for a few minutes longer, and gradually she relaxed. Then, just when I was sure she was asleep, she turned her face toward me.

It started as one of those "Don't worry, here's a little tenderness and brotherly affection" kisses. That didn't last long. She wrapped her arms around my neck and pulled me against her with a sudden strength.

The first time is rarely the best; there are too many accommodations that must be made to unfamiliar limbs, to attempted caresses that go wrong, and—most vital—to the intricacies of timing, of response and pace. But this first time with Celia was one that we both still remember and talk about. For all of its rawness, its unexpectedness, that morning so long ago on a sofa in the Tokyo Press Club represents a high mark that has rarely been reached, even after all these years.

"Oh, God," she whispered. "I thought I'd go right out through the ceiling. It's been so long."

"Don't talk about it," I said, my face against the warm curve of her breast. "It's bad luck to talk about it."

"Just like a man. Ravish a girl's virtue and then you don't want to talk about it."

"Frankly," I said, falling into her mood, "I feel a little ravished myself."

She pulled back under the spread. "Listen, Congressman, if that's a crack . . ."

"No," I said, putting up my hands. "Believe me, Celia, I am incredibly touched, in all ways. I can't imagine how I could have been so lucky."

"I assure you," she said, "I do not go around sleeping with people on five hours' notice."

"Neither do I."

"But we both did."

"Yes," I agreed, "we both did."

She sighed. "Now you *will* think I'm brazen—I even want to again."

When I reached for her, she gave me a slap. "Not *now*, you sex fiend. I meant later. Tonight. And maybe tomorrow night. And—"

Into her hair I said, "Shhh," and she understood.

Celia was brushing her hair. She wore the orange kimono I'd bought her in Tokyo so long ago.

She turned to face me. Her body had aged well. She was broader in the hips, but her waist was still small and her breasts had not sagged. "Did you say something?" she asked.

"I guess so. I was daydreaming about Tokyo. Sorry."

"Why be sorry? Those were wonderful days. I think about them often."

"I know. But this isn't the time. I don't know why he did it, maybe he's up to mischief, maybe not, but the President has given you a clear beat on the biggest story of the year. If you release at six A.M. sharp, you'll beat the five-bell bulletins by at least a minute."

She put the brush down on the vanity table and held out her hands to me. "Oh, Mouse," she said, "what have I done to you? You're turning into a newspaperwoman's husband."

"What else did you have in mind?"

She lifted her arms and the unbelted kimono fell open. Beneath it, unrestrained, was the soft, rosy body I had loved so long and so often. "How about me being just a senator's wife?"

As she moved into my embrace and her lips brushed against my ear, she gave a little laugh and whispered, "Besides, love, we'll be through by five."

"Don't be too sure," I told her.

She made a sound that was half laugh, half sigh, and the kimono slipped down her body to form an orange pool around her feet.

At ten of six, the kimono again wrapped around her loosely, Celia picked up her direct-line phone to Trans-World International.

"Seth," she asked, "are the lines all hot?"

A pause, then she said, "Get ready for a five-bell bulletin. I want you to give me a go at exactly six A.M. No, I can't tell you. Yes, I *know* there's an emergency meeting of the General Assembly. Just be ready to go at six."

She put the instrument on hold and went into her work room. I had made myself moderately decent in my old terry-cloth robe. While she moved purposefully around the room switching on equipment, I plugged in the big half-gallon coffee urn and began the ritual of measuring out the specially ground Colombian brew we both prefer to the hermetically sealed, colorfully packed, characterless mixtures you find on the supermarket shelves.

Those few visitors lucky enough to be invited into Celia's private domain invariably react as if they've been led into the master control center at Cape Kennedy. And no wonder. Four TV monitors are set into one wall. Three are tuned to each of the major networks. The fourth is hooked into a video-tape recorder mounted beneath it. Three ordinary audio recorders, with huge ten-inch reels, flank the video deck. Whenever news is breaking, Celia has the audio machines recording every word received over the air—and at particularly tense moments, she records the picture as well.

"This is the next best thing to being three places at once," she told me once. "It doesn't take the place of legwork, but it sure as hell helps."

Whatever it accomplished for her, Celia must have been doing something right. When the total number of newspapers carrying her TWI column passed two hundred, I stopped counting. I have no exact idea how much money she earns; I don't want to know. We made that agreement long ago—no mingling of funds, no arguing about who pays for what. *I* pay, and that is that. If she wants to blow us to a two-week retreat at Little Dix Bay down on Virgin Gorda, that's fine with me and I will lounge around the sand like a beach lizard soaking up planter's punches. But she is not to spend her own funds on so much as a can of beans for the house.

The one exception to our rule is this room. She pays for her own equipment and telephone calls. She has to: one month of her long distance charges would put my bank account out of business.

The non-stop talkers were already busy on the networks. I have often wondered what peculiar form of education creates these charming gentlemen with their eternal mouths. Knowing that in just five minutes or so, the truth, whatever it is, will be revealed, they still fill the airways with meaningless speculation—half-truths, guesses, background information ("The last time, Dave, an emergency session of the Assembly was called was in 1970 when . . .")—anything to keep from committing the most unforgivable sin of all, allowing dead air.

I remember one exception to this rule: in 1963, when the assassinated John F. Kennedy lay in state under the Great Rotunda of the Capitol, the camera focused on the flag-draped casket. All through the long night, the only sound heard was the shuffle of tired feet as the throngs passed the bier. That silence was more eloquent than a million words.

Now, Celia sat down at one of two IBM Selectric typewriters arranged beside each other on a long typing table near the heavily draped window. Her fingers flew over the keyboard, the little metal ball whirled and danced against the yellow paper. The sweep second hand of the Western Union clock lacked twenty seconds of six A.M. when she pulled the paper out of the typewriter and pressed a button that put the telephone onto conference, which meant she could talk without picking up the receiver. She pressed another series of buttons and the audio recorders began spooling their magnetic tape past the recording heads.

The coffee was ready. I poured both cups. She nodded her thanks, sipped, and said, "Are you there, Seth?"

"Standing by, Miss Craig."

"I read nine seconds."

"Close enough," he said. "Wait for my 'Go.'"

On the TV monitors we could see the Assembly Hall of the United Nations, filling with delegates. Two of the three sets had a white title over the picture, "Live from the UN."

"Coming up on 0600," said Seth's voice.

"Have your operators send the copy straight out as I dictate it," said Celia.

"Yes ma'am," said Seth's voice. "Stand by. Four. Three. Two. One. Go."

In the background I could hear the teletype operators sending a five-bell signal—the alert to warn receiving newspapers and broadcast stations that an important story is coming. At the same time, Celia began reading her copy.

"Special Bulletin, by Celia Craig," she read. "A top Washington source" (journalese for the President but not for attribution) "revealed today that the Defense Department has secretly installed two squadrons of Third Generation Safeguard Anti-Ballistic Missiles on the island of Honshu, Japan. The ring of missiles, with their atomic warheads, are said to protect Tokyo, Yokohama, and other major Japanese cities. However, such installation violates the terms of the Peace Settlement with that nation, and specifically violates the Japanese Constitution, which forbids atomic warheads on Japanese soil."

She paused, and sipped at the coffee. On the monitors a confused clump of men were climbing to the speaker's rostrum. I nodded my head toward them and Celia smiled, then continued:

"An emergency session of the United Nations General Assembly was begun at six this morning. A reliable source indicates that the People's Republic of North Korea will accuse the United States of aggressive provocation, and will demand that the missiles be removed. Not since the thirteen days of the Cuban Missile Crisis have the United States and the Communist Bloc been involved in such a desperate confrontation. Official sources have declined to comment on what the response of the United States will be to this disclosure. Endit."

She finished her coffee, said, "Thanks, Seth. Be talking to you later," and broke the connection. "Now," she said to me, switching on the sound of one of the TV monitors, "watch this. It ought to be fun."

The picture, which showed a group of men forming on the

rostrum, cut suddenly to an announcer, sitting in a booth over the General Assembly floor.

"A bulletin has just been handed to me," he said. "A prominent Washington columnist . . ."

("Bastard!" Celia hissed. "The least he could do is use my name!")

". . . has just revealed that a high official source stated . . ."

Then, word for word, he read the copy my wife had just dictated. "Stay tuned to this station," he urged, "for more news as it happens. Now, back to the General Assembly, live from the United Nations."

"The new journalism," Celia complained. "My beat may give our papers a bare five-minute lead in getting out on the street, if that. In the old days we'd have had a clear two or three hours."

"What now?" I asked, looking at my watch. "I'd better get over to the Hill by nine. We'll be having a special session or two of our own, if I know our Majority Leader."

"Stick around for another hour, love," she said, touching my cheek. "It may be the only time we'll have together for a while."

She stood behind my chair, bent over, and planted a soft kiss on the top of my bald pate.

The doctors have told me that they can find no organic cause whatever for my baldness. It came on me two years after I married Celia. One day I had as much hair as Ringo Starr; the next, my comb started pulling it out in clumps. Within a month I was completely bald.

"Don't let it bother you," Celia had said. "I always had a yen for Yul Brynner anyway. If you buy a toup I'll leave you."

I didn't buy a hairpiece—but I wore my hat every chance I got, until one day, a few months after he had been beaten by Eisenhower, Adlai Stevenson cornered me in the new Senate Office Building and, patting his own hairless scalp for emphasis, told me, "Hugh, it's all right—in fact, it's desirable— for a politician to be able to make people laugh. If you think that photo of the hole in my shoe was an accident, you'd better think again. But he should never be a figure of fun. Make them laugh with you, not *at* you, which is what they're doing now. Throw away that damned hat—you're not the only bald man in the world, or even in Congress. And stop taking your head so seriously. At least, the outside of it."

His advice stuck. For a while I wondered if my hairless state might be blamed on accidental exposure to radiation back in 1945, perhaps when I flew the first atomic mission to Japan. But the doctors assured me that was impossible.

Although I felt naked at first, I began to flaunt my bare scalp, and after a while it felt natural. Finally, after a couple of sessions with a shrink, I accepted that the cause was psychosomatic. Never underestimate the power of the mind . . . especially a mind that has a guilty conscience.

"Here we go," said Celia, providing a welcome interruption to my train of thought.

David Albright, Great Britain, President of the General Assembly, rapped for order and said, "The Honorable Delegate from the People's Republic of North Korea has called this special emergency session of the Assembly to reveal what he terms a situation detrimental to world peace, and to propose a resolution."

There was some talking back and forth about the procedure of the session, but it was obvious that Kar Nu Han was going to get the floor eventually. Meanwhile, messengers were scurrying up and down the aisles, delivering folded bits of paper to the delegates.

"My story," Celia said, a little proudly. "It's interesting that practically everybody in New York knows what Kar Nu Han is going to say before he's even said it. And it's only now that the delegates are getting the word, five minutes after the rest of the world."

"I think I'll start dressing," I said.

"Leave the door open so you can hear."

"I'll turn on the bedroom set." For some reason, this always seems to irritate Celia. I have often suggested to her that we turn the mortgage over to her equipment, since it seems to own the house anyway. Such suggestions are met with thin lips and lukewarm coffee for a day or so.

I doubt that any man completely understands women. Their minds operate on a different wave length than ours. You joyfully accept them on your own, logical level ("I don't want any favors. Treat me like a man.") then: Bam! Some illogical, unexpected, unearned bolt out of the feminine blue lays you cold. I remember a lyric from a musical comedy of the sixties, a charming little play titled *I Do, I Do,* with Mary Martin and Robert Preston. Celia and I had gone to see it to celebrate our own wedding anniversary; we'd been told to expect an ode to happy marriages. Well, it certainly wasn't any ode to *ours.* There was a song in which the couple agreed to calmly discuss each other's failings, so as to improve themselves. Robert Preston went through a perfectly logical instruction on how to balance household accounts—only to be answered by Mary Martin's devastating and unanswerable counterattack: "You chew in your sleep." *You chew in your sleep!* What logical response can a man make to such a charge?

Although I knew it galled her, I turned on the bedroom set. Kar Nu Han was speaking rapidly in Korean. His voice was low, the simultaneous English translation riding over it.

To me all simultaneous translators sound like Alistair Cooke. This one also had an annoying habit of fighting dead air with "uh's."

"The—uh—United States—uh—has committed an act of aggression—uh—that leaves—uh—the People's Republic of North Korea—uh—no alternative but to place this—uh—matter before the court of—uh—world opinion." And so on.

As I struggled into my trousers, the speech continued.

"Incontrovertible evidence proves that the imperialistic forces of the United States of America have secretly established operable missile bases on western Honshu. Such provocative action can have only one aim—to attempt to frighten and dominate the People's Republic of North Korea.

"Gentlemen, must a small, peaceful nation such as ours cower under the sword of the aggressor? Does only might make right? Our borders have been violated by espionage ships, our air space has been overflown by spy planes. And now our cities, our factories, our very lives come under the atomic warheads of aggressive missiles, smuggled into a neutral nation in the dark of night and erected with all the stealth of a saboteur planting an infernal device to explode his peaceful neighbors into bits.

"We, the People's Republic of North Korea, charge the United States of America with constructing nine offensive missile sites, five of which are now operational.

"The United States has stolen into our back yard, like a burglar in the night, and erected offensive weapons with which to threaten our very existence.

"What are we to do?

"Are we so friendless, so alone, that there is no alternative but to surrender to the invader?

"Our purpose in coming to this assembly is not to present ultimatums—although we ourselves have been presented with a nuclear ultimatum—but to seek understanding and accommodation. Our purpose is not to draw mighty armies up against one another—although the deadliest army of all has been drawn up against us—but to seek peace and an end to strife.

"It saddens my heart to say so, my honored colleagues, but there are those who observe, perhaps with good reason, that this august gathering is an eagle without wings, a tiger without claws.

"Therefore, speaking for the People's Republic of North Korea, and for those nations which have already bespoken themselves to our cause, I must reluctantly promise that, unless the deliberately provocative and aggressive missiles are withdrawn from Japanese soil within two weeks from this moment, that is to say, exactly 1130 hours, Greenwich Mean Time, August 16, that a state of war between the People's Republic of North Korea and her allies, and the United States of America and her allies shall exist.

"That is my statement. There is nothing to debate."

He stepped away from the podium. The camera was close enough to show that the slim, brown man was perspiring heavily. I didn't blame him. I was sweating myself.

Fastening my necktie, I went back into Celia's room. She was banging away on the Selectric. I cleared my throat. She heard me, but gave that little shrug of her right shoulder that said clearly, "I love you but I'm working my ass off, so clear out." I kissed the back of her neck and went outside, wiped the mist off the Mustang's window with a paper towel, and started the drive into downtown Washington.

It was already hot—almost as hot as it had been in the South Pacific so long ago when I was a nineteen-year-old bombardier with his sweaty finger pressed against the first nuclear button.

Tinian, Marianas Islands—*May 29, 1945*

How can I describe those days when war was a kind of glory, when youth was all around us and death was a noseless specter who waited in the officers' club and took our buddies away on missions to nowhere? Oh, we never glamorized our very real heroism and our fatalistic sense of duty the way Van Johnson and Spencer Tracy did in the rash of flier films like *A Guy Named Joe* and *Thirty Seconds Over Tokyo*.

When those films showed up at our outdoor movie theater, where we sat on coconut logs under the stars (unless it was raining, which was most of the time, in which case we sat under our ponchos, feeling the rain pound against the rubberized fabric), we hooted Van Johnson with glee. Actually we were envious of his good looks and his civilian status. Most of us liked Tracy, and since he was over the hill for draft purposes, we awarded him a respectful disdain as he flew off to his various Valhallas.

But the actor we all had to watch out for was Keye Luke,

who often turned up as a Japanese fighter pilot. Luke was very good at choking out the mouthful of chocolate syrup, or whatever it was the movie people used for blood, and he usually got the chance to demonstrate this proficiency once in every flier movie. But this was not enough for the Sniper.

Somewhere on the island of Tinian a band of uncaptured Japanese marines was hiding out, and one of them, armed with a telescopic rifle, lived only for the moment when Keye Luke would appear. That was the signal for all of us to duck while the outraged Jap put six quick rounds into the screen. We were never able to catch the sniper, and no one really wanted to, I guess. Not only did he have a reckless sense of humor, he apparently knew the films better than we did. One night, tired of patching the screen, the projectionist edited Keye Luke out of the movie. Undaunted, the Jap sniper put six rounds where Luke *should* have been.

Tinian is a long, very flat island whose only fame until the war had been as home for the largest leper colony in the Pacific. But in 1945 it was a base for the most spectacular airstrip in the world. Seabees had bulldozed most of the already flat coral and yellow earth into a monstrous strip that allowed three B-29s to take off at the same time. Across a narrow channel, Saipan had another bomber strip, and Guam, a hundred miles away, had two more. Most of the war material—and most of the men—scheduled for the ultimate assault on the Japanese islands were piled up here in the Marianas.

My God, how young we were! Most of the pilots were barely old enough to vote, and navigators and bombardiers were usually a year or two younger than the pilots. Of course, ours was a peculiar kind of youth: as dealers in death, we came to know old No-Nose well, and in a kind of paranoia of self-preservation, demonstrated a peculiar camaraderie with him. When a plane went down with no chutes visible, the word emanated from the debriefing room as if by osmosis; and by the time we got back to the Quonset hut, still choking from the raw bourbon the flight surgeon dispersed from his musette bag, all the belongings of the missing men had vanished and the mattresses were stripped and rolled up on the bare springs of the GI bunks. The only thing we could count on was that within a day or so another four fresh-faced kids direct from flight school, wings still glittering, would show up and move into the empty bunks as happily as if they had been shown to a suite at the Fairmount.

We never talked about those who did not come back. We did not have any of those Hollywood battleground bull sessions in which someone (usually William Bendix) would puff on a cigarette (usually a Camel) and say, "Gee, when I get back to Brooklyn, you know what I'm going to do? I'm going to get me a steak *that* thick, smothered with onions, with three scoops of vanilla ice cream on the side. . . ." We had learned our movie lesson well; we knew that every time Bill Bendix started talking like that he went out on a patrol and got stuck with a bayonet, or got himself burned up in an exploding tank, or machine-gunned by some nasty Nazi.

When the United States Marines captured Tinian in June and July of 1944, it was as if God were sending the leathernecks ashore as personal emissaries to demonstrate the horror of war. Less than two hundred marines were killed in the five-week battle. But 8,000 Japanese died. There must be a moral there. Maybe it's that a ton of TNT, a dozen canisters of napalm, and three hundred pounds of shrapnel are tougher, any day in the week, than one Japanese soldier armed with a bolt-action rifle.

Correspondents called Tinian the biggest aircraft carrier in the world. North Field was, at least in 1945, the longest operational strip on earth. At one time, 2100 B-29s roosted along its edges, like great silver goony birds lazing through the hot afternoons.

Our outfit, the 509th Composite Group, had landed on May 29, 1945, aboard the ship *Cape Victory*. As we steamed up to the pier, the radio room turned on the loudspeakers and let us listen to a broadcast they were picking up from Tokyo Rose.

"Welcome, young men of the 509th," she said in those soft tones that wooed Americans all over the Pacific. "You are the latest sacrifices to the war machine of imperialistic Washington. Don't you boys wish you were home now? I know you are thinking of your girls and your wives. But how long do you believe they will wait for you? Isn't it better to live peaceful lives in your own country than to die on some nameless Pacific shoal? Your government will not even tell you what you are dying for. Oh, *we* know why you have come to Tinian. And that is why it is all so sad. Because many of you *will* die. For nothing! It makes me so sad. . . . Would you like to hear one of the songs your girls are listening to now? Listening . . . but with whom?"

One thing you had to say for Tokyo Rose: she always had the latest platters from the Hit Parade. This time she played Freddy Martin's popular version of the Chopin Polonaise, "Till the End of Time."

> *Till the end of time . . .*
> *Till each mountain disappears,*
> *I'll be there with you*
> *To care for you*
> *Through laughter and through tears.*[1] . . .

Some of us jeered and told the radio loudspeaker what we'd like to insert where in Tokyo Rose. But others were quiet. Away from women so long, it was oddly pleasant to hear a female voice—even one of the enemy's.

Most of the air crews were flying out with the 509th's B-29s a few weeks later. But several crews had been sent aboard the *Cape Victory* to begin flying as observers with the 21st Bomber Command of the 20th Air Force.

One of the things you get used to in the army is leaving buddies behind. You swear you'll "keep in touch"; but the intervening miles and months destroy the most passionate friendships, and soon you cannot even remember the name or the face of your barracks-mate.

Tim Bond, who had washed out of pilot training a week

1. Copyright 1945 by Anne-Rachel Music Corporation, New York, New York. Used by permission.

before the ax fell on me, was one such friend. Once he left the big Air Training Command Base at San Antonio to attend navigation school in Kansas, we both knew that the chances of our ever "looking each other up" and quaffing mug after mug of beer in back-street gin mills were almost nil. We exchanged addresses, but it was an empty gesture. Even the optimism of youth could not delude us that our friendship would survive the trauma of Shipping Out.

But long before I found myself on Tinian, Tim Bond and I had been reunited—surprised, delighted, suspicious of the good roll of the dice—at a barren airfield located in the Utah desert.

Wendover Field was only 125 miles from Salt Lake City, which to a fun-seeking bombardier was like being 125 miles from Alcatraz. I got off the train at Salt Lake, made a disappointing survey of the city's female potential, and found the nearest bar to see if my forged Class A pass would convince the bartender I was of drinking age. To my surprise he didn't even ask for my ID. I was sipping a beer when a slim figure emerged from the gloom and pounded me on the shoulder until I spilled Schlitz all over the countertop. "Hot damn! Mac, is it really you? What are you doing in this crappy town?"

"Tim! Hell, I'm assigned to some outfit called the 509th Composite Group. I'm just waiting for transportation out to the base."

Tim waved for another beer and leaned forward conspiratorially. "Take my advice," he said. "Go AWOL. Get yourself captured by the Germans. Stalag 14 is better any day than Wendover Field. I've only been there two weeks, and I'm ready to turn Arab."

We drank and talked and played "Hey, whatever happened to So-and-So?" until we realized it was time to eat, and went off looking for a restaurant. Somewhere on a side street we found a hamburger joint. Tim talked and gestured between bites of the greasy, lumpy sandwiches.

"Hugh, I'm not kidding about that place. Listen, there's a

36

story that when a new pilot arrived he looked out at the frigging desert and said, 'My God, what do you guys do for fun around here?' The adjutant said, 'Mostly, sir, we get drunk.' So the pilot asks, 'But what about . . . ah . . . sex?' Well, the adjutant just pointed out the window and, high up on a hill, the pilot saw a mangy, shaggy female camel. 'Hell, no!' he says. 'I'll never get *that* hard up!'

"So the weeks drag by and the pilot gets hornier and hornier, and nervouser and nervouser, and one day he can't take it any more. He lets out a yell, jumps out the window, runs up the hill and socks it to that old camel. When he's through, and pulling up his pants, he notices that everybody on the base is gathered around staring at him. 'What the hell are you guys looking at?' he says. 'You told me that's what *you* do!' And the adjutant shakes his head and says, 'No, sir, what *we* do is ride her into town and park her outside the whorehouse.' " Tim choked over the last bite of his hamburger. "Yes sir, Mac, there are times out there at Wendover when that mangy camel starts looking really *good*."

I don't remember much more of that night, because we got really drunk. When the last bus left for the base, we had been put aboard it by two angry MPs who disapproved of young fly-boys pissing in the Mormon fountain.

The next day we made the happy discovery that we'd been assigned to the same air crew, aboard a fresh-from-the-factory B-29. Tim was navigator, and I was her bombardier.

Carved out of the desert, with mountains on all sides, Wendover was perfect for a secret project. When Bob Hope's USO company played there, he looked down his ski nose at the base and said, "Welcome to Leftover Field."

When freed for a rare weekend, we had two delightful choices: Salt Lake City, or Elko, Nevada, a hundred miles west. In Salt Lake we could look at the Mormon Temple; in Elko, the gambling casino. Tim invariably headed for Salt Lake. I suppose he had a yen for music. I, realizing that I stood a much better chance of getting booze in easy-going Nevada, despite my nineteen years and fuzzy upper lip, usually opted for Elko. A few years ago, when Barry Goldwater invited me to fly right seat in a new commercial jet he was trying out, we flew up from Arizona and made a stop at Elko. It was the same old place. The years between had not changed it one damned bit so far as I could see.

But back in 1945 Elko was the best I could find, and I made the long trip four times during the months I was stationed at Wendover.

Few if any of us on the flight level knew why we had been chosen for servitude at this outpost. Nor did we know what we were supposed to be doing. I remember one day when I was killing time walking down the flight line, kicking rocks and hallucinating a cold beer, I heard noises coming from an open hangar door.

Inside, a crew of mechanics were busy stripping a B-29. They had already removed all the guns and were now ripping out the armor.

A tech sergeant came over.

"Sorry, Lieutenant," he said. "This area's restricted."

I hauled out my ID. "I've got a flight line pass."

"No good in here, sir."

"I'm not in there," I said, irrationally angry. "Why are you ripping up that airplane?"

"By your leave, sir," he said, and pulled the heavy door shut in my face.

That night, in the Officers' Club, I cornered Major Rosy Cooper, the executive officer.

"How the hell are we supposed to fight a war without guns and armor?" I asked. "What do we do, throw rocks at them and sit on our flak vests to keep from getting our asses shot off?"

"Don't ask, Mac," he said. "You have no need to know."

"I have a need to know if I'm going out on some kind of frigging suicide mission. An urgent need!"

"Take my word for it," he said, and bought me a beer. "We know what we're doing. For our job, speed and maneuverability are worth more than guns and armor."

"Who the hell needs speed and maneuverability at 30,000 feet?"

Rosy Cooper looked at me in a way that reminded me his shoulders supported gold major's leaves while my own trembled under a mere lieutenant's silver bars. I shut up and drank my beer.

Two days later I found out why the ships had been lightened. Our outfit had fifteen B-29s—and every one had been stripped down to the bare metal. My plane was designated number twenty-seven until her first flight, after which Tim Bond renamed her in honor of certain events he found hard to forget.

We were flying five miles up, straight and level, on a simulated bomb run. Our ground speed was around two hundred knots. The pilot, Captain Charles (he *had* to be called "Tex") Ritter, came on the intercom and said, "Everybody strapped in good?"

None of us were, of course, but we all said "Roger." Who the hell straps in on a practice run?

"Here we go," said Tex Ritter.

I locked in my bombsight and flew the plane for a little while by adjusting my sight controls. The cross hairs crawled across the desert floor five miles below. When they bisected a highway crossroad, I hit the release.

"Bombs away," I said.

Control of the airplane passed automatically back to Ritter. I was leaning back, relaxing for the trip to base, when I heard all four engines go to maximum power and the nose of the big plane pointed almost straight down. Since I wasn't strapped in, I went right up to the overhead and banged my forehead against the plexiglass. I was still grabbing for handholds when Ritter brought the B-29 out of the dive, and I remember thinking that the wings were probably going to come off. He had old number twenty-seven in a steep left bank. The earth rotated past her nose. In a matter of seconds we had turned completely around and were going like hell on a course 155 degrees reciprocal to our original heading.

I heard the training officer's voice on the command channel. "Pretty sloppy," he said. "You took thirty-nine seconds. Thirty's the limit."

I heard Tim Bond swearing furiously. He seemed to be discussing Ritter's ancestry.

"Everybody all right?" the pilot asked.

All of us reported in except Tim. The skinny navigator used words that none of us suspected he knew.

"What's wrong back there?" Ritter demanded.

"I'll tell you what's wrong," Tim yelled. "What's wrong is that this goddamned chemical john didn't flush right, that's what the hell's wrong. And when you shoved this bastard's nose down, the whole goddamned thing backed up. My compartment looks like the bottom of a latrine trench."

He said considerably more, but everyone was laughing so hard that he was blanked out on the intercom.

That night we were all sitting around in the officers' club drinking 3.2 beer and discussing a name for old number twenty-seven.

Ritter voted for *The Honey Bucket,* but most of us felt that was too Oriental. It was finally Tim himself who, scrubbed but still faintly aromatic, said, "There's only one name for her, and that's what she is. *The Busted Flush!*"

As I said, we were young, and filled with dreams of glory. War was a game. Deadly, brutal, terrifying—but a game all the same. So, as part of the game, we put a scatological name, *The Busted Flush,* on the machine of destruction that was scheduled to bring atomic fire to Japan.

It seemed funny at the time.

Somehow I'd gotten the idea that Utah and Nevada and places like that were deserts, where the sun burned down and bleached the longhorns' bones white, and all that nonsense. So it didn't seem right to be up to our knees in snow, even though it was Christmas Day.

The wind, boiling down from the mountains, caught up the snow and threw talcum-fine bits of ice down our necks as we scampered from barracks to mess hall for the big Christmas dinner the 509th mess sergeant had laid on for us. The big room was festooned with paper streamers, bright red and green and yellow, and the mess sergeant had decked himself out in a Santa Claus outfit, including beard and a belly that was half pillow, half mess sergeant.

This was the one day of the year that officers and enlisted men ate together. Families were invited too. That was the reason for the mess sergeant's outfit. He passed out bright red stockings filled with candy and hard nuts and bubble gum (the post commissary had never heard of bubble gum: it had to be smuggled back from Salt Lake City and Elko by good-natured couriers), along with a small toy or two.

Since most families on Wendover were those of civilian-soldiers, there was only a light sprinkling of army brats. But you could recognize them a mile away, wearing cut-down uniforms with sergeants' stripes or captains' bars, flaunting their fathers' ranks. It was a tradition that the son of, say, a sergeant, would never wear higher rank, although there was certainly no military regulation to keep him from promoting himself all the way up to five-star general.

Ordinarily the army brats stayed away from the civilian-soldier kids, whose fathers dreamed only of earning enough points to be discharged and get back to their bakeries or service stations or night classes in electrical engineering. In fact, most of the brats were sufficiently snobbish to not even like each other.

But on Christmas these and other tensions were at a minimum. Thanks to a rumor that our ten best airplanes were going to be taken to Cuba for special training, we'd been breaking our humps practicing what had come to be known as the "Tokyo Two-Step"—the peculiar maneuver that had baptized poor Tim Bond with the contents of our chemical latrine. I was sure that *The Busted Flush* was up there in the top ten.

None of us knew at the time why we were trying so hard to perfect a maneuver that seemed to make no sense. Later, of course, when we learned that we had been training to drop an atomic bomb, it all fitted together. The eggheads had figured out that a bomb dropped from 30,000 feet would be hurled by the slingshot effect more than three miles ahead of the drop point before it reached detonation altitude 2,000 feet above the target. The reason for shoving the nose of the B-29 down was to trade altitude for speed, and the reason for heading off on the 155-degree course was simply to get our asses out of there before the shock wave could catch up and tear off our wings.

The brass must have spent many a troubled night while we snored peacefully in our racks. At that time no nuclear device had ever been exploded, and atomic theory was rough enough so that all calculations could be completely off. For all they really knew, even eight miles from ground zero the B-29 might easily be enveloped in the fireball.

This was my first operational assignment. A year before, in my first year at Harvard, I had gotten up one morning, looked out at the gently drifting snow, and wondered what the hell I was doing there bucking for a law degree that might not mean anything in two years. Safe from the draft because of a partially detached retina in my left eye, I had never really felt any obligation to serve. All I had to do was look around me, to see how many young men were being spared for one reason or another. None of us was particularly ashamed of it.

That's what makes it so hard to understand why I got up that particular morning and, looking down at the undergraduates scurrying across the Yard through the snow flurries like furry black gnomes, decided to catch the next train home to Cleveland, where, as usual, my father was barricaded behind his copy of the *Plain Dealer*, from which he only came up for air and to eat and work. Other natural processes always included the newspaper, for it usually vanished into the bathroom with him.

I told him what was on my mind, and he listened thoughtfully. Finally he got up and, for the first time in my life, poured me a drink. True, it was only a tiny dollop of Scotch with a huge amount of soda, weak fare indeed compared to the mugs of bootleg whiskey I had choked down at Harvard, but it was from my *father!*

"Hugh," he said, "most of us are afraid of being called corny when we say things that mean a lot to us, or sound idealistic. I'm selfish enough to want you to stay out of this war, because you're my only son and I don't want you hurt or killed. But I don't own you, you're a full human being with free will." He handed me the drink and, embarrassed, I took it. "You know, don't you, that Doc Martin recommended we leave your eye alone. That retina's only partially detached. You can still see. But there's a good chance that the operation could fail and then you wouldn't have any vision left there at all."

I wish I could recall saying something brilliant, but to the best of my memory I shuffled my feet and choked on the Scotch as if I'd never had a drink before and said, "Yeah, but I still want to do it."

"Are you sure you don't want to think about it a little longer?"

"If I think too long, I'll chicken out."

My father looked at his watch. "Doc's probably at the club, lying about the long-term capital gains he's going to take this year. I know for a fact that he took a bath selling steel short because he thought the war would be over by now. Let's drive over and have a drink with him."

The bartender at the country club pointedly looked the other way as I tackled my second drink in my father's presence, and Dr. Martin chewed me out for being six kinds of idiot, wanting to get my ass shot off when I could keep it snugly warmed within a pair of Radcliffe legs. But even at nineteen I knew enough to see he was proud of my decision.

It took me seven weeks flat to wash out of pilot's training, and I had a choice then of becoming a navigator, becoming a bombardier, or accepting ground status. The last was out, and I'd never been too good on map reading in the Boy Scouts, so I opted for bombardier. To my instructor's surprise (and, secretly, my own) I had an incredible knack for the job. My manipulation of the Norden bombsight put me number one in my class. So, when Colonel Paul Tibbets was talent-scouting for his 509th, my 201 file found its way to his desk, and the next thing I knew I was freezing my tail off in Utah.

The training was intensive and, to fliers accustomed to salvo bombing, peculiar. The day before Christmas we flew over the Salton Sea in southern California. The 509th had set up a drop zone there in the manmade lake which, at more than two hundred feet below sea level, had few inhabitants to observe our practice sessions. Down along the edge of the desolate shores they had set up a complex array of cameras, and technicians photographed the different bomb casings we dropped into the target area. But what seemed odd to us was that we were dropping one bomb each trip, just one, and we knew that one had better go exactly where it was supposed to.

It would have taken an idiot to miss the obvious: we were practicing to drop some kind of superbomb.

But the young, at least in 1944, did not worry about the consequences of their actions. We were practicing to drop a superbomb; therefore we would go somewhere and *drop* one. That was that.

And so on Christmas Eve of 1944 I pressed the button that dropped a dummy bomb casing into the Salton Sea, then lay back against my parachute and read a copy of *Doc Savage Magazine* until we touched down, at which time I showered, ate, then went to the officers' club and got falling-down drunk.

Dinner—that is to say, lunch—is the big meal in the army. Few of us had the stamina to go to breakfast Christmas Day, so when noon rolled around we were hungry enough to forget our hangovers. We brushed off our best ODs, polished our brass, spit-shined our shoes, gave our wings one extra stroke with the blitz cloth, then wrapped up in the overcoats that had, we swore, been fashioned from horse blankets, and dashed through the frigid wind to the mess hall.

The mess sergeant gave us all a merry "Ho-Ho" from behind his cotton whiskers but decided we were too old to come in for the hard nuts and bubble gum. I didn't mind: I had my own personal supply. On my last trip to Elko I had bought every piece of bubble gum on the main drag, extracting a dozen pieces from the bag as my courier's fee.

There are many bad things about military food. The reconstituted eggs are perhaps the worst sight ever to greet a sleepy eye at four A.M. The creamed beef on toast lives up to its nickname, "shit on a shingle."

But there is nothing remotely wrong with the army's holiday meal. You would not get better turkey at the Waldorf. In fact, I have eaten Christmas turkey at the Waldorf, and I greatly prefer the army's. The sweet potatoes are glazed and orange-yellow with little crunchy bits of brown sugar clinging to the edges. The giblet gravy is a brown swimming pool for chunks of turkey liver and gizzards. But it is the cranberry sauce that I remember best. Do you recall that Thanksgiving in the early sixties when millions—myself included—went cranberryless, fearing contamination from a Jersey bog's pesticide? Well, I swear, had I known that those cans of Ocean Spray contained the same cranberry sauce I got at Wendover Field, Utah, I would have cheerfully accepted the protestations of the Cranberry Institute and chomped my way through at least a pint of the stuff.

Mince pie! Hot, spicy, tangy on the tongue! Coffee! Real coffee, so scarce in that fourth year of the war—freshly made, not pre-boiled and allowed to sit, fermenting, for hours. Individual paper bags filled with nuts and a McIntosh apple, a navel orange, a dozen pieces of hard candy. Plus a package of cigarettes. Camels, of course.

Ah, war. It was wonderful.

That night the CQ came into my room with his flashlight. He put its beam in my face and shook my shoulder. I struggled out of sleep, half drunk, conscious that the floor was littered with quart bottles of Budweiser, most of them empty, and that I could be court-martialed for drinking in the BOQ.

The charge of quarters, a quiet, slim sergeant named Malloy, ignored the evidence.

"Lieutenant McGavin?"

"Yeah?"

"Are you Lieutenant McGavin?"

"Malloy, you know damned well I'm Lieutenant McGavin. What time is it?"

"I'm sorry, sir, they told me to ask to be sure. It's 0300. Sir, can you get dressed and come down to the orderly room?"

"What the hell for?"

"There's a message for you, sir." He paused. "I think it's important."

My heart took a dive into my stomach. This is when they always come for you—at three in the morning, when the spirit of a man is lowest, when God is off somewhere else, and you are the most alone you'll ever be.

My mother is dead, I thought. She had been suffering for years with a myocardial insufficiency that made her turn blue when she walked half a block. I swallowed at a lump in my throat as I laced up my boots and tugged on my field jacket. At nineteen you may think you are a man, but the child is only an eyeblink away.

It wasn't my mother at all. Coming home from the club, my father had smashed up the car and killed himself.

While Celia and I waited for the teletype wires of Trans-World International to heat up, President Howard Foster was down in the White House basement relaxing with a quick swim in the heated pool he had repossessed from the press corps.

Like all Presidents in moments of crisis, Foster had established a circle of advisers. On various occasions they were called "the Group," "the Defense Cabinet," and "the Rat Pack." This last was for private consumption, and did not appear on the Security Council's Action Memorandum 321, which dubbed the circle "The Executive Committee responsible for coordinating the activities of the Executive Branch" and went on to order regular meetings at nine A.M. in the Cabinet Room, with extraordinary meetings to be called at the President's discretion.

But to the members of the Executive Committee, "the Rat Pack" it was. They were:

ARTHUR RAND, Vice-President;

SOL CUSHMAN, Secretary of State;

MARTIN KUHN, Attorney General;

PAUL RYAN, Director of the Central Intelligence Agency;

HARRISON NEAL, Ambassador-at-Large;

GENERAL OSCAR BURTON, Chairman of the Joint Chiefs of Staff:

PHIL HEPBURN, Special Assistant to the President for National Security;

plus deputies for several of the department heads who kept notes and were prepared to stand in for their superiors.

The first Executive Committee meeting commenced at a quarter of six. Although each of the men present had been

47

warned of what was coming, Kar Nu Han's United Nations speech had half a dozen adults shouting like children.

"He's deliberately misrepresenting the capabilities of the missiles!" said General Burton.

"There's one point he didn't misrepresent," Martin Kuhn, the Attorney General, said. "We're out on a limb, legally. If Japan asks us to take those birds out of there, we don't have a leg to stand on."

"Japan won't ask us to take them out," President Foster said patiently. "For Christ's sake, we didn't sneak those missiles into the country. Premier Ito knew all about them and agreed in principle."

"Principle is one thing," Kuhn persisted, "but actual signed documents are another. You can insist Ito said, Fine, come ahead with your missiles. But if you don't have it on paper what have you got?"

"Why don't we just take them out?" asked Sol Cushman. Before Foster could answer, the Secretary of State held up his hand and went on: "Oh, I know, I agreed previously that their installation was an effective political-military ploy, but we've gotten ourselves caught now. Let's take our lumps and withdraw before the thing escalates."

"We can't take them out," said Foster.

"There's no doubt that we're going to get a black eye from the world press over this," said Harrison Neal, Ambassador-at-Large. "When Kennedy invoked the Monroe Doctrine to justify his Cuban quarantine, the world knew he was actually responding to an overt disturbance of the status quo. Allowing Russian missiles in Cuba would have tipped the scales too far in favor of the Communist Bloc. We're in the same spot now, and this time the world is going to say *we've* played dirty."

"The Russians won't say that," replied the President.

"They may," said Sol Cushman. When Foster looked at him sharply, he added, "Sorry, sir, but we don't have any signed paperwork in that area, either. Premier Nabov may find himself with his back pushed to the wall. In that case, he has to condemn our action, particularly in view of the North Korean threat to declare a state of war if our missiles aren't removed."

General Oscar Burton growled, "Any time we let a tenth-rate power like North Korea order the United States around—"

"Unfortunately," said the President, "the situation is such that at least one first-rate military nation is backing North Korea's play."

"China is in it for sure," said Paul Ryan, speaking for the first time. The director of the CIA was a small, slim man who looked as if he might be a violinist. "There's been a tremendous amount of radio traffic between Peking and Pyongyang in the past month. If you remember, sir, in my briefing of July 24, I warned that the Chinese were penetrating our weather-station cover story."

"Of course you told me," said the President. "But goddamn it, why do you think we put those birds there if we didn't want the Chinese to know about them?"

"Well," said the CIA man dryly, "they sure know about them."

Phil Hepburn, the President's special assistant on national security, referred to a sheaf of notes. "Mr. President," he said, "our readouts give us a sixty-seven-percent probability that, no matter what the Red Bloc says, they're just bluffing. China's posture, nuclear-wise, is much better than it was in the sixties, but our second strike megadeath projection would still leave her devastated. Also, Chairman K'ang has been pursuing a relatively moderate course for the past two years. He finally seems to have his own national problems under control."

"Phil," said the President, "that's the same readout that persuaded me to put the Safeguards into Japan in the first place. Except the last time you quoted it to me, the bluff ratio was over eighty-five percent. What shrank it?"

"New information," said Hepburn. "Our projection was based on the expected Chinese response to gentle, persistent pressure from all sides. But if the pressure weakens, for instance from the Soviet sphere of influence, naturally the figures change."

"Has that pressure weakened?"

"Slightly," admitted the President's assistant. "Not because of anything the Soviets have done, but rather because of what they haven't. We expected an instant response confirming the defensive nature of the missiles on Japan. Their satellite photos, for instance, would have established conclusively that the sites are ground-to-air ABMs rather than offensive ground-to-ground weapons. By withholding that information from the Chinese, the Soviets have changed our projections."

"God preserve me from all projections," said the President. "After the Bay of Pigs, John F. Kennedy swore he would never trust the experts again. And I'm beginning to feel the same way. So now we've got a better-than-thirty-percent chance that the Chinese will empty out their holes, and for all we know, the Russians along with them."

"There's still an almost-seventy-percent projection that they won't," said Hepburn.

"Today. What about tomorrow? Or even this afternoon? Those funny figures of yours keep changing."

"I can't help that, sir. When the input changes, the output has to change too."

"I know, Phil," the President said quietly. "I'm not really blaming you. Well, my friends, here we are. We've got a tiger by the tail. What next?"

"Take the ABMs out," said Sol Cushman.

Howard Foster looked at his Secretary of State and shook his head slowly. "We can't, Sol. Believe me. Any other suggestions?"

The Vice-President, who had not spoken until now, said, "What are the U.S. casualty projections if the Chinese empty their holes?"

"First strike?" Hepburn asked.

"Naturally. We'd never hit first."

Hepburn consulted his files. "If it's only the Chinese, we read out eighteen point seven megadeaths."

"Eighteen million, seven hundred thousand dead," the Vice-President repeated.

"That's assuming a fifty percent knockdown by our ABMs," said Hepburn. "Of course, if the Chinese attack is coordinated with one from the Russians, our knockdown shrinks to around ten percent, and the casualty total runs just under a hundred and fifty million." He looked up. "But the remaining eighty million would probably lose half of their survivors due to hunger, disease, and—frankly—intercommunity warfare over the remaining food supplies. A year after the strike . . ." Here the assistant shuffled through several papers, "Give or take half a million, let's say thirty million Americans would be left."

Martin Kuhn, the boyish, freckled Attorney General, threw his yellow pad down on the table. "What in the name of God are we doing? Mr. President, we're guilty of a crime in the eyes of every civilized nation on this earth. We have been caught at it, and given a chance to get the hell out without suffering the consequences. So what are we doing sitting around here calmly discussing a situation in which the best we can hope for is that the United States of America will be hurtled back to the population level of 170 years ago, with half of the land permanently blighted by radiation? Let's take those missiles out of there and accept the consequences. It won't sink the Republic. We've survived worse."

"Are you through, Martin?" asked the President.

"I guess so," said Kuhn.

"Anybody else?"

"Mr. President," said Arthur Rand, "as Vice-President, I'm accustomed to acting in your stead, whether or not I agree with your position, and whether or not I know why you're doing what you do. Right now it seems obvious that you know something I don't—something nobody in this room knows except you. Is that correct?"

"It may be, Arthur," said the President.

"Is there any chance of your telling us what it is?"

"Not a chance in the world."

"Then I agree with the Attorney General," said Arthur Rand. "I don't know why we put those damned things in there to begin with. I think the risk far outweighs the gain. China's been around for a long time. We'll figure out some other way to contain the Yellow Peril."

"Noted," said the President. "Anybody else?" There was no

answer. "All right, come on, who else wants to take the missiles out?"

Martin Kuhn and Arthur Rand raised their hands immediately. Then, after some hesitation, Sol Cushman and Harrison Neal put theirs up too.

"I abstain," said Paul Ryan.

"I say leave them in," said General Oscar Burton.

"As do I," said the President. He looked around. "Well, one abstention, four say to take the missiles out, two to leave them in."

Arthur Rand gave what sounded like a sigh of relief, but before he could speak, the President went on:

"Unfortunately, gentlemen, this committee is not a democracy. I am glad to have had your fresh views, but this is one time when the majority does not rule. Those missiles stay."

Up on the Hill I had my own problems. The United States Senate has been called the most exclusive club in the world, and in many ways that statement is true. But every club has rules, and I was breaking the most traditional one: Thou shalt not rock thy party's boat. There I was, a Democratic senator, defying our Democratic President's position on the ABMs—particularly treasonous in view of the morning's events.

Having been elected in New York State, I know from painful experience how powerful the political machine can be. I have watched it thrust third-rate men into national prominence —and suck truly great ones into oblivion. But, oddly, I have somehow managed to keep myself clean of the worst manifestations of the machine.

Now the word was out this morning: Stop McGavin.

The venerable Majority Leader, Senator Jake Dobsen, caught up with me in the cloak room. He arrived through a flurry of Senate pages, the usually self-possessed young men scattering right and left.

"Hugh, you old som'bitch," said Jake, "let's you'n me set a spell."

Bad news already—when Jake Dobsen put on his Kentucky colonel accent, you were in Trouble.

He snapped his fingers for coffee. It arrived instantly.

"The body politic," Dobsen began, "owes its life to the people. The people elect the body politic; the people nourish it; the people succor it in illness and respect it in health. In turn, the body politic *owes* the people; it owes the people true representation in accordance with the people's wishes; it owes allegiance to the welfare of the people; it owes the people the virtues of humility and patience, of forebearance, and most important, loyalty."

I sipped at my coffee. It was vile. "Jake," I said, "the answer is No."

"Hugh, you—" He stumbled over the double-vowel sound; it is the curse of my life. I have often thought of changing my first name to Sam. "You wrong me, you wrong me every way. Have I asked you to go against your conscience? Have I asked you to abandon your principles?"

"You're just about to, you old fraud," I said, grinning. I found it impossible to get mad at Jake Dobsen. In his thirty years on the Hill, I doubt if he had ever made one personal enemy. Thousands of impersonal ones, yes, men who cursed at the mention of Jake Dobsen—but who would have given a pint of their blood instantly if the old man ever needed it. "Jake, I have an airplane to fly tonight. And if you keep feeding me this battery acid the commissary calls coffee, I'll be too nervous to handle the controls."

"How is Celia?" the genial monster asked, changing tactics in mid-breath.

"Flourishing," I said. "She sends her regards."

"That brilliant woman," he said. "Brilliant and beautiful. Ah, you lucky dog."

"Get to it, Jake," I said. "I've got a feeling things are heating up on the floor. We ought to be in there."

"You never had children, Hugh?"

"You know we don't, Jake. What's that supposed to mean?"

"My son is a major in the Air Force, did you know that? He's stationed on Formosa, liaison with the Nationalist Air Force. And *he's* got children—they're with him and Martha, of course. I think about my son, and about *his* sons often. That's what this old world is all about, isn't it? Our sons, and our sons' sons."

The old bastard was hitting low. Celia and I had tried every way known to medicine to have children; the medics checked us both out constantly, found nothing wrong with her plumbing, and millions of active sperm in mine. But, with vague mutterings of "intrauterine acidity" or "psychological insufficiency," they threw up their hands and said they didn't know what the hell was wrong—it just looked like I wasn't ever going to be able to knock up my wife, and why didn't we resort to artificial insemination, or adoption, or just forget the idea of kids. Adoption was out: neither of us was particularly hung up on the idea of raising kids—we wanted to raise *our* kids. We'd tried the artificial insemination route twice, but the messy business of collecting my semen and the injection of it into her made us both feel like throwing up. So there we were, with Celia nearing the end of her child-bearing years, and nothing in sight.

"I agree with you in principle, Jake," I said. "But we differ in what's best for our various sons, real or imaginary. I've spent the past twenty years listening to people complain about the idiocy of the arms race. I believe the Third Gens in Japan are a symbol of this idiocy, and if a first step is ever going to be taken anywhere, that's where it should be."

"Why do you think we took the calculated risk of putting those missiles over there?" Dobsen said, dropping the Kentucky accent. "Our understanding with the Soviets was that if we were able to contain China, a bilateral arms de-escalation could begin. Premier Nabov—"

"It isn't going to work that way, Jake," I told him. "As long as those nuke warheads are in Japan, the world's walking a tightrope. My position is that I want them out of there, and to hell with the dignity of the Administration. We made a mistake —but rattling more nuclear sabers isn't going to undo it."

"Damn it, boy," he said, "Don't you suppose there's a *reason* for going eyeball to eyeball with China?"

He stopped and sucked in his cheeks.

"Suddenly," I said, "I begin to get the idea that the President and now you have deep, important things on your minds, and you aren't letting anyone else in on the secret. What the devil's going on?"

"Nothing," he said. "So your mind's made up, Hugh? You're still going to Europe tomorrow after all I've said?"

"Jake, look at it my way, please. Earlier this morning I had Foster making the same pitch, and now here you are, and all either one of you will say is Lay off, McGavin, but we can't tell you why. *Trust* us."

"That's just what you ought to do, boy," he said. "We wouldn't steer you wrong."

"You ask me to give up everything I believe in and offer in exchange a vague, we-wouldn't-steer-you-wrong copout? Listen, this isn't a game of Monopoly. I know there've been times in the past when we came dangerously close to a nuclear exchange, but I'm convinced that we've never been closer than we are today. Now how can you ask me to back off from my convictions and trust you when you won't give me one goddamned piece of hard information?"

"You know, boy," he said, "you're right up there in contention for that big job. Oh, I know you think Artie Rand's got the straight line for the nomination—but that's only so if the President taps him. If Foster doesn't make a big deal out of it, it's anybody's guess who might get the delegates. You'd have as good a chance as anyone else."

"Jake," I said, "are you trying to bribe me?"

"Wouldn't dream of it," he replied. "I'm only laying out facts. Fact: Rand is a good man, but you're just as good. Fact: Foster hasn't been *that* popular a President. Truth is, the party might be in better shape running a man less associated with Foster's policies than Arthur Rand. Big fact: Foster is still President, and as long as he is, the party has to stand behind him. The party won't sit still for mavericks running off on their own and fertilizing our doorstep. Take my word, Hugh, nothing's going to happen over this business in Japan. I'll tell you this much—if it gets down to the wire, we'll pull out. I have the President's word on that. Now that's not to get around, do you hear me?" He spread his hands. "So why can't you go along with us? Wait until you've got that big office on Pennsylvania Avenue, and then you can run things the way you want. In the meantime, keep your head down, boy—otherwise you'll get so many people mad at you that you won't have a chance in hell at the convention."

"You old bastard, you *are* trying to bribe me! Why, Jake? What's so important about my stand on the Third Gens and the arms race all of a sudden? I know you well enough to see that you don't like what you're doing now. Jesus, can't you see what this issue's doing to us? You're standing there lying to me, and you know that I know it, and you're so committed you still can't back off. That's what's happened to the whole damned world, ever since that first atomic bomb fell."

Jake Dobsen took out a thick, fat cigar and rolled it between his fingers. He crinkled it near his ear, swirled it under his nose, and inhaled deeply. Then he bit off one end, spat the chunk of tobacco onto the thick rug, and ignited a kitchen match with one thumbnail.

"That's been it all along with you, hasn't it, boy? You've been carrying a poke of guilt around ever since you got out of the Army Corps back in 1946. You saw all those movies of Hiroshima and Nagasaki, and that's what wakes you up in the middle of the night." He offered me a cigar. I shook my head. "Do you think we don't know what you've been through? But we all had jobs to do in the war, and some of them were worse than what you went through. I was in command of a regiment in Burma, and the things we had to do still snap me out of sleep like a colt on a rope. But we had to win. And the rules of the game haven't changed. We have to win now, too. So as much as I understand how you feel about the bomb and the part you played in dropping it, we can't let our compassion for your pain get in the way of winning. Because, boy, in this game, the losers don't get a second chance."

"Thanks, Jake," I said. "But any guilt I may have about Hiroshima and Nagasaki is shared by a couple of hundred thousand other guys. It doesn't bother me much more than a burr under a colt's saddle, if you understand that simile."

"It's not a simile, it's a metaphor," he said without smiling. "And don't try to shit a shitter, Hugh. Maybe those other guys built the bomb and supported its delivery—but *you* dropped it."

"Maybe I did," I said. "But there's one thing you can say about the bomb I dropped."

"What's that?"

I put my empty coffee cup down and started for the door. As I went out toward the Senate Floor, I turned my head and said, "Mine didn't work."

Havana, Cuba—*January 6, 1945*

After receiving word of my father's death, I took an emergency furlough—with the understanding that I had to get from Cleveland to Havana on my own initiative if I wanted to participate in the Cuban training program. I wanted to, all right, desperately, because only ten of the B-29s had been chosen for the mission, and competition for the actual combat order was getting tight.

My worries about getting down to Cuba were the best thing that could have happened to me at the time. I was too busy to grieve. The funeral details tumbled over each other like cornflakes coming out of a Kellogg's package, and suddenly it was time to drive out to the airport and board the Military Air Transport Service C-47 that would take me as far as Maxwell Field in Montgomery, Alabama.

My father had been in the ground for over a week, and my brother, Kevin, had gone back to school. Melissa, my sister, was staying at home with our mother—she would skip the spring term at Juilliard, where she was studying music composition. The thing I remember most about those ten days at home

is a recurring melody from a piano piece Melissa was composing. She had progressed to a point about three minutes into
the composition and gotten stuck. She kept playing those three
minutes and stopping, playing and stopping—a sad, distant,
foreign-sounding melody that still visits me in my dreams. Melissa never finished her training, and today she does not even
have a piano in her home. One evening during the Kennedy
Administration when Leonard Bernstein was visiting the White
House, I told him about the way the melody recurred in my
dreams. He listened to me hum it, went directly to the piano
made famous by Harry Truman, and played it—beautifully,
accurately, and just as I remembered it. A CBS reporter made
a tape and sent me a copy, which I, in turn, sent to Melissa.
She wrote back saying it was beautiful—and asking me if I
knew who the composer was.

I was delayed for a day at Maxwell Field in Montgomery,
waiting for another plane to take me to Miami. I wandered
around the quiet, tree-shaded streets, up the long hill to the
Alabama Capitol Building. At the time I was an ardent F.
Scott Fitzgerald fan, and I imagined the author walking these
same streets while he was courting Zelda. Somehow, despite
the flood of khaki uniforms—on women as well as men—Montgomery still seemed to belong to the last century. I ate huge
servings of fried catfish, and made out in the front seat of a
Ford coupé with a typist who worked for the Alabama Supreme Court. We had met four hours before in the Golden
Bell Lounge, around the corner from the Jefferson Davis Hotel,
where you could buy 3.2 beer and spike it with your own
bourbon from a paper bag. We both promised to write; neither
of us did, and I never saw her again.

The flight to Miami finally materialized, a hedge-hopping
nightmare in a PT-6 training plane with a rock-happy marine
who had just returned from three years in the South Pacific.
He had half a case of beer in the front cockpit with him, and
as the liquid worked its way through his ample belly, he re-
filled the empty cans and heaved them over the side, trying
to make direct hits on the passing rooftops.

In Miami the air traffic officer told me my chances of getting a flight to Cuba were slim. So I paid an off-duty corporal twenty dollars to drive me to Key West in a shiny, new-looking Model T Ford that chugged patiently along the overseas highway, sounding as if it were powered with wound-up rubber bands. The accelerator lever was on the steering wheel, and the horn made a delightful *ooo-gah* sound.

At Key West I was lucky. The ferry was loaded and ready to go, and ten minutes after I walked on board, we were in the Straits of Florida, on our way to Havana.

I beat the 509th to Batista Airfield by two days, and had that time to wander around Havana, enjoying the sunshine and the high, rounded behinds of the Cuban girls. I was short on money, so I stayed out of the fancy night clubs and gambling casinos. One little bar I found had a cool, quiet feel, so I sat there for a while drinking the rich Cuban beer and rereading *The Great Gatsby*. Someone sat down next to me after a while and said, "That was Fitzgerald's best. Are you stationed here, Lieutenant?"

He was a big barrel-chested man with the kind of beard you end up with when you don't shave for a few weeks, and a crinkled, laughing squint to his eyes.

"I just got in from Montgomery," I said, and without knowing why, added, "Fitzgerald's wife came from there."

"Yes, I know," he said. We talked about Scott Fitzgerald's other novels for a few minutes, and then he surprised me with a question. "Lieutenant, are you any good with machine guns?"

"Not very," I said. "Why?"

"I suddenly have an itch to go out on my boat and shoot some sharks. I never had an Air Corps gunner aboard before."

"I'm a bombardier."

"Even better. We'll bomb the bastards. What do you say? We might even find a sub."

"I don't think so," I said. "I'm really on duty, but my outfit hasn't shown up yet."

"In that case, let me buy you a drink," he said. He waved at the Cuban bartender. "Two specials," he called, "and then keep them coming." He stuck out his hand. "Professor Hemingstein is the name."

I gave mine, and he got my knuckles in the old bone-mashing grip and squeezed until I winced; then he let go, laughing. The drinks came—tart, filled with shaved ice, delicious.

"Daiquiris," he said. "I hold the record here. Sixteen at one sitting."

"They're good," I told him.

He had picked up the Fitzgerald book and was shaking his head. "Poor dumb lovable bastard," he said, half to himself. "He killed himself as surely as if he had put a gun to his head."

"What?" I asked stupidly. "Who?"

"A gun. Scotty. Lieutenant, you've got good taste in books."

"I like to read."

"Did you ever read *For Whom the Bell Tolls?*"

"No, but I saw the movie. With Gary Cooper and Ingrid Bergman."

"My God, boy, isn't she one hunk of woman?"

He gave a great laugh and belted me on the shoulder with his fist. "Fly-boy, I like you. Are you hungry? Hey!" he yelled. "What the hell's happened to the service in this place? Where are the shrimp?"

The bartender made a helpless gesture with his hands. "But you did not order the shrimp."

"I *always* order the shrimp! Pronto!"

"Yes, señor," said the bartender. I could see there was no rancor between them, that this was a game they played.

He opened the book to the last page and squinted at it, then took out wire-rimmed GI-issue glasses and put them on.

"Best damned glasses in the world," he said. "Got them from the medics in England. I just got back from there."

"Are you in the service, sir?" I asked.

"Nope. Just a camp follower." His lips moved silently as he read the last paragraph of *The Great Gatsby*. He put the book down with a thump. "Jesus, that's a great ending. Scotty *was*

Gatsby, you know. That was really both of them out there looking across the bay at that little blue light that neither one
would ever be able to reach."

"What do you teach?" I asked.

He looked at me sharply. "What do you mean?"

"You said you're a professor."

"Well," he said slowly, "you might say I teach about things
that are real. At least, real to me. Things like hunting and fishing, to name a couple."

Puzzled, I said, "You mean you're sort of a guide?"

He roared with laughter, pounding the bar. The bartender,
mistaking, ran over and tried to explain that the shrimp were
already being boiled. The Professor waved his hand back and
forth, discounting any complaint, and nearly choking on his
amusement.

For a while he questioned me in sharp detail about my
job. I couldn't tell him anything about the Norden bombsight,
but there was nothing classified about the principles of aerial
bombardment, and he listened with intense concentration as I
discoursed on trajectories and rate of fall and all of the technical stuff I had been memorizing myself only a few months
before.

"There'll never be another war like this one," he said as
the shrimp arrived. They were pink and smelled tangy and
hot. I had never seen a shrimp in its shell before, and I did
not know what to do with it.

My new friend picked up a whole shrimp—head, shell, and
tail—and popped it into his mouth. He made great crunching
sounds as he chewed it up. He said nothing, but his eyes
watched me carefully. I copied what he had done, felt the shell
shattering between my molars, and almost choked on the sharp
fragments as I tried to swallow. Without saying anything, the
bartender snapped the head off one of the shrimp with his
thumbnail, then pulled on the flukes of the tail. Out popped
the naked, shell-less shrimp meat I was accustomed to finding
in my infrequent shrimp cocktails at fancy restaurants.

The Professor continued eating his shrimp with their shells

on while I followed the bartender's example with mine. They tasted better than any I'd ever had, and I said so.

His mouth full of chunks of shell, the Professor said, "That's because these are still alive when they go in the pot. Never freeze shrimp. Kills all the taste."

We did not approach his record of sixteen daiquiris, but when I weaved my way to the door shortly before midnight, we had passed ten. In the interim the bar had filled for a couple of hours; everyone who came in seemed to know the Professor. Around eleven it had emptied out and now we were the last ones left, the bartender yawning as we moved to go.

"Got to get back to the base," I mumbled.

"I'll put you in a cab," said the Professor, and next thing I remember, I was at the gate to Batista Airfield and the sentry was asking for my pass.

I couldn't find it, and the driver kept telling the guard, "All right, all right, he friend of Papa." I didn't understand what was going on, but I finally located the travel orders in my breast pocket and got passed through. At the BOQ, where I had left my B-4 flight bag earlier in the day, I lurched out of the cab and began fumbling for my wallet.

"No, no," said the driver. "Papa pay." To my drunken amazement, he got back in the car and drove away.

The next morning I was awakened by a banging on my door. When I opened it, a small Cuban boy was there with a large brown paper bag. "Are you the lieutenant McGavin?" he asked.

"Yeah," I mumbled, looking out from the dizziness of my hangover.

The boy handed me the bag, said, "Papa send this," and then took off before I could fumble out some change or ask who the hell Papa was. I sat down on the rumpled bunk and, because it seemed easier than opening it, ripped the paper bag down the side. A book fell out on the OD blanket, along with two bottles of Cutty Sark scotch—an incredible treasure in January of 1945. I put the bottles on the pillow carefully, and looked at the book.

It was *For Whom the Bell Tolls,* and its flyleaf bore an inscription: "One day we must go after those sharks. Meanwhile, stay well and come back to the Floridita any time you are in town. Your friend, Ernest." I turned the book over; the photograph on the back cover was that of a younger but very recognizable Professor Hemingstein.

Well, I never said I was particularly smart at nineteen, did I?

Once the training got under way, we started dropping what some joker named Pumpkins. Each bomber carried only one Pumpkin—a huge metal ovoid weighing 10,000 pounds. What was even more amazing to us, we began flying missions singly.

This went against the entire history of high-level bombing. Formation flying is all that had kept the daylight-bombing B-17s from being cut to ribbons by German fighters once our planes had overflown the range of their protective fighters. By staying in tight formation, each bomber commanded a certain arc of sky; and just as the Roman soldiers massed shoulder to shoulder with shields joined and spears extended, the bomber formation provided protection against attacking interceptors.

But in Cuba we went out alone and made long over-water flights, culminating in a drop of the Pumpkin on some Caribbean island. Once the rest of the group arrived, we were restricted to the base; so I never got back to the Floridita. But we had many bull sessions in our corner of the Officers' Club, and by the time the training was over we had all figured out what was happening.

"You men are the best the Air Corps has today," Rosy Cooper told us at one briefing. "Your mission is so secret that you are not to even dream about it, let alone write letters to your folks. In case any of you were wondering why Lieutenant Bagley never arrived in Havana, let me tell you. He had one beer too many in Wendover the night before we left and started talking about our flights to the Salton Sea. Lieutenant Bagley is now the motor pool officer on a charming island in the Aleutians called Adak. I am told that Adak is touched by the sun one day in every eighty-nine during good years, and not at all during bad ones. Do you get the message?"

We did, and watched what we said in our letters, knowing they were going to be censored anyway. But there is no rule that can prevent bull sessions in the back of the Officers' Club, and it was not very long before we had all decided that our target would be Japan, because of the intensive over-water practice; that we were going to be carrying a very new and unusual kind of bomb, because of the Pumpkin; and finally, that it was going to happen pretty soon, because of the intensity with which our training was being carried out.

We hated to leave the tropical splendor of Cuba to fly back to Wendover Field, where ice and slush still slicked the runways, but the main force of the 509th was scheduled to sail from Seattle on May 6.

To say that we found ourselves unwelcome on Tinian would be understating it. The 509th, once it was fully formed into "Project A," was supposedly isolated from the rest of the island. There were fences around our compound, and sentries with carbines and mean-looking dogs. By then, those of us who had been flying regular missions with the 20th Air Force had been pulled off them and sequestered inside the fenced-off compound.

We were warned sternly not to associate with our fellow fliers—a warning more honored in the breach than in the observance—but we still felt resentment and suspicion around us. Despite the relatively low losses the regular missions were taking, there were still men dying on the strikes against Tokyo and Yokohama, and the buddies of those men who never came back took out their anger and frustration on the 509th. So far as they could see, we were pampered and, worse, given milk runs to fly, while men who had been in the Pacific years longer than we had were ditching shattered aircraft in the ocean.

Day after day we would crawl into *The Busted Flush*, fly 1500 miles, drop a single bomb—a Pumpkin filled with conventional explosives—and return to base. The Japanese were so short on planes and antiaircraft shells that they deliberately ignored us, although after Major Claude Eatherly diverted from his cloud-shrouded target and attempted to drop his practice bomb down Emperor Hirohito's chimney in the Royal Palace, the nightly broadcast from Tokyo Rose noted: "You American boys must be disturbed to know that after flying a B-29 bomber all the way to Japan and risking death a dozen times, your arms supply is so depleted that you were only able to drop one bomb, which landed harmlessly in a vacant lot near Tokyo Station." She then played "Don't Fence Me In," followed by an orgy of Hit Parade goodies, including "Sentimental Journey" and "Mairzy Doats."

By now the nicknames of the atomic bombs had caught up with us, and we were using them. The long, slender, more conventional bomb was called the "Thin Man" and had actually been named after President Roosevelt; the chubbier, round one was called "Fat Boy" after Prime Minister Winston Churchill. When the Thin Man was redesigned and became shorter, it was renamed "Little Boy."

History tells us that Little Boy was a uranium device, while Fat Boy used plutonium. At that time, of course, we had no idea what it was that we were practicing to drop—but it was already common knowledge on Tinian that we were fooling around with a bomb that would make a hole so big it would take ten bulldozers ten years to fill it up.

Washington, D.C.—*August 2, Now*

When I came out of the Cloak Room, I found a heavy stack of papers on my Senate Floor desk. One was red-flagged, which meant top urgency. It was on ordinary blue memo paper, and read:

> Boss: I've come up with a project none of us ever heard of that seems to have eaten up nine billion dol-

lars since 1964, when my files begin. There's evidence that it was around even before then; am checking. Code name on it is Project JF and that is absolutely all I have been able to find out. Check with me before you leave the country and maybe I'll have more.

Jack

"Jack" was John Sherwood, my special assistant. He had been rummaging through the files, digging out information for my speeches on the arms race. A roly-poly little man, with fairly long pale hair, Jack looks as if he might be a hotel clerk. But behind the butter-and-eggs face with the sleepy eyes is one of the fastest and most incisive minds I have ever known. Jack's usual way to present startling information is to clear his throat over his favorite beverage, a ten-to-one martini, and say, By the way, did you know Adolf Hitler was actually Jewish? If he had resorted to a terse memo on this mysterious Project JF, the odds were that he regarded it as a big item. I made a note to call him as soon as the Senate session was over.

With many of the senators out of town, the Floor was only half-filled, but I knew this was a large turnout under the circumstances. When I had arrived, the Vice-President was absent from his seat, but as I was reading Jack's memo he hurried in.

Jake Dobsen made a long, impassioned speech, which boiled down to the same one he had given in the Cloak Room. The Senior Senator from Illinois rose and asked if the President was asking for extraordinary powers with which to handle the emergency, and the Vice-President replied that the powers already held by the President seemed adequate to handle the situation, but he thanked the Senator from Illinois for his courtesy in asking. He added, darkly, that it was unfortunate there were always one or two mavericks too independent to pull with the team, rebels who insisted on going their own way even when their actions might be adverse to the policies of their government. Good old Artie Rand was looking directly at me as he spoke.

Nothing was really resolved at the session. There was talk of troop call-ups. One senator who asked what the President was going to do about the North Korean ultimatum was told that the President was "considering" it. Questions as to whether or not we were going to pull out the missiles were met with evasion.

In all, a typical Senate session. We adjourned shortly after noon, and Arthur Rand almost broke his leg getting around the desks to catch up with me.

"How about lunch, Hugh?"

"I don't think so," I said. "I've got a lot of desk-clearing to do if I want to fly out of here tonight."

"Walk with me, then." We went out, no doubt presenting a picture of two old friends engaged in pleasant conversation. But the Vice-President was leaning on me even harder than Jake Dobsen had.

"Howard is really concerned," he told me. "Hugh, if you insist on going through with your speeches against the ABM program, the reaction might ruin you in this town."

"Arthur, if our government has gotten to a point where I can be ruined for following my conscience, I'd just as soon be ruined."

"The President's authorized me to make you an offer."

"What kind of offer?"

"Cancel your trip. Get sick. We'll give you a suite at Walter Reed if you want it. Or you and Celia can go down to Virgin Gorda for a couple of weeks."

"During a crisis like this? That'd look nice to the voters."

"Hugh, the President doesn't care *where* you go. Just promise to lay off the ABMs for the next two weeks."

"And?"

"He'll take the missiles out. Quietly, without fanfare, but the Chinese will know they're gone."

"When?"

"Next week."

"Why not tomorrow? What's the point of inflaming the issue by waiting a week if he's going to take them out anyway?"

"He wants to keep the pressure on China as long as he can; you know that."

I shook my head. "Not good enough, Arthur. Even if he

took those birds out tomorrow, there's still the whole Third Gen program. The crisis in Japan has only brought it to a head."

We were walking past the Robert Taft Memorial. The day was hot and humid as only a Washington day can be. I have always wondered why George Washington let himself be talked into moving the capital away from Philadelphia. I suppose the thought of having a whole city named after him was too tempting. It always seems to rain when I go to Philadelphia, but on any given day I will take the weather in the City of Brotherly Love over that in Washington.

We crossed the street. The Secret Service men were trailing us discreetly, but they were closer than usual, nervous about the Vice-President walking out in the open the way he was. "Look," I went on, keeping my voice low, "I don't understand all this heat from Foster. I've met him head on before, on issues he cared much more about than this ABM thing. You win a few, you lose a few, but I've never seen any reason for rancor or vindictiveness. Why is this one so different?"

"Because we're in a crisis, Hugh!"

"Bull. We've been in one continuous crisis for the past twenty years. You'll have to do better than that."

"We haven't been threatened with a declaration of war unless we knuckle under to a fourth-rate power."

"I agree that the Koreans got a little melodramatic," I said, "but even if they hadn't, once those missiles were revealed, world opinion was certain to call for their removal."

"Don't be too sure," said the Vice-President.

"No," I said, "I won't. I'm not sure about anything any more. I feel as if I got up on the wrong side of the planet this morning. This isn't the United States I know. I'll tell you something, Arthur. I'm glad the Koreans found out about those missiles. Because otherwise I probably would have had to blow the whistle myself."

"That would be treason," he said.

"Perhaps. Now we'll never know."

"Shit!" he exploded. It shocked me so much that I stopped in mid-step. I had never heard Arthur Rand so much as curse.

"Such language," I murmured.

He did not smile. "Why won't you listen to us, Hugh? What makes you defy us when you know the President must have a vitally important reason to ask you to stand down from your position? He likes you, he respects you. And you're right, you've disagreed violently before and he's taken it like the professional he is. Can't you see this time is different?"

"Do *you* know why, Arthur? Has he told you?"

He paused before answering. "No," he said finally. "I think he started to once. And he's referred several times to a sealed document that I am to open the instant he should die or cease to exercise the powers of his office."

"Where is it?"

"The bag man has it."

The bag man, a warrant officer, carried a black satchel containing all of the daily codes needed to press the nuclear button, and was never more than a few feet from the President. When the shift changed, the bag was passed along to the new officer.

"What if something happens to Air Force One and the bag goes down with the plane?"

"There's a duplicate in the White House Top Security safe," he said. "Look, I'm curious too, but if the man doesn't want to tell me, no one can compel him. Meanwhile, he has instructed me—not asked, but instructed—to persuade you to cancel your trip."

"Sorry, Arthur. The trip's still on. Foster made some threats this morning, which he later took back. And now you seem to be suggesting he's going to stop me by whatever means necessary."

"No, I'm not," Arthur Rand said. "But I can tell you this —if you insist on defying him, he'll withdraw any support you might have expected from him at the convention in Salt Lake City. And that's a quote."

"Frankly, I never thought I'd get much support from him anyway," I said. "I honestly believed he was going to throw it to you."

"Not me, Hugh. I've been next to him long enough to know

that I don't want his job, and that's between you and me. But he senses it."

"That doesn't mean he agrees with you," I said. "Sorry, Arthur. You're going to have to go back and tell him I wouldn't budge. Maybe if he hustles he can get my flight certificate cancelled before I take off tonight, and if he does I'll just take commercial flights. I doubt he'd have much luck lifting my passport, but he can always try."

The Vice-President shook his head slowly and waved for his limousine, which had been following us. I stopped at the smoke stand and bought a package of Sail tobacco, stuffed my pipe, and rode up to my third-floor office, where I found a telegram waiting for me from the FAA informing me that my pilot's license *had* been suspended pending an investigation into irregularities in my last physical: Foster's way of giving me a gentle slap on the wrist, a warning that he was prepared to be as rough as he had to.

I dialed Jack Sherwood's number and, when he answered, asked him to join Celia and me for lunch at Harvey's. He said he would see us at one, and that he had some more information for me. He sounded excited.

I spent twenty minutes trying to clear my desk, gave it up as a bad job, and left a note for Miss Bancroft to call the airfield and cancel my lease on the Lear jet, then get me on a commercial flight to London. The cancellation, I reflected glumly, would cost me a nice penalty. While I was writing, the telephone rang.

"Mouse," said Celia, "I can't make it for lunch. Something's come up."

"Too bad," I said, and told her about the odd coincidence of my pilot's license being suspended. She cursed in a most unladylike way, and I laughed.

"I'm going out commercial tonight," I said. "That is, unless Foster's had my air travel card lifted too."

"He probably has," she said. "Hugh, be careful. There's something more to this than just the confrontation with North Korea. Foster's playing for keeps."

"So am I, Ceil. Look, if you want to get off here, I won't mind."

Her voice hardened. "What exactly do you mean by 'get off here'?"

"Nothing personal, baby. But if this position of mine is going to foul you up at your job, there's no need for you to get splashed with the mud they're throwing at me. Go ahead and write anything you have to."

"Many thanks for your faith and trust, old buddy," she said, and hung up.

Women. Now I would spend the afternoon wondering where she was and whether I would see her before I set off around the world. No, not really. Angry as she might be, Celia would never do that to me. There were little unspoken rules in our battles with each other.

I dialed her private number at home. It rang, and a recording of her voice came on: "Miss Craig is not in. If you will give your message when you hear the tone, you have sixty seconds."

The beep came, and I said, "Ceil, I don't need sixty seconds. I'm sorry. I love you. Look, call Bancroft and find out what flight I'm on. I'll wait in the bar until five minutes before flight time. Kiss."

It made me feel a little better. I checked myself in the mirror, looked in the closet to be sure Miss Bancroft had packed my old B-4 bag. They really built those things. Mine had been issued in 1944, and when I was mustered out in early 1946, I'd shamelessly stolen it. The 20th Air Force insignia painted on it was cracked and fading, but the bag itself was still alive and well. That's the difference between real canvas and miracle plastic fabrics.

Jack was waiting outside Harvey's on Connecticut Avenue. "Just got here," he said. "Celia inside?"

"She couldn't make it."

"I'm not sorry," he said. "No offense, boss, but this is the kind of thing I'd be uneasy talking about around reporters, even one who happens to be your wife."

71

"In that case," I said, "let's be sure to get one of the debugged tables."

He laughed, but it was strained. The truth was, none of us was really sure how many public places in Washington were wired for sound.

"Drink?" I asked.

"Not now."

"I think I'll just have the chopped steak," I said. "Along with asparagus." I have to follow the low carbohydrate route to keep my suits fitting.

"I admire your willpower," Jack said sadly.

He took out a sheaf of papers and spread them on the table as soon as the waiter was gone. Looking around for hidden mikes, he said, "Testing, testing, one, two, three."

I gave his joke the small chuckle it deserved, and he began. "Would you believe that we have spent an average of eight hundred million dollars a year since 1945 on a project that no one knows anything about?"

"The JF thing?"

He nodded. "It's classified Top Secret, Need to Know, Eyes-Only. The money comes out of a special Presidential appropriation, and it started with Truman, in September, 1945."

"The month the war ended."

"Right. Well, as far as I can check, there's not a goddamned word anywhere about what this project is. The appropriation has gone up some years, down others. Last year, it hit a billion, one million."

I whistled. "That's a lot of special appropriation."

"And it's been consistent, for thirty years more or less. Do you know how much dough Project JF has eaten up in that time? Almost twenty-five billion bucks. That would buy a lot of peanut butter sandwiches for those kids in Appalachia." He picked up a celery stick and bit into it savagely. "Where do they *get* money like that? And how do they hide it from us?"

"Government's big business, Jack. Last year the total receipts from all sources came to over two hundred billion dollars. Siphon off a little here, a little there, and you can bury eight hundred million pretty easy."

"Well, they've been doing it," he said, finishing the celery stick and turning to a scallion. "Boss, these Xerox copies cost me three hundred bucks, and I wouldn't have gotten them even so except the young lady in question happens to agree with you that the whole military-industrial complex has gotten out of hand."

I mentioned the secret document the President had prepared for Arthur Rand. "Do you suppose that could be connected with Project JF?"

"I'll try to find out," Jack said. "Wouldn't surprise me, considering the consistency of this thing. Look at the guys involved—every President from Truman on, Democratic or Republican. And not a peep out of any of them. They've been rubber-stamping this special appropriation every year, boom or bust, upswing or recession. It doesn't surprise me that Foster would want Rand to know about it if something happens."

I sighed and picked up the Xerox copies. "Can I have these?"

"Eat them if you're captured," he said. "I promised my contact I'd show them to you and then personally tear them into shreds and flush them down the john."

"So you're a liar."

"Among other things," he agreed.

I watched the approach of our lunch. "Are you really hungry?"

"Not a bit," said my assistant. "What I want now is a drink."

"Me too," I said. Pleading an emergency call back to the Senate, we paid the surprised waiter and ducked around the corner for two fast scotches.

"I'm spooked, boss," Jack said. "I heard about your pilot's license. The word gets around fast. Foster isn't bucking for any public relations image today. He's passing the word that if you get out of line, you're to be busted. Watch it, hey? I'm too old to break in a new senator."

"Let him try," I said. "The day when a President can intimidate a United States senator hasn't arrived yet. When it does, I'll move to Mexico."

"You'll play hell getting elected next term," Jack said. "You won't be able to raise a dime for the pay toilet."

"Maybe by then I'll be on Pennsylvania Avenue myself, and I'll pass a bill outlawing pay johns. I've always thought they were just a means to enforce segregation anyway."

"I still worry about you," he said. "I don't like the idea of you brooming all over the world single-handed."

"This is out of my own pocket, friend," I said. "If you want to see Gay Paree, buy your own ticket."

"If that's all it takes for me to go with you, I'll go in hock to Diner's Club right now," he said seriously.

I touched his shoulder. "Thanks, Jack, but I was only kidding. I've got to move fast and in God knows what directions. It's London first, then Paris, and from there on make your own guess. But I appreciate the intention."

"Okay," he said, walking me out to the street. "But take care. If you get sloughed, I'm out of work. And as I said, I'm too old to look for another job."

At the curb, waiting for a cab, I said, "We'll use your phone for contacts."

"It's bugged. No kidding."

"What choice do we have?"

"Call this one," he said, scribbling an Arlington, Virginia, number on the flap of a matchbook. "New girl friend. Political science major, first job, tremendously interested in workings of government."

"Good lay?"

"Fair, but needs breaking in. Seriously, boss, unless they're tailing me twenty-four hours a day, no one knows I'm seeing this babe. I've only been out there twice."

"Okay, it can't be any worse than your place. But you've got to be there at a certain time every day."

"Make that nine A.M. and it'll be no hardship at all."

"0900 hours Arlington time," I agreed, smiling.

74

As a cab saw my wave and began making a U-turn, Jack said, "Isn't it hell when we have to move like criminals to keep our government from spying on us?"

I said nothing.

Tinian, Marianas Islands—*August 1, 1945*

Although Major Claude Eatherly never dropped an actual atomic bomb, the myth insists that guilt over what he helped do at Hiroshima caused his post-war problems: periods in various mental wards, attempted suicide, and such crimes as petty larceny and arms smuggling.

I knew Major Eatherly, although not well, during the training period at Wendover and later on Tinian. A finer pilot would have been hard to find. His B-29, *Straight Flush*, was supposedly named after that high-ranking poker hand. But I always took it as an oblique slam at *The Busted Flush*, since Eatherly's crew said the major never flew a plane rough enough to spill a glass of water, let alone rupture a chemical latrine.

Most of the ships' names had personal connotations. *The Great Artiste*, which was fitted out as a laboratory instrument plane for the Hiroshima and Nagasaki raids, was supposedly named after the legendary powers of her bombardier, Captain Tex Beahan. Captain Frederick Bock's plane, which would drop the Nagasaki bomb with another pilot at the controls, cried out for the name, *Bock's Car*. Colonel Paul Tibbets remembered being warned by everyone in his family that learning to fly would surely result in disaster—except his mother, who had said calmly, "Go ahead and fly. You'll be fine." Her maiden name was Enola Gay Haggard, and number eighty-two became *Enola Gay*.

On June 18, in Washington, President Harry S Truman had

met with a group of his military and civilian advisers. Attempting to find a solution to the war in the Far East—and aware of continuing, but so far unsuccessful, peace overtures by both sides—Truman said, "As I understood it, the Joint Chiefs of Staff are still of the unanimous opinion that the Kyushu operation is the best solution?"

This meant an amphibious invasion of the Japanese mainland, an operation certain to take half a million lives. Secretary of War Henry Stimson agreed with the Joint Chiefs, but added, "I think there is a large submerged class in Japan who do not favor the present war and whose full opinion and influence has not yet been felt. I feel something should be done to arouse them and to develop any possible influence they might have before it becomes necessary to face them on the beaches."

After further conversation, Truman agreed that the Joint Chiefs should proceed with the Kyushu operation.

It was then that John McCloy, Assistant Secretary of War, changed the history of the world. He declared that the idea of invading Japan was "fantastic," and suggested instead, "Why not use the atomic bomb?"

This opened a new argument, about whether the ethics of civilized warfare dictated that Japan should be warned before using such a weapon. It was reiterated that the bomb had not been tested, and no one was even sure it would work. Truman reaffirmed his approval of the amphibious invasion, and the meeting adjourned with the understanding that work on the bomb would be hurried along.

So the 509th flew its practice runs for a mission that might never happen, with a bomb that might never work, while the entire Pacific swarmed with preparations for what would be the bloodiest assault known to mankind.

The thriving sugar cane business built up on Tinian by the Japanese had given way to the huge runways of North Field. The lepers were out of sight and out of mind.

Since the island was shaped somewhat like Manhattan, the Seabees had laid out the wide asphalt roads to correspond with the city's streets. We had an Eighth Avenue, a Forty-second

Street, and a Broadway. The 509th's barbed wire enclosure was located roughly at Columbia University, in upper Manhattan.

We went to the outdoor movie theater every evening and tried to forget the crazy Jap sniper who might one day tire of shooting at Keye Luke and aim his weapon at one of us instead. We (that is, those of us who were officers) were entitled to buy one bottle of liquor a week for $1.30, but it did not go as far as you would think, because custom dictated that the booze be shared with the enlisted members of the crew. When your life depends on a man's skilled hands, you do not hesitate to split your whiskey ration with him.

Occasionally we flew missions and dropped a Pumpkin on Japan, and although sometimes we circled for minutes after the drop, we were never able to see that the huge bomb had done much damage. Meantime, the fliers of the 20th Air Force who drew the day-in, day-out missions against the Japanese homeland, sustaining regular losses, increased their resentment against us.

On their way to briefings, at two in the morning, they let out their anger by tossing rocks over the barbed wire fences, against the tin roofs of our Quonset huts. In the middle of the night, when you had just managed to go to sleep despite the heat building up inside your mosquito net, the clang of a good-sized chunk of coral against the Quonset's roof made you think you were inside a kettle drum.

Some unsung hero of the 20th Air Force wrote an ode to our misunderstood presence. Called "Nobody Knows" it was mimeographed and distributed all over the island—especially in the mess halls of the 509th. We laughed it off, but the humor had a bitter undertone to it, and it touched our hidden feelings of guilt. By then we were starting to lose our pride in being the elite, to wonder if there was something wrong with us that we were sheltered and protected so.

I still have a crinkled, yellowing copy of the poem, and at one time even tried to find the man who wrote it. My efforts were unsuccessful. But whoever he is, and wherever he is, I can tell him now that he hit a sore nerve in the men of the 509th.

NOBODY KNOWS

Into the air the secret rose.
Where they're going, nobody knows.
Tomorrow they'll return again,
But we'll never know where they've been.
Don't ask us about results or such,
Unless you want to get in Dutch.
But take it from one who is sure of the score,
The 509th is winning the war.

When the other groups are ready to go,
We have a program on the whole damned show.
And when Halsey's Fifth shells Nippon's shore,
Why, shucks, we hear about it the day before.
And MacArthur and Doolittle give out in advance,
But with this new bunch we haven't a chance.
We should have been home a month or more,
For the 509th is winning the war.

At this time in Washington, a target list was being drawn up. Kyoto, the Japanese shrine city, was originally on the list. Secretary of War Stimson crossed it off, substituting Tokyo. "We don't blow up temples unless we have to," he told his aides. But General Hap Arnold, wanting Kyoto as a target, put it back on again. Stimson erased it a second time. The final list had Tokyo at the top, followed by Kokura, Osaka, and Kobe. Hiroshima and Nagasaki were not mentioned.

On Tinian General Curtis LeMay and a number of officers from the Project A group met and formed the "Tinian Joint Chief of Staff" to plan for the first drop.

In the meantime the rocks rained against our tin roofs; we fought mosquitos and flies, swilled beer from cans half rusted by the salt air, and snarled at our enemies, the fliers of the 20th Air Force.

Then, on July 16, 1945, halfway around the world from our

tropic island, three men lying in the New Mexico desert saw the sky light up with the brightness of a thousand suns. The uranium bomb, the Thin Man, was considered so foolproof that it was not even tested. But that dawn at Alamogordo the plutonium device, the Fat Man, detonated successfully; and as Vannevar Bush, James B. Conant, and General Leslie Groves clasped hands silently, the atomic age moved from theory into stark, terrifying reality.

Preparations on Tinian took on a feverish pitch. We did not have to be told that the crews were being trimmed down to a select few. Those of us who delivered the Pumpkins most often knew we were at the top of the list. No one had yet told us officially that there was anything bigger in store for us than the Pumpkins themselves. No one had to.

At that time, our crew list looked like this:

> PILOT—Captain Charles "Tex" Ritter
> CO-PILOT—1st Lieutenant Ben Heller
> BOMBARDIER—1st Lieutenant Hugh McGavin
> NAVIGATOR—1st Lieutenant Tim Bond
> TAIL GUNNER—S/Sgt. Joe Kingsly
> FLIGHT ENGINEER—S/Sgt. Norman Percy
> RADIO OPERATOR—S/Sgt. Phillip Bowie
> RADAR OPERATOR—S/Sgt. Tom O'Neal
> WAIST GUNNER—Sgt. Tom Barnes

Later, on the actual mission, we would be carrying three more officers as supercargo:

> WEAPONEER—Captain Meredith Rogers, USN
> ASSISTANT WEAPONEER—Lieutenant Paul Randolph, USN
> ECM (Electronic Countermeasures)—1st Lieutenant George Murphy

These last three did not fly on any of the practice missions. It made us slightly uneasy, even after all these months, to be unarmed except for S/Sgt. Joe Kingsly's tail guns. Ordinarily the B-29 is heavily armed—hence the nickname "superfortress."

Central Fire Control gunners working from midship were normally able to concentrate a fierce screen of .50 caliber slugs on any attacking fighter. Now, the only way we could shoot at an enemy was first to run away from him.

To make matters more interesting, Kingsly was under orders to report to the base photo lab on every non-flying day, where he was undergoing instruction in photography.

"Lieutenant," he said to me one day, "I don't know what I am any more—a gunner or a fashion photographer."

Issued an impressive camera, a Rolliflex with twin lenses and unlimited film, he practiced his art on us. He also practiced on every test mission, shooting dozens of pictures of the Japanese homeland as we sped away from it. Some of them were amazingly good. I cannot say the same for the portrait he made of me, standing in such a way that a coconut palm appeared to be growing out of my head.

As the tension increased, we let ourselves drift into a strange isolation. Instead of being curious about what kind of Pumpkin we were carrying to Japan, we actually went out of our way to avoid looking at it. The human subconscious was at work, screening out a truth we did not want to know. Even here on Tinian, three officers who disregarded the prohibition about talking of our work found themselves instantly on aircraft bound for such paradises as Malaya and Wake Island. None of us, so far as I know, had any attacks of conscience or moral reservations about what we knew we were training to do. Our self-imposed distance from knowledge provided self-preservation. No one wanted to sit out the war on Wake, a miserable little aircraft stopover which rises no more than six feet above the waves halfway between Honolulu and the Marianas.

One night near the end of July, I was sitting in front of the Quonset hut when the fliers of the 20th Air Force came by with their chunks of coral. The missiles clanged against the roof, and then one came a little too close for comfort, thudding into the sand just inches away from my combat boot. I got up and went over to the fence.

"Listen," I said, "fun is fun, but don't hurt me, fellows. I'm being saved for better things."

"That's what we hear," growled a flier, all wrapped up in his flight suit and heavy leather jacket. While it was tropical on Tinian, at 30,000 feet the temperature outside a plane's thin aluminum skin is seventy degrees below zero. "Is this barbed wire to keep you in, or us out?"

"They don't want our minds contaminated by all your cursing and evil talk," I said.

He spat. "Kid, I've been out here for nineteen months. I've flown one tour of forty missions, and I'm halfway through my second. How many have you flown?"

"Five," I said. "But we can't all be heroes."

"What are you guys up to?" he asked, dropping his voice and some of its exaggerated hostility.

"I don't know."

"Crap!" he said, mad again. He would have said more, but an MP came down along the edge of the fence: "Move along there. No talking."

"Well," said the flier, starting off, "let us know when you've won the war."

"Sure," I said. I went back to my perch on the Quonset hut steps, but the cigarette tasted lousy so I crushed it out against the white coral sand and went inside to try and sleep.

I was half undressed when I heard the first of the B-29s roaring down the runway. There was something subtly wrong with the sound of its engines. I ran outside. The plane rose into view over the palm trees that surrounded our compound. It was in a climbing turn, and two engines seemed to be cutting in and out. The moon was bright and I could see the plane clearly. It lowered its port wing, then fell off swiftly in what looked like a slip and disappeared out of sight behind the palms. There was a bright orange flash, and then the sound reached me, a *KA-WHOOOOM!* that was as much air pressure as noise. The orange flash turned into a column of oily black smoke and flame that rose hundreds of feet into the humid air.

The other B-29s continued their takeoffs; they would fly seven hours to Japan and seven hours back. By the time their crews returned, the bunks in the Quonset would be stripped and the mattresses rolled, and all the personal belongings would have been taken away.

Distantly, I heard the wail of a crash truck. It didn't matter. When a B-29 carrying 2,000 pounds of bombs and a full fuel load explodes, there is nothing a crash truck can do—no, nor a burial squad, either, because whatever is left, if anything, is like a chunky, charred, two-foot-long fire log.

I went back to bed, but it was a long time before I slept. I thought I could smell the burning plane.

Dulles International Airport—*August 2, Now*

My B-4 bag was checked through to London; my ticket was in order. I had been assigned Seat A-6, which gave me the options of sleeping, reading, or looking at the movie. I had a pocketful of traveler's checks, credit cards, and cash. My passport—still untouched, so far as I knew, by the ubiquitous hand of the President—was in my pocket.

The only thing missing was Celia. I checked my watch. Fifteen minutes before I had to hustle. Usually, at Dulles, they put you in a big buslike gadget called a mobile lounge and drive you out to the plane. My VIP status relieved me of that inconvenience, but the BOAC courtesy driver had warned me that I had to be in his jeep no later than five of eight.

Suddenly her arms wrapped around my neck.

Her face pressed against mine. It was wet and cold.

"Mouse," she said. "I'm sorry. I'm a bitch. Forgive me."

"You're forgiven," I said. "Stop crying. Here's a martini."

"It looks dead," she said, sitting down.

"No offense intended, but it's been waiting quite a while. It's probably half ice-water by now. I'll order another."

"Don't. There isn't time." She sipped at the sweating glass. "Oh, my dear, what a day. You don't know what's going on."

"I can guess. They've had everybody after me but the ghost of George Washington, and he's probably warming up in the bullpen."

"I don't mean that. Didn't you hear? *Pravda* condemned the presence of our missiles in Japan and called them a serious challenge to world peace."

"So," I said, sipping my own watered-down drink, "Nabov chickened out on us. Well, it was to be expected. What else did the Russians say?"

"That Foster has embarked on a dangerous adventure which could lead to ominous consequences. A fairly hard line, but something tells me they've avoided putting the button on it. If they really wanted trouble, they'd have gone just a little bit further."

"They went far enough," I said. "Ceil, I've got to hurry. Listen—I'll be in touch as often as I can. Anything I want you to know that shouldn't be broadcast all over town, I'll pass along through Jack Sherwood. He thinks he's got a safe phone, and maybe we'll be able to talk without being overheard."

"Big Brother is listening," she said glumly.

"Jack's own words," I said. "Baby, I hate to go just now. But you know if I have to make a choice between getting the nomination and coming out for what I know is right, there's only one way I can go."

"Of course I know. Why do you think I love you? Who wants the White House anyhow?"

"*I* do," I admitted. "But not on just any terms. Keep that in mind when it appears your nutty husband is committing political suicide over there."

"Are we all paid up?"

"Yes, but we still have five minutes."

"Which," she said, "I would rather spend outside in the twilight where maybe I could give you a proper goodbye."

We went out through the special gate and stood in the shadows. The BOAC driver looked the other way.

"God, Mouse, I'm going to miss you," Celia said, pressing up against me. "I wish you weren't flying. You know how it scares me. In my heart, I know the Wright brothers were wrong."

"This is a *British* plane," I said. "Come here."

She wrapped both arms around my head and pulled me down to her waiting mouth. In seconds, I was aroused. She felt me, and drew away a little.

"Nope," she whispered. "Can't have you smuggling that on board for the stewardesses."

"BOAC has stewards," I mumbled.

"Even worse," she said, dabbing at my lips with her handkerchief. Then the tears burst forth and she seemed small and defenseless—not at all the unflappable Washington columnist.

"Oh, Hugh," she said, "I wish I could go with you."

"So do I," I said, meaning it. The BOAC driver "accidentally" brushed his elbow against the horn. It made a tiny, furtive beep. It was time to go.

"Take care of yourself," Celia said.

"You too."

I was already in the jeep when she called, "Hey, Hugh!"

"Yeah?"

"Catch!" She tossed a package at me. It arched past the driver's startled face and fell into my hands like a football. "A little present. Open it on the plane."

Over the sound of the engine I bellowed, "Many thanks!"

"Sir, we really must go," said the driver.

"Right," I said. "Sorry." I waved at her again as the jeep made a sweeping turn and headed out to the waiting jet plane. The mobile lounge passed us on its way back.

At the plane, the driver said, "You'll have to go up the crew ramp, sir."

"No trouble," I said, and thanked him. Carrying Celia's package under one arm, I climbed up the narrow steps.

"Welcome aboard, Senator," said a steward. "I'll show you to your seat."

I followed him back past the gallery and into the first-class compartment, where I slipped into my seat and fastened my belt.

A light on the bulkhead that had read "Lounge Occupied" went out. A man came down the aisle and took the seat beside me.

"Hello, Senator."

It was Phil Hepburn, the President's Special Assistant for National Security.

"Hello, Phil," I said. "Going somewhere?"

"London," he said. "The President thought it might be a good idea if you had someone along to take notes."

"Shove it, buddy," I said. "I can't stop you from following me around, but I don't have to talk with you."

He rubbed his high forehead. "I just take orders."

"I don't," I said, irrationally angry beyond whatever provocation Phil's presence might have provided. "And I don't like being spied on."

"Look," he said calmly, "if it makes you any happier, I'll stay out of your sight. But don't kid yourself—I'll be around. It just seemed to me it might be friendlier to travel together instead of playing follow the leader, but if you want it that way, okay."

When he started to get up, I pulled him back by his sleeve.

"Never mind," I said. "I know it's not your fault. Let's have a drink and tell lies about the good old days."

"I don't drink any more," he said, "but I lie very well indeed."

"That's right, you had that operation."

"That operation, as you put it," Phil said peevishly, "removed two feet of my colon, all of it pickled in gin. I'm lucky not to be going to the bathroom in a plastic sack. But don't let me ruin *your* cocktail hour."

"You are a sweet man," I said, feeling the plane move. "Let me know what you most enjoy eating and can't any more, and I'll be sure to order it. Anything except carbohydrates. The drinking man's diet, you know."

Cheerfully he said, "May you rot in hell."

We both fell silent, feeling the huge airliner hurtle down the runway, shuddering on the edge of being airborne. The wheels broke away from the concrete, and the lights of Dulles International dropped away beneath us.

"You never get over it, do you?" said Phil.

I gave him a puzzled look. Silently, he pointed at my feet. Without knowing I had been doing it, I was manipulating nonexistent rudder pedals. I grinned and relaxed my feet.

"I do the same thing when I'm riding in someone else's car," Phil said.

"Thanks to your boss, I'm not really flying this thing," I said. "What would you have done? Tied yourself on the tail with a rope?"

"I don't know what you're talking about," he said slyly. He nodded at the package. "What's that?"

"I don't know," I said. "Celia tossed it at me as I was running for the plane."

I tore the paper away. Inside, wrapped in tissue, was a huge, fuzzy, grinning velvet mouse.

"What the hell is that supposed to mean?" said Phil Hepburn. "A toy mouse?"

"I couldn't explain it," I said, smiling.

The President's Situation Room was shut down except for the big world map that filled one wall, flickering with telemetered updates of troop and missile positions.

Howard Foster had dismissed the Situation Room staff, and was sitting quietly in the dim room with General Oscar Burton, Chairman of the Joint Chiefs of Staff.

"Mr. President," said the General, "I'm beginning to feel like a first-rate idiot, rampaging around yelling Sic 'em!"

"Penalty of rank," smiled the President. "Part of the routine has to be that the military is chomping at the bit to empty the holes and use those missiles, restrained only by a sane, sensible civilian hand on the reins."

"I feel like Curtis LeMay," groaned Burton.

"Then now you know how *he* felt," said the President.

"Are you trying to tell me LeMay wasn't really advocating preventive nuclear strikes?"

Foster shrugged. "Figure it out for yourself," he said. "But you have to admit that the test of any strategy is its success or failure. So far, ours has succeeded."

The General got up and examined the flashing red dots over western Japan on the map. "So far," he said. "But we may have pushed them one step too far this time. My information is that China has gone to Condition Yellow, just one step to Standby—which, of course, is just one below Condition Red."

"That was the purpose of this maneuver," Foster reminded him. "We wanted to see how far they'd go. If our calculations are right, they'll never hit that Red Alert."

"And if they do?"

"We crawl out of Japan on our bellies, apologizing all the way. But then, as much as I've resisted it until now, we start opening up those warehouses at the Dugway Proving Ground."

"And you call the military bloodthirsty? Jesus, Mr. President, even an atomic bomb is more selective than that stuff at Dugway. Remember a few years ago, when an accidental leak from a spray plane killed 6,000 sheep in Skull Valley? That nerve gas was carried miles from where it was supposed to be. Suppose those 6,000 sheep had been 6,000 Indians on the Skull Valley Reservation? Or suppose the wind had been blowing the other way, toward Salt Lake City?"

"Why are you chewing *me* out, General?" asked the President. "That was an Army goof-up."

Burton tapped the map with a pointer. "Well, this one isn't an Army goof-up. What do we do if the Chinese empty their holes without going up the ladder through Standby and Red? Suppose they just push the button without any further escalation?"

"They won't," said Foster. He sighed. "Anyway, if they did, at least we'd know. We're pretty sure already about the Russians, France, and Great Britain. China's been the big question mark. I have Premier Nabov's word that even if China empties her holes, Russia won't join in the strike. And we can survive a first strike from China."

"I assume you're not serious," said the General. "That is, I assume you're not willing to trade eighteen million American dead to find out whether or not China's willing to push the button."

"There's no reason it should go that far," said the President. "If we learn for a certainty that China is *prepared* to fire her missiles, that will tell us all we need to know. What we'll probably find out is that she isn't, in the final analysis, willing to go that far. Then the status quo will be back to normal again and we can all breathe a little easier."

"Mr. President," said Burton, "how much do you know about the development of the atomic bomb?"

The President smiled. "I honestly believe I could pass a course in nuclear physics by now. Why?"

"Back in the middle forties, when the eggheads were trying to figure out how much plutonium it took to make a critical mass, there wasn't any easy way to get an answer. So some poor bastard spent a couple of weeks sitting at a steel table with two chunks of plutonium and a screwdriver, tickling the dragon's tail."

"Tickling the what?"

"That's what they called the experiment he was making. The room was full of Geiger counters and recording equipment, and what this guy did was to shove those two chunks of plutonium closer and closer to each other while the Geiger counters went crazy. He wanted to see how close he could get to critical mass, but he had to be careful not to reach it, because if he had—"

"I think I get the point," said the President.

"Well," said Burton, "isn't that what we're doing now? Tickling the dragon's tail, seeing how close we can get before it gets mad, turns around, and burns our heads off?"

"General," said the President, "if the dragon has teeth, that's exactly what we're doing."

"Well," said Burton, "don't forget that guy at the steel table tickled once too often. He died nine days later from the overdose."

Sixty-seven-year-old Mikhail Nabov, Premier and Chairman of the Central Committee of the U.S.S.R., sighed and examined the latest series of communiqués which had been handed to him.

"Everything is going according to plan," he said. But when one of his officers agreed, he added, "Why, then, has this great weight settled itself on my back? I knew the risks involved in this project, and we all agreed it was wise to accept them. We must take China's measure. But in the back of my mind something is saying, 'No, no, we have made a mistake.' Gentlemen, I have learned never to ignore that little voice. It lives in a world where there are no 'arrangements,' no 'understandings.' It is a quiet voice that believes in one goal only—self-preservation. And now that voice is telling me that we may have made a serious error."

Mikhail Nabov looked around the room, at his staff and his advisors, and said, "We must present an appearance of readiness to the world. Bring our missile complexes to Standby and begin the countdown."

In Tokyo a small, thin man entered the offices of International Telegraph on the Ginza.

"I would like to send a message, please," he said. "It is to the Honorable Senator Hugh McGavin in Washington, D.C."

"Please fill out this lamentable but necessary document," said the clerk behind the counter.

Squinting through round, thick glasses, the man printed laboriously in English.

THE HON. SENATOR H. MC GAVIN,
WASHINGTON, D.C., U.S.A.
ESTEEMED SIR I HAVE VALUABLE INFORMATION CONCERN-

ING YOUR NOBLE POSITION ON NUCLEAR WARFARE STOP PLEASE CONTACT THE UNDERSIGNED AT HIBYA HALL TOKYO.

YOSHIJE NAKAMURA

The clerk counted the words. "Please pay two thousand, four hundred yen, Nakamura-san."

Nakamura paid and went back onto the hot pavement of the Ginza. He felt inside the pockets of his shabby suit. Now he had less than 10,000 yen, or twenty-eight dollars, between him and starvation.

The clerk looked after him, smiled, and turned to the teletypist.

Touching his forehead, he said, "*Baka na hito*. The crazy one."

In Peking, Chairman K'ang Na-Soong sat alone in a small room, cooled by a breeze that blew over a small rock garden and a lily pond. Holding a brush delicately in his hand, he drew small birds on a long strip of rice paper.

The bird flies, he thought, and the wind is angry.

Another stroke.

The man on earth sees the bird and feels the wind.

Another.

If the bird should fall, the wind will rejoice.

K'ang sipped from a fragile teacup, bent over his drawing again.

The man will pick up the tiny creature and feel its heart flutter against his palm.

When the wind blows harder, the man will feel cold and hurry inside.

If he leaves the bird by the path, the wind may freeze it.

If he takes the bird inside, the waiting cat may feast.

Can he make the bird fly again?

He throws it into the air.

The bird may fly. Perhaps it will make peace with the wind.

Or it may fall. And the cat will be waiting.

Which is it to be?

Chairman K'ang stepped back from his painting. It is what it is, he thought.

He rang a tiny silver bell.

A servant hurried in.

"Bring me General Lui-han," said the Chairman. "Inform him that I wish all information about the American missile bases in Japan."

The servant bowed and left. K'ang Na-Soong turned to pick up the painting, but the wind had blown it into the pool, and it was sinking out of sight in the water.

A hand was pulling at my shoulder. I struggled up from sleep.

"Hugh?" said Phil Hepburn. "You were talking in your sleep. Something about an alarm bell going off."

I rubbed my forehead. "Sorry," I mumbled.

"It's all right," he said. "I'm just as glad to have had an excuse to wake you up. I don't know what else you do good in the sack, but let me tell you, Senator, you hold the world's championship for snoring."

Tinian, Marianas Islands—*August 2, 1945*

"Jeez, Lieutenant, you take the cake for snoring," the CQ said, the echo of his whistle still blaring in my ears. "Up and at 'em. Drop your cocks and grab your socks."

It was two in the morning. We had another mission scheduled for today. The sour smell of mildewed canvas and sweating men filled the Quonset hut. We staggered outside and down the walk made of crushed white seashells to the latrine, which had a wooden wall waist high for modesty's sake but was open otherwise to the elements. There were two long rows of wooden benchlike ten-holers which were scrubbed down daily with lye soap and lemon powder by the fatigue details. Along one wall were homemade tin urinals. Everything emptied into a huge underground reservoir which had been blasted out of the living coral by the Seabees. When the level reached a point where quicklime could no longer control the odor, the latrine would be filled in and a new one opened.

A few feet away along a concrete walk was the group shower—another waist-high wall for modesty. The water was cold. It would be years before hot water came to Tinian.

As we attended to our bodies we could hear the cry of night birds feeding on flying insects.

We still had no clear idea of what we were going to do, or when we were going to do it. Information regarding the bomb was in short supply. General Douglas MacArthur, who shared command of the Pacific War with Admiral Chester Nimitz, had been given the word only the day before, on August 1. General Carl "Toohy" Spaatz, head of the Strategic Air Force, made a special flight to inform the General personally that a superweapon had been brought into his command and that a military group, the 509th Composite, had been formed to deliver it without MacArthur's being informed of either.

"Tell me a little more about this bomb, General," MacArthur said, sucking on his famous corncob pipe.

"It works," said Spaatz. "They tested the first on July 16 at Alamogordo, New Mexico. The yield was equivalent to 20,000 tons of TNT."

"20,000 pounds of TNT?" MacArthur said, misunderstanding. "That's the pay load of ten B-29s. Very good."

"I said 20,000 tons, sir," said Spaatz. "It'd take two hundred B-29s to deliver that much destruction."

MacArthur sat quietly for a moment. "You know," he said thoughtfully, "this is going to change our notions of warfare."

MacArthur always was one for understatement.

Showering next to me, Tim Bond tried to work up a lather with the yellow GI-issue salt-water soap and cursed, as he did every morning.

"Goddamned salt water," he mumbled.

"Nervous in the service?"

"Rock happy," he agreed. Rinsing, he said, "Mac, where do you think we're going today?"

"How about San Francisco?"

"That's an idea," he chortled. "I'll make a mistake on the heading. By the time Tex wakes up we'll be halfway to California."

"What do you say when he notices the sun is rising in the west?"

"Hell, this is the Far East *The*-ater! Everything is ass backwards here."

After lathering up and trying to get clean under the salt-water shower heads, you were supposed to get all the soap off and then step under the single fresh water head to rinse away the salt. A bored pfc was on duty to make sure no one took his entire shower with the precious fresh water. He was dozing this morning, and I let the delicious, sweet liquid pool in my armpits and groin.

"Come on," grumbled Tim. "Save some for the workers."

We dressed and made our way to the mess hall, "The Dog Patch Inn," where, in honor of the fact that we were flying a mission, we were served real eggs instead of the usual reconstituted ones. There were sausages, too, and oatmeal with chunks of margarine melting in it. The coffee was black and freshly made.

We ate quickly, and tucked bits of toast and little sausages wrapped in napkins into our flight suit pockets to flesh out the soggy box lunches we would find on board *The Busted Flush*.

"What kind of Pumpkin are we hauling today?" Tim asked over his second cup of coffee.

"Don't know," I mumbled through my oatmeal. "Didn't ask."

"Well how the hell am I supposed to compute wind drift and gas consumption if I don't know how much weight we're carrying?"

"See the chaplain," I said.

Actually, I did know which Pumpkin we were carrying. It was the slim, torpedo-shaped "Little Boy." We had carried Little Boy for the past two missions—but I saw no point in talking about it, especially when the everpresent intelligence officers were all around me.

We wandered over to the briefing hut and stubbed out our Camels in the #10 cans that had crossed the Pacific carrying tomatoes or fruit cocktail, only to end their days filled with sand as GI ashtrays. Rosy Cooper himself briefed us, and it was just what I had expected. We were to rendezvous at Iwo Jima, arrive over Tokyo at 0900 hours, drop our Pumpkin in Hibya Park, across the street from Frank Lloyd Wright's Imperial Hotel.

"Don't hit the hotel," Cooper warned. "Not only are there a bunch of neutral dignitaries living there, the Architects' Association would never forgive you."

Two of us were going out tonight: our own *The Busted Flush* and *Bock's Car*. We had Tokyo, and Bock had Kobe.

"This is the life," Tim said as our weapons carrier growled its way across the runway to *The Busted Flush*. "Up early in the morning, hit the sky for some good fresh air, exercise your sphincter muscles trying not to shit when the flak comes up, then back to do sitting-up exercises batting away the mosquitos. When this war is over I'm going to run the same routine as a packaged tourist attraction. I'll be a millionaire by the time I'm thirty."

I made a walk-around under the open bomb bay doors to check the Pumpkin. As I had known, it was Little Boy, and all the connections and mechanisms seemed all right. Our pilot, Captain Ritter, joined me.

"What do you think's in that thing, Mac?" he asked.

"A couple of hundred pounds of H.E., I'd judge, from the impact marks."

"What the hell are we doing flying 3,000 miles to drop two hundred pounds of high explosive?"

"Tex," I said earnestly, "do you want to set up light housekeeping on Wake Island? Those shooflies aren't kidding. A loose lip may not sink a ship, but it'll sink you, in some crummy jungle that even Tarzan wouldn't have."

"It's a hell of a war," he sighed.

We got aboard and waited for the green light from the tower. Tex took every foot of the runway before he rotated the yoke slowly and *The Busted Flush* eased into the sky, passing over the blackened carcasses of B-29s that had not made that vital transition from concrete to sky soon enough. Huddled in my position in the transparent nose, I saw the blackness that marked the end of the runway rushing toward me; as always I whispered, without realizing it, "God, let us get off one more time and I'll never ask anything again." I did not know that my throat microphone picked it up, despite the fact that I had not spoken aloud, and that everyone on the bomber heard me. It was years later before one of them told me about it. At the time, each of the other men had a version of my not-so-silent prayer to occupy his own mind with, and no time to be concerned with mine.

Our first leg to Iwo Jima was flown at 9,000 feet, and since there was nothing else to do, most of us just settled down and napped. Tex Ritter had the ship on autopilot, and I was never completely sure that *he* didn't sleep too.

With the battle of Okinawa over, Luzon secured by the Allies, and things going very badly in Japan's remaining outposts in China and Manchuria, the Japanese government had secretly been suing for peace for several months. In later years I was horrified to learn how a series of misunderstandings and misinterpreted communications had extended the war for extra bloody weeks. Had those messages been understood by both sides and acted upon, the atomic bomb might never have been dropped.

But on July 16, when Fat Boy was tested in the New Mexico desert, the administration of the United States was committed either to total destruction of the Japanese military machine, or to unconditional surrender. It was the "unconditional" that caused all the trouble. The Japanese were willing to accept all the normal penalties of defeat—but that key word, which, had they known it, was subject to various interpretations by the victorious Allies, was the stumbling block. Without some guarantee that the position of the Emperor would be respected, and that the outlying Japanese islands would not summarily be turned over to an occupying Russian force, those Japanese in favor of surrender could not make themselves heard in their own homeland.

At Alamogordo, the Fat Boy, or "The Gadget," as it was then called, was suspended from a metal tower a hundred feet high. The scientists, none of whom knew for sure what the yield of the device would be, had formed a pool into which each put a dollar. The eventual winner was Dr. Isadore Rabi, who guessed 18,000 tons of TNT.

But before the detonation, Dr. Enrico Fermi, the first man ever to split the atom, was scurrying about the blast site placing bits of torn paper in strategic locations. "Bah on your machinery," he informed the surprised technicians. "I will tell you the accurate yield before your devices stop oscillating."

At exactly 5:30 A.M., Mountain Daylight Saving Time, a monstrous green super-sun rose over the New Mexico desert, flooding the barren landscape with an eerie, fiery glow never before seen by human eyes.

The fireball rose rapidly to 8,000 feet above the huddled men, while Dr. Fermi, a determined man who would not be cowed by either instruments or atomic flame, watched the antics of his tumbling bits of paper.

Dr. Julius Robert Oppenheimer described his reactions to the blast by quoting from a book of sacred Hindu writings:

> If the radiance of a thousand suns
> Were to burst at once into the sky
> That would be like the splendour of the Mighty One.
> I am become Death,
> The shatterer of Worlds.

In later years, the radiance of this day would shatter him,

too, when he opposed the hydrogen bomb and was stripped of his security clearance.

Meanwhile, Dr. Fermi was measuring the displacement of his bits of paper and furiously manipulating a slide rule. True to his word, before the readouts of the instruments could be taken, he announced, "20,000 tons of TNT."

It took the machines two days to confirm his findings.

Those minutes on the New Mexico desert remain in the minds of many observers as a deep, almost mystical experience. William L. Laurence, science editor for *The New York Times*, wrote: "If the first man could have been present in the moment of creation when God said 'Let there be light,' he might have seen something like what we saw."

Harvard scientist George Kistiakowsky saw death rather than birth. He was positive that in the final seconds of the world, the last man would see something quite similar to that fiery moment.

Secretary of War Henry Stimson, who was in Potsdam, Germany, received a coded message:

DOCTOR HAS JUST RETURNED MOST ENTHUSIASTIC AND CONFIDENT THAT THE LITTLE BOY IS AS HUSKY AS HIS BIG BROTHER. THE LIGHT IN HIS EYES WAS DISCERNIBLE FROM HERE TO HIGHHOLD AND I COULD HAVE HEARD HIS SCREAMS FROM HERE TO MY FARM.

This revealed that the bomb blast could have been seen as far away as Stimson's Long Island Highhold summer house 250 miles from Washington. The assistant who sent the message lived on a farm fifty miles from the Capitol; the sound of the explosion could have been heard at that distance.

Still smarting from the demands Stalin had made at Yalta, Stimson confided to his diary, "We do not need Russia any more."

On July 24 President Harry S Truman met with Soviet Premier Josef Stalin. Through a trusted interpreter he informed Stalin, "We have developed a new weapon that has unusual destructive force."

"The Germans were able to destroy millions of Russian

lives with nothing more than panzers and starvation," Stalin commented.

"You don't understand," President Truman persisted. "We can end the war with this weapon."

"Good," said Stalin, projecting a bored disinterest. Puzzled, Truman returned to his quarters and held an emergency meeting with Stimson.

The following day, at the Ceilienhof Palace, a handsome brownstone building near the rubble of bomb-shattered Berlin, the Secretary of War met again with the Premier. Stimson told Stalin that the United States welcomed Russia's participation in the war against Japan.

"We worked well together in bringing the Nazi tyrant to his grave," said Stalin. "Let us work equally well in toppling the Japanese aggressor."

Translated loosely, that meant, "What's in it for me?"

Stimson knew that the atomic bomb would be used soon; he knew, too, that Stalin knew. But neither man voiced his knowledge openly. Diplomatic protocol dictated against it. Without saying so in words, Stalin wanted to know how much of the fallen Japanese Empire would be spoils for the Soviets. Also without using words, Stimson tried to let Stalin know that the game had changed, that Russia's intervention was no longer a vital issue.

Near the end of the conversation, Stimson became aware of a disturbance in the adjoining room. The door opened briefly, and he caught a glimpse of what looked like a motion picture camera fallen against it. The interpreter said, "No newsreels allowed," and the door shut again. Stimson meant to mention the incident to the President, but it slipped his mind, and so it would be years before anyone became aware of Stalin's unusual fascination with motion picture cameras.

The meeting ended with some semblance of agreement, and on July 26, 1945, the Potsdam conference concluded with the issuance of an ultimatum to the Japanese Empire.

Of the thirteen points, the final one was the trigger that ultimately sent the atomic bomb to Japan.

POINT THIRTEEN: We call upon the Government of Japan to proclaim now the unconditional surrender of all Japanese armed forces, and to provide proper and adequate assurance of their good faith in such action. The alternative for Japan is prompt and utter destruction.

Dozing on my plexiglass perch aboard *The Busted Flush*, returning from a Pumpkin drop in Tokyo's Hibya Park, I had no inkling whatsoever that *I* was that threatened instrument of prompt and utter destruction.

London—*August 3, Now*

I have always wished for the time to be a tourist in London, and have never had it. I would trade four pages in the Congressional Record for the privilege of paying my fifty cents and gawking at the Tower of London, or wandering lazily through the British Museum on Great Russell Street, eyeing the Rosetta Stone, and studying the original manuscript describing Samuel Coleridge's dream-inspired Xanadu. I have never had the time to check out Madame Tussaud's wax replica of President Howard Foster and his jovial companions in the Chamber of Horrors.

Westminster Abbey, Parliament, the Changing of the Guard at Buckingham Palace—to me these last tattered vestiges of history clinging to the remnants of the British Empire have been only blurred façades outside a speeding car as I was hustled from one appointment to another.

This day was no different; my appointment with Prime Minister John Phillip Hawkins at Number Ten Downing Street permitted me barely enough time to freshen up at my hotel and crawl wearily into the official car the Prime Minister had sent for me. I was at the Hotel Inverness Court, which I knew was originally a secret hideout set up by Edward VII for his mistress. Ten minutes from Piccadilly, this former town house has a bar that was once a gilt-and-white-decorated theater, and the place is filled with columns, crystal chandeliers, fireplaces. When Celia first saw it, in 1964, she cried, "It's Toad Hall!"

Phil Hepburn was closer in, at the Royal Hotel on Upper Woburn Place. "Maybe they don't check *your* expense account, friend," he said, stepping into his cab, "but mine gets the finetooth comb treatment. Besides, it gives me a kick to get a good room for eight bucks."

"I'll see you," I said.

"You bet you will," he told me.

Two bobbies were standing guard outside the three-story brick building at Number Ten Downing Street. They examined my credentials, and one touched the doorbell.

A young man in a gray business suit opened the door.

"Ah," he said. "Senator McGavin. Just on time."

As he led me inside, he kept up a running undertone of polite comment: "I hope you had a pleasant flight. Ah, good. You have caused us a bit of trouble, you know."

"What kind of trouble?"

He wagged his finger. "Ah, perhaps I had better let the P.M. tell you about it. He's in there, sir. Just go right in. Would you like coffee?"

Shuddering at my memory of English coffee, I said, "Would you happen to have any cold buttermilk?"

Unperturbed, the young man answered, "If not, sir, we can pop around the corner and find some. Thank you."

I thanked him for thanking me, and went into the study.

One of the nice things about being my age, and having achieved some manner of recognition in relatively early years, is that you knew everybody *when*. For instance, I knew John Phillip Hawkins when he was an assistant vice-consul in Washington, and the two of us sat often on his back lawn drinking Whitbread ale and singing dirty songs. Hawkins was especially fond of "The Good Ship Venus," and his very favorite verse went:

> And there was Tommy Kipper . . .
> 'E was a cheerful nipper.
> 'E stuffed his arse
> With broken glass
> And circumcised the skipper!

In fact, I have one such serenade preserved on tape; now, looking at John's face—aged with time and worry, and yet underneath the sagging flesh there was still the boisterous Johnny of long-ago Washington—I had a mischievous impulse to burst out with a chorus.

I didn't, of course. Senator Hugh McGavin held out his hand and, with all dignity and protocol, greeted Prime Minister John Phillip Hawkins.

"Good to see you, Mac," he said. "You seem to have created a proper flap."

"So your man said. What's it all about?"

He tilted one eyebrow. "You are most assuredly ambassador without portfolio."

"President Foster?"

"His spokesman. I got the impression your Administration would take it as a personal favor if we were to heave you into the Tower and stretch you on the rack."

Carefully, I said, "The President is understandably disturbed about the incident with North Korea."

"Aren't you?"

For a moment the years between us lowered, and it was as if we were back on the dew-misted lawn in Washington.

"Johnny," I said, "I'm so scared that my arms and legs feel empty. It's like someone sneaked into my veins and drew out all the blood. I'll never forget sitting in the Senate, helplessly watching Lyndon Johnson drift us deeper into the Vietnamese war. I feel the same way now. We're on a head-on collision course with Red China, and if either one of us blinks, we'll smash together with an impact that might destroy the world."

"Your buttermilk, sir." It was the young man in the gray business suit. I thanked him and he went out of the room, not quite backwards, not quite bowing his way out, but giving the impression of both.

"John," I said, "I've told you about Tinian."

"Yes. Often."

"Were we right? Some said we should have demonstrated the bomb's power in an open field. Others said we had to surprise the Japanese. But what has always terrified me was that *we*, those of us who actually dropped the bomb, never got a vote at all. When I took off for Japan I had no more real understanding of what was riding down there in the bomb bay than I had of nuclear fission. I was a hired hand, and what I was hired for was to push that red button when my bombsight lined up with the target."

"We've been through all this, Hugh," he said. "If it hadn't been you, it would only have been someone else. The machine was programmed for destruction. It doesn't really matter who pushed the button."

"In other words," I said, sipping my buttermilk, "it was inevitable."

"Well, wasn't it?"

I fumbled out my pipe. "Yes, I suppose it was. And that's why I'm frightened now. The arms race has gotten out of hand. There are men who say seriously, without jokes and without exaggeration, that the United States has become dependent on a war economy—that the whole ABM thing is just one more example of collusion between the military and the defense industry. That we're making Krupp look like a kid with a string of Chinese firecrackers."

The Prime Minister smiled. "I can see why your President is reluctant to allow you out without a keeper."

"Don't worry. I have one. He's probably lurking across the street right now with a laser spy beam."

"I shouldn't be concerned about that," said Hawkins. "Our

bobbies may look diffident, but I assure you they're extremely efficient." He leaned forward and struck a match for my pipe, then settled back. "All right, Hugh, why have you come to me?"

"I'm looking for help," I said. "I knew about the Third Gen ABMs in Japan a couple of weeks ago. Originally, I planned to shame the Administration into taking them out. Well, all that's past now. But Foster may still need some prodding to yank them. I don't know why, but he's determined to push K'ang right to the wall. And I'm not sure K'ang will let himself be pushed."

"How can I help?"

"Destroy your bombs. You have no constructive use for them. You don't have the nuclear capacity to bring us, or Russia, or even China anywhere near a trade-even point. Any use you might make of them would be a spastic, last-revenge gesture."

"Granted," he said. "With the bomb, we're only a second-rate power. But without it, we'd be down there with the locals in fifth place. You might say, Hugh, that the bomb is our Gibraltar. Surely anyone in his right senses knows we have no more use for Gib than we do for those blasted monkeys that foul the whole blessed rock. But when Franco tried to force us out, we faced him down—and I'm afraid, old boy, that the same is true of our bomb. It isn't much, but it's ours, and that's the way things are."

"That's not the way they have to be. Make the gesture."

He took out a thick, black cigar and lit it. As he puffed, fleecy gray clouds of smoke wreathed his face.

I sat silently. My nerves felt painfully stretched.

"All right, Hugh," said the Prime Minister. "Let me pose a hypothetical question. Suppose you become the next President of the United States."

"Not likely."

"*Suppose*," he insisted. "Suppose then that I come to you and say, My old friend, I am afraid for the world and you can help by destroying your nuclear capability. Now, mind you, I

103

cannot guarantee that the Soviets or China will destroy theirs, nor can I even guarantee to destroy my own, for I speak as an ambassador without portfolio. But I ask you to strip yourself of your most powerful weapon as a demonstration of leadership and conscience. As President, what would you do?"

"I'd try to have you committed," I said glumly.

"I'm sorry not to be more encouraging," he said. "I'm on your side, old boy, but I can't leap out the window with you. What we both need is a fire ladder, so we can climb down to safety. That's your real job, Hugh. Find that ladder. I'm just as anxious to get out of this burning building as you are."

"All right," I said. "Leave it for a while. How about the ABMs in Japan? What's your government's position going to be on them?"

"One of genteel horror," he said. "They are a deliberately provocative gesture against China."

"Of course," I said, "even Third Gen ABMs aren't ground-to-ground. They're ground-to-air."

Hawkins snorted. "Tell that to the bloody marines, chum. If they don't hit anything in the air and come back to earth, they can be made to explode, can't they?"

"I suppose so."

"So here's where you stand. You have an ultimatum from North Korea. At any moment now you will probably receive a demand from the Japanese Diet to get your blasted ABMs off their tight little island. What price cataclysm?"

"Only Foster knows," I said, "and he's not telling."

"Ah, Mac," he said softly, "what a mess. Take the advice of a friend. Don't hunger after that job on Pennsylvania Avenue. Your friend Foster is undoubtedly going through the tortures of the damned, doing what he thinks is right, compelled to keep his own counsel, taking decisions that he would rather leave to the next fellow, gambling with stakes that no one man should possess. It's a thankless job, my friend—take it from one who knows."

In another room, a bell tinkled. "Let's have a bite," Hawkins said. "Time enough later to solve the problems of the world. I suppose you'll be giving a press conference?"

"I have to. And, I'll be saying some of the same things I said to you."

"I wouldn't expect anything else," he said, leading me into the dining room.

"I'll probably be using words like 'indecisive' and 'reactionary.'"

"Love pats," he growled. "You should hear some of the things I've been called by the Consort. Now there's a man with a gift of language. I believe he could turn an Italian fishmonger green with envy."

We sat down. "How's Celia?" he asked.

"Feisty as ever. She's right in the middle of this missile thing. She had a clear scoop on it."

"Reporters don't say 'scoop' any more. They say 'beat.'"

"You don't tell me, Mr. Prime Minister," I said, feeling a little less tense.

"*That's* the Hugh McGavin I remember," he said. "I was beginning to fear you'd gone and become a statesman. Horrid. Don't let them corrupt you, Mac."

The meal was simple: a clear soup, rack of lamb with mint jelly, tossed salad.

We went back into the study for coffee laced with brandy, and I took one of Hawkins' ferocious cigars.

"Go ahead," he had insisted. "One lungful of Cuban tobacco won't contaminate you."

"Okay, but only because I'm weak," I said. "That shows you what kind of man Jack Kennedy was. No one loved a good Cuban *puro* better than he—but he embargoed Cuba and cut them off without a whimper."

"Yes, but what do you do this time? If the Japanese turn against you, do you stop listening to transistor radios?"

"Very funny."

"Seriously, old cock, do you think this Cook's Tour of yours is going to have any real effect, other than publicizing the divisiveness within your own party?"

"I have to do it, Johnny. Look—have you ever been seriously ill?"

"Roaring hangovers after every Embassy ball."

105

"Not that," I said, laughing. "And not colds or flu. I had pneumonia once. I *knew* I was sick. It was unlike any other feeling I'd ever experienced. There was a dreadful, certain knowledge of doom. Well, I got up one morning a few years back and knew for a certainty that our world, and particularly my own country, was desperately ill, and that it was time to call in the doctor with his miracle drugs. But just like me when I had walking-around pneumonia, the world keeps insisting there's nothing wrong that a good tonic won't cure.

"Well, it's too late for Geritol. We're trapped in a closed circle that grows smaller by the hour. But if I can break the pattern, if I can help get us off this crazy merry-go-round, maybe we can use our talents and resources for something worthwhile instead of plotting to blow each other up."

"Good luck," he said softly. "My best wishes go with you."

"But you can't help?"

He shook his head. "It may be true that the British Lion has become somewhat feeble, but he's still too frisky to submit to having his teeth pulled."

The two of us blew cigar smoke at the ceiling. "All right," I said finally. "I'll just have to start somewhere else."

His next question surprised me. "Mac, have you ever seen an atomic bomb explode?"

"I saw one of the Bikini tests."

"But you weren't at Hiroshima or Nagasaki."

"No. Why do you ask, Johnny?"

"No reason, old boy. I suppose I wondered what it was like to see one of our precious atomic devices used in anger."

"Probably no different than watching people die under fire bombs or with napalm eating away at them. The bomb isn't any different; it's just bigger."

The Prime Minister of Great Britain examined his cigar before answering. A string of smoke curled up from its half-inch of gray ash.

"No, Mac," he said finally. "The bomb *is* different."

When *The Busted Flush* returned from its mission to Tokyo one day, we were met by Major Rosy Cooper and a tall man who was introduced as Charles Kern of *Collier's* magazine.

"Mr. Kern is providing pool coverage for the press," Cooper told us, "along with Bill Laurence of *The New York Times.* He's cleared all the way up, so you don't have to worry about what you tell him."

"You guys seen the Trinity films yet?" asked Kern.

Tex Ritter looked at me, at the sky, then back to Kern. "What's Trinity?"

"We're briefing the men tonight," Cooper told Kern. "They'll see the films then."

Kern took the front seat of our weapons carrier; Rosy Cooper drove off in his jeep. "I'll be with you guys for the next couple of days," said Kern. "Just forget I'm around."

"Have you ever been shot at?" Ritter asked, crawling into the back of the vehicle.

"What do you mean?"

"Our gang is funny," said my favorite pilot. "There's only one membership requirement. You have to have been shot at without shitting in your pants."

"Oh," said the reporter, trying a laugh that came out more like a croak. "What would you say if I told you I flew with Jimmy Doolittle when he hit Tokyo—"

"I'd say you were a loudmouthed liar," said Tex. "I know for a fact there were no correspondents on that mission."

"Just asking," said Kern. "But hell yes, I've been shot at."

"Did you shit your pants?"

"Once," said the reporter. "When an LST I was in took a direct hit off Tarawa."

"*You* were at Tarawa?"

"Want to see my clippings?"

"Never mind," said Ritter. "Welcome aboard."

Kern took his outstretched hand. "Thanks," he said. "Well, how does it feel?"

"How does *what* feel?" I asked.

"You're?"

"McGavin, bombardier."

"Glad to meet you. How does it feel to be chosen to drop the first atomic bomb?"

"What's an atomic bomb?"

He stared at me. "What's an atomic bomb?" He shook his head. "You've got to be kidding."

The weapons carrier started up with a jerk.

Tex asked, "Any of you guys know what an atomic bomb is?"

There was a chorus of Hell no's, and the *Collier's* man groaned. "What have you been practicing with?"

"Pumpkins," I said brightly.

"Happy Hallowe'en," Kern muttered. "Okay, forget everything I said. If the C.O. finds I let the cat out, he'll probably have me shot at sunrise."

"Are you sure you've got all your facts straight?" Tex Ritter asked. "I heard the C.O. was going to lead the first mission."

"He *was*," said Kern. "But High Command ordered him to stand down. If something goes wrong, they don't want to lose their group commander."

"And we're expendable," mumbled Tim Bond.

Off the runway, the weapons carrier turned up "Broadway" toward the 509th stockade.

"What's this 'Trinity' you mentioned?" I asked.

"Code name for a test they ran in New Mexico," said the reporter. "They tested your Pumpkin there a couple of weeks ago."

"Nobody tells us nothing," Tim Bond said, hugging his precious case of instruments to his chest as he swayed with the motion of the weapons carrier.

"So what's an atomic bomb?" asked the radio operator, S/Sgt. Phillip Bowie.

"Don't you ever read *Amazing Stories?*" asked S/Sgt. Tom O'Neal, the radar operator. "That's what Buck Rogers drops on those Kryptons. Blows their asses to smithereens."

"Knock it off, men," said Ritter. "They're just mean enough to have planted this guy on us to see if he could get us talking. Anyone here want to go to Wake Island?"

We rode in silence the rest of the trip.

Unknown to us, Charles Kern was dead right: the decision to drop the atomic bomb had been made, and *The Busted Flush* picked out of the hat. Part of the choice was due to my steady record of direct hits with the Pumpkin, part to Ritter's superb flying.

The Japanese were short of all necessary war material—but one thing they were *not* short of was men. Later estimates suggested that more than five million uniformed men were available to meet an Allied assault against the Japanese mainland. And behind those five million, armed with clubs, pitchforks, and beer bottles filled with gasoline, were another twenty million civilians ready to die for the Emperor.

American casualties for the assault were estimated in the area of half a million men. Had the Japanese invasion been carried out, it would have been the bloodiest chapter of recorded warfare.

2,000 planes had been hoarded by the Imperial Air Force to meet the attack. Hundreds of torpedo boats and even small skiffs were packed to the gunwales with high explosives for suicide runs against the Allied troop ships. The Japanese strategy was to attack the troop carriers, to cause as much death and injury as possible, hoping to blunt the resolve of the attacking forces.

Even with these discouraging facts in hand, there was still considerable agitation in high Allied circles about the morality of dropping the atomic bomb on populated centers. Doctor

Albert Einstein—who, through a personal letter sent to President Roosevelt in 1939, had been almost single-handedly responsible for the origination of the Manhattan Project—was now convinced that the bomb was not needed. Germany was defeated; Japan on her knees—so from Princeton came Einstein's plea that the world be spared the Pandora's Box of nuclear warfare.

Facing the specter of half a million American casualties, President Harry S Truman felt he had no real choice. The bomb had been developed as a military weapon, and it would be so used.

One camp of scientists held out for a demonstration of the bomb's power on an unpopulated area. But, argued others, fissionable material was in short supply. There was uranium for two Little Boys, and only enough plutonium for two Fat Men. It would take weeks to refine more.

If a demonstration in an unpopulated spot revealed the secret of our weapon without being sufficiently powerful to shock the Japanese into instant surrender, the next bomber headed for Japan might find enough resistance rising against it to keep the mission from succeeding. Given enough desperation and forewarning, the Japanese could be expected to shoot down any B-29, no matter what the cost.

Therefore the military leaders were determined that the bomb be dropped without warning and without disclosure. Then, if it failed, nothing would be lost.

The crew of *The Busted Flush* got in four hours of sack time, ate breakfast, and gathered in the briefing hut. The main briefing for the other crews would be held later.

"You men are special," Rosy Cooper told us. "You're going out first, and I don't mind saying I'm more than a little envious."

He introduced Captain Meredith Rogers of the United States Navy.

"I'm your weaponeer," Rogers told us. "I don't doubt that

your curiosity has been running high as to what kind of weapon we've been practicing for. Okay. Now you find out."

The lights clicked out. A movie projector began to grind.

On the screen what looked like a barren moonscape was suddenly flooded with light. A round ball of flame grew, and began to rise into the air. Shock waves rippled vertical white lines of tracer smoke. The film was silent; except for the whir of the projector, the room was dead quiet.

The lights came on.

"It's hard to tell from that film exactly what happened," Captain Rogers said, "but those are movies of the weapon you've been training to drop."

"It looked like a thermite bomb," said Tex Ritter.

"Captain," said Rogers, "how high would you say that cloud went straight up?"

"A couple of hundred yards," said Ritter.

"Eight miles," said Rogers. "With nothing in the picture to give you scale, it's hard to see how big the blast really was."

"So that's why we've been doing the Tokyo Two-Step," said Tim Bond.

Cooper stared at the ceiling of the Quonset hut, trying not to laugh.

"If you mean your evasive maneuvers, you're right," said Rogers. "You see, we don't even know exactly how strong the shock waves are going to be. Our test bomb was exploded on a hundred-foot tower. Your drop will go off at 2,000 feet. The entire ground-shear effect will be different. So the best procedure is to haul ass the minute you let the beast go." He waved at the projectionist, and a color slide appeared on the screen. It showed a mushroom-shaped cloud towering over the desert, glowing with orange and purple shadows.

"This is vital," said Rogers. "Stay out of that cloud. "Don't even go near it. It's radioactive as hell."

"You mean like when you can't have babies?" Tim Bond asked.

"That's sterility, you clunk," I said.

"He could be right," said Rogers. "We don't know much yet about the effects of radiation on the human body. The safest thing is just to stay away from it."

S/Sgt. Phillip Bowie, the radar operator, asked the question. "Sir, is this one of those atomic bombs?"

Captain Rogers looked at him sharply. "Where did you hear that term?"

Bowie shrugged. "I read *Amazing Stories*," he said. "They've had atomic bombs ever since I can remember."

Rogers smiled tightly. "Well, Sergeant, this isn't science fiction. All I can tell you is that this weapon has the power of 20,000 tons of TNT."

"*Tons?*" I asked.

"Tons."

"That ought to make a nice little hole," I said.

"Lieutenant," he said, "would you remain behind after the briefing?"

"Yes, sir," I answered. Now I'd done it. Shot my mouth off when I should have kept quiet.

"Your takeoff is going to be hairy, Captain Ritter," said Rosy Cooper. "You'll be overloaded right up to the red line."

"Don't worry about us, Major," Ritter said.

"All right. Your course will take you to Iwo Jima, where you'll join up with Major Milburn and his *Happy Hooligan*. He'll be carrying instruments and scientists to record the effects of the bomb. Your altitude to Iwo will be 5300 feet. The weather planes will take off at 0130 hours. They'll radio conditions at your primary and secondary targets. It's absolutely necessary that you have clear visibility so we can see how the weapon performs. Lieutenant McGavin, you can use radar to check your reference points, but you must bomb visually. Understood?"

"Roger."

"Your takeoff will be at 0300 hours. Ritter, don't get fancy. Use every inch of that runway. Don't take any chances."

"Got you, sir."

And so did the rest of us. If 20,000 tons of TNT exploded on takeoff, there wouldn't be any Tinian left.

Captain Meredith Rogers read our minds. "It's small comfort to you," he said lightly, "but don't worry about blowing up the island if you go in on takeoff. That's why I'll be aboard. I won't fuse the bomb until we're safely airborne."

"Gee, thank you, sir," said Tim Bond. It broke us up.

"Don't worry, son," said Rogers. "I've been practicing."

"At ease," Cooper said when the laughter started up again. "At Iwo you'll rendezvous with Major Milburn, then climb gradually to 14,000 feet. Hold that altitude until an hour from target, then go on up to 32,000 for the bomb run. Got that?"

"Yes, sir," said Ritter.

"Questions?"

"Just one," said our pilot. "What *is* the primary target?"

Rosy Cooper looked at him a long time before saying quietly, "Tokyo."

London—*August 3, Now*

"Thank you, Senator," said the man from BBC-TV. The lights began to go out in the ballroom.

"Thank *you*," I said, mopping my forehead with a Kleenex. Even with the air conditioning working full blast, TV lights heat a room up to tropical temperatures in minutes.

Phil Hepburn came over as I climbed down from the small stage.

"You were in top form," he said. "That bit about the world looking to Great Britain for guidance in conscience was sneaky. What did Hawkins say when you used it on him?"

"Ask him yourself," I said.

"You look hot," he said. "Let's go for a walk."

"No thanks."

"I think it might be a good idea. We can talk about a communication I've just had with Castle."

"Castle" was Secret Service jargon for the White House. It had come into fashion for government personnel to show their in-ness by using code terms for personnel and places.

"All right," I said. "Ten minutes."

For the convenience of the press, I'd held my conference at the Savoy. We strolled outside, and in a few minutes were walking through Trafalgar Square.

"The Russians have made their move," Hepburn said casually.

"Oh?"

"Their missiles are on countdown. They've gone to Standby."

"How do you know?"

"Scrambled communication with Lancer."

Senselessly angry, I flared, "I thought they retired that code name when Kennedy was shot."

He shrugged. "They're using it for Foster now," he said. "But if you prefer, I won't."

"I prefer."

"All right. I talked with the President for ten minutes. He told me that our spy satellites show unusual activity all along the Baltic missile complex. Those, as you know, are the holes aimed directly at North America."

"Was there any communication directly from Nabov?"

"None. The hot line is so quiet, we're starting to wonder if it's been disconnected."

"I see. And what has our response been?"

"We've gone to Yellow. The nuke subs are all running on sealed orders, with instructions to fire if they're unable to make contact with Washington during their regular listening periods."

"So if we have an unusual sun spot period to louse up radio, those idiots will push the button."

"Of course not, Hugh. The subs have four different ways of communicating, and there's not the faintest possibility of all of them going out at the same time. That is, if Washington is still in business."

"Is this Soviet reaction more of Foster's grand design?"

"I couldn't say," Hepburn said blandly.

"What's the message to me?"

"The President urges you to consider the seriousness of the situation, and return to your desk where you're needed."

"The same old song."

"And the same old answer?"

"The same old answer."

"I'll tell him."

We turned down St. Martin's Lane.

"Celia sends her best," he said casually. "She was with the President when I spoke with him."

"What did she say?"

"Just hello. And she wishes you'd come home."

"Don't kid me, Phil."

"I'm not. That's what she said, word for word. 'Tell Hugh I wish he'd come home.'"

"Thanks," I said.

"None required. Through sleet and snow and gloom of night . . ."

"The faithful company rat completes his appointed rounds."

At the corner of Drury Lane, he stopped. "Well, Senator, I'll leave you here. I'm sure you can find your way home alone."

"Reporting in to your boss?"

"Going back to Bond Street," he said. "Suddenly I have this overwhelming urge to buy a suit on Savile Row."

"I doubt if they're on Diner's Club," I said.

He grinned and headed back toward Trafalgar Square. I hailed a taxi. "Inverness Court," I told the driver and then sat back, stuffing my pipe.

"Begging your pardon, gov-ner," said the driver, "but you're an American?"

"That's right."

"Would you be willing to pay your hire with U.S. dollars? At," he hurried to add, "the official rate, of course."

"If you want. Why?"

He turned around long enough to wink. "I can get a nice markup on U.S. dollars on the market, sir. You know how it is."

"Yes," I said, thinking of the Prime Minister's comment about the tired British Lion, "I know how it is."

I gave him a dollar over the fare on the meter and he thanked me fervently. There were several messages and a telegram waiting for me inside. I opened the telegram in the elevator.

> CAN YOU COME TO TEL AVIV DAY AFTER TO-
> MORROW QUESTION OF UTMOST IMPORTANCE
> STOP COLONEL BRIGHT-HAMILTON WILL CON-
> TACT YOU AND SPEAKS FOR ME STOP ALL PER-
> SONAL REGARDS
>
> LEVI BERNARDI

The day after tomorrow was August 5. I wondered what Bernardi wanted. I remembered enjoying his company in 1967, when I was President Johnson's special envoy to Israel. Bernardi, a stocky, nervous man, had been second in command to General Dayan at that time. Elected Prime Minister of Israel in 1971, he had maintained a hawkish attitude toward the Arab states since taking office.

In my room I kicked off my shoes and threw my jacket over the back of a chair. The management of the Inverness, bless them, had catered to my American insanity by providing a pitcher of ice water. I took a glass from the bathroom, dug into my suitcase for the plastic flask of Cutty Sark, and poured myself a double. Slopping water over the top of the glass, I sat down near the telephone and glanced through the other messages.

There were courtesy calls from acquaintances in London. The fourth said, "Please inform the Foreign Secretary of the Republic of France when he may call upon you," and gave a number.

Well, France was next on my list anyway. I gave the number to the hotel operator, and after the usual bombardment of "Hallo's" and a disconcerting "I'll knock him right up for you, sir," from my operator, I reached Raoul DuPré.

"May I come around and see you, Senator?" he asked. "This evening, if possible?"

"Certainly," I said. "Perhaps you would like to have a drink somewhere?"

"No, no," he said. "May I come directly to your hotel? Say, at six?"

"Six is fine," I said. He welcomed me to Europe, and I told him how glad I was to be here, and we hung up, still muttering empty compliments to each other.

Now down to business. I gave the operator the number Jack Sherwood had written on a book of matches and said I'd talk to anyone who answered. It was now almost five: eleven A.M. in Arlington, two hours after I'd promised to call.

"There will be a slight delay," said the operator. I thanked her and hung up. My shirt had wilted. I took it off and rubbed myself down with a towel, sipping at my scotch-and-water.

The telephone rang. I picked it up expecting to hear Jack Sherwood. Instead, a clipped, British voice spoke.

"Colonel Bright-Hamilton here," it said. "Senator McGavin?"

"You're talking to him."

"Did you receive Prime Minister Bernardi's wire?"

"Just now."

"I was wondering if I might pop around and speak with you. At your convenience, of course."

Apparently it was Talk-to-McGavin Night. I sighed. This one wouldn't want a drink either.

He didn't. "S'pose we make it after dinner?" he suggested. "I'll be by with my car and we can take a drive."

"Nine o'clock?"

"Nine is wizard." He thanked me, I thanked him, and we hung up.

The playing fields of Eton had scattered alumni far and wide, But, *wizard?*

The telephone rang again. Arlington, this time. The connection was none too good, but I could hear a voice on the other end and was in no mood to risk losing contact altogether, so I shouted, "Jack?"

"Yes. I've been hoping you'd call." Then something garbled.

"I can't hear you, Jack. What's happening? I heard the President's been talking to Celia."

The connection improved, and he said, "That's what I told you, boss. Listen, all hell's broken loose back here. Any chance of you coming home?"

"You too? What's going on, anyway?"

"You never saw such heat in your life. The FBI had me up most of the night. And as you may have guessed, this line is now wide open."

I had a crazy impulse to throw the intelligence crew into frenzied action by telling Jack to initiate Plan Nine and set off the charges under the White House, but restrained myself. A sense of humor is not an employment requirement for joining the FBI.

"What are they doing to Celia?"

"Nothing that I know of."

That was a relief. "Then why did she say she wished I'd come home?"

"She did? When?"

I told him about Hepburn's message.

"She's probably upset by what they're doing to *you*," Jack said. "I didn't know she'd gone over to see the President. But now that I think of it, knowing Celia, I'm not surprised."

"What do you mean, doing to me?"

"I bet you didn't know there was a big wad of Mafia money in your last campaign war chest."

"Who says so?"

"Right now the Attorney General's office says so. The story broke early this morning, but it was all over town last night. Nobody's accusing you of anything, of course, but Marty Kuhn swears he'll get to the bottom of it right away."

"Ouch," I said. "Well, if it happened, it happened. I knew

118

nothing about it, and I'd swear none of my staff did either."

"You'll come out clean in the end," Jack agreed. "But that'll be after the nominations. The big day's August 18, in case you forgot."

"I didn't forget, but there's an ultimatum that comes due before that. By the eighteenth, the last thing any of us may be worrying about is who gets nominated."

"You're calling the shots, boss. But they're playing dirty. Aren't you going to do anything about it?"

"I don't think so," I said. "Listen, tell Celia not to worry, Jack. I can take care of myself."

"Let's hope so."

"Can I call you there tomorrow?"

"Better not," he said. "Mara got a little upset when the FBI went through her medicine cabinet. Ten minutes after she'd told them we were just good friends, they found her pills. She's in the bedroom now packing. I think she's going back to school to take a graduate course in government. Mara doesn't like the way the real thing works."

"Okay, I'll call you at the office from now on. Eleven A.M. your time."

"Right. Goodbye, boss."

"Goodbye, Jack." Then, too quickly to think the better of it, "Goodbye, Mr. President."

As I hung up I could hear Jack Sherwood laughing across the Atlantic.

My drink was empty. I built another, and returned the courtesy calls. Yes, it was nice to be back. No, I was sorry, but this was a work trip and I'd have to take a raincheck. Next time without fail. Fine, I'll say hello to her for you.

Click.

I put on a fresh shirt and was adjusting my tie when a gentle tap came at the door. I opened it. A bellboy stood there with a bucket of ice.

"Your ice, sir," he said. Before I could answer that I hadn't ordered ice, he put one finger to his lips. "I'll put it over here, sir, if you don't mind."

- As he did, he pointed at a slip of paper on the tray. I picked it up:

> For purposes of security I have taken another
> room. This young man can bring you here.
>
> DuPré

"No," I said. "I don't mind. I was just going to take a walk before dinner anyway."

"Very good, sir," he said. "Thank you."

He left, and I put on my jacket, meanwhile looking around the room. It was hard to believe they'd bugged the Inverness.

The bellboy was waiting in the hall. He nodded, and set off down the heavily carpeted corridor at a brisk pace. At the fire stairs he held the door for me, led me down a flight, then out into another hall and to a door where he knocked once.

"Come," said a voice.

The bellboy opened the door, nodded at me again, tightened his lips when I reached into my pocket.

"Please sir," he said.

"Thank you Peter," said DuPré. "We shan't need you any more tonight."

The imitation bellboy nodded and closed the door.

"How are you, Senator?" asked the French Foreign Secretary. "Sorry about the Interpol routine, but one never knows."

"You're early," I said.

"Yes. You'll be back in your room by six, at which time I shall telephone and break our engagement."

"Who are you trying to outwit?"

He shrugged, the French tilt of the shoulder that says eloquently, "No one could be expected to know, but there is a very slight suspicion that if anyone does know, that someone is me."

"We have twenty minutes," I said. "Is this in connection with my visit to your country?"

"Yes. I watched you on BBC today, and I gather that your visit to France has the same object. You wish to enlist our support in ending the arms race, in destroying the nuclear stockpile. You desire to use our good offices to help persuade the United States to remove her missiles from Japan."

"Yes."

"You have come a long way for nothing, my friend." I started to speak but he raised his hand. "No, hear me out. It is impossible for my nation to publicly support your mission. At great expense and sacrifice, France has become the first nonaligned nuclear power. Why do you think we withdrew from NATO? That was no idle gesture of pique on DeGaulle's part. With the United States and Great Britain rattling their bombs on the one side, and Russia and China bashing theirs about on the other, France was able to break the stalemate."

"National pride had nothing to do with it," I said dryly.

That shrug again. "Perhaps," he said. "But we are losing time. Let me say, speaking for the President of France, that while we are in sympathy with a reduction in the arms race, we have not yet seen specific proposals with which we can align ourselves. And until we do, we have no intention of reducing our own nuclear capacity. As for the situation in Asia, we no longer have holdings or aspirations in that part of the world. We shall remain silent in an affair that is none of our concern."

"That's laying it out," I said. "In that case, I don't suppose a visit to Paris would be fruitful."

"Ah, no, my friend. I have just told you what the official position of France will be. But take my word for it, your trip to our nation will be of great interest despite that official position."

"How?"

"I could not tell you if I knew. My instructions were to advise you of our official position so that you would not be shocked and angry when you met that position publicly. But I was also to assure you that the President is anxious to speak with you privately, and that you will find what he has to say most intriguing."

"Intrigue," I said, "is the secret ingredient behind all successful farce."

"We invented the form," he agreed amiably. "So. Shall I tell the President to expect you in the morning?"

"Yes," I said. "You've got my curiosity up."

"Precisely my intention," he said, looking at his watch. "Now, my friend, it is time for you to return to your room and we will perform act two of our little farce."

I shook his hand. "I'm not sure what I'm thanking you for," I said, "but thanks anyway."

He gripped my hand. "I, *mon ami,* thank you for fighting this battle. As Foreign Secretary, my views are those of my nation. But as a man, I wish you luck."

"War is too important to be left to the generals?"

"One of your American colleagues said much the same thing," smiled DuPré. "Albert Wohlstetter. '*Peace* is too important to be left to the generals.' I agree. Good luck, my friend."

We shook hands again and he let me out into the hall. I went back up the flight of stairs and opened the door.

The imitation bellboy was replacing a pile of shirts in my dresser drawer.

"Oh, good evening sir," he said, unperturbed. "I was just checking to see if everything was all right."

"Everything's fine," I said.

"Yes," he answered, nodding at me as he slid toward the door, "it seems to be."

"Let me give you a tip."

"Oh, that isn't necessary, sir."

"I think it is," I said, moving close to him. "I won't be needing you any more." As I said it, I clenched my fist in front of his nose. "Take the rest of the evening off."

He smiled slightly and said, "That's very generous of you, sir. Good night."

I closed the door a little harder than I should have. Apparently, for all of his good wishes, Raoul DuPré wasn't leaving anything to chance. Then, as I looked across the room, I had to smile.

On the bureau near the ice bucket with a little note taped

to it reading "Thank you for allowing me to visit" and signed "Peter" was a bottle of seventy-year-old Martell brandy. Ah, the French.

The telephone rang. It was DuPré.

"Senator McGavin?" he said. "I am most dreadfully sorry, but an important meeting is continuing into the evening. I shall be forced to cancel our appointment."

"I understand."

"Its only purpose was to welcome you formally and to wish you a pleasant visit to my country. Will you accept my good wishes now, and forgive my discourtesy?"

"There's nothing to forgive," I said, picking up the bottle of brandy and examining its label. "Thank you for your call. You may inform your government that I'll be arriving on the ten A.M. flight to Orly."

"I shall do so. Good night, Senator."

"Good night, Mr. Secretary."

So much for the intrigue. I made a quick check of my belongings to make sure the bogus bellboy hadn't taken anything, and then went down for a cold martini before dinner. I had plenty of time. My next mysterious visitor wouldn't be arriving until nine.

Tinian, Marianas Islands—*August 3, 1945*

At nineteen, when you come head-on against Authority you're either rebellious or you're scared. That night on Tinian, I was scared.

"I didn't mean to mouth off, sir," I told Captain Meredith Rogers. We were alone in the briefing hut. "I just said what popped into my head."

"Forget it, Lieutenant," he said. "I didn't ask you to stay behind so I could chew you out. I want to talk about the mission."

123

"Oh."

"Since you're going to drop this thing, I thought you ought to know a little more about how it works."

"I know they've been putting it together over in the assembly area," I said.

"That's supposed to be a secret."

"It's hard to keep a secret on an island this small."

"Well, we originally intended to have the bomb completely assembled for takeoff. But those last two B-29s going in on takeoff changed our minds. So I'm going to fly with you, McGavin, and complete the final assembly in the air. Lieutenant Randolph will assist me, but I want you back there too. Anything can happen before we reach the target. The more you know, the more chance you can help if something happens to Randolph or me."

"Yes sir. Is there any chance of getting a look at this thing? So far, all I've gotten is rumors."

"Why not?" he said.

We got into a jeep and drove over to the assembly area.

The weapon was on a bomb carrier, surrounded by high brass and civilians. The lowest rank I saw was major. Everybody saluted everybody else, then Captain Rogers took me through the crowd to where the bomb was sitting, nestled into the carrier's cradle.

It looked only superficially like the Pumpkins we'd been dropping. It was more than ten feet long and almost three feet around. The whole bomb casing was dull gray except for the nose, which was polished to a chrome-like finish.

"Tungsten steel," said Rogers, tapping it. "Won't crumple under air pressure during the drop."

Scribbled all over the gray gunmetal part of the casing were messages to the Japanese, the most memorable of which was "Hirohito eats shit."

"What·are those?" I asked, pointing at four antennae that projected from the bomb's tail.

"Radar pickups," said Rogers. "They're hooked up with one

of the fusing mechanisms. I'll explain them in detail on board, when we're arming the bomb."

We walked around the bomb once more. I felt numb, unreal. It's one thing to train for a mission—another to see the weapon lying ominously in its cradle like an obscene ten-foot cigar of steel. How many times since that night on Tinian have I lain awake, asking myself, Would I have dropped it if I'd known what it was really capable of doing? "Atomic bomb" was just a term out of *Amazing Stories*, something you dropped on the Kryptons. It's one thing to be told, "Stay away from that cloud, it's radioactive"—another to learn what radioactivity did to the torn bodies of the survivors, how it twisted their genes to produce monster children for decades.

A million men were spared by the quick end of World War II. But what of the thousands of women and children who did not live to welcome their men home again?

I was only acting under orders.

But saying that doesn't help much when you are snapped out of sleep by the tenth nightmare you've had that month, a nightmare that never changes its sound . . . the strident, insistent clanging of an alarm bell.

When we got back to the Quonset hut for the regular briefing, it was filled. The crews of the weather planes and the instrument ship, *Happy Hooligan*, were all there, yawning in the humid night air.

The air-sea rescue officer showed us on his map where picket ships were located in case we had to ditch. He indicated safe landing strips on Okinawa, cautioned the pilots to dump surplus gasoline in the event of a forcedown.

"Buddy," muttered Tex Ritter, "if I've got gasoline left, I ain't landing."

The communications officer informed us that for this mission, the 509th Composite Group's Special Bombing Mission 312, the radio call signal would be changed from Zebra to

Jimmy Durante, and that a radio watch would be kept on all operable channels. "Bomb ship takes priority," he said. "Anybody hears Jimmy Durante calling, get the hell off the frequency."

The operations officer went through the takeoff order and rendezvous procedure, then told us that *The Busted Flush* would be flying to rendezvous at 5,300 feet instead of the usual 9,000. This created a puzzled buzz in the hut. One of the men from *Happy Hooligan* leaned over and whispered to me, "How come?"

I shrugged. I knew, but I wasn't talking. The air at 9,000 feet would be a little rarefied for three guys working in the unpressurized bomb bay, arming Little Boy.

The chaplain finished the briefing with a prayer. He was Lutheran, but all of us bowed our heads anyway—Catholics, Baptists, Jews, and atheists alike.

"Almighty Father, who wilt hear the prayers of those who love Thee, we pray Thee to be with those who brave the height of Thy heavens and carry the battle to our enemies.

"Armed with Thy might, may they bring the war to a rapid end that once more we may know peace on earth.

"May the men who fly this night be safe in Thy care and may they be returned safely to us. We shall go forward, trusting to Thee, knowing we are in Thy care, now and forever. Amen."

Thirty minutes later the three weather planes took off simultaneously. Major John Williams' *Frankie and Johnny* would scout Tokyo, the primary target. Captain Erwin Coffee's *Koffee's Kup* was headed for Osaka; Captain Harry Marshall's *Diamond Lil* for Kobe. We watched enviously as they were airborne in less than 5,000 feet of runway.

"I used to think 10,000 feet of strip was a lot," complained Tim Bond. "But we're 15,000 pounds overweight."

"You heard Tex," I said. "He told the Colonel not to worry."

"It's not the Colonel who's worrying," said Tim. "Its *me*."

A B-29 weighs over sixty tons. That's a lot of dead weight for the molecules flowing over the curve of the wing to haul

126

up into the air. I had been flying for more than a year, but I still would sit in my bubble and look back at the wings flexing in the turbulence and, squeezing my eyes shut, shudder. With a five-ton bomb in the forward bay and 6,000 gallons of fuel aboard, we were prime candidates for one of those greasy orange fireballs I had seen so often in the night when an overloaded bomber tried to claw its way into the sky and stalled out over the shattering coral hummocks. I am sure that our no-nosed friend stood close to us that night. We felt the coolness of his leather jacket against our naked forearms; his breath offended our nostrils as insects whined around our ears and the night birds called; above all, his invisible presence crept into our veins and made our limbs weak.

The weather planes disappeared into the darkness. The flat drone of their engines echoed distantly, then faded.

We checked our gear and got on the weapons carrier that would take us to *The Busted Flush.*

"That's a hell of a way to keep a secret," Ben Heller grumbled, pointing.

Our B-29 was floodlighted with a glare that could have been seen from 50,000 feet. Three huge searchlights were trained on her. She sparkled and shone like a Tiffany window.

"What the hell's going on?" demanded Tim Bond.

The area around the plane was jammed with cameramen, most of them carrying Speed Graphics or tiny Leicas. Several huge motion picture cameras were set up on tripods. Three Signal Corps men ran around with hand-held movie cameras.

"Where the hell have you guys been?" demanded Tex Ritter. "They want to take a group shot of us."

"Has it occurred to you," complained Tim Bond, "that old Keye Luke may be up there in the boondocks waiting to make a group shot too?"

"He only shoots at movies," said Heller. "We're gonna be famous!"

The nine of us grouped up before the plane, in front of the drawing of an overflowing john and the name, *The Busted Flush.*

"How about the other guys?" someone yelled from the press gallery.

Embarrassed, Captain Meredith Rogers came forward. With him were the assistant weaponeer, Lieutenant Randolph; and Lieutenant George Murphy, the ECM man. They fell in at one end of our formation, and the flash bulbs began to go off.

"Maybe they're taking all these pictures to remember what we looked like," grumbled Tim Bond. "Somebody may know more than we do."

"Hey," called the waist gunner, Sergeant Tom Barnes, "are these going to be in *Life* magazine?"

"You'll be lucky to make *Yank*," said S/Sgt. Norman Percy, the flight engineer.

"Okay," yelled one of the cameramen. "Now just act natural. We want to get some individual shots."

"How natural?" Percy wanted to know.

"Just do what you usually do before a flight."

Percy nodded, strolled over to the plane, zipped open his fly, and urinated on the nose wheel.

"Knock it off!" yelled an officer we didn't know. "Don't anyone photograph that. Sergeant, what do you think you're doing?"

Calmly shaking off a few drops, Percy replied, "Sir, they asked me to do what I usually do before a flight. This is what I usually do."

The officer made a choking sound. Tex Ritter stepped up to him and said seriously, "He's telling the truth, sir. It's our good luck trick."

He was lying through his teeth. No one had ever seen Percy pull such a stunt. I had to bite my lip to keep from laughing.

"But—" sputtered the officer, "it's—unsanitary. It'll rot the rubber."

"I never thought of that," Ritter said. "Sergeant! Knock off rotting the rubber."

"Yes sir!" Percy bellowed, stamping his feet English-style and coming to attention with his pecker hanging out.

"Zip up, zip up," Ritter said in a voice strained from trying to hold in his laughter.

The cameramen swarmed all over us. Point at the bomb bay, Lieutenant. Wave at the cockpit. Check the tires.

"Not *that* one!" choked Ritter, avoiding the glistening puddle of Percy's urine.

What are you thinking about? Nervous? How many missions does this make for you? Do you have a girl? Play football? Any idea what result this will have on the war?

I escaped the worst of the mob and stood near the forward hatch with Captain Rogers.

"I'll be goddamned," he said, shaking his head at the confusion around us. "Don't those idiots know that our Japanese friends out in the boondocks have radios?"

"Rifles, too," I said, thinking of the sniper.

"Suppose they signal Tokyo that we're making a big fuss about this particular mission? They could put up enough fighter cover to blast us out of the sky. It's only because they think we're weather planes that we've been getting away with these flights up to now."

The vision of a squadron of Zeroes rising to meet us sent chills down my already sweating back. With all our armor stripped away and only the tail gunner to protect us, we would be cut to ribbons.

Rogers had said something. "What?" I asked. "I wasn't listening."

"I said, can I borrow your pistol?"

"What pistol?"

"Don't you have a pistol? I thought all flight personnel were issued hand weapons."

"Oh, *that* pistol." I rummaged in my flight bag. "It's in here somewhere, I think. I haven't seen it for a while." Finally I found it, under a pile of maps.

Rogers took it, a snub-nosed .38 revolver.

"Looks rusty to me," he said. "Will it work?"

"I think so," I said. "I never tried it."

"Let me keep it for the flight," he said. "If we're forced

down I can't be taken. I'm the only one on board who knows exactly how the bomb is constructed."

I stared at him, mouth gaping open. He sounded like something out of one of those John Wayne movies—but I could tell he wasn't kidding. If we went down, he really intended to shoot himself.

He flipped open the cylinder and checked the six cartridges. Their brass casings were green with mold.

"Jesus, McGavin, you don't take very good care of your weapon. This damned thing might not work at all."

Before I knew what he was doing, he flipped the cylinder back, pointed the .38 into the air, and squeezed off a round.

Everyone froze. It was like one of those tableaux you see at religious festivals—a hundred men all caught in odd, strained positions. Then, after a silent eternity, while the echoes of the pistol shot still bounced off the runway, the cameramen and the brass started diving for the boondocks. A bird colonel rushed up and demanded, "What happened?"

"A little accident," Rogers said. "I didn't know it was loaded." He put the still-smoking pistol into the knee pocket of his flight suit.

Now the photographers seemed more eager to pack up their equipment and get out of the floodlights than to continue recording our sweating faces for posterity.

Lieutenant Paul Randolph, the assistant weaponeer, joined us.

"Everything okay with the little black box?" Rogers asked.

"Copesetic," said Randolph. "I installed it myself this afternoon. Just got through checking it out."

"What black box is that?" I asked.

"An instrument panel that monitors what's going on inside the bomb until you release it," said Rogers.

"What the hell do you mean, what's going on inside?" I yelped. "What could be going on inside the bomb? Are you telling me it's going to be ticking away down there during the flight?"

The two Navy men gave each other knowing grins.

"Don't worry about it, McGavin," said Captain Rogers. "I'll explain the whole thing to you once we're airborne." He looked at his watch. "Paul, it's getting about that time."

"Might as well," agreed the assistant weaponeer.

"See you later," said Rogers, waving a casual farewell at me as they strolled off.

Most of the photographers had gone now. It was less than an hour to takeoff. It is at such moments that you start asking yourself what the hell you're doing here.

This is the hour of dread, the hour in which you can go rock happy and wrap your arms around a palm tree and refuse to board the aircraft. It has happened too often for any of us to feel immune from it. And when it does, we look with pity and submerged envy at the babbling wreck of a man who is led away from the flight line. We will never see him again. When a flier cracks up he is transferred within the hour, and from then on it is as if he never came back from a mission.

This is the hour when we search our souls and find little there to reassure us of immortality. As we bow our heads and listen to the chaplain's prayer, the best we can hope for is that Whoever it is up there, He will not decide to play a nasty trick on us this mission; that if He feels frisky, He will turn His attentions to someone else.

This is the hour when the fresh eggs we ate with such relish turn to sour curds in our stomachs, and the coffee burns backwards, up into our throats with every belch. Some of us vomit on the hardstand, spewing the yellow eggs and brown coffee over our boots. Some of us commute rapidly back and forth to the latrine, our rectums burning with an almost liquid diarrhea that will itch and torment our behinds for the next fourteen hours. Some of us lean casually against the plane, smoking Camels in defiance of the "No Smoking" signs all around.

This is the hour when the only sign that means anything is the one that reads, "G.P. Loaded," indicating that the plane is fully bombed and ready for flight. Our issue hack watches tick relentlessly toward that moment when we will be hurtling down the runway, approaching V-1, the point of no return when we are committed to a takeoff whether or not it can succeed. The huge bomber moves at 250 feet a second; after V-1 there is not enough runway remaining to abort a takeoff and stop. The blackened hulks of unlucky B-29s dot the coral island like the vulture-picked skeletons of some gigantic species of bird.

Now it is nearly time.

Captain Meredith Rogers returns, carrying two heavy metal cans. Lieutenant Paul Randolph helps him stow them in the aircraft. They are followed by four MPs with automatic rifles.

Time, which has moved so slowly, begins to accelerate. Suddenly there is not enough left to complete our preparations for flight, and we move hurriedly, checking off our printed lists with insane efficiency. The sweep hands of our watches speed up, blur, whisk us into the future that we dread.

The heavy hatch clangs shut. We are twelve working fliers and one passenger, the *Collier's* man, Charles Kern, who has arrived at the last minute waving orders personally signed by the Commanding General. We are all strapped in for the takeoff—all except for Kern who, since there is no seat for him, lies in the padded thirty-foot tunnel between the forward and aft compartments of the bomber with his feet in the air, braced in the observation bubble the navigator uses for shooting stars.

"North Tinian Tower, this is Jimmy Durante Two-Seven. Request taxi and takeoff instructions. Over."

The answer crackles in my headphones. "Jimmy Durante Two-Seven, this is North Tinian Tower. Your runway is B for Boy, I repeat, B for Boy. All other runways are inactive. Don't worry about traffic. The sky is yours. Over."

"Many thanks, North Tinian Tower. Are we cleared for takeoff? Over."

"Jimmy Durante Two-Seven, you are cleared for takeoff. Good luck, you guys. North Tinian Tower out."

"Jimmy Durante Two-Seven out."

Tex Ritter taxies *The Busted Flush* onto Runway B, creeping to the very edge of the hardtop, where it joins the white coral sand. We sit there for a moment while he runs up each

132

of the four engines separately and tests, one after the other, the four primary magnetos, then the four back-up mags, then all four sets together.

"Less than fifty RPM drop," reports S/Sgt. Percy.

"Okay, men," says Ritter, "hang on."

Slowly, he lets the engines out until it sounds as if they are going to rip themselves out of their wing mounts. With both Ritter and Ben Heller standing on the brakes, the big airplane shudders and quivers as the huge propellers claw the air and try to move the ship forward.

"Now!" yells Ritter.

The brakes released, the tires squealing against the runway, *The Busted Flush* begins to move.

The pale runway lights streak toward me like a shower of blue meteorites. Far ahead, I see a blackness where the runway stops and the Pacific Ocean begins, and as it rushes toward me the B-29 bounces and settles, bounces again and settles. We are losing runway fast, and the plane shows no signs of becoming airborne. The blackness is so close I can almost reach out of the bubble nose and touch it. The engines make a groaning sound, and the blue lights fall away beneath us—none too soon, because then I see the phosphorescent whiteness of breakers and we are over the water at a height of less than fifty feet.

"Thank you, Lord," I think—and say—and my throat mike broadcasts it throughout the plane.

London—*August 3, Now*

Colonel Phillip Bright-Hamilton, the Israeli representative, was a caricature. His shaggy brown tweeds were rough enough to rub the paint off metal; the monocle screwed into one eye was obviously plain glass; the bristly moustache would have done any RAF officer proud.

"Senator," he said, taking my hand limply.

Naturally his car was a Rolls. As we got in, Bright-Hamilton said, "I thought a drive down toward the Channel would be nice. The sea air is refreshing at this time of year."

"Whatever you say, Colonel." I settled down in the comfortable seat. I confess to a great love for this particular symbol of the inherited-money rich. My heart broke when Rolls introduced the "owner driven" model. It was an era ending.

As the driver engaged the gears, the Colonel kept up a chatter of small talk about the latest scandal backstage at the Court of St. James's. But when the car slid around a curve, he gave a grunt, popped the monocle out of his eye and said, "Thank God. I'm getting tired of that routine."

"Colonel!" I said. "What happened to your accent?"

"Senator, if you want an accent, I should give you an accent that would take you back to Delancey Street. Mr. Accent, that's the cross I bear. This year, Colonel Bright-Hamilton. Next year, maybe a fisherman on the Bosporus. Iss nussing. Except I'd better cultivate a taste for beet soup."

He fumbled at the built-in bar. "Jews are supposed to be temperate drinkers, so I put the goys in their place by boozing them under the table. Want a demonstration?"

"Unfair," I said. "I've got a two-martini lead on you, not to mention a bottle of the worst red wine I've had this side of Mexico."

He dumped bourbon into a plastic glass, dropping in a chunk of ice. "Do I know what you mean!" he laughed. "I was with the flying squad that went out into the jungles to bring back Herr Oberleutnant Kraken last year. The French wine in Mexico City costs an arm and a leg and didn't travel well; the local stuff costs merely an arm, and plates your stomach with zinc. Do you know they age that stuff with *chemicals?*"

"Why the Colonel Blimp act?"

He gave me a wide smile. "Why not? You'd be surprised to learn how many people give Colonel Bright-Hamilton a wrinkled nose, and pay no attention to anything he says or does.

Look," he said, swirling his drink around in the plastic glass, "let's put the tochus on the table. Then we can drink."

"Fine."

"Bernardi wants you down in Tel Aviv. Bad. Don't ask me why, but he told me you can be trusted. So I'm going to tell you everything I know, and rely on you to keep quiet—even in Israel. Okay?"

"It's a deal."

The Rolls-Royce purred through the night as he spoke quietly, punctuating his speech with sips at the bourbon.

"It had to come, and it came now. We're getting ready to test our own atomic bomb. Bernardi knows your views on the bomb, and on the arms race. Believe me, Senator, the last thing Israel wants is to step up the cost of making war."

"In that case, why do you want a bomb?"

"We don't. But we've *got* a bomb. What are we supposed to do? Stick it in the ice box? Anyway, we're going to test the bomb whether or not you like the idea. So the question is, will you come down and take a look at it?"

"Why should I?"

"Because—and here's where I go out on the guessing limb —I think Bernardi hopes your report might wake people up. Senator, if *we* can get enough fissionable material to put together a bomb, don't you think we know the Arabs can't be more than a few years behind us? I bet your President gets the runs every time he thinks about Castro finding himself with a couple of chunks of plutonium. There's nothing hard about making a bomb—it's getting the plutonium that's difficult."

"So," I said, lighting my pipe, "you're putting on a demonstration in hopes it will convince the world that nuclear proliferation has gone far enough?"

"Something like that."

"I have to say, I don't like the idea of nuclear weapons in the Middle East."

"Senator, you don't have to like it. I'm telling you the facts of life."

135

"Can I have some of that bourbon?"

He made me a drink as the car slid through the darkness. Sipping it, I said, "There's more."

He nodded. "There's the part we don't like to think about. We don't like remembering that the two most notorious atomic spies were Jews."

"What's that got to do with Israel developing a bomb?"

"Maybe we wanted to show you we can do it without spies."

"Colonel," I said, "bull."

He laughed. "All right, maybe it is. But it's no bull that what happened to the Rosenbergs has been a thorn in our sides all these years. We've got a dream that goes, Wouldn't it be funny if what the Rosenbergs sold the Russians wasn't worth a damn? What if there wasn't any secret at all?"

"That doesn't sound funny to me," I said. "Although they would still technically have been guilty of espionage, I doubt if the death penalty would have been invoked. As it was, of course, we know that the information the Rosenbergs gave the U.S.S.R. moved their nuclear timetable up at least five years."

He put his monocle back in and scowled at me like Erich von Stroheim. "You haven't bought much of what I've said, have you?"

"Not much."

"All right. Put it on this basis. What do you have to lose? You may pick up support for your viewpoint. At the worst, you blow a couple of days."

"When do I have to be there?"

"The morning of the fifth. Day after tomorrow."

"I have to be in Paris tomorrow."

"We can fly you out tomorrow night. We've got a VIP Boeing 727. You can even fly right seat if you want."

"Bribery? I'm not qualified on anything bigger than a Lear."

"Who's to know? How about it, Senator?"

What the hell? The whole voyage was mad. What harm could a side excursion into another bad dream do?

Bright-Hamilton said he'd contact me at my hotel in Paris.

The jet would be ready to fly me out of France any time after midnight.

We turned back toward London, without ever having gotten close enough to Brighton to smell the cool sea air.

The clerk began shaking his head before the man approaching the desk at Tokyo's Hibya Hall was close enough to speak.

"A thousand apologies, Nakamura-san," the clerk said, "but there are no messages for you."

"I am expecting a cable," said Yoshije Nakamura.

"There is none. I beg your forgiveness."

"But it has been an entire day. Are you sure?"

"Regrettably so, Nakamura-san."

"*Domo arigato,*" said Nakamura. "Thank you."

"*Domo se ma sen,*" replied the clerk, bowing. "You are very welcome."

Premier Mikhail Nabov rubbed shaking fingers against his eyelids. "The American satellites have transmitted their photographs of the Baltic," he said. "Has there been any inquiry from Washington?"

"Nothing, Comrade," said an officer.

Nabov frowned. "My small voice continues to warn me of danger. Has there been any change in the posture of the Chinese?"

"They are still on Yellow," said the officer.

"What is Foster planning?" mused the Premier. "It is time he made his move. Why is he waiting?"

The question did not require an answer. Patiently, the officer waited.

"What is the status of our countdown?" Nabov asked.

"X minus two hours and holding," said the officer. "Our standing orders require a hold at this point unless we receive direct orders from you."

"How long can we hold without having to begin the countdown again?"

"Indefinitely."

Nabov sighed. "Very well," he said. "Continue the hold, but be ready to resume counting when I give the word."

The officer saluted and left the room. Nabov rubbed the back of his neck.

"Be still, little voice," he whispered.

"Where's Phil?" the President asked, as Executive Meeting Number Four began in the White House Situation Room.

"Still in Europe," said the Vice-President. "Otherwise, all present."

"Good. First, our intelligence reports that the Russians are holding at X minus two hours. Correct, General?"

"Yes sir," said General Oscar Burton. "Of course, they could fire right now without continuing the countdown if they wanted to."

"Where do we stand?"

"Half of SAC is airborne. The nuke subs are operating under sealed orders, checking in with us every hour for the Go–No Go. All Minuteman sites have tucked in, on full operational readiness. We can move any time you give the order."

"What are the projections if we preempt?"

Reading from a blue-bound report, Burton said, "Overkill on the magnitude of three times for the U.S.S.R. We've got the Russian population centers and military complexes bracketed with our MIRVs. There's no way they could knock them all down. Our computer readouts indicate that enough will get through to destroy the targets three times over."

"Beautiful," said the Secretary of State. "That's all we need. Why all this talk of a preemptive strike? You know we aren't going to preempt."

"It's just one of the contingency plans we've worked up," said Burton. "Besides, if we spot an enemy attack coming our way, we've still got time to empty our holes, and the effect on him would be the same as if we'd preempted."

"What about China?" asked the President.

"We'd take out their major population centers," said Burton, "but unless we used the dirties, at least sixty percent of the population would come through. They're so decentralized, you see."

"The dirties," said Sol Cushman, "the weapons with cobalt casings."

"Yes sir. Fallout from them would destroy all life at least five hundred miles downwind. Frankly, there'd be great danger to India and most of Southeast Asia if we used dirties on the Chinese."

"Paul," the President said to the Director of the CIA, "did Phil turn the bluff ratio information over to you?"

"Yes sir."

"Where do we stand now?"

"Not very well, sir," said the CIA man. "The probability of their bluffing is now less than fifty percent. Forty-eight point nine, to be exact."

"So there's a fifty-one percent chance the Chinese will fire."

"As of now, sir," said Ryan. "The only bright side to it is that they're still holding at Yellow."

The President tapped his fingers nervously on the table for a moment. "All right," he said. "I presume the committee's recommendation is the same, that we pull the ABMs out of Japan."

"Yes sir," said a chorus of voices.

"No sir," said General Oscar Burton. "Leave them there. Put more in, if we get time."

"Thank you, gentlemen," said President Howard Foster. "I appreciate your advice. For the time being, I'm going to maintain the status quo. The missiles stay."

Celia sat alone in her work room. The TV monitors were dark. The tape spools motionless. All of the telephones turned off, electric typewriters unplugged.

An envelope, torn open, lay on the floor. Its contents, a single sheet of paper, were on the desk before her.

On the letterhead of the Trans-World International Syndicate, a short message was typed.

139

Miss Celia Craig,
1801 N Street,
Washington, D.C.

August 3

DELIVER BY HAND

Dear Miss Craig:

Persistent reports of political activities on your part have placed this Syndicate in the embarrassing position of having to defend actions which we have no sympathy for, and which as newspapermen we feel are antagonistic toward the public interest.

Accordingly, under Clause 14-D of your contract, this Syndicate hereby terminates your employment.

Sincerely,

Jonathan West, *President*

And under the typewritten message, a handwritten scrawl: "Sweetie, why don't you sue us? I'd love to get you under oath on a witness stand. Jon."

Outside, the sun was trying to make its way through the early morning Washington smog. Down the street a dog barked. It was just another muggy morning on N Street.

Celia dialed Jack Sherwood's apartment number. Ten rings later, she put down the telephone.

On the front page of *The Washington Post*, my face stared up at her. The headline read: SENATOR MCGAVIN LINKED WITH MAFIA. A long story, written by Celia's rival at the Syndicate, listed speculations and might-bes as if they were hard fact.

"Oh, Hugh," said Celia, "Why aren't you here?"

I never got out of Orly Airport.

After being met by a small army of reporters and television cameramen, making my speech about disarmament, fielding questions about the missiles in Japan, disavowing any knowledge of President Foster's plans in the Far East, and expressing puzzlement over the Attorney General's report linking me with the Mafia, I was led to a quiet VIP lounge on the third floor of the Air France building.

The door was guarded by four soldiers. My escort tapped at it, and when I stepped inside I came face to face with the President of France.

"Good morning, Senator," he said in a booming voice, only slightly accented. "Come, have some coffee with me."

He waved my escort away, shut the door. "Now," he said. "We can relax. How was your flight?"

"Smooth," I said. "Sir, I'm surprised to see you here. I intended to come to you."

"Poof!" He dismissed protocol with an airy wave of his hand. "I know that your time is short." He poured a demitasse and handed it to me. "I made this myself," he said, quite seriously.

I tasted the coffee. "It's excellent."

He smiled. "My policies are often attacked. My coffee, never." He sipped at his own. "Now, may I tell you why I wanted to speak with you personally?"

"Secretary DuPré told me your government would not be able to offer any public assistance to my mission."

"Senator," he said, "do you know anything about a Project Jesus Factor?"

"Project JF? I think so."

"A very expensive project, is it not?"

141

"So it would seem," I said carefully. "And very secret. How did you learn of it?"

He shrugged. "Let it be said that you and I are interested in the same things. Do you know what this Project Jesus Factor is?"

"No."

"Nor do I," he said. "But I am convinced that when you learn what this mysterious project is all about, you will be closer to achieving your aims."

"Forgive me, sir, but I am convinced that you know more than you're willing to say."

"Of course," he said blandly. "My concern for France takes precedence over the assistance I would like to extend to you. Perhaps if you would answer a question or two?"

"If I can."

"The atomic bomb," he said. "You have seen it explode with your own eyes—not on film, or described by a third party?"

"I saw a test," I said. "It was impressive."

"Did you see a bomb?"

"I beg your pardon?"

"Did you see a bomb? A bomb dropped from the air? Or did you see a device suspended from a tower?"

"I think it was dropped."

"Are you sure?"

"They said it was an air drop," I told him, trying to remember. "Why? What are you getting at?"

"Nothing," said the President of France. "Let us say I was attempting to discover why you have this tremendous hatred for the bomb."

"I've got my reasons," I said. "Sir, what do you want from me?"

"Nothing, my friend. But perhaps when you find out the truth about your Project Jesus Factor, you would be kind enough to speak with me again."

"If the project comes under the heading of national security . . ."

"Of course, of course," he said, raising his hand. "But should your discovery be in the interests of world peace?" He sipped his coffee slowly. "I truly wish I could be more open with you. As it is, the only advice I can give you is to remember that, when you see what you see, or think you see, things are not always what they seem."

Puzzled, I said nothing.

He stood. "I have received a personal communication from my old friend Levi Bernardi. He informed me of your visit to Israel."

"Did he tell you why I'm going?"

"Not in so many words. Since I knew our meeting here would be a brief one, I informed Prime Minister Bernardi that his aircraft could pick you up earlier than planned. I hope this was not presumptuous of me. Certainly the hospitality of Paris is yours."

"No, you were right, sir," I said. "Time is short."

"It is now eleven-ten," he said. "The Israeli jet will be here by noon. Of course, they can wait if necessary. Would you join me for lunch?"

"With your permission, sir, I think I'd better leave as soon as possible. It's a long flight."

"Certainly." He held out his hand. "Senator, I wish you God-speed and good fortune with your mission."

"Thank you, sir."

"My aide will attend to your baggage. And please return soon. The next time, bring your charming wife. My regards to her—I remember her well from my last visit to your country."

"I'll do that," I said. Deftly, the President of France had guided me out the door. The interview was over.

When *The Busted Flush* reached 5300 feet, cruising altitude for the first leg of the flight, Captain Meredith Rogers' voice came over the intercom.

"McGavin?" he said. "Ready to go to work?"

"Yes sir," I said. "See you in the forward bay."

Every man aboard the B-29 was busy. The flight engineer was adjusting engine RPMs and propeller pitch, fine-tuning the four giant engines until they meshed in perfect synchronization. Our pilot, Captain Ritter, was rechecking all the flight controls before he put the plane onto auto-pilot. Behind us S/Sgt. Joe Kingsly, the tail gunner, tested his guns. They sounded like a stick being dragged along a picket fence.

I joined Rogers in the forward bomb bay. It was crowded; the Little Boy almost filled the huge compartment. We were squeezed onto a narrow walkway beside it.

"Paul, can you hear me?" Rogers asked. He listened for a moment, then nodded. My own intercom was not plugged into the bomb bay outlet, so I heard nothing. "Fine," Rogers said. "I'm going to unplug the intercom for a while. Don't get worried. I'll be back to you when I'm ready to start work."

He reached over and pulled out his own plug. Then, to my horror, he took out a cigarette and lit it, casually leaning against the bomb. When he offered me one I shook my head.

"McGavin," he said, "that enlisted man back there at the briefing was right. This is an atomic bomb. In theory, it's the simplest kind of weapon—but setting it off is complicated. That's why it's so big. Most of this hardware is timing and fusing mechanisms."

"Where's the TNT, or whatever it is that makes the explosion?"

He indicated the buckets that had been brought on board the plane just before takeoff. "In there. One bucket contains forty-two percent of the uranium, and the other one has the rest of it."

"Uranium?"

"It's a fissionable metal, heavier than lead. Under normal conditions, uranium emits radioactive particles. But slowly, not in an explosion."

"Like radium?"

He nodded. "Except it's safer to handle. I can pick the uranium up in my bare hands—in fact, in a few minutes I will. You might get burned if you put a piece under your pillow all night, but the amount of radioactivity uranium puts out won't hurt you unless you're exposed for several hours."

"What makes it explode?"

"Critical mass." I looked at him stupidly. "Take a given amount of uranium—say, for argument, a pound of the stuff —and it'll just sit there, emitting a steady stream of radioactivity, but it won't explode. Then add another ounce—only one ounce plus the original pound—and you achieve what the physicists call critical mass. The radioactive particles being thrown off hit other particles, and in just a matter of milliseconds, trillions of particles have hit trillions of other particles, and the whole damn thing blows up. They call that a chain reaction."

Today the theory of atomic fission is taught in every high school physics course. But to me in 1945 it was as if Flash Gordon had returned from the planet Ming and was describing how his death ray worked.

Rogers touched the side of the bomb. "This big bastard," he went on, "is just a huge gun barrel. We put one chunk of uranium down here, at the nose. We put the other one up at the tail. It's shaped like a bullet, maybe six inches around. There's a high explosive charge behind it, and when the bomb is set off, that charge explodes and shoots the uranium down a wooden tunnel at a thousand feet a second. The uranium slug hits the other chunk, you reach critical mass, and boom. Got that?"

It sounded simple enough. So simple that I wondered why someone else hadn't already thought of it.

"Theoretically," he said, "that should be all we have to do. But just to be safe, we use Little Abner." He showed me a small metal device. "This is what we call an initiator. At the moment the uranium slug hits the uranium rings down here in the nose, Little Abner emits a shower of neutrons, just to make doubly sure the chain reaction begins."

Earnestly I said, "I only studied law. I take your word for it."

He laughed. "Any questions?"

"How do you know this thing will stop when it uses up the uranium? What if it starts working on the earth and blows everything else up too?"

"We used to worry about that. When they ran the Trinity test in New Mexico, there was a real fear that once the dragon started flaming he wouldn't stop until he'd burned everything. But it didn't happen."

Glumly, I said, "I wish I'd stayed at Harvard."

"Ready?"

"Yes sir."

We plugged in our intercom cords. "Paul?" said Rogers. "Do you read me?"

"Loud and clear."

"Radio operator?"

"Yes sir?"

"Plug me into the command circuit. I'll report directly to Tinian."

"You're hooked up, sir."

"Tinian Special Group A, this is Jimmy Durante. Do you read me? Over."

A crackle of static, then, "Jimmy Durante, we read you five by five. Over."

"We're ready to start tickling the dragon's tail. Do not respond to my communications until further notice. Radioman, keep this channel open, even if I stop talking." He turned to me. "Okay, McGavin, here we go."

I held a flashlight while he used an ordinary screwdriver to take several panels off the side of the bomb. He had a large case, from which he removed components as he needed them.

"Inserting radar proximity fuse," he reported. "Paul, what does your little black box say?"

"Proximity fuse connected and functioning," Lieutenant Paul Randolph reported from the flight deck.

Rogers took up another small unit. "Inserting atmospheric pressure fuse," he said. "Paul?"

"Red light," said Randolph. "Jiggle it around."

"Shit," said Rogers. "A half million dollars' worth of special hand-tooled parts and you have to jiggle them." But he jiggled.

"Green light," Randolph reported. "Atmospheric pressure fuse connected and functioning."

"Inserting time fuses," said Rogers.

"Green light," came the reply. "Connected and functioning."

"Any one of these fuses could set off the beast," Rogers told me, switching off his intercom. "But for safety's sake, they have to trip in sequence before the bomb will explode. First, the time fuse doesn't permit anything to start working until fifteen seconds after the bomb leaves the bay. After forty seconds or so of free fall, the atmospheric pressure fuse will sense that the bomb is around 2,000 feet above the target. That's when the proximity fuse goes into action. It pushes out radar signals that bounce back from the ground. The nineteenth pulse triggers the high explosives and Little Abner. We had a hell of a time finding a radar wavelength we were sure the Japs weren't using—it could be embarrassing if they triggered the bomb while we were still carrying it. Okay, now I'll set the proximity fuse."

He switched on the intercom. "Jimmy Durante here," he said. "Setting radar frequencies on proximity fuse." He made several adjustments.

"Frequencies check out," said Randolph.

Rogers showed me a slip of paper on which a string of numbers were written. "They thought of everything," he said, with a smile. "Rice paper." He popped it into his mouth and chewed. "Delicious. But I prefer fortune cookies."

"All fusing systems green," Randolph reported over the intercom.

"Hand me that bucket," said Rogers. I did. It was heavy.

He removed the lead cover, reached inside and took out a slug of dull gray metal. Carefully, he seated it near the tail of the bomb in a fitted chamber that matched the slug exactly.

"Placing slug," he reported. He bent over, picked up a paper-wrapped object, obviously heavy, and slid it into the breech, behind the uranium slug. As he screwed thin wires to connectors projecting from the brown paper, he said, "H.E. charge in place. Connecting firing cables."

"Green light on H.E. charge," said Randolph.

Rogers stepped back and mopped his sweating forehead with a sleeve. "That was the moment I didn't like," he said. "There's almost fifty pounds of high explosives there, and one spark of static electricity could have set it off."

He lifted the other bucket and removed a ring-shaped piece of metal.

"Inserting rings," he said.

"Green light on rings."

"Inserting initiator."

"Green light on initiator."

"Okay," said Rogers. "Give me a couple of minutes to settle down, and we'll check out the circuits." He switched off his intercom. I did the same. This time when he offered a Camel, I took it. "We're almost done," he said. "But this is the tricky part. What I've got to do now is put direct current through each one of these circuits, but making sure that at least one circuit in the sequence is always disconnected, so the juice can't go all the way and set off the explosive charge. Got that?"

I had it. We finished our cigarettes and hooked up the intercom again.

"I have disconnected the proximity fuse circuit," he said.

"Proximity fuse shows disconnect," Randolph answered.

"Hitting the juice," said Rogers.

"Stage One reads green."

"Juice off," said Rogers. "Now I've disconnected the atmospheric fuse."

"Atmospheric fuse shows disconnect."

"Hitting the juice."

"Stage Two reads green."

"Juice off. Disconnecting H.E. detonator."

"Detonator shows disconnect."

"Hitting the juice." There was a pause. "Hitting the juice."

"Sorry, Captain," came the reply. "I read red on Stage Three."

Rogers cursed. "Juice off. I'll trace the circuit."

I held the flashlight close while he fumbled through a maze of varicolored wires.

"Son of a bitch!" he swore. "Look at that, McGavin!" I looked, but could see nothing unusual. "Some clown nicked this blue cable with his side cutters, just enough to weaken it so it would break when moved. Hand me those wire strippers and electrical tape."

5,000 feet above the tossing Pacific, as *The Busted Flush* streaked toward Iwo Jima, Captain Meredith Rogers stripped the broken cable back at both ends, twisted the wires together with a pair of pliers, wrapped the bare surfaces with black electrical tape, and stepped back. "Juice on," he said, throwing a toggle switch.

"I get a green light on Stage Three," said Randolph.

"Good," said Rogers. "Juice off. All stages check out." He nodded toward me. "Think you could go through that sequence if you had to?"

"I'd hate to try, but I guess I could."

"I hope you don't have to. Give me a hand with those panels."

We replaced the curved metal panels and screwed them down tightly.

"Okay," he said. "Only one more step, and from then on it's up to you."

He disconnected a cable that ran from the side of the bomb into the wall of the bomb bay, then threw a small switch located behind one of the tail fins.

"Little Boy's running on his own battery power now," he explained. "The only thing still hooked up is Lieutenant Randolph's black box, and that'll disconnect automatically."

"When?"

He looked directly at me before answering.

"When you push the bomb release button."

Tel Aviv—August 4, Now

The flight to Israel took us down over Venice and the Adriatic Sea, past Athens and Crete, across the Mediterranean. We made a flat approach over the water and a screeching landing at the big Sde Dov airport outside Tel Aviv.

It was the golden time of evening, when the shadows are long and dark blue against the reddish sand. The modern high-rise buildings were blinding white, with a red halo of sunlight against their western edges. They stood out starkly against the violently blue sky.

Except for a few moments over the Mediterranean when I slid into the right seat and experimented with the controls, I declined the pilot's offer to fly co-pilot. But I sat in the flight engineer's position for the landing. As we approached the airport at treetop level, I said, "You certainly fly this thing right onto the ground."

Busy as he was, the pilot turned and grinned. "Self-defense," he said. "You never know when there might be some Arab commando down there with a recoilless rifle. This way they don't have time to draw a bead."

"I thought the situation had quieted down."

"It's quiet, but that doesn't mean they're sleeping. Wheels down."

I heard the dull thump of the wheels lowering and locking. Now the pilot was engrossed with his cockpit check, so I watched the approaching airstrip and listened to the quiet, confident conversation between the fliers.

I have always felt most at home in the presence of men who make the sky their domain. Despite the glamorous fly-boy image made popular in the thirties and forties by Tailspin Tommy and Milton Caniff, the average pilot lives in a world of empirical truths: if a rudder cable is frayed and parts during flight, his aircraft will crash and most probably he will die. He cannot rely on any other man completely. He makes it a point to examine that rudder cable himself—perhaps not on every flight, but often enough so that he will not be surprised by a preventable failure.

This Israeli pilot was good. He greased that 727 right in just above the palm trees and slid onto the runway without a bump. It was like landing on glass. He put the fan jets into reverse, and the plane shuddered as ground speed dropped.

Instead of taxiing over to the terminal building, he followed a jeep to a low hut near the end of the runway. When he chopped the throttles, a half dozen white-coveralled ground crewmen swarmed over the plane. Two shoved a loading ramp up to the forward hatch.

"Nice flight, Captain," I said to the pilot, shaking his hand.

"My pleasure," he said. "You ought to get your multi-engine rating. These things are fun to fly."

"I can barely afford gas for my Supercub," I said. "In fact, I may have to take up soaring when I get home again. There's a rumor I may be unemployed."

"You can always come to work for El Al," he said. "We'll start you off as a flight engineer."

"Don't joke," I said, "I might be glad to get it."

"Good luck," he said. "Seriously, I hope you succeed at what you're doing. I flew for the RAF before I emigrated, and if I told you about the near misses we had, it'd turn your hair white."

"Not mine," I grinned, patting my shiny pate.

"Sorry, Senator. Anyway, keep up the good work. I've got four kids."

"I'll do my best," I promised.

Waiting for me at the foot of the steps was a slim man in khaki. He wore the insignia of a major.

"Senator McGavin? Welcome to Israel. I am Major Kiesler."

"Na'im me'ohd," I said.

"Ah, you speak Hebrew!" He launched into a speech, the words whistling over my head like arrows.

"Hold on," I said. "I just used up all the Hebrew I own. I got that out of a guide book."

One of the 727's crewmen staggered down the ramp carrying my lumpy B-4 bag. "Shall I take this to customs?" he asked Kiesler.

"No," said the Major. "Put it in the car." Then, to me, "Senator, Prime Minister Bernardi asks me to convey his best wishes, and to beg his forgiveness for not being able to see you tonight. Could you dine with him tomorrow evening?"

"I'll be happy to."

"Unfortunately," Kiesler went on, looking embarrassed, "the Prime Minister will not be in Tel Aviv. He will be in Dimona, near the Wilderness of Zin in the Negev."

"That's all right," I said. "I don't mind going down to Dimona."

"You must be tired. There are several alternatives. You can stay in Tel Aviv tonight—there is a fine suite at the Dan—or, if you prefer to be on the beach, the Hilton. Then, tomorrow, we can either drive to Dimona, or fly to Beersheba and drive from there."

"If we drive, does the route take us through Jerusalem?"

"It can."

"How about driving down tonight? This is my first chance to see the Old City—the last time I was here, the Jordanians were still in possession, and I left before your troops moved in. Then we could drive on down to the Negev tomorrow afternoon."

"Very well," he said. "But I would suggest that we dine before leaving Tel Aviv. The restaurants in Jerusalem are not very good, and they are tremendously expensive."

"In that case," I said, "we'll sign Bernardi's name."

Kiesler gave me a look that made it clear he did not know whether or not I was joking. "As you wish, Senator," he said. "My orders were to place myself at your disposal."

"Do you have to go back to your headquarters to pick up anything?"

He shook his head. "I have a complete kit in the car." He led me to the pale gray Citroën parked near one of the huts. I waved farewell to the pilot and slid into the car. It was hot and stuffy. Major Kiesler beckoned an enlisted man over.

"Telephone ahead to the King David Hotel in Jerusalem," he said. "Reserve a suite for Senator McGavin and a single room for me. Then notify the Prime Minister's aide that we will be staying in Jerusalem tonight and arriving in Dimona tomorrow afternoon."

"Yes sir," said the enlisted man. He saluted. Kiesler returned it and got in the car.

"We are going to Jerusalem," he told the driver.

"Yes sir," said the driver.

From behind, the khaki-uniformed, short-haired driver could have been either sex. When she turned, I saw she was a young woman.

"How do you do, Senator?" she said. "My name is Barbara."

"Na'im me'ohd," I said, "and let me warn you that's all the Hebrew I know."

She laughed. "Your accent reminds me of Charlton Heston."

"Is that a compliment or a knock?"

"A compliment."

"Once the car is moving," Kiesler said pointedly, "turn on the air conditioning."

"Yes sir," Barbara said, starting the motor. As we drove out of the airport, she engaged the air conditioning. At first it flooded the rear seat with hot, muggy air, but then it began to cool us. There was a peculiar, foreign smell. I've noticed that somehow cars seem to smell like the countries in which they are driven. This particular odor was not unpleasant—there were slight traces of smoke, of spices, and growing flowers.

"Do you want to drive through the Carmel Market and Independence Park, Senator?" she said.

"No thanks, Barbara. I've seen most of Tel Aviv. Why don't you take the most direct route?"

153

"Then I'll use Haifa Road. We'll cut down to Kibbutz Galuyoth and pick up Jerusalem Road there."

"Very good, driver," said Major Kiesler. He reminded me of a prim, very proper instructor I had known years before at Harvard. Since there was no real authority in the man, he had to rely on the authority he wore.

The blue twilight was upon us. The skyline of Tel Aviv seemed speckled with yellow fireflies. As we drove south, I remembered my first visit to this bustling city long ago, when Tel Aviv was virtually empty of men—most had been called up for the 1967 war. Somehow the city continued to function, manned by women and men too old or young to fight. Now, with peace several years old in the Middle East, I hoped the impending test of Israel's atomic bomb would not wreck the balance of power so completely that the United Arab Republic would succeed in persuading the Soviets—or worse, China—to provide them with nuclear weapons. It was just this sort of proliferation that I hoped to prevent.

As we turned onto Jerusalem Road, the city around us was peaceful and quiet. Many of the pedestrians we drove past wore Arab burnooses. Children played at the side of the road. I stretched, yawned, and thought of home.

I must have slept, because the next thing I knew was the gentle whisper of music from the car's radio. Major Kiesler was snoring beside me. I coughed and reached for my pipe.

"Does the music disturb you?" Barbara asked.

"No," I mumbled. "I must have dozed off."

"You were tired," she said. "Shall I turn off the radio?"

"Leave it on," I said. "I don't listen to enough music."

She laughed softly. "You would if you lived in Tel Aviv. They call it the city of transistor radios. Every student in the park has one held to his ear."

"What's that playing now?"

"The Israeli Philharmonic. They're doing the Saint-Saëns Organ Symphony. I have it on a recording."

I had finished stuffing my pipe, and fumbled for a match. She saw me in the rear-view mirror, and pushed the cigarette lighter on the dashboard.

"That thing won't work in a pipe," I said. "Here they are."
I cupped a match in my hand and puffed away at the rich
Sail tobacco. Beside me, Major Kiesler mumbled and threw
out one hand that nearly knocked the pipe from my mouth.

"Barbara," I said, "would you mind if I rode up there with
you? The Major's a restless sleeper."

"Not at all," she said. The car slowed and stopped. I got
out. It was good to stretch my legs.

We were in a sea of darkness, somewhere between Tel
Aviv and Jerusalem. Barbara switched off the headlights and
got out too. Above me, the stars were bright points of light
punched through the tent of night.

"Where are we?" I asked.

"The Valley of Ayalon. We passed Ramla a little while ago.
But I did not think you would want to be awakened just to
see the Tower of Richard the Lion-Hearted."

"Not really," I said, puffing on my pipe. "What's so special
about the Valley of Ayalon?"

"Why do you think there is anything special about it?"

"Something about the way you said the name. It's the way
I'd say, 'This is the Grand Canyon.'"

She laughed. "Our valley is tiny compared to the Grand
Canyon. But you are right. According to the Bible, this is where
Joshua stopped the sun long enough to drive off the Amor-
rheans. And it is said that Samson lived here."

"While he still had his hair, I hope."

"Are you sensitive about hair, Senator?"

"My lack of it, you mean? No, not any more." I told her
about Adlai Stevenson straightening me out.

"It must be wonderful," she said, "to know men like Mr.
Stevenson."

"Not really. After a while, you don't think about *who* they
are. You talk with them, you eat and drink with them, you
travel with them—and you find that, like Mr. Stevenson, they
have holes in their shoes too."

"I do not think I could be so blasé," she said.

"Why not? You're talking to me now, aren't you? Of course,
I'm only a junior senator, but—"

"You cannot see me shaking in my shoes," she said.

I reached out and touched her arm. She *was* trembling.

"Maybe we'd better get going," I said.

"Yes," she said. "If the Major wakes up he will be angry."

As the car picked up speed, I asked, "How much further?"

"We start the climb soon. This road is called the Highway of Courage. It was built under Arab fire in 1948. If it were daylight, you would be able to see the burned-out wreckage of automobiles and armored cars that were shelled by the enemy. Hundreds of lives were paid for this road. And now the tourists litter it with their beer cans."

"They do the same at Gettysburg," I said. "Barbara, are you in the army, or what?"

"I am what they call a *chayelet*."

"Which means?"

She giggled. "Girl soldier, more or less. We are obliged to do military service at the age of eighteen, for twenty months. The boys must serve for twenty-six. And unlike your country, there are no deferments for academic studies. Only if you are ill, married, or pregnant are you excused. We complain, but it is an honor to be a *chayelet*."

She touched her head. "The only thing I miss," she said, "is the long hair I used to have. The regulations forbid the hair to touch the collar. So a *chayelet* either wears her hair gathered on top of her head, which is very hot in the summer, or has it cut as I did. The first thing I shall do when I am discharged is to let my hair grow again."

"How far off is that?"

"Ten months."

"Then you're only nineteen."

"For a sabra, nineteen is old enough to work, to bear arms."

Remembering where I had been and what I had done when I was nineteen, I wondered why it seemed so young to me now.

"I wish it were not so dark," she complained as we sped through the night. "You would be able to see the Yaar-ha-Kedoshim on your right."

"What's that?"

"The Forest of the Martyrs. We have planted six million trees there to remember the six million who died under Hitler. It is so beautiful, it takes your breath."

"Do you know Jerusalem well?"

"I go there often. My sister is married to a dentist who has his practice near the Hadassah Hospital. I will stay with them tonight. It is lucky I have relatives there. Otherwise I would have to report to the barracks, and they insist on bed check at eleven P.M."

I smiled. It had been a long time since I thought of bed check.

"Do you keep civilian clothes at your sister's?"

"Yes. Why?"

"I wondered if you'd like to have dinner tonight with a bald-headed United States senator?"

"Oh, I couldn't." But her voice sounded disappointed.

"Why not?"

"The Major . . ."

"Let me handle the Major. If you were a filthy rich tourist, with all the money in the world, and no problems with bed check or snippy little majors, where would you go tonight?"

"You'll laugh at me."

"I promise not to laugh."

"I absolutely adore Italian cooking. There's a restaurant on King George Street called the Gondola. But it is terribly expensive."

"The Gondola it is," I said. "When do you think we'll be through checking in at the King David? You'll need time to go to your sister's and change."

"It will be after nine," she said. "But—if—well, if we do have dinner, it would be faster for you to take a taxi to the restaurant and I will meet you there."

"Fine," I said. "It's settled." I wrote the name of the restaurant and "King George Street" in my pocket notebook.

The music played softly in the Citroën as we talked quietly of America and of Barbara's hopes to visit there someday.

Then the road widened out to four lanes, and before I knew it we were at the gates of Jerusalem. As the sound of exhaust popped against the stone walls, Major Kiesler stirred in the back seat, then sat up suddenly.

"Where are we?" he demanded.

"Entering Jerusalem, Major," said Barbara.

"Senator," he said disapprovingly, "you shouldn't be riding up there."

"Sorry," I said. "I didn't want to disturb your rest."

"Stop the car, driver," he ordered. She did.

"I like it where I am," I said.

Barbara shook her head slightly. "No," her lips said without sound.

I got out and crawled into the back seat beside Kiesler. "Major," I said maliciously, "you snore like a buzz saw."

"You should have wakened me," he said, as if his snoring was my fault.

"Let's go straight to the hotel, Barbara," I said. "I've got a dinner engagement and I don't want to be late."

"Oh?" said Kiesler. "I didn't know you had friends in Jerusalem."

"I do. So hurry, driver."

"Yes sir," she said.

The King David Hotel was all its name promised. The style of its façade was a mixture of Victorian and Oriental. Two Arab boys seized our luggage and hustled it inside.

"Remain here, driver," said Kiesler, "in case we need you."

"I'm sure we won't be needing her tonight, Major," I said. "Why can't she just take the night off?"

She looked to Kiesler for permission. "Oh, all right," he said. "Go ahead. But be here at eight in the morning. And don't use the car for your personal trips."

"Yes sir," she said. "Good night, Senator."

"Good night, driver," I said, winking at her.

"Blasted *chayelets*," Kiesler complained as we went inside. "Not an ounce of discipline in the lot of them."

"Too true," I said. "Youth is wasted on the young."

"We've a fine suite for the Senator," the clerk announced. "It faces the east garden, and you've a lovely view of the Old City."

"Many thanks," I said. "And thank you, Major, for your help. I'll see you in the morning."

"Are you sure you wouldn't rather have dinner here?" he asked nervously. "The Regency Grill has an excellent beef strogonoff. And there's a view of the Oriental gardens from the cocktail terrace."

"You go right ahead," I said. "Now, I've got to hurry, Major. Good night."

"Very well," he said, visibly reluctant to leave me. But the bellboy led me toward the elevator while Kiesler was still signing the register. As the doors closed, I gave him a great big smile.

The suite was luxurious. From its small terrace I could see a cluster of lights that must have been the Old City. The furnishings were carved from rosewood and covered with intricately patterned brocade.

I took a quick shower, put on a fresh suit, and went down to the main desk.

"Can I change some dollars?" I asked the cashier.

"Yes sir. The rate today is three Israeli pounds to one U.S. dollar."

I gave her two fifty-dollar traveler's checks. She hesitated.

"What's wrong?"

"Nothing," she said. "But I might suggest—if you're going to make purchases in the shops, most of them will give you a fifteen percent discount if you pay with traveler's checks or foreign currency rather than Israeli pounds."

"That's all right," I said. "But thanks anyway."

She gave me three hundred pounds, in five-pound notes. I said good night and went out to ask the doorman to hail a cab. He smiled at the U.S. quarter I gave him.

"The Gondola on King George Street," I told the Arab driver.

"Fifteen pounds," he said instantly.

"How about five?"

"Tourists!" he snapped. "They would rob their mothers and leave them to starve. Twelve."

"Eight."

The driver called on heaven to witness his wretched estate in life, in which he was obliged to provide transportation for foreign millionaires at less than the cost of his petrol. "Ten pounds," he said finally.

"Ten including tip," I said.

The offer must have been acceptable, because he floorboarded the ancient Ford and we careened through the narrow streets of Jerusalem, horn blaring. The driver kept up a constant screech of invective against the terrified pedestrians.

He skidded to a stop in front of what looked like an apartment building.

"The Gondola," he announced.

"Are you sure?"

"It's inside," he said scornfully. Suspiciously, I got out and gave him two five-pound notes. Without a word of thanks he sped away, burning his tires against the cobblestones.

He had brought me to the right place, however. Through the apartment building entrance I found a small easel with "The Gondola" lettered on a heavy card.

The restaurant walls were hand-rubbed blonde wood panels, with huge murals depicting a glorified Italy. The carpeting was thick and soft. I looked around. The place was nearly empty.

I sat at the bar and ordered a gin and tonic. As I sipped it, I did a little mental arithmetic. It was almost nine, which would make it around two in the afternoon in Washington. I would be back at the King David in plenty of time to catch Jack Sherwood at his office.

"Hello," said Barbara. I had not seen her approach, and her voice startled me.

I stood up. "You don't look like a *chayelet* to me," I said.

She had changed into a sheer, knee-length dress, tied loosely at the waist with a scarlet sash. A single strand of pearls curved around her neck.

"Thank you, Senator," she said.

As I beckoned for the maître d', I said, "Look, if I can call you Barbara, you can call me Hugh."

"I couldn't!"

"You can and you will. Try it."

She pursed her lips as if she were going to whistle and, in a small voice, said, "Hugh."

"Good. Now let's eat."

We were taken to a small table in the corner, with a huge candle burning in its center. A waiter hurried over with my drink. Barbara ordered a Cinzano and, self-consciously, we began reading the gigantic menu.

"What kind of Italian food do you like best?" I asked.

"Spaghetti," she said, looking down at the table. "It's all I know."

"Will you let me order for you?"

"I would like you to."

I nodded at the waiter and he hurried over.

"A single order of fettucini. Then for the main course, veal scallopine, and on the side some linguine with red sauce."

"Scallopine?" asked Barbara, when he had gone. "Fettucini? Are they like spaghetti?"

"Fettucini is three-thousand-percent carbohydrates," I told her. "And linguine is even worse. You are going to see a man gain twenty pounds before your very eyes. But I can't hold out any longer. Thank you, Barbara, for giving me an excuse." I caught the wine steward's eye and nodded him over.

"Chianti?" he suggested.

I shuddered. "Do you have a good unbruised Bordeaux?" He nodded, and I told him, "Put it in a bucket to chill. And don't give me that horrified look. Do you know what room temperature is in the cellar of a Bordeaux castle?" He made a confused gesture and hurried away.

"It is fun being with you," Barbara said, sipping her vermouth. "I feel—protected."

"You? I should think you'd be protecting me."

"I can shoot a rifle accurately," she said. "And I was taught to creep up behind a sentry with a knife."

161

She smiled. "But they did not teach me how to order wine, or what is fettucini."

"You can't know everything at nineteen."

"I think you did. What were you doing when you were nineteen?"

Slowly, I said, "I was flying airplanes."

"You were in the army?"

"Yes. It was a long time ago."

"Did you kill many of the enemy?"

"I was in the group that dropped the first atomic bomb on Japan."

She looked down at her glass. "Oh. That must have been dreadful for you."

"It was worse for the people it was dropped on."

"Yes, but you were at war. Do you blame yourself for it?"

"Change things around a little," I said. "Let's say I was a guard at Buchenwald and I was ordered to herd a thousand Jews into the ovens. Refusing would only put me in the oven too. Yet afterwards, you could call me a war criminal. Couldn't you?"

"But that was different."

"How? Were the civilians in Buchenwald any more innocent than the civilians in Hiroshima?"

"I see," she said. "So now you try to destroy the bomb."

"Yes. Not so much because of any guilt I feel myself, but because, having been involved personally, I know how easily good men can be forced to do evil things. All war is terrible —but wars of annihilation are too easy to start today. I believe we must roll the clock back to a less violent age."

"Hugh," she said sadly, "I think you can never do that. Violence has been with us always. These streets, the desert around the city—the hills of Golgotha—all are drenched with blood. And yet this place is the cradle of Christianity."

"I'm not trying to make humanity nice," I said. "I'm too cynical for that. But let's make it a little harder to kill one another. As it stands now, one finger on a button and civilization goes up in smoke."

The wine steward rushed at us from one side of the room, bearing the wine. A waiter wheeled over a cart with a spirit lamp and a chafing dish and began tossing the fettucini.

"It smells delicious," said Barbara.

"It is," I told her. I watched as she ate, and her spontaneous happiness, her wondering amazement at the newness of it all, her intense gratitude for such small gifts all combined to make me feel warm, and smugly proud. There was a dance or two in the old McGavin yet!

After dinner it still seemed too early to go back to the hotel. "Can we do any sightseeing at this ungodly hour?" I asked. "I'm wide awake and it's too nice a night to waste."

"Some of the Old City is very lovely at night," she said. "We can get a taxi and visit the Wailing Wall. That is my favorite spot. It is the symbol of what every Jewish soldier fought to achieve."

"Let's go."

I paid the check—sixty Israeli pounds. Barbara was horrified. I shrugged. "Twenty dollars. Not a fortune."

"For you, Senator," she said, smiling. "But that's almost a month's salary for a *chayelet.*"

There was no hassle with the taxi driver this time. Barbara spoke quietly but firmly to him in Hebrew, then turned to me with satisfaction. "He wanted ten pounds," she said, "but when I told him I was a soldier, he agreed to four."

"Miraculous," I said. I told her about my bargaining with the driver from the King David Hotel, and how pleased I had been to knock five pounds off his asking price.

"He gave you the right name," she laughed. "Millionaire tourist! You should have paid him six pounds instead of ten, and he would have been happy."

The taxi lurched through the narrow streets. Many of the walls were pockmarked by bullets and shell fragments.

"I know I am always saying this," she said, "but if it were not dark, you would be able to see David's Tower. But at least —look! That is the Holy Sepulchre. The last five Stations of the Cross are there. Tomorrow, if we have time, we will come back and enter the Old City through St. Stephen's Gate. We will begin with the First Station, where Pontius Pilate questioned Jesus, and then follow the stations along the Via Dolorosa."

To me, the Holy Sepulchre seemed low and dingy. But I did not say so to Barbara. Her face was suffused with happiness, and I was glad that I had invited her to join me for dinner. I felt a soft stirring of quiet desire for her, and amused myself with that old masculine mental game of "What if. . . ?"

The taxi stopped. "We will walk from here," she said.

I gave the driver a five-pound note, took the change, and followed Barbara.

We entered a courtyard through a narrow street, and stood before the Wailing Wall. To me, it was just another high, rough-hewn barricade.

"These blocks of stone came from the temples of Herod and Solomon," she said. "For centuries Jews came here to weep over the destruction of the temple, and for their own wandering lives."

"You make a very nice guide," I said. "What's next, *Chayelet?*"

"If we go around that end, we can see the Mosque of Omar."

"Fine," I said. "Is he the one with a loaf of bread, a glass of wine and thou?"

"Senator," she said, smiling, "one day you are going to stop trying so hard to make jokes, and then I think you will say something very important."

I started to answer, but that was when a little Fiat sedan came around a pock-marked building and roared past. What looked like a tin can hurtled from the car's window, bounced on the cobblestones, and tumbled toward us.

"Run!" screamed Barbara.

I reached for her arm, and then the night flared with an eye-searing burst of flame. She smashed back against me and we both fell down on the slippery stones.

Distantly, I heard men shouting, and when I opened my

eyes I saw khaki-uniformed soldiers running toward us. I sat up and bent to help Barbara to her feet.

"My God," I groaned. "What the hell was that?"

She did not answer. She never would again. The blast had caught her full in the abdomen. Her slender body had shielded me, and though my hands and arms were awash with her blood, my suit gouted with it, there was not a wound on me.

The doctors would not believe I was unharmed. Reluctantly they released me in Major Kiesler's custody.

"Now I will have to inform the Lieber family about her," he complained.

I looked at him stupidly.

"Lieber?" I said. "Was that her name?"

Over the Pacific—*August 4, 1945*

We sighted Iwo Jima at 0534, rising out of the early morning mists like a blue-purple whale breaking through the oily surface of the Pacific. The island seemed calm and peaceful, Mount Suribachi's volcanic cone thrusting skyward on the northern end. There was nothing visible from the air to remind us of the bloody fighting that had taken place down there less than six months earlier.

Our rendezvous with *Happy Hooligan* was made without incident. Tim Bond chortled a little, as he always did when his navigation had been perfect.

Now we climbed to 9,000 feet for the second leg of the mission. The flight deck and the compartment amidships were pressurized at an effective altitude of around 8,000 feet, so we did not have to wear oxygen masks—although they were on hand in the event of the ship's being holed by flak or fighter fire. From now on, unless we went on oxygen and depressurized the entire plane, we were cut off from the Little Boy in the forward bomb bay. Our only contact was through Lieutenant Paul Randolph's little black box.

"Radio silence in effect," announced S/Sgt. Phillip Bowie. This meant we would be out of touch with Tinian and the weather planes—except that when they radioed reports on target visibilities, ostensibly to the Tinian weather group, the messages would in reality be directed to us.

"Guess I'd better get to work," said a strange voice. It took me a moment to recognize it as Lieutenant George Murphy, the electronic counter-measures officer.

With radar an accepted tool of war, most missions tried to outwit the Japanese radar by scattering "chaff"—streamers of tinfoil—during their approach. But for the next few days, during the scheduled atomic missions, all bombers had been forbidden to use chaff. High Command wanted to be absolutely sure that Japanese radar could be tracked accurately, so the ECM man aboard the attacking B-29 would know instantly if the enemy had switched to a frequency that might trigger the bomb's proximity fuse.

We were still so far away from the mainland that there was virtually no chance of any radar signal reaching us. But Murphy bent over his instruments anyway, and would remain at them until Little Boy was released.

Rogers came up and joined me in the greenhouse.

"How's it going?"

"Fine, sir."

"Nervous?"

"About what?"

He nodded back toward the bomb bay. "Our friend."

"Captain," I said, "it's your problem whether or not it works. I just push the button."

"Good," he said. "That's what I like to hear. See you later."

He left, and I sat alone for a while. Then the *Collier's* man, Charles Kern, took his place.

We talked for a while, about my home in Cleveland and my studies at Harvard. No, I didn't have a steady girl friend. Sure, I'd like one—but the pickings on Tinian were pretty slim. After the war? I would probably finish school on the GI Bill, and get my law degree.

"That shouldn't be too long," he said. "That monster back there ought to put the Japs out of action in a couple of days."

I stared at him. Through all the training, through all the practice runs, through the briefing, and through this first part of the mission in which I had helped arm the bomb, I had never thought that we had anything more here than just another bomb, however powerful. We would drop it, and then we would drop some more, and the war would go on. It had simply never occurred to me that we carried, riding heavily in our forward bomb bay, the means to end the war.

"What's the matter?" he asked.

"Nothing," I said. "I guess I never thought the war might be over so soon."

"Two weeks," he said. "Three at the outside."

"I'll be damned," I said.

"Your name will be in the history books. Didn't you think about that either?"

"No, can't say that I did."

"When they print the name of the man who dropped the first atomic bomb, that's you. First Lieutenant Hugh McGavin. Your kids will read it, and your grandchildren."

"It's just another mission."

"Lieutenant, it's the first mission of its kind. The face of war is changing today, and you're the guy who's pushing the button. That's what war's going to be from now on—pushing buttons. Do you know how many people that thing can kill?"

"Quite a few, I guess. I never thought about it." That, too, was true. You think about hitting targets—peculiar configurations of buildings and streets are your aiming point. You do not think about people down there, screaming and burning and dying.

"Two hundred thousand. Quarter of a million. Who knows. But take my word for it, Lieutenant, what you're doing today is going to end the war."

"I hope so. It's just too bad that you have to kill so many

167

people to do it. Why don't we just blow the top off Fujiyama, to show the Japs what we can do to them, and maybe they'd quit."

"Don't worry about it, McGavin. Just do what they tell you. They know how to run this war."

"All right, but who's 'they'? General LeMay? General MacArthur? President Truman? Look, don't quote me on this, but do you think Truman knows anything about B-29s? I mean, has he ever flown in one?"

"Probably not. What are you getting at?"

"Just that when it comes to dropping bombs, I probably know more about it than the President of the United States. Because *I'm* doing it, and I do it good, and he never has. Do you get what I mean?"

"No."

"Well, nobody asked me if this bomb was a good idea. I don't think they actually asked *anybody*. If they had, we might be going about this differently."

"Lieutenant, you're what? Nineteen, twenty? You can't even vote yet. Leave politics to the politicians, and generaling to the generals."

"They leave the missions to me," I said, angry. "It's my ass that gets shot off, not theirs. I ought to have something to say about what goes on."

"Lieutenant," he said, "when your name is in the newspapers and the history books, remember that Charlie Kern did you a big favor. I'm going to forget everything you said. Because, kid, you sound like some kind of Red nut."

"And you sound like a horse's ass," I said. "Write what you want, Mr. Kern. But get the hell out of my compartment."

"Sure," he said. "Just don't get nervous. The next few hours are going to make you famous." He left.

On the intercom, I heard Randolph say, "Captain Rogers? I have a green Christmas tree on the board. All systems are Go."

"Keep watching it," said Rogers. "What's the temperature now in the bomb bay?"

"Ten below zero," said Randolph.

"Brrr," said Rogers. Someone else on the circuit laughed. "Radar operator?" Rogers asked.

"Yes sir?"

"Is your scope operating properly?"

"Right on the beam."

"Okay. Now, no matter what happens, don't look up from that hood when we make our drop. We want to know what the explosion looks like on radar. Got that?"

"Yes sir."

"Captain Rogers," said Ritter's slow voice, "I'd appreciate it if you'd check with me before giving orders to my crew."

"Sorry, Captain," said the Navy man.

"O'Neal, you do what Captain Rogers said," Ritter went on. "As for the rest of you, they say this thing can blind you. I'll let you know when to put on your goggles. Be sure to wear them."

This was the first mission on which we had not been allowed to carry charts, in case we were forced down before dropping the bomb. I hoped that Tim Bond had the approach to Tokyo memorized.

The flight droned through the lazy morning hours. The clouds far below us were blazing white. Looking down at *Happy Hooligan*, flying five hundred feet below and in front of us, I could see the white con trails streaming back from the plane's wing tips.

S/Sgt. Phillip Bowie, listening intently on 6.195 kilocycles, said, "Weather reports coming in, sir."

I could hear the fast bursts of code—too fast for me to copy, although I had my novice ham license. This stuff was arriving at twenty words a minute.

"*Diamond Lil* reports Kobe has sixty percent cloud cover," Bowie said. "Conditions fair for visual bombing."

"Roger," said Tex Ritter.

Some more code, and then Bowie said, "*Koffee's Kup* reports Osaka CAVU." Ceiling and visibility unlimited. In the next few hours, Osaka might die because of her nice weather.

Another burst of code. "Here's *Frankie and Johnny*," said the radio operator. "Tokyo is CAVU."

"Tokyo it is," said Ritter. "Everybody hear that?" There was a chorus of assents over the intercom. "We're going to drop this baby right down Hirohito's old kazoo. Climbing to 32,000. All stations report in."

"Bombardier reporting in, sir," I said. "Everything fine."

The other men reported as I fiddled with my Norden bombsight. I wasn't sure how big Hirohito's kazoo was, but I was pretty sure I would be able to hit Tokyo Station, two blocks from the Emperor's palace.

Dimona, Israel—*August 5, Now*

"We do our best, but it's almost impossible to keep those guerrillas from infiltrating," said Prime Minister Levi Bernardi. "They usually toss their bombs into crowded restaurants and schools. It was your bad luck that you were on the street when they happened to pass."

"It was worse luck for the girl," I said. "I feel guilty as hell. If I hadn't asked her to show me around we wouldn't have been there."

Bernardi shook his head slowly. "No man is God," he said. "The bomb could just as easily have gone through the window of her car as she was driving through the Mandelbaum Gate. My advice to you, my friend, is to try to forget."

We were sitting in a comfortable air-conditioned apartment in Dimona, a small, almost doll-like town that somehow looked collapsible. The new concrete building in which the apartment was located was one of the few solid structures there.

Major Kiesler had vanished after delivering me to the Prime Minister's aide. We were driven down from Jerusalem by an Israeli sergeant, a bearlike man who had appeared at the King David Hotel shortly after nine A.M.

Ironically, I had been back at the hotel showering in plenty of time to put my call through to Jack Sherwood. I was in a foul mood, though. And it did not help to look down at the luxurious tiled bath and see Barbara's blood swirling through the drain between my feet.

"Boss," Jack said, "AT&T may get me for profanity, but I've got both good news and bad news. The bad news first. This year we've got nothing to eat but buffalo shit. Now the good news. We've got *plenty* of buffalo shit."

"Very funny," I said. "What's it supposed to mean?"

"Marty Kuhn got an update on that Mafia connection of yours, and found out the story was full of holes. You're off the hook on that one. Marty's making nasty noises like there's a good possibility the whole thing was a goofup by an unnamed Washington bureau whose initials are FBI."

"Kuhn's an honest man," I said. "What's the bad news?"

"Your everloving got a tin can tied to her by Jon West over at the syndicate."

"How? She's got a contract."

"He invited her to sue them."

"I'll be a son of a bitch," I said. "That bastard on Pennsylvania Avenue won't stop at anything, will he?"

"The word is, he's just begun to fight," said my assistant. "Boss, watch out. He's a mean mamu. But don't worry about Celia. She says to tell you she loves you and that this thing may be good because now she can get in your corner officially. Leave a number where you can be reached, and she'll get back to you in an hour or so."

I gave him the number and he whistled. "Jerusalem? You get around, don't you?"

I told him about the bomb, and about Barbara Lieber, and he began to chatter nervously. I cut him off with, "Listen, it was just one of those things. But make sure Ceil knows that I'm all right before it comes in over the wires. Got that?"

"Okay, boss, but you're *sure* you're okay?"

"Positive. Say, has Phil Hepburn turned up back there?"

"Not that I know of. You lose him?"

171

"I haven't seen him since London."

"You don't think he had anything to do with what happened tonight, do you?"

"Hell, no," I said, then stopped. *Was* I completely sure?

"Okay," said Jack. "But watch yourself. Now, for a moment, can I talk about mundane things? Like future employment, for instance?"

"Shoot."

"The convention's August 18, remember?"

"I remember. And the North Korean ultimatum expires the sixteenth. So there may not be any Salt Lake City left by the time the delegates get there."

"What I want to know is, are *you* going to be there?"

"I'll think about it. Is there anything I should know now about the situation in Japan?"

"Foster's going up to New York tomorrow to address the UN. Meanwhile, the Third Gens are still sitting there and the Prez hasn't said a word about taking them out. China's on Yellow, Nabov's holding his countdown at two hours."

"What's our response?"

"Just standing by, waiting to see what happens next. I get the feeling that despite the countdown, nobody's really worried about the Russians. This isn't the first time they've done it. After all, they counted all the way to fifteen minutes when General Merrill smashed down the East German barricades on the Berlin autobahn last summer."

"Okay, Jack, thanks for the information. Anything else?"

"I guess not. So long, boss."

I hung up and went into the bathroom to splash water on my face. Then I lay down and closed my eyes.

All right. Now Barbara Lieber would never let her hair grow long or listen to Saint-Saëns again. What about all the others? They numbered in the hundreds of thousands. They, too, enjoyed looking at beauty and listening to music.

Yes, but I never saw them. Their blood did not smoke on my hands and soak through my Dacron-and-cotton permanent-press suit. ("We can wash that out before it stains," Major Kiesler had said.)

The telephone bell was a distant signal. I came awake yelling.

"There's something wrong in the bomb bay! The alarm . . ."

But I was alone in my suite at the King David Hotel in Jerusalem, and it was only the black-and-gold telephone on the night stand.

When I picked it up, Celia was on the other end.

"Darling? Are you all right?"

"Yes, baby, I'm fine. It's good to hear your voice. I've been lying here getting the willies."

"I heard. Oh, Mouse, it must have been awful. That poor girl. Did they catch whoever did it?"

"I don't think so. They think it may have been a group of Jordanian commandos from the east bank. Listen, hon, I'm all right. But what about you?"

"Jon West fired me," she said calmly. "Which is fine by me, now that I've gotten over the shock. I just gave a press conference in which I threw the blocks to that sanctimonious bastard in the White House. Between what he tried to do to you and what he succeeded in doing to me, he's burned up all his brownie points. If I want it, I've got four pages in *Life* to lay out my accusations. And frankly, dear, I am sorely tempted. I could come up with facts about Foster's Administration that would make Bobby Baker look like a boy scout. But what I'd rather do, if you'll let me, is climb on board and toot *your* horn a little. Where are you going from Jerusalem?"

"I've got a meeting with Bernardi. I'd better not say where on the phone. After that I'm not sure. Why?"

"Can I join you? I had a call from the *Times*, and they'll foot the bill for a series of pieces on your trip from my viewpoint. Why don't I fly to Tel Aviv and hook up with you there?"

"I don't know, baby," I said. "I miss you like the dickens. But . . ."

"I've got my own passport," she reminded me. "I can come anyway if you're going to be hard-headed about it."

"Settle down," I said. "Come ahead. I'm sorry. It's just that I don't know what my plans are from here. We might turn around and fly right back to the States."

"I'll put up at the Hilton," she said. "And Mouse, be careful. Please."

"I will," I said. "Kiss?"

"Kiss," she said, and broke the connection.

The sweat was cold on my forehead. A thought had struck me when Celia asked to join me: if she had been here tonight, it would have been her in the courtyard instead of Barbara.

Bernardi and I were sipping rich, black coffee. We talked about old friends, men we both knew from those frantic days in 1967. He listened carefully as I went over my reasons for seeking nuclear disarmament and nodded.

"I would like nothing better," he said. "You know, my friend, even after the three wars we have fought with the Arabs, Israel is still an object of humor in some circles. We probably abet that laughter. I remember driving past Oron, perhaps ten miles from here, with Ben-Gurion, and we passed the nuclear reactor near the Great Crater. Leonard Bernstein was with us—he had come to conduct the Philharmonic. He said, 'That must be the nuclear plant,' and Ben-Gurion turned almost purple. 'It's a textile factory!' he shouted. 'It's a textile factory!' That has become one of our standing jokes. Now whenever anyone drives past, everyone shouts, 'It's a textile factory!' So perhaps we foster the humor. However, that is why this test is so important. When the tiny, slightly humorous state of Israel can detonate an atomic bomb, it is time the world looked to its course."

"What do you plan to do after the test? Renounce the bomb and destroy your stockpile?"

"No, Senator. And rest assured I have considered the rami-

174

fications of disturbing the balance of power in the Middle East. There is always the possibility that the communists will provide Nasser with his own nuclear devices. In that case, I suspect it would be my duty to order a preemptive strike."

"Then you aren't helping one bit," I said. "In fact, you're increasing the tension. And for what? You've reached an accommodation with the Arab nations."

"An uneasy one," he said. "If you doubt that, remember what happened only last night."

"Then why did you want me here? You don't need me to report on your demonstration. The press can do that."

"You have a unique association with nuclear weapons, Senator," he said. "I felt that it would be beneficial to the world if your voice were the one to describe our achievement. Linked with the cause you espouse, this may be the wedge you need to drive sanity into the thick skulls of our world leaders."

"Yours included," I said harshly. "What makes you think France or Britain would give up their bombs as long as you hang onto yours? Someone has to make the first move. And that's why I came all this way. You're in a unique position, too. You don't really need the bomb. All right, you've developed it. But you can make the gesture of renouncing it without hurting your own defensive posture a bit."

"Perhaps. Of course, there is always another alternative."

"What's that?" I asked.

"Our bomb might not even work."

Tokyo—August 4, 1945

A few miles from the Japanese coast, we switched off our Identification-Friend-or-Foe device. The IFF was a small transponder that kept friendly antiaircraft units from firing at our blip on their radar.

"Land ho," said Ritter in the cockpit.

We had made landfall at 0819. The Japanese islands, capped by cumulus clouds, were dead ahead.

"Okay, gang," said our pilot, "put on your flak suits."

We struggled into the heavy body armor. On the flight deck, the men ordinarily sat on theirs, but there was always the possibility that a burst would send shrapnel straight through the plexiglass nose, so I wore mine. Of course, if I ever had to bail out into the sea, I would have sunk like a lead weight.

"Don't forget your goggles," said Ritter. "You can wear them on your foreheads now, but when you hear a buzz in the intercom, get them over your eyes fast and keep them there until I tell you to take them off."

We had all been issued special Polaroid glasses. They were shaped like the goggles skin divers wear, and their heavy quartz lenses admitted only purple light. With them on, you could barely distinguish the shadow of your hand against the sunlight outside. I was the only man on board *The Busted Flush* who would not be wearing goggles at the moment of release. I needed to work my bombsight without their protection.

"How's the little black box, Paul?" asked Captain Rogers.

"Christmas tree," said Randolph. "All green."

"Bomb is Go, Captain Ritter," said Rogers.

"Got that, Mac?" asked Tex Ritter.

"Yes sir," I said. "Tim, how long to IP?" The Initial Point, where the bomb run was started, was when I would take over the B-29. At our speed the IP would be about fifteen miles from the target.

"Twenty-five seconds," said Tim Bond. "How about that, troops? I got you here right on the nose!"

"Two merit badges," said Ritter. "Okay, settle down. Mac, the minute you make your drop get those goggles on."

"Roger," I said.

"Oxygen masks all hitched up to the emergency bottles?" asked Ritter. This was an idea he had come up with after being told of the bomb's power. There was a possibility that the blast

176

might shatter our windows, causing depressurization. At six miles above sea level, that would be fatal without oxygen.

The crew reported affirmative on the oxygen.

"Hey," said the *Collier's* man from his position near Central Fire Control, "I haven't got a mask."

"I'll let you share mine," said Sgt. Tom Barnes casually.

"Ten seconds, Mac," said Tim Bond.

I made a minor adjustment to the complicated Norden sight. It felt cold through my kid gloves. I racked focus until the cross hairs jumped into sharp relief against the harbor sliding past 30,000 feet beneath me.

"Course, 280 degrees," said Tim Bond.

"Stand by, Mac," said Ritter.

"Standing by."

"She's all yours!"

"Got her."

Now I flew the huge aircraft by the tiny adjustments I made with my bombsight. By turning the controls to place the cross hairs on a road below, I caused the autopilot to make delicate manipulations to ailerons and rudder that kept the B-29 on course.

It was like looking at the photo-maps we used in training. The city sliding past beneath me was unreal; it was only a target.

I did not think of people at that moment, of pain and terror and death. I thought only of doing my job. My eye searched for the aiming point, a landmark several miles this side of the drop point, Tokyo Station, in the heart of the city.

Then I saw it, a small circular park surrounded by a moat. "Stand by," I yelled over the intercom. "I've got the aiming point."

It crept into the middle of my bombsight, crawling toward the place where the black lines crossed. Then it was there, and I punched the button that started the automatic sequence of releasing the bomb.

"Sixty seconds!" I called.

"Everything green!" said Lieutenant Paul Randolph.

A steady buzzing tone filled our earphones. It was transmitted to *Happy Hooligan*, flying on our right wing; to the weather planes returning to base; even Tinian Tower picked it up.

I felt the plane quiver slightly as the bomb bay doors opened.

Then *The Busted Flush* lurched, as Little Boy was released automatically by the timing mechanisms.

"Bomb away!" I shouted.

"Hang on!" yelled Tex Ritter.

The steady tone in our earphones stopped the second the bomb broke its connections with the plane.

Ritter jammed the nose of the bomber down. Below me, I could see Little Boy tumbling past, yawing and heaving at first, then stabilizing as the tail fins bit into the air.

Four parachutes floated past: instrument packets, released by *Happy Hooligan*. Their radioed information would record the bomb's effects and transmit them to the instrument plane.

Detonation was scheduled for exactly twenty-eight seconds from the moment of release. As *The Busted Flush* lurched at being relieved of the five-ton weight, I started the sweep second hand on my hack watch.

Now we were on a 155-degree course away from the drop point, diving, all four engines clawing at the thin air with maximum power.

"Twenty, twenty-one, twenty-two . . ." I heard over the intercom.

My hands were shaking. I stuck them under my armpits and tried to warm them. Clear-air turbulence buffeted the plane.

My God! I had forgotten to close the bomb bay. It must be costing us at least twenty miles an hour in speed. I shoved the lever forward.

Ritter said nothing. Perhaps he had not noticed.

"Twenty-five," said the voice. "Twenty-six, twenty-seven . . ."

"Grab hold!" yelled Ritter.

"Twenty-eight, twenty-nine, thirty . . ."

I looked at my watch. He was counting fast. We still had three seconds to go.

Inside my head, I could hear them ticking away.

Tick.

Tick.

TICK.

I clutched my handholds.

TICK. TICK.

"Thirty-five," said the voice on the intercom.

"What the hell's wrong?" yelled a voice. It was mine.

"Kingsly," Ritter called to the tail gunner, "what do you see back there?"

"Nothing, sir," said Kingsly. "These damned goggles black everything out."

"Forty," said the relentless voice.

"It's a dud," I whispered.

"Who the hell is that?" roared the pilot. "Everybody stay off this channel. Captain Rogers?"

"Yes sir?"

"What's wrong?"

"I don't know. It should have gone off sixteen seconds ago."

"No sign of Jap radar interference," said Lieutenant Paul Randolph.

"Shit!" said Ritter. "Kingsly, uncover one eye. What do you see?"

"Four—no, five parachutes. One's pretty low."

"That's Little Boy," I muttered.

"The low parachute looks like it's on fire," the tail gunner reported. "Yes sir, it is. It's going down faster now. I can't see it any more."

"The son of a bitch didn't work," Ritter said. "We came all this way for nothing."

"It's worse than that, Captain," said Rogers. "It not only didn't work, now the Japanese have it."

There was a long pause, then Ritter's voice: "Tinian Tower, Tinian Tower, this is Jimmy Durante. Over."

Tinian acknowledged, and our pilot said, "Little Boy struck out. Repeat, Little Boy struck out. Returning to base. Out."

The B-29 flew south, with the sun streaming in the windows. Far below us, the Pacific sparkled and gleamed.

"Gentlemen," said Tex Ritter after a long silence, "we have gone and put our asses in a sling."

Mitzpeh Ramon Proving Ground, Israel—*August 6, Now*

It was just dawn, and the early morning sun was still out of sight behind the jagged desert *mezas*, eroded stone sentries like those in our own Painted Desert.

Driving south from Dimona, we had found ourselves suddenly in the *regh*, a barren waste of sun-scorched rock and sand. From inside our air-conditioned car, it looked rather like a moonscape in the pre-dawn darkness.

"Alas," said Bernardi, "we haven't reclaimed *all* of the desert yet."

By the time we got to the proving ground several miles west of the village of Mitzpeh Ramon, a small town that teetered casually on the very edge of the monstrous crater Mactesh Ramon, it was light enough to see the surrounding countryside better.

"This is the Zin Desert," said Bernardi. "The story goes that when the Children of Israel reached this point, they rose up against Moses and said, 'Why have you made us come up out of Egypt and brought us into this wretched place, which cannot be sowed; nor bringeth forth figs, nor vines, nor pomegranates, neither is there any water to drink?' And I can't say that I blame them."

"This wretched place, I gather, is where your demonstration takes place."

180

"It does," he said. "The prevailing winds at this time of the year will take any fallout downwind into the desert, which we've cleared of nomads for fifty miles. But there shouldn't be much. We've gone out of our way to make a clean bomb."

Looking out the narrow windows of the bunker, I could see the drop point four miles away as clearly as if it were a photo mural just outside.

"The glass darkens in relationship to the light striking it," said Bernardi. "There's no risk of being blinded by the burst."

"How long have we got?"

"Six minutes."

"I have to say you seem to be running things pretty casually." There were only two other men in the bunker.

"Oh, these are the VIP quarters. The worker bees are in the main blockhouse, running around like mad."

He pointed at a tower perched on a distant knoll. "That's the target," he said. "We're delivering the bomb with a French *Mirage*. The detonation is set for six hundred feet, to keep the shock wave to a minimum. Of course, if we were striking an actual target, the altitude would be higher."

"Yes," I said, remembering. "Around 2,000 feet."

I stuffed my pipe and lit it. "You must have been able to miniaturize your detonation system to carry the bomb aboard a *Mirage*."

"The yield is relatively low," he said. "Say approximately the same power as your Hiroshima weapon. 20,000 tons of TNT. More or less, of course."

"Of course," I said, sucking at my pipe.

One of the officers said, "Mr. Prime Minister, we have the *Mirage* on your command circuit."

"Good," said Bernardi. "Major Goldman? Can you hear me?"

"*Ken, Adon Prime Minister*," said a voice from a loudspeaker.

"Please use English," said Bernardi. "We have an honored guest this morning."

"Yes sir," said the voice, in what is called a Mid-Atlantic accent.

"Is everything all right?" asked Bernardi.

"Yes sir. We are ready to commence."

"Good luck, Major."

Bernardi turned to me. "Now," he said. "We wait."

"The *Mirage* is on our radar," said one of the officers.

"Thank you," said Bernardi and turned to me. "It won't be long now."

"I can wait."

"I have heard," he said casually, "that your bid for the Presidential nomination may not be as hopeless as first it seemed. I think that it would be a good thing for the United States to have a man like you in command."

"There's where you've got it wrong, sir," I said. "It may appear to the casual observer that the President commands," I reminded him, "but he does so only with the advice and consent of the legislature."

"Still," he persisted, "he has broad powers. What would you do if you were President? Would you listen to your own advice and abandon your nuclear capability?"

"I doubt it," I said. "But I know that I would do everything in my power to achieve some kind of mutual de-escalation."

"Escalation. De-escalation." He sighed. "The words we use today."

"Thirty seconds," said one of the officers.

"Well," said Levi Bernardi, "you may be about to welcome another member into the nuclear club."

"Twenty seconds."

"All systems on automatic," reported the pilot over the loudspeaker.

"Ten seconds."

"With the money spent on this bomb," Bernardi said slowly, "we could have reclaimed another twenty square miles of the *regh*. And it would have provided food for at least 10,000 people."

A shrill tone burst from the loudspeaker.

"Bomb away," reported the pilot.

"There!" said Bernardi. "Do you see the parachute?"

I saw it—twin half-circles of orange-and-white nylon, high above the target.

The pitch of the tone from the loudspeaker increased. Then there was a piercing, warbling sound.

"Detonation," said Bernardi.

Instinctively, I closed my eyes. But there was no explosion; no sudden flood of light.

"Look," Bernardi said.

A red, smoking flame climbed the shroud lines of the parachute. It reached the nylon, consumed it, and a tiny object fell into the desert.

"Isn't that what happened to *your* bomb?" Bernardi asked softly.

Tinian, Marianas Islands—*August 4, 1945*

Twelve hours and nineteen minutes after *The Busted Flush* had lifted off Tinian's 10,000-foot runway, we touched down again, rolled over to our hardstand, and Ritter cut the throttles.

The big four-bladed propellers slowed, flashed in the afternoon sunlight, and stopped.

All of the brass were waiting for us: the CO, of course. And General Carl "Toohy" Spaatz, head of the Strategic Air Force, along with General Nathan Twining and several other generals and admirals I did not recognize.

The brass were embarrassed: they had gathered at Tinian to award us medals.

We piled into a cavalcade of weapons carriers and were sped to the debriefing hut, where we lined up for a shot at the urinal. The usual bourbon and lemonade was waiting for us in stainless steel GI pitchers.

Rogers and I sat at the same table. Relentlessly the interrogator took us step by step through the procedure of arming the bomb, trying to find out where, if anywhere, a mistake had been made. He had a wire recorder, and twice he used it to play back the radio messages Rogers had sent from the bomber.

"Dammit," Rogers kept saying, "the bastard was green all the way. That bomb left the bay in perfect operating condition. Something must have happened to it on the way down."

Three hours later we broke for a meal and four badly needed hours of sleep; then we were back at it for the rest of the night.

We had the morning off, but were restricted to quarters; and after noon chow, the interrogators questioned us again. This time they were rough.

"Why did you do it?" mine demanded. "Was it your conscience? Admit it, you didn't want to kill, isn't that right?"

Wearily I repeated, "I didn't do anything except my job, Major. I watched Captain Rogers arm the bomb, and then I spent the rest of the mission in my compartment. How the hell could I have fouled things up?"

"You're through in this Air Corps, you know that, don't you, Lieutenant? So why don't you make it easy on yourself. We can throw the book at you if you don't cooperate."

I was still protesting my innocence when a civilian came into the room and whispered into my interrogator's ear. The Major looked unhappy, then he stood up.

"Okay, Lieutenant," he said. "That's all. You can go."

"You mean you believe me?" I blurted out.

"I have to," he said. "We just got word from *Diamond Lil*. They released another Little Boy over Kobe."

I knew what he was going to say, but having to hear it to make it real, I waited.

"That one didn't work either," the Major said bitterly.

"Did you bring me all this way to show me a bomb that you knew wasn't going to work?" I asked Bernardi.

"You were surprised when it did not explode," he said slowly. "You really thought it would."

"Of course I thought it would."

"Yet this is not the first time you have seen an atomic bomb fail."

"I can't talk about any other bombs I've seen, sir," I said. Every one of us who had participated in the Tokyo and Kobe missions had been forced to sign declarations of secrecy that were later incorporated into the National Securities Act and were still in effect.

"I trust," Bernardi said, "that you are familiar with the Jesus Factor."

"A research project my government has been supporting for quite some time," I said.

"The Jesus Factor is more than just a project," said Bernardi. "It is an effect. You have just seen it in action. According to all scientific theory and knowledge, that bomb should have exploded. What prevented it from doing so was the Jesus Factor."

Standing in the Negev Desert, so near the paths walked by Christ, the term sounded odd and blasphemous.

"All I can say, sir," I said, "is that you must have done something wrong when you assembled your bomb."

"Perhaps," he said, looking at the sweep second hand of a large clock on the wall. "But watch that tower out there. In just a few seconds—"

"Nine . . . eight . . seven . . ." said a voice over the loudspeaker.

"What?" I asked, surprised.

"Four . . . three . . . two . . . one . . ."

A man-made sun flared in the desert. The light-sensitive windows darkened instantly, and I saw the fireball itself, and then the perfect circle of the shock wave as it sucked dust up from the desert floor.

It took several seconds for the sound to reach us. Inside the bunker it sounded like a distant roll of thunder.

"Within minutes," said Bernardi, "the world will know that Israel has successfully tested an atomic device. But have we successfully tested a *bomb?*"

I almost did not hear him. My mind had flashed far away and long ago, to a coral island in the Pacific.

Tinian, Marianas Islands—*August 6, 1945*

President Truman's voice was flat and toneless, distorted by the short-wave transmission, as he said, "The world will note that the first atomic bomb was dropped on Hiroshima—a military base. We won the race of discovery against the Germans. We have used it to shorten the agony of war, in order to save the lives of thousands and thousands of young Americans. We shall continue to use it until we completely destroy Japan's power to make war."

There it was. At last. Now, at the war's end, we of the 509th were free to mingle with the rest of the 20th Air Force. Truman had said it for us: we didn't give a damn how many Japanese lives were saved. It was our own that concerned us. The jubilant fliers of the 20th Air Force filled us up on free beer until we waddled like pregnant ducks.

"By God, Tim," I gurgled, "we made it! We got through this bastard alive!"

"How about nu'her beer?" he said.

Half drunk, Tim and I went to the outdoor movie. We smuggled four cans of warm beer in under our ponchos, and drank it as we watched a Rita Hayworth and Gene Kelly movie, *Cover Girl*. When it was over, we stood up on the coconut logs, stretching, and Tim Bond laughed.

"Buddy," he said, "we finally did it. The war is over."

Before I could answer, a startled expression appeared on his face and he seemed to lose his footing. I reached over to catch him, and he fell slowly into my arms. From a jagged wound in his throat blood spurted against my hands.

"Tim!" I yelled. Two more men went down before the projectionist doused the lights. I tried to stop Tim's bleeding, but then it stopped by itself and he was dead.

Our sniper had not remained satisfied with the shadow of Keye Luke.

Mitzpeh Ramon Proving Ground, Israel—*August 6, Now*

I looked down at my shaking hands—so clean now, so free of blood—and I saw Tim again, and the girl Barbara, and I felt as if I had stepped back out of myself, as if I were only an audience looking on.

The failures over Tokyo and Kobe, the announcement of Hiroshima and Nagasaki, the tests at Bikini and all the years between them, and this moment in the desert blended together—and without knowing how I knew, I *knew*.

"My God," I whispered, watching myself from a vast distance, hearing the words and saying them too:

"The atomic bomb doesn't work!"

BOOK TWO

Chain Reaction

When you have designed and built the best missile the human mind can devise, installed a complete back-up system, and run every detail through the computers a dozen times getting a Go readout every time; and you put your bird on the pad and press the button and the damned thing doesn't work—then, my friend, you have met the Jesus Factor.

—Traditional missile lore, passed down from engineer to engineer

The Negev Desert—*August 6, Now*

"My friend," said Bernardi, "you just can't go barging into the United Nations shouting 'The atomic bomb doesn't work.' All you know for sure is that *Israel's* doesn't work. An atomic device works, yes. But the air drop you saw this morning is the third bomb we've tested, and not one has gone off. Our telemetry shows us that everything functions perfectly, right up to the moment of critical mass when chain reaction should begin. Then, instead of exploding, the warhead turns white-hot and melts down."

"Yet your tower shot exploded."

The Prime Minister nodded. "Interesting, isn't it? It makes you wonder how many other air bursts failed, while tower shots succeeded."

I had not told him about the Tokyo and Kobe misfires. I knew I did not have to.

"The reason I wanted you here," he said as we drove north toward Beersheba, "is that for years now there have been persistent rumors that Hiroshima and Nagasaki were not the only Japanese cities to come under atomic attack. Tokyo is mentioned in all of these rumors, and several months ago I spent an interesting evening with a former *Collier's* reporter who swears he flew on a mission to Tokyo, in which you were the bombardier, and that the atomic bomb you dropped did not explode."

"Charlie Kern," I said. "I wondered what happened to him after *Collier's* went out of business."

"He has taken up drinking as a career," Bernardi said without humor. "Ordinarily I would not give credence to anything a man like Kern said. But much of his disconnected ramblings tied in with information I had already received from other sources. So I noted what he said, discounting most of it and filing the rest away for future reference. After our first two air bursts failed, I decided to stage this little demonstration. Because of your public views on the arms race and your private connection with the development of the bomb, you seemed a very necessary guest. I do not think I was wrong."

"What if I go blabbing to the press that your bomb didn't really work?"

"Go ahead," he said, smiling. "There were many representatives of the world press present this morning. They all think that the parachutes dropped by the *Mirage* were instrument clusters to record the force of the device itself—which, according to their briefings, went off exactly on schedule."

We rode silently for a while. Then I asked, "Do you know for a fact that the bombs of any other nation do not work?"

"No, nor do I now know even after my own test. There are still many questions to be answered. How do you explain away Hiroshima and Nagasaki? Those cities were hit with *something*. Perhaps we are both wrong—perhaps there *is* a bomb, and you and I have been mere observers to some prank of fate today."

"You mentioned the Jesus Factor."

"I know of the project by that name which is being operated secretly by your government," he said. "And of course, I know what the name signifies—it refers to any unexplainable malfunction of a theoretically perfect device. I am aware that the United States has spent huge sums of money on Project JF, and I know also that both France and Britain have similar projects. The British call theirs 'Victoria,' and the French, with somewhat dubious humor, have dubbed theirs 'Bastille.' As for the Russians and the Chinese, I have only rumors."

"I think I had better talk with my President," I said. "Do you have a scrambler circuit with Washington?"

"No, but there is a United States communications vessel a few miles off the coast. It has been our guest several times in the past few years. I can have you flown out by helicopter."

"Thank you," I said. Then: "You don't play around, do you? You really want to see this thing stopped."

"Yes," he said. "I do not know if my own tests, and my suspicions of the others, are in any way proof of what you and I both now privately believe. We may be fooling ourselves. But, Hugh, can you imagine a world without the shadow of nuclear holocaust over it? For more than twenty-five years we have lived in fear that some lunatic might push the button to destroy us all. Ending that fear in one moment of truth—what a dream!"

"I just don't know," I said. "My head is spinning. I've got to talk with Foster."

"My plane is waiting at Beersheba," he said. "We will fly to Tel Aviv, and meanwhile I will have the communications vessel alerted for your arrival."

The desert unreeled past us, jagged rocks and lifeless sand.

Was I mad as a hatter?

I knew the bomb this morning had not exploded. Of course, I had only Bernardi's word that it *was* a bomb. It might really have been a packet of instruments, as the other observers thought.

But what of the Tokyo bomb?

Perhaps it was just what it seemed: an accidental failure.

And the Kobe bomb?

The same.

Because if there was *not* a workable atomic bomb, what had destroyed Hiroshima? What had leveled Nagasaki?

And why would a bomb work on a tower and fail when suspended from a parachute? And did that mean that warheads attached to missiles would malfunction too? If so, what were we *really* doing in Japan with our ABMs?

I would have to get Jack Sherwood cracking on Project Jesus Factor right away. With the knowledge I had gained this morning, it should be easier to break the project open and pry out the truth.

Once I got to a safe radio, Howard Foster was going to have some tough questions thrown at him.

What had Prime Minister John Hawkins really been after

when he asked me if I had ever seen an atomic bomb explode?

And the President of France had asked me virtually the same question. Had these men been trying to tell me something? Or trying to find out how much I knew? Whom could I count on for help now that I had opened the first door?

I would have to be careful. Too much disclosure might weaken my own country's defensive capability without necessarily advancing the cause of peace.

I must have dozed, because suddenly we were entering Beersheba, the capital of the Negev. We drove past the Arab *souk,* where sleepy, cud-chewing camels dripped saliva, watched over by veiled Bedouins.

The city itself was large, with apartment buildings looming beside ancient Arab huts.

Word of the successful test had preceded us. The narrow streets were jammed with waving, cheering people. Bernardi waved back as our cavalcade swept through the city and headed for the airport, where a twin-engine jet was ready for us.

An hour later I was in the El Al pilots' lounge in Tel Aviv, sipping a cold beer and waiting for a chopper to take me out to the communications ship, the *Edward White.*

I checked with the Hilton; Celia had not arrived yet. I left word that I would be back by eight. Then I finished my beer and lit a pipe, my feet propped up on a stool. It would be nice to sleep, I thought. After a day or two of traveling, no matter how much sleep I get, I am always tired.

A uniformed El Al clerk came over.

"Senator, your helicopter is here."

I followed him to the pad outside the terminal. The chopper was a Navy four-seater, its blades still windmilling. I ducked under them and shook hands with the pilot. He looked incredibly young, like a grown-up Charlie Brown with a freckled nose and a baseball cap a size too big for him.

"Welcome aboard, sir," he said. "I'm Lieutenant Harper."

"Hugh McGavin. Do you have takeoff clearance?"

"Yes sir. Buckle up, please."

I cinched the belt tightly across my lap and took a deep breath. I have never enjoyed flying in helicopters. For one thing, they *lean;* and another, they fly sideways, and you always feel as if you are going to fall out through the bubble nose. In a small craft like the one I was in, the blister extends down almost to your feet, and you get the distinct feeling that you are riding on a broomstick with nothing else between you and the ground.

Lieutenant Harper took the chopper up at an angle. In a few seconds we were over the white-capped water and gaining altitude as we swept out to sea.

"The *White*'s about forty miles straight out, sir," he said. "It won't take long."

"How long have you been out here, Lieutenant?"

"This tour? Seven months. But I put in a hitch on the *Enterprise,* too. When she went back to the States, I shipped over to the *White.*"

"You must like the Mediterranean."

"Senator," he said brightly, "I like the Italian chicks, that's my dark secret. I may never go home."

I laughed. Some things never change.

The flight was uneventful. A few miles offshore, an Israeli Skyhawk circled us curiously. Satisfied, its pilot gave us a jaunty wave, pointed his ship skyward, threw in the afterburner, and disappeared straight up.

"You don't get much gas mileage that way," Harper commented.

We talked flying for a while. Then the *Edward White* came into sight, and he concentrated on his approach.

From the air the ship looked like a floating antenna. Dipoles, yagis, and radar dishes sprouted all over the superstructure. At the *White*'s stern, there was a large platform with a target painted on it—the helicopter landing pad.

Harper put the chopper down neatly, and two enlisted men chocked the wheels. A lieutenant commander was waiting for me outside the painted target.

"Commander Elliot, sir," he said. We shook hands.

"I need a top-level scrambled circuit to Washington," I said.

He led me to a small room crammed with radio gear. A petty officer stood up when we entered.

"Chief Yarborough's cleared for Top Secret," said Elliot. "How private is this message?"

"All the way," I said. "Sorry, Chief. No reflection on you. Once you hook me up with Washington and sync up the scramblers, I'd like to be left alone in here."

"Yes sir," said the petty officer.

"Commander Elliot, if there are any monitoring devices in here, I want them disconnected,"

"There's a slow-speed tape recorder," he said. "We ordinarily record every transmission."

"Not this time, if you please."

Elliot nodded, and Yarborough threw a switch. The reels of the tape recorder mounted in the wall stopped turning.

"Where in Washington, sir?" asked Yarborough.

"The White House. Situation Room. Priority One."

He stiffened. "Yes sir," he said. He and Elliot avoided looking at me. They both knew what Priority One meant.

"I've got the White House," Yarborough reported. "I'm syncing up the scrambler circuits now."

There was a warbling tone from the loudspeaker. He adjusted a control and the warble gradually disappeared until a single note sounded.

"All synced, sir," Yarborough said.

"Thank you," I said, sitting down at the microphone. Yarborough left.

"Let me know when you're through," said Elliot.

"I will," I said. He left too.

"White House, this is Senator Hugh McGavin," I said. "Do you read me?"

"Five by five, Senator. This is Colonel Bracken. Where's the fire?"

Although our voices sounded clear to us, anyone else listening on the frequency would have received only a garbled series of clipped musical notes.

"I have to speak with the President."

"Stand by, sir," he said. "I'll try to get through to him."

For a few minutes only the steady tone from the speaker let me know that I was still receiving Washington. I fumbled out my pipe and sucked at its stem.

Colonel Bracken came back on the air. "Senator," he said, "I have the President."

"Is he there in the Situation Room with you?"

"Yes, I'm here, Senator," said Foster's voice. "What's this all about?"

"Mr. President," I said, "this is a matter for your ears only. May I ask you to clear the room and to turn off all monitoring and recording devices?"

There was a short pause, then Foster's voice: "Do it, Colonel."

"Yes sir," said Bracken.

"The room's not clear yet, Hugh," said Foster. "How are things with you?"

"Bored with traveling," I said. "And of course, it's hot here. But I understand it's been even hotter in Washington."

"You might say so," he said. Then: "All right, we're alone. Now what's this all about?"

"Howard," I said, "can we drop the titles for a few minutes and talk turkey?"

"Fine with me."

"I've just come back from the Negev, where Israel set off an atomic device."

"Yes, we know. Our instruments picked it up, and of course we got clear photos from our satellites."

"Yes, but the explosion wasn't from a bomb. It was caused by a device on a tower."

"What's the difference?" he said carefully.

"The difference," I said, "is that so far Israel has been

197

unable to detonate a bomb in the air. They've tried three times, and each time the warhead melted down instead of exploding. Yet the tower shot succeeded on the first try."

"Who have you spoken to about this?"

"No one. Prime Minister Bernardi was with me at the test, and seemed to think this failure of air bursts is not unique to Israel. In point of fact, I know it is not. I was over Tokyo, you will remember, and I know about the Kobe failure, too."

"Just what are you asking me?"

"Howard, what is Project Jesus Factor?"

"That's on a Need to Know."

"Is it an attempt to produce a bomb that really works? Have we been hoaxing the world all these years?" He did not answer. "Howard? Are you there?"

"Senator McGavin," he said slowly, "you are stumbling around in areas that are critical to this nation's survival. I ask you to abandon your activities."

"So we're back to Senator, Mr. President," I said. "All right. But I think I'm entitled to some answers."

"Give it up, Hugh," he said, a new note—almost of pleading—in his voice.

"I can't," I said. "You should know that I can't."

The static crackled for a few seconds. Finally he said, "All I can tell you is that our civilization has never stood in greater danger than it does at this moment. And your meddling might be just enough to push us over the edge."

"Meddling? Trying to de-escalate the arms race, trying to get those missiles out of Japan? Howard, what are those Third Gens *really* doing there?"

"Come home," he said. "Come back to Washington, and we'll sit down and hash this out."

"I don't know if I'm ready to come back yet. In view of what's happened here, I think I ought to talk with France and England again."

"Don't!" he said. "Listen carefully, Hugh. I warn you, if you repeat your suspicions to anyone else, it could be disastrous. What would it take to convince you you're wrong?"

"Explode a bomb in the air."

"Our treaty with Russia prohibits us from testing in the atmosphere."

"Then I guess that's about it."

"No, wait," he said. "Can you stay in Tel Aviv for another day?"

"I suppose so."

"Let me think. There must be some way we can get together. I'll work it out and have Phil Hepburn get in touch with you."

"All right. Where is he, incidentally?"

"What do you mean, where is he? Isn't he in Tel Aviv?"

"The last time I saw him was in London."

There was a long pause. "Listen, Hugh," he said, "I'll get back to you soon. Where are you staying?"

"The Hilton."

"Right. But remember what I said. For God's sake, keep quiet."

"I'll do my best," I said. "But I hope we straighten this mess out soon."

"My communications man is coming back into the room," he said. "Take care of yourself, Senator."

"You too, Mr. President. Over and out."

When I lifted my arm from the table, it left a damp imprint. I went out on deck, joined Commander Elliot in his cabin for a cup of terrible Navy coffee, and then flew back to Tel Aviv, where an air-conditioned limousine was waiting for me, my battered B-4 bag in its trunk. I was in the Hilton by seven-thirty.

"Has Mrs. McGavin checked in?" I asked.

"Yes sir," said the clerk. "Shall I ring her?"

"No," I said.

On the third floor I motioned for the bellboy to be silent and tapped on the door.

"Who is it?" her voice called.

"Western Union," I said in falsetto.

She opened the door, her hair loose, a hairbrush in her hand.

"Mouse!" she shrieked.

"Silly broad," I said. "There ain't no Western Union in Tel
Aviv."

Tel Aviv—*August 6, Now*

We never made it out for dinner. Around ten, after showering
together, we telephoned down to room service for scrambled
eggs.

"Get some ham," Celia whispered. "I always feel so de-
liciously *evil* eating ham in Israel."

We had a half bottle of wine with the eggs; and afterwards,
sitting on the terrace under a full moon, looking down at the
phosphorescent waves curling up along the beach, I stroked
her hair.

"I'm sorry I got you all bollixed up, baby," I said. "When
we get back I'll have a little visit with our friend Jon West."

"Don't bother yourself," she said. "Let him simmer in his
own cowardice for a while. The word's out that he let Foster
pressure him. That will hurt Jon worse in the newspaper business than anything we could do."

"Speaking of Foster, I called him today."

"Collect, I hope."

"He wants me to come back to Washington and see if we
can work things out."

"I hope you spit in his ear."

"I told him I wasn't coming back yet. But he's upset. The
Israeli test today changes everything."

"I'll say. If Levi Bernardi can have a bomb, almost anybody can have a bomb."

I was tempted to tell her that maybe *nobody* had a bomb.
But I didn't. If the news leaked out, I didn't want to have
Celia involved.

"Oh," she said, "I've got a suitcase full of mail and junk for you. Jack sends his regards, and he gave me a sealed envelope to guard with my life. He said to mention Project JF to you and you'd know what it was."

She handed me a brown manila envelope sealed with transparent tape. I ripped it open and took out a sheaf of Xerox copies. Clipped to them was a note from Jack:

> *Boss—here's the latest stack of memos I could get on Project JF. You'll notice that all this stuff is highly classified, so if you get nabbed, say you found it in a pumpkin. In the absence of any further word from you, I am going to see how much deeper I can get into JF.*
>
> *Jack*

The first memo, a smeared, almost unreadable Xerox, went:

TOP	FOR YOUR EYES
SECRET	ONLY

HEADQUARTERS,
509th Composite Group
San Francisco, Calif.
APO

TO: Commanding Officer, Manhattan District
FROM: Major Roseman Cooper, Executive Officer, 509th Composite Group
SUBJECT: Disposition of fissionable material

1. Your command has already been advised of the malfunctions at Tokyo and Kobe. Both of those bombs were uranium 235, and exhausted our supplies of that fissionable material.

2. As detailed in my memo of August 9, our supplies of plutonium fissionable material were dispersed at Hiroshima and Nagasaki.

3. In view of the Japanese suit for peace, this unit will not require further supplies of plutonium. The

request for the next allocated shipment is hereby canceled.

4. Allied personnel entering Hiroshima and Nagasaki should be warned to take suitable precautions against radioactivity. Because of the manner in which the plutonium was dispersed at those cities, there will probably be considerably more lingering radiation than at the Trinity test.

I looked for the August 9 memo. It was missing from the stack. I muttered a curse.

"Excuse me," said Celia. She got up quickly and went inside. I flipped through the rest of the papers. Most of them were addressed to General Groves, although several were from him to the President. They spoke chiefly of money, of sums that added into the billions as I glanced through the memos. And one name kept reappearing.

The Jesus Factor continues.

We haven't licked JF yet.

Jesus Factor still with us.

Thought we'd succeeded, but the Jesus Factor cropped up again.

And one, personally scribbled by John F. Kennedy, read, "Check into a French project named 'Bastille.' It sounds a lot like our own JF."

I finished my drink and went looking for Celia. She was in the bathroom, and through the closed door I heard retching sounds. I tapped.

"Baby, are you all right?"

"Just a minute," she said, coughing. I heard water running, then the sound of a toothbrush. I went over and put the stack of memos in my briefcase.

The bathroom door opened. Celia was smiling, but pale.

"What's the matter, hon?" I asked.

"Nothing," she said. "I drank like a fish on the plane, and all the excitement and then the wine—it's just too much for a working girl to take."

"Maybe you'd better lie down."

"What about you?"

"I'm going to sit out on the terrace for a while. I've got to stop running for an hour or so and just think."

"Go think then," she said. "I'm going to take an Alka-Seltzer and read a while."

I kissed her. She tasted pepperminty.

Outside, the night air was warm. A gentle breeze came in over the Mediterranean.

I lit my pipe and sat there for a long time. The wording of Rosy Cooper's memo bothered me.

In referring to Hiroshima and Nagasaki, he had mentioned plutonium being "dispersed."

What did "dispersed" mean?

I wondered where Rosy was now. I knew he was a lieutenant general in the Air Force, getting close to retirement age. I jotted his name in my notebook. The next time I spoke to Jack, I'd ask him to track Rosy down.

My pipe went out, and I discovered I was out of matches. Besides, a swarm of mosquitos had begun shooting landings on my naked scalp. I went back inside.

Celia was asleep. She had put a large manila envelope on the coffee table and scribbled a note on hotel stationery:

> *Mouse—here's the rest of your mail. Please go through it tonight so I can have you to myself tomorrow.*
>
> *C.*

Although Jack had already screened the mail, most of it was routine. One telegram, however, had a handwritten note clipped to it.

> *Boss—I had this guy checked out and he used to be one of the top nuclear physicists in Japan. Then he started going around saying that Hiroshima and Nagasaki were not destroyed by atomic bombs. They had him in a loony bin for a while; apparently he's on the loose again. But it's just weird enough that I thought you might be interested.*

The telegram read:

ESTEEMED SIR I HAVE VALUABLE INFORMATION CON-
CERNING YOUR NOBLE POSITION ON NUCLEAR WARFARE
STOP PLEASE CONTACT THE UNDERSIGNED AT HIBYA HALL,
TOKYO.

YOSHIJE NAKAMURA

A few days before I would have chuckled and sent Nakamura my usual polite brushoff letter. But not now. Not after
this morning in the Negev.

I picked up the telephone.

"Operator," I said, "I want to send an overseas cable. To
Tokyo."

Tel Aviv—*August 7, Now*

"My name is Gene Scudder," said my early-morning visitor.
"I'm with the State Department."

Mr. Scudder had arrived at a most inopportune moment.

"He'll go away," I'd said to Celia when he tapped at the
door. "Whoever it is, he'll go away."

He did not go away. "The hell with him," I said. But it was
no use. The moment was past. I wrapped myself in my robe,
stuck my feet into Mexican sandals, and went out into the
sitting room to receive my unwelcome guest.

"We've got a telephone," I said. "You might have called."

"I tried. The operator said it was off the hook."

"Oh," I said, remembering. "All right, Mr. Scudder. What
can I do for the State Department?"

"The President has asked me to speak with you, Senator,
about Phil Hepburn."

"Is he in jail or someplace else suitably removed from others?"

Scudder did not smile. "He's dead. The London police found his body in the Thames late yesterday. His throat was cut. He'd been in the water for at least twenty-four hours."

Poor Hepburn. What a lousy end for an essentially gentle man. I hoped he had at least enjoyed his shopping spree on Savile Row.

"It might have been robbery," said the State Department man. "But of course that's what they would want us to think."

"Who's 'they'?"

"We thought you might be able to tell us."

I nearly hit him. "Listen to me. Hepburn may not have been a buddy of mine, but I respected him as a man. So don't come sliding around here with your insinuations. You couldn't pin the Mafia on me, so now you'd like to try murder? Go back to your boss and tell him no sale."

Flushed, he said, "Please, Senator, there is no cause for anger. I was merely inquiring—"

"Is that all you have to say?"

"No. The President has asked me to remind you of a promise you made to him yesterday concerning your silence on certain classified matters."

"I remember," I said. "He practically threatened to have me prosecuted for treason. Well, Mr. Scudder, I'm a little tired of being threatened. Why don't you go back to your cipher room or wherever it is you hang out and inform the President that I don't give one fart in a windstorm whether or not I get the lousy nomination! Tell him further I'm only keeping my mouth shut because I want to be sure I'm not hurting my country, not because of his threats. But if I decide that it isn't my country which is in danger, but merely Howard Foster's Administration, he can count on headlines that will have the people screaming for impeachment. Do you think you can remember all that, Mr. Scudder?"

"Bravo!" said Celia, emerging in a pale yellow dress.

"My wife, Celia Craig—Mr. Scudder of the State Department. Mr. Scudder is just leaving."

His lips pressed tightly together, Scudder bowed slightly to Celia and left.

She kissed me. "What a tiger," she said. "Did you mean all that, or were you just mad because he interrupted us?"

I laughed. "Both. What the hell is it with Foster? He isn't the first President who's had opposition to his plans."

"Don't expect *me* to defend him," she said. "I hope you sink the bastard."

Dressing, I said casually, "How would you like sukiyaki for dinner?"

"In Tel Aviv? What do you eat when you go to Japan, blintzes?"

"I thought we'd fly to Tokyo today," I said. "I got an interesting cable from a Professor Nakamura and wired him back last night. I want to hear what he has to say."

"Nakamura?" she said. "He's the guy Larry on the *Post* wanted to run an item on. For a while he was running around saying Hiroshima and Nagasaki weren't destroyed by the bomb. What does he think we did to Hiroshima? Hit it with a stick?"

"It might be interesting to find out. After breakfast, I'll see what we can do about airplanes. Oh, and remind me when I call Jack, I want him to track down a General Cooper."

"Rosy Cooper? The one you knew in the 509th?"

"That's him."

"Save the dime. I saw his picture in *Time* a couple of months ago. He's stationed on Guam. He's commanding officer of a bomber base there."

"You're sure?"

"Big beefy guy with a white handlebar moustache?"

"Yes."

"I'm sure, Mouse. You know I don't forget things like that."

"Guam," I said. "I hear the Japanese tourist industry is doing a booming business on Saipan. We shouldn't have any trouble getting a flight from Tokyo to Guam."

"If I may be so crass," she said, "how are we affording all this?"

"God helps those who carry Air Travel cards," I said. "Although paying later might be painful. Something tells me I'll never be able to slip it past the watchdogs on the Hill. Anyway, isn't the *Times* springing for you?"

"Nope," she said cheerfully. "You sounded so grumpy about it, I thought I'd try being a wife on this trip instead of a reporter."

I kissed her. "Somehow," I said, "I like you better that way. But if you feel Nelly Bly creeping up on you, let me know. We may hit a few things I wouldn't like to see in *Life*."

"I'll give you fair warning," she said. "Now how about some breakfast? We world travelers need our energy."

We found a table on the restaurant's terrace, overlooking the sea. Celia gleefully ordered a double serving of bacon to go with her poached eggs. I settled for juice, pastry, and coffee.

"I'll be right back," I said. "I'll get the travel girl working on our reservations."

Conscious of the probability that I would be paying for these tickets out of my own pocket, I told the travel agent that we would be going to Guam as well as Tokyo, and to work out the most economical ticketing. On the way back to the terrace I picked up a newspaper.

The lead story, naturally, covered the nuclear test in the Negev. One subhead stated there had been a flood of negative reactions from other nations. The United States in particular condemned Bernardi for increasing tension at this critical time.

As for the missiles in Japan, the Administration was still "studying" the situation. Foster had gone before the United Nations to say bluntly that the matter was an internal affair which concerned only the United States and Japan. He was booed from the gallery. The Communist Bloc had boycotted his speech.

In Japan the Diet was in special session. Premier Ito faced a vote of confidence that might remove him from office. Ito had made no public statement since the discovery of the missile placement, and the press consensus was that he was stalling for time.

In China mobilization continued.

On page thirty-two I found the only good news of the day: Snoopy finally got the Red Baron in his sights. The Baron managed to make it back to his own lines trailing smoke, as our hero gave him the salute reserved for a worthy opponent.

"Maybe we'd do well to stay on Guam," Celia said, glancing at the headlines. "As the Eskimo said watching the missiles go over the North Pole, 'There goes the end of civilization as *they* know it.' "

The travel girl came over carrying a yellow pad. "Senator," she said, "I am sorry to disturb you, but you said you were in a hurry. There is an El Al jet leaving in two hours which connects with a jet for Saipan. From there it's a local flight to Guam. If you miss that Saipan flight, it will be three days before the next one."

Celia dabbed at her mouth with a napkin. "The blur you see heading for our room is the Senator's official suitcase packer."

"Then you want the noon El Al flight?" asked the travel girl. "And the connection to Saipan?"

"Yes," I said. "I planned to see someone in Tokyo, but we'll catch him on the way back."

"I'll have the tickets in thirty minutes," she said. "Meanwhile, I'll call El Al and confirm your passage and connection with JAL in Tokyo for Saipan."

I thanked her, paid the check, and went up to the room. Celia was folding her clothing neatly and replacing it in the round leather hatbox-like affairs she uses as suitcases.

My B-4 bag, still packed, was hanging in the closet. I grunted as I took it down, tossed it on the bed.

"I wish you'd get a real suitcase," Celia complained.

"Ha! Look who's talking."

On the way to the airport, Celia waved out the taxi window. "Farewell, Tel Aviv," she said. "Maybe one day I'll get to see more than the road to and from the airport."

The flight to Tokyo took eleven hours. We were on the ground at Tokyo International Airport for ninety minutes, during which time I phoned Hibya Hall and left word for Professor Nakamura that I'd see him in a couple of days. Then we were over the blue Pacific en route to Saipan.

The trip which had taken seven hours in our primitive B-29s had shrunk to two. As we circled for landing, we passed over Tinian at about 5,000 feet, and for the first time in more than twenty-five years I looked down at the Manhattan-shaped island that had been the jumping-off point for 2,000 B-29s. I could barely see the scar of the runway. The jungle had moved in on it almost completely.

As our baggage was unloaded, I pushed my way through clusters of chattering Japanese tourists to the Marianas Airways counter and asked about flights to Guam.

"I'm sorry, you just missed today's flight," said the clerk.

"My watch is still living in Tel Aviv," I said. "What time would that be here?"

"One P.M. was the flight, sir. It's one-thirty-four now."

I booked us on the next day's flight, and we got a jitney taxi which took us to the Cliff Hotel. It was a modern building hugging the side of Army Hill, looking down at Beach Red where the U.S. Marines took over 4,000 casualties in 1944. Far out in the water was the rusting hulk of an amphibious tank, still sitting where it had been hit by Japanese artillery more than a quarter of a century before.

After six hours of sleep we got up, staggered to the dining room, and ate fresh fish and exotic fruits. Then we weaved our way back to bed for another long nap, and woke up at one A.M., wide awake and ready to take on the world.

"There must be some night life on this island," Celia said. "Let's find it."

The desk clerk was not very optimistic. "Bloody Mary's is usually open after midnight," he said. "I'd call for you, but they have no telephone."

"We'll take a chance," I said. We went out and woke up a sleeping taxi driver. When I named our destination, he pulled back his lips in a knowing grin.

"Miss Mary's going to be mighty happy to see you folks," he said.

"Why?"

"Because these days all she gets is Japanese tourists and the U.S. Coast Guard. Not ten dollars among them. Yes sir, you're going to be mighty welcome at Bloody Mary's."

As we drove off, Celia hugged my arm. "Maybe she'll sing 'Bali Hai' for us."

Saipan, Marianas Islands—*August 9, Now*

"I," said Celia, "am going back to bed." It was dawn, and we sat on the hotel patio, watching the sun streak the clouds with red and purple. "I know the natives are supposed to be friendly, but Miss Mary overdid it."

"We don't have to be at the airport until twelve-thirty," I said. "I was thinking I might go over to Tinian this morning and look around."

"Why don't you do that, Mouse?" she said. "I'll check us out of here and meet you at the airport."

"Want to come with me?"

"I'd love to, but I just can't," she said. "My stomach feels like something you make soap in. I'm up to here with Miss Mary's Coco Locos. I just want to get under those sheets."

"Come on," I said. "I'll tuck you in."

As we walked slowly to our room, arms around each other, she said, "Don't get any fancy ideas. *I'm* going to sleep."

"You're safe with me," I said. "I just want to put on some khakis. No point in messing up a good suit in the boondocks."

"Mmmmm," she said.

"Goodnight," I said, unzipping her. Mechanically, she slipped out of the dress. I guided her to the bed and she sank into it with a satisfied groan. By the time I finished changing, her breathing was deep and regular. I kissed her forehead and closed the door quietly.

When I asked the clerk about getting over to Tinian, he said, "You take a taxi to South Pier. Then there's a ferry service, but it costs ten dollars."

"That's all right," I said. I left a ten-thirty call for Celia, woke up another taxi driver, and we started south along the single-lane highway that circles the island.

Saipan was just waking up. Tiny chickens scurried out from under the brightly colored flamboyant and hibiscus plants, racing across the road just in time to escape our wheels. On their way to the fields, farmers led gigantic water buffalo by ropes through rings in their noses. Many of the huts had roofs made from metal advertising signs—Coca-Cola, Dutch Cleanser, and Clabber Girl Baking Soda messages shared space with newer signs in Japanese.

The sun was already warm when we pulled up at South Pier. The taxi driver honked his horn three times, and a shirtless native wearing tattered blue pants cut off at the knees came over.

"This man wants to go to Tinian," said my driver.

"Ten dollah," said the native. "And three dollah an hour for waiting and another dollah for using the jeep."

"You've got a jeep over there?"

"War surplus. It's stuck in first gear, but it runs."

"I'll take it," I said. I paid off the taxi and followed the native to a small boat with a single Whirlwind outboard motor mounted on its stern.

"My name is Juan," he said as we pulled away from the pier. Ahead, shimmering over the water, I saw the low hump of Tinian.

"Call me Mac."

"Were you stationed on Tinian?"

"Back in the war. I imagine it's changed."

He spat into the water. "Nobody much there any more," he said. "There's a little copra, and one farmer raising goats. The leper colony moved away a long time ago. I come over here sometimes to get away from those Jap tourists. It's worse than during the war. At least the Jap soldiers built roads and kept to themselves. But the tourists are all over the place, snapping pictures, digging in the sand for souvenirs. They caught one at the airport trying to take home a human skull."

"I wouldn't think you were old enough to remember the war."

"I'm ovah sixty, man." He spat again. "I remember the war good. That's why it doesn't seem right to have all those Jap tourists here."

We landed at a small jetty, and he tied up the boat. He fumbled in a cigar box and took out a distributor cap. "I keep this so that goat farmer don't use my jeep."

The jeep was in a grove of coconut palms. It had once been olive drab, and I could still see the white star and some of the identification numbers against the rusty metal. It was easy to believe that this vehicle had been here since the war; perhaps I had even ridden in it on the way out to the flight line.

Juan put the distributor cap in place, closed the hood, and ground the starter. "Where to?"

"Let's drive down the runway."

"Not much left of it," he said. We bounced through the low vegetation and came out into an area of grass and twisted bushes. "This is the edge," he said. We drove another hundred feet and he stopped. "There it is."

We were near the water. I looked the other way and saw the shape of the long runway receding from us. Most of the concrete was covered with vegetation. I could see the rough outlines, and that was all.

The place where we were sitting must have been just about

where *The Busted Flush* had broken away from the runway that night so long ago. Over to the left was where I had seen the B-29 crash. All along here had been Quonset huts and neat walkways made from crushed shells. Now there was only jungle.

"Drive up to the other end," I said.

The jeep whined in first gear as we bounced along what was left of the runway. We passed a large mound covered with bushes.

"Old wreck," Juan said. "They left ten, fifteen of them here. The jungle just grew up on top of them."

I could recognize nothing. All the landmarks I remembered so well were gone. Trees had grown where there had been none. I wondered how long it took a coconut palm to grow.

Near the end of the airstrip I had Juan stop the jeep. Although nothing looked familiar, I knew I had to be near the 509th compound.

"I'm going to walk around a little," I said. "I'll meet you back here."

"I'll wait in the shade," he said, driving under a coconut palm. "If you're not used to this sun, stay under the trees. It's hot."

"I'll watch it."

I left him in the jeep smoking a homemade cigar. Fifty feet away and he was out of sight behind the jungle growth.

The ground was littered with coconut shells and fallen palm fronds. I picked my way through the trees, finding nothing. I was almost ready to go back to the jeep when I saw a rectangular patch of low grass in the higher vegetation.

I kicked at it and discovered concrete underneath. Following its edge, I came to a place where it had cracked open. I shoved chunks of coral into the hole, and they fell into darkness.

This was one of the twenty-hole latrines, sealed over by the Seabees more than a quarter of a century ago. I unzipped and took a leak into it. In the trees above, a bird noticed me and shrilled a warning.

Now that I knew where I was, I imagined I could trace the compound's streets. There—that mound might once have been a Quonset hut. There was the orderly room. And there —yes, that was the briefing hut.

Wandering in the jungle of my memories, I came to a slope that curved gently down toward a circular field of grass. As I walked down it, I kicked at chunks of rotten logs.

This had been the outdoor theater. Here on this hill we sat, young and thin, watching John Wayne and Humphrey Bogart.

And Keye Luke. . . .

Standing there with the tropic sun dappling down through the coconut fronds, I thought I could hear the distant rumble of powerful engines. Surely I would see them soon, breaking through the clouds—great formations of bombers, black against the morning sky. From one plane three flares would arch down signaling there were wounded aboard. And now they would peel out of formation and float down toward the two-mile-long runway, landing gear outstretched and reaching for the earth. . . .

A distant horn blared. I did not know how long it had been blowing. It honked three times, paused for several seconds, and honked again.

I picked my way toward it. When I came out onto what was left of the runway, Juan was standing up on the jeep's seat.

"We might as well go back," I told him. "There's nothing else here I want to see."

"Thought you might have gotten lost back there," he said. "It's easy to get mixed up in that jungle."

"Yes, it is," I agreed.

Guam, Marianas Islands—*August 9, Now*

The inter-island flight took less than an hour. Our plane, a twin-engined turbo-prop, flew at 3,000 feet. Celia and I sat in the rear, by the door. The only other passengers aboard were half a dozen young Japanese couples. Apparently Saipan and Guam were the Japanese jet set's Acapulco and Riviera.

I had spoken with Rosy Cooper that morning on radio-phone. "Of course I remember you!" he said. "Best bombardier the 509th ever had." He promised to have a driver meet us at the airport.

Now, looking down as the turbo-prop circled for landing, I saw that the airport was obviously a converted military field. I remembered that there had been four on Guam during the war: the small, originally civilian Naval Air Station at Agana, the island's capital; Harmon Airfield, which was used by cargo planes; and North and Northwest Fields, both of which serviced B-29s.

Literature provided by the stewardess informed us that Guam was a free port, where we could make tremendous savings on perfumes, liquor, and cameras.

"One bottle of Chanel," I told Celia. "That's my limit, so don't get your hopes up."

General Rosy Cooper was waiting for us.

"It's too bad," he said, "that we didn't have that magnificent head of skin back on Tinian. We could have used it for a landing beacon."

Rosy had always been heavy, but now he must have been close to three hundred pounds. I immediately felt better about my own battle of the bulge. "How've you been, Rosy," I asked him.

"Hanging on, tooth and nail. The Air Force thinks I ought to spend my last command on some dinky training base in

Kansas. But I foxed them. I've got my paper work so fouled up here, they'll have to let me stay on another year just to get it straightened out."

"I don't want to take up too much of your time," I said, "but I guess you know what I've been up to."

We got in his staff car and he told the driver, "My quarters, Hank." Then, to me, "Sure I know. It does my old heart good to see you kicking those die-hards in their lard asses—pardon me, Mrs. McGavin."

She smiled. "You ought to hear what I call them."

"I guess I could have contacted you by letter or phone, Rosy," I said, "but I had to be in Tokyo anyway, and I couldn't resist making the old trip one more time."

"Anything I can do," he said. "I never was a hawk, you know. If you can get us back to the good old days of stabbing and shooting each other instead of doing it with missiles, you wouldn't hurt my feelings any. When do you have to get back to Tokyo?"

"Tomorrow."

"Then we'll have dinner together. Wait until you see our Officers' Club. It's like the Waldorf."

"Do you ever see any of the old outfit?" I asked.

"No, not for five or six years," he said. "I guess you know Tex Ritter bought it in Vietnam?"

"I heard."

"The crazy bastard!" he exploded. "He had no business flying combat at his age. But I guess he never got over having to prove himself because of Tokyo."

"What happened at Tokyo?" asked Celia.

"We had a bad mission," I said, giving Rosy a warning look. "Ritter was a career man, and he took that stuff seriously."

"Here we are," said Rosy as the car slid into a port beside a handsome house that seemed to be all screened porches.

A plump Guamanian woman opened the door for us. She took Rosy's service cap and nodded as he introduced her: "Maria, who keeps this place from turning into a rat's nest."

He looked at his watch. "Mac, you and Celia'll want to freshen up. Let Maria make you a gin and tonic. I've got to

216

go over to HQ for a few minutes, but I'll be back by four and we can start some serious drinking and talking."

"Since I have a feeling I'm going to be excluded from that particular activity," said Celia, "maybe your driver can take me out to explore some of this duty-free shopping I've heard about?"

I smiled at her. "*Two* bottles of Chanel," I said.

In our room, after the driver had delivered the luggage, Celia closed the door and came close, sniffing.

"I don't know what you did over on that island," she said, "but you smell just like a goat."

"They had some very friendly goats there."

"The shower," she told me, "is through that door."

The water cascading down on my head, pleasantly cool against my sunburned scalp, spattered against something else. I turned and bumped into Celia. Her nipples were erect, and as she pressed her breasts up against me, she whispered, "I got to feeling kind of goaty myself."

"That's some woman you've got there," Rosy said as we watched his staff car backing out of the driveway, taking Celia on her shopping expedition.

I nodded. "Sometimes I wake up in the middle of the night and look at her for an hour, asking myself how I could have been so lucky. Of course, I'm a disaster at cards."

"So I remember," he said, motioning me back inside. "Well, there's the booze and we've got a couple of hours. Shall we get to it?"

I took the drink he offered and sat down in one of the bamboo chairs. "Rosy," I said, "first, you ought to know that I have a Q clearance. You can check that with a signal to Washington."

"I did after your call from Saipan. I didn't think you had come all this way to discuss the weather."

"Good," I said, "because what I want to talk about is still classified. You remember my Tokyo mission."

"How could I forget it? I thought the C.O. was going to take off under his own power. Toohy Spaatz had come all the way from Honolulu to give you guys a medal, and you blew it. Oh, yes, that was a memorable afternoon."

"Then there was the Kobe mission," I said. "Same result. Zero."

"Don't remind me," he said. "For a while there I had a very strong hunch that the entire 509th was going to be shipped to the Aleutians."

"Luckily, Hiroshima bailed us out," I said. "And then came Nagasaki, and the war was over."

"The timetable was close," he said. "We had to beat Japan before winter set in, and that meant we had to go on the beaches in late September. Lots of men are alive today who wouldn't be if it weren't for Hiroshima."

"I suppose you heard about the Israeli test?"

"It made headlines in *Stars and Stripes*."

"I was there. Rosy, they dropped it by parachute and it was just like being back over Tokyo."

"What do you mean?"

"It didn't explode."

"*Something* exploded."

"A tower shot. Prime Minister Bernardi told me he had tested three air bursts and none of them functioned."

"Mac," he said slowly, "what's this got to do with me?"

"Tell me what really happened at Hiroshima."

"You know what happened there."

"Do I?"

"We dropped a twenty-kiloton bomb and killed a hundred thousand people," he said. "Except for its having ended the war, it was nothing to be proud of."

"You're saying *Enola Gay*'s bomb exploded?"

"Of course it exploded, Mac. I don't know why yours didn't work, but take my word, the one over Hiroshima did the job."

I opened my briefcase and took out the memo he had sent to General Groves in 1945. "What did you mean by 'dispersed,' Rosy? That doesn't sound like what you'd say in describing an explosion."

"Where in hell did you get that?"

"Never mind. But I can tell you this: Rosy, I don't believe we really dropped a bomb on Hiroshima. At least, not one that exploded. Does that make me nuts?"

"It qualifies you for a checkup," he said. He turned and stared out the window.

"Rosy, how do you *know* we exploded a bomb at Hiroshima? or Nagasaki?"

"Other than the fact that we destroyed the cities, that we have photographs of it, that a couple of hundred thousand people died—other than that, I don't *know* anything. How do you know you're on Guam? This might be Staten Island."

He sipped at his drink. "Besides, Mac, I saw Nagasaki. That's one I can tell you about from personal experience."

"I didn't know you flew that mission."

"Well, I did, in *Bock's Car* with Chuck Sweeney at the wheel. Do you know that by then the scientists were getting so upset by what we were doing, they taped a message to the instrument cluster?"

"What did it say?"

He got up and took down a thick book bound in brown leather. "I copied it down for my journal," he said. "Here it is. Dr. Luis Alvarez, who was working with us, remembered the name of a scientist he had studied with at the University of California in 1938. A Professor Ryukochi Sagane, who was back in Japan during the war. Here."

He handed the heavy book to me, and I read:

Headquarters
Atomic Bomb Command
August 9, 1945

TO: Prof R. Sagane
FROM: Three of your former scientific colleagues during your stay in the United States.

We are sending this as a personal message to urge that you use your influence as a reputable nuclear physicist to convince the Japanese General Staff of the terrible consequences which will be suffered by your people if you continue in this war.

You have known for several years that an atomic bomb could be built if a nation were willing to pay the enormous cost of preparing the necessary material. Now that you have seen that we have constructed the production plants, there can be no doubt in your mind that all the output of these factories, working twenty-four hours a day, will be exploded on your homeland.

Within the space of three weeks, we have proof-fired one bomb in the American desert, exploded one in Hiroshima, and fired the third one this morning.

We implore you to confirm these facts to your leaders, and to do your utmost to stop the destruction and waste of life, which can only result in the total annihilation of all your cities if continued. As scientists, we deplore the use to which a beautiful discovery has been put, but we can assure you that unless Japan surrenders at once, this rain of atomic bombs will increase manyfold in fury.

I handed the book back to Cooper. "Did Professor Sagane ever get the message?"

"Not that we know of. You know, the mission was almost aborted, because *Bock's Car* had a malfunction of the fuel transfer pump in the lower-rear bomb bay, so we were carrying six hundred gallons of fuel that we couldn't use, or even get rid of. That made it pretty tight. But it was decided that the mission had to proceed because of the psychological pressure it would put on the Japanese. We barely got off the ground. Fifty feet less of runway, and I wouldn't be here.

"We dodged clouds all the way up to Japan. The weather was lousy. Our primary target was Kokura. It was hazy over the target, and we started getting flak. We made three passes, but the bombardier couldn't find his drop point. And we had absolute orders not to bomb by radar. The antiaircraft fire kept getting closer and closer, and then we saw fighters trying to get up to us."

"So you went to Nagasaki?"

"Yes. We thought of hitting Tokyo, but we had no orders. And Nagasaki was on the list as a secondary target. It was stretching our fuel to the limit, but we went."

"Did you see the drop itself?"

"I saw the flash, through those purple goggles. We had only enough gas left for one bomb run. Even then, we were out of luck in getting back to Tinian, and it was anybody's guess if we'd even make it as far as Okinawa. The city had almost total cloud cover. A big argument started. Although we weren't supposed to bomb by radar, some of us said hitting the target by radar was better than dumping the bomb in the ocean. Our bombardier swore he could put Fat Boy within a thousand yards of the aim point. But then a hole opened up in the clouds, so we lined up on a big stadium and let it go.

"We hauled out of there, and about a minute later the whole sky lit up. We turned back to look, and it was just like the movies of Hiroshima. A big cloud, all red and purple and yellow, was boiling up. Then we saw the shock waves coming —they made the air look like ripples in a lake. There were five of them, and I didn't think we'd make it through. It sounded like somebody was beating on the side of the cockpit with sledge hammers. Some of the crew thought we were taking flak. Somehow, the plane held together. Meanwhile, that bastard of a mushroom cloud was coming up right underneath us. I remember saying, 'Let's get the hell out of here,' and we made like a scalded dog. We were over six miles up, and that cloud still went right past us. It ended up ten or eleven miles high."

"And you actually saw it?"

"Of course I saw it. By then the fuel situation was getting critical, so we hauled ass. There was a real chance that we might have to ditch, but with the tension off it didn't bother us. We alerted the air-sea rescue people and headed down the chain of islands between Kyushu and Okinawa. You can imagine how happy we were to learn that, because of the extra time we'd taken to get to Nagasaki, the air-sea folks had packed up and gone home. They thought we were already back on Tinian. And that goddamned tower at Yontan Field on Okie wouldn't answer our calls. When we got there, the sky was full of P-38s and B-25s. We didn't have enough gas to go around the circuit even once, so we shot off flares to alert the stupid bastards. As you might expect, nobody paid the least bit of attention. The radio operator was hollering 'Mayday' and getting no response. Finally we shot off every flare we had, twenty-four of them, all shapes and colors. It looked like the Fourth of July. And we went down into that rat's nest, dodging P-38s. We hit the runway doing better than a hundred, and halfway down it two engines quit. They were out of gas. That's how close it was."

I puffed at my pipe. Rosy got up and stood, hands on his hips, looking out at the late afternoon sunlight.

"Yes," he said softly, "I saw Nagasaki. If Hiroshima was anything like it, I'm glad I wasn't there." He turned and faced me. "Mac, I'm sorry I couldn't help you. But that's the way it was. Where the hell did you ever pick up such a notion? Sure, I wish the bomb didn't work too. But it does, and I guess we've got to live with it."

"Yeah," I said, "I guess we've got to."

Dinner was unpleasant. Rosy drank too much and began to talk loudly about the way the military had become civilianized. He had small respect for defense contractors, and made this clear to everyone within fifty feet, over the concerned shushes of the club manager.

"Do you know how many ex-field grade officers they've got working at Lockheed?" he demanded. "More than two hundred. You know they didn't hire those men because they liked the color of their hair. Contracts today are awarded on the basis of who you know."

"Lockheed may sue you," I said.

"It's not just Lockheed. Hell, they're all the same. Remember when the Navy ordered a batch of deep-water rescue subs for two million bucks apiece? They ended up costing eighty million dollars each. I know there's a lot of research and development, but how do you go from a bid of two million to an actual cost of eighty? Is it any wonder our taxes are out of sight? Everybody in Washington has an ax to grind, and they're grinding it on our hides. When guys like you and me aren't around any more, there's going to be nobody to stop them, and we'll end up with a country that's run like Venezuela. You won't be able to tell the difference between a GI and a civilian. I may be an old fogey, but I still think the purpose of the military is to defend the nation, not *be* the nation."

"I agree, Rosy," I said. "But hold it down."

"*You* hold it down," he said. "I'm on my way out to pasture. Done my job, and now it's time for the gold watch and the pension. Pretty soon nobody's going to tell me what to do any more. Then I won't have to lie to friends."

"What do you mean, lie?"

"Forget it," he said, straightening. "Just had a little too much to drink. Funny. Can't take it like I used to."

"It's late," said Celia, looking at her watch. "And the plane leaves at seven A.M."

"Home," said Rosy Cooper. "I'll get my driver and we'll go home."

He got up and stumbled from the dining room.

"He's a sad man," Celia said later, as we lay quietly in the guest room back at Rosy's quarters. "It's terrible to get old and have your world pass you by."

"I'm bothered by him," I said.

"He didn't tell you what you wanted today, did he?"

"No," I said. "He didn't."

Everything changes but memory. It had been more than twenty years since I had walked the streets of Tokyo, yet somehow I expected to find them the same as they had been so long ago.

They were still a jumbled mixture of East and West. Colorfully flowered kimonos brushed against gray flannel suits. Gleaming Toyota sedans honked angry horns at rickety bicycles, piled high with crates of chickens or cases of saki. But the city itself was new and modern.

We checked into the new Imperial Hotel, with its twin towers, across the street from Hibya Park. There, aeons ago, I had blown a hole in one of the baseball fields with a test Pumpkin.

The designer of the new Imperial knew the Japanese compulsion for privacy. The hotel's corridors were narrow and twisting like catacombs, full of strange turns and cul de sacs. He might have taken a few lessons from Frank Lloyd Wright, who built the first modern Imperial back in the twenties.

I have always been amazed at how well the Japanese adapt to their overcrowded existence. Even on the packed streets, they are isolated from each other by a formal, ritualized politeness. The person who bows first, the number of handshakes, the loudness of hissed *Domo see ma sens* and *Ah so desukas* are rigidly prescribed. The first means roughly, "You are so wonderfully welcome," the second, "Yes, I understand." If you have these two phrases firmly in hand, you can practically conduct a fluent Japanese conversation.

I remember one sultry summer day during the Korean war, when I was courting Celia. As I crossed the wide boulevard our occupying forces had renamed Avenue A, I heard a tremendous commotion and saw, to my horror, an old Japanese woman lying on the streetcar tracks. A trolley car was inches away from her.

The commotion came from dozens of angry Japanese commuters who were jammed into the trolley car and hanging out over its running boards. They were shouting at the woman, urging her to get out of their way. Impassively, with the stoic determination of the old, she squinched her eyes shut even tighter and remained in front of the heavy steel wheels.

My companion, a Japanese newspaperman, caught my arm when I started toward her. "No, Hugh-san," he said. "Soon the police will come."

As he drew me away, I said angrily, "What the hell kind of country is this? That poor old woman is trying to kill herself and everybody's mad at her for lousing up their trolley schedule. Why doesn't someone help her?"

Patiently, he explained. "Only the authorities would dare help her. If you or I were to prevent her from committing *jisatsu,* self-murder, we would be responsible for her life from then on. The old woman knows this. I do not know what problems have made her decide to part with life, but if you prevent her, they become your problems. That is why the passengers were angry. They have accused her of attempting to trick them into saving her. She should have been more dignified. An old woman is supposed to use poison, or leap from a high place. That way no one else is involved."

"Nice place you've got here," I said sourly.

"It is necessary in a country so small with so many people," he said. "The most terrible crime is to invade another's privacy. Whoever touches that old woman will be doing so, and that is why we must leave it to the police, who have the immunity of the state protecting them. In earlier times, before the war, the problem would have been solved very simply. The brakeman would not have seen her in time to stop. In that way, no one would be inconvenienced, no one would risk responsibility, and the old woman would have achieved what she wanted."

It was eleven A.M. when Celia and I checked into the Imperial. I called Professor Nakamura and agreed to meet him in the bar at one that afternoon. We sent the bags upstairs, and Celia and I took a short walk down the familiar streets. Without saying, we both knew where our meandering was leading us.

Where Shinbun Alley and the Press Club had been was now a new apartment building.

Celia sighed. "Nothing is sacred."

"Maybe they didn't know."

"It should have been made into a shrine." Then, in a softer voice, "Oh, hell! Hugh, we're getting old."

Looking at the apartment building, I said, "I guess we are."

"It's got so all the sales clerks are younger than I am. They look respectful and call me ma'am."

"I have a guaranteed prescription for what ails you," I said, waving down a taxi. "Imperial Hotel, *doazo*," I said.

"Yes sir," he answered. "If you will be so kind, I am speaking English. I am student at Waseda College."

"See?" said Celia. "Even the cab drivers are younger than we are."

The driver practiced his English on us all the way back to the hotel, thanked us profusely when we paid the two hundred yen on the meter and tipped him another hundred —which made the ride come to less than a dollar.

I led her to the bar and said, "Two martinis, on the rocks, very dry. Twist of lemon."

"Oh, no, Mouse," she protested. "I swore off martinis."

"This is an emergency. We've just discovered we belong to the Geriatric Generation. Besides, the way things are going, I feel like getting a little plotzed."

"Don't forget Professor Nakamura."

"I'll stay rational until we've had lunch, but then watch out, baby. It's about time we kicked up our heels anyway."

Celia touched my cheek and said, "Mr. Senator, you may just be right. Let's scandalize Tokyo."

"It's a deal." The martinis came and I lifted mine. "To scandal."

"You're a dirty old man." She lifted her glass higher. "May you never change."

"Nor you," I said. We sipped. It was a perfectly awful martini, awash with vermouth. "Boy-san," I said to the bartender, "about this glass of vermouth. . . ."

Celia put her hand on my arm. The bartender was obviously anxious. I relented. "*Ichi bon*," I said. "Number One." He beamed happily and I felt like Santa Claus.

"There's nothing wrong with vermouth," Celia said. "I used to drink it straight in college."

"When I was in college," I said, "I drank bootleg white lightning. It was terrible. The faculty warned us it would make us go blind. They were wrong, thank goodness."

"All it did was make hair fall out," she said sweetly.

"Here's to spankings," I said. "Surest way in the world to silence a shrewish woman."

We both enjoyed the game. Part of the fun lay in the fact that we knew it was possible to go too far and discover ourselves in a genuine fight. Neither of us welcomed fights, but when they happened, the air got cleared. And the making-up period was always delightful.

A uniformed bellboy came into the bar, placing folded copies of a newspaper before each of us. I opened mine—*The Nippon Times,* Tokyo's English-language daily.

"PREMIER TO ADDRESS DIET," read the headline.

Looking over my shoulder, Celia said, "I'm amazed he's been able to hold out this long. It's obvious he's been playing for time."

Other front page stories reported that North Korea had reiterated her demands in the UN General Assembly, charging, "The United States of America has not made a single move in the direction of peace. Instead, her warmongering leaders have cast down the gauntlet, declaring that the offensive missiles in Japan are an internal affair of the United States and the Japanese people. There is hard evidence that the United States has prepared for a preemptive strike against the People's Republic of North Korea. Such a strike would be ill advised. Our friends in Asia would not let such an act go unpunished."

The statement was continued to the back of the paper. I started to turn to it, but Celia stopped me.

"Look at this," she said, pointing at a small article near the bottom of the front page.

The headline read, "SENATOR'S AIDE ARRESTED FOR ESPIONAGE."

"Holy Christ!" I said. "It's Jack!"

I read, "John Sherwood, personal aide to Senator Hugh McGavin, candidate for the Democratic Presidential nomination, was arrested today in Washington on charges of espionage.

"Top Secret documents were found in Mr. Sherwood's possession, according to the Attorney General's office. Mr. Sherwood refused to explain where he had gotten them.

"Senator McGavin, who is on a world tour promoting nuclear disarmament, was unavailable for comment."

"That lousy bastard," I said.

"I take it you are referring to our distinguished President," said Celia.

"Jack must have gotten nabbed trying to get some more stuff on the Jesus Factor," I mumbled.

"The what?"

"Forget it, hon. It's something that's tied in with this ABM bit. We found a secret project that's eating up money like a rat in a cheese factory."

"Mr. Senator, sir," she said, saluting me, "I beg to inform you that you have just lost a wife but gained a reporter."

"Nelly Bly is back?"

"In the flesh. Mouse, what *do* you have in that briefcase?"

"Secret documents," I said. "The same kind of stuff they nabbed Jack for."

"It isn't particularly smart to leave stuff like that lying around hotel rooms."

"No," I said, "I guess it isn't. You know, I mentioned some of those papers to Rosy Cooper yesterday."

"He wouldn't have called Washington. He's your friend."

"A very unhappy, guilty-looking friend. Face it, Ceil, that's how they nabbed Jack—Rosy blew the whistle on me, and since I wasn't around, they grabbed Jack." I stood up.

"Where are you going?"

"From now on that briefcase isn't going to be out of my sight."

"What good will that do?" she asked. "If you chain it to your wrist, they'll just cut your hand off. Hugh, I don't know what the hell's going on, but it scares me. Can't you get off here? You've done all any man could do."

"Ceil, there's still one big question I have to answer for my own peace of mind."

"You always were stubborn," she said. "All right, buddy boy, get yourself arrested or beat up or killed."

"I'll be right back," I said. "It's almost time to meet Professor Nakamura anyway."

"*You* meet him," she said. "I'm going to sit here and get drunk."

I tried to kiss her, but she turned her face away. There wasn't any point in arguing. I went up to the room and checked the briefcase to see that it still contained the Xerox copies, then returned to the bar with it.

Celia was gone. I looked around. There was a flurry of excitement in a small room near the cigar counter.

She lay on a couch, pale and still. A waiter was pressing a wet cloth to her forehead.

I pressed my way through the crowd. "Celia!"

She tried to sit up. "Oh, Mouse," she said, "I'm sorry. I don't know what hit me. I felt sick, and when I got up the room started spinning around like a top. I guess those martinis were a mistake."

I nodded the anxious manager over and asked for the hotel doctor. He set off, almost at a run. I knelt beside my wife and touched her face. She was not feverish. The color was coming back to her cheeks now, and her eyes found mine.

"I'm sorry," she repeated. "All that gin on an empty stomach."

"Sure, baby," I said. "You just lie still."

"Don't look so scared," she said, trying to smile. "I haven't had a heart attack or anything. You never heard of the vapors?"

"Yes," I said. "I heard of them in Tel Aviv. Now, you take it easy or I'll belt you one."

"Yes, boss," she said in a tiny voice.

I held her hand until the doctor arrived. He was a European

with a thick German accent. He introduced himself as Doctor Frank Brandt and hastened to add that he was Swiss. That hadn't changed in twenty years. During the postwar period, Japan had been filled with "Swiss" expatriates running restaurants where you could get excellent schnitzel and dark beer.

Doctor Brandt, although he paid scant attention to me, was gentle and reassuring with Celia.

"The jet airplane is harder on the stomach than most of us know. Do you think that you can go leapfrogging over continents without suffering some upset? Come, there is nothing wrong with you that sleep and some soup cannot cure."

Sitting up, she said, "I hate soup."

"So much the better," said the doctor. "With each spoonful, you will remind yourself that if God had wanted jet planes to fly, he would have equipped them with propellers."

"Is there any law," she said, "against substituting brandy for the soup?"

Doctor Brandt snapped his fingers. "Cognac!" he demanded. "*French* brandy. *Honto!*"

The bartender fell over his feet getting to the bottle of Martel. He returned with half a pony of the rich brown cognac.

"Mmmm," said Celia, sipping it. "Think I'll get sick more often."

"Let me help you to your room," said the doctor.

I started to say that I would go too, but he cut me off with a sharp look and an almost imperceptible shake of his head.

"Ceil," I said, "I'd better wait here for the Professor."

"Of course," she said, "I'm all right. I'll just lie down for an hour. Maybe I'll even try the doctor's soup."

She left with him, steady on her feet, but looking forlorn, helpless, childlike.

"Senator McGavin?" asked a voice. I turned and saw a short, very thin Japanese man. His collar was inches too big for his neck, and as he held out his hand, I saw that the cuffs of his shirt were frayed and discolored.

"Professor Nakamura?"

"*Hai.*" He bobbed his head. "I am sorry. Perhaps I should return later?"

"No," I said. "My wife just suffered a slight indisposition. It's nothing serious. But maybe we'd better skip lunch. Could we have a drink instead?"

"Certainly," he said. "Would you like to stay here? Or, there is a lovely rathskeller in Hibya Park."

I could sense what was bothering him. He figured he was going to be stuck with the check, and he was obviously not equipped to pay Imperial Hotel prices.

"Let's try the rathskeller," I said.

He hurried along beside me as we went out past the front desk, across the street, and through the low, gray wall into the park. The paths wound through beautifully landscaped little hills, covered with rock gardens and tiny temples. Despite the sun overhead it was cool and pleasant under the trees.

The rathskeller was actually an outdoor beer garden in the center of the park. The Japanese waitresses were dressed in Tyrolean shorts and blouses, with tiny caps perched on their jet-black hair.

"Professor," I said, "you must allow me. I have nothing but thousand-yen notes, and I have to get change."

"Oh, no," he protested. "You are my guest."

"We are both guests of the United States government," I said firmly. "I'm on an expense account." It sounded convincing.

"Very well," Nakamura said, "in that case . . ."

We ordered seidels of beer, and when a portly Japanese man went by carrying a plate of steaming pig's knuckles and sauerkraut, I said, "Maybe I could handle some lunch after all. That looks good."

We both ordered the knuckles and kraut. So much for my dreams of delicate sashimi and tempura.

"Senator," he said, "I have watched your work with great interest. And today, with the world tottering on the edge of a nuclear chasm, it is men like yourself who offer our only hope. But—and I do not know how to say this—I believe I know certain facts that affect your position strongly."

"I think I know what you're trying to say," I told him. "You don't think Hiroshima and Nagasaki were hit by atomic bombs."

"I cannot speak for Nagasaki," he said, "but I was at Hiroshima, working at the National Institute for Cancer Research. And I can assure you, Senator, that whatever destroyed Hiroshima, it was certainly *not* an atomic bomb."

"Why are you so sure?"

"Like most nuclear physicists," he said, "I was aware at that time of the theoretical possibility of an atomic bomb. But then, in the primitive dawn of nuclear science, amassing the necessary fissionable material for a bomb seemed beyond the resources of any single nation."

"Maybe it was," I said. "Britain and Canada had spent hundreds of millions before the U.S. spent a dime. We built on top of their work."

"Even so," he said, "I do not believe the morning of August 6, 1945, saw an atomic device exploded over Hiroshima. I was there, you know."

His beer was almost gone. I waved for two more. Meanwhile, the food arrived and we attacked it. I found it delicious. Nakamura pretended indifference, but it was obvious that he was desperately hungry.

"I wish," he said, "that we could go to Hiroshima. There I could show you what I am trying to describe."

"Why can't we?"

"It is more than a thousand kilometers."

"An hour by jet. Professor, if you've got something to show me in Hiroshima, let's go. We can be there this evening."

His face was almost shining with excitement. "It has been years since I saw Hiroshima," he said. "Senator, I am now an old man and I have not been well—but I am not insane. I have always known what I saw, and it is those who refuse to listen to me who are insane."

I had my doubts, but my visit to Hiroshima had been long delayed. It was time I went there and faced up to whatever it was that had been waiting for me all these years.

"Fine, Professor," I said. "Do you live far from here?"

"Only a few blocks," he said. "I—I have an address at Hibya Hall, and sometimes I stay with friends. . . ."

He had said it all. Hibya Hall was a mail drop and a

storage locker for him, and he slept wherever he could find an empty straw mat.

I gave him a ten-thousand-yen note. Twenty-eight dollars. "Keep a strict expense record," I said, "because I'll be turning this in to my government. Take a cab, get your suitcase and whatever you'll need for a day or so, and meet me back at the hotel in an hour. Is that enough time?"

Holding the money as if it were something strange that had fallen into his hand, he said, "Yes, of course."

"I'll book us on a plane for Hiroshima this afternoon. We'll start as soon as you get back to the Imperial."

He tried to thank me, but I waved him away. "I'll see you in an hour." I paid the bill and went back to the hotel. As I passed the desk, the clerk beckoned to me. "Dr. Brandt is in the bar, sir. He asked to see you."

The doctor was sipping a champagne cocktail.

"How's my wife?" I asked.

"Resting," he said. "Do not be alarmed, Senator. She is perfectly all right."

"What was the trouble?"

"We had a very pleasant talk, Mrs. McGavin and I," he said. "She is a most amazing woman."

"Doctor, I have a great deal of respect for the medical profession, but if you could please start answering my questions . . ."

"Typical reaction," he said. "The plumed male, thinking the world circles around him alone."

"Doctor—"

He held up a hand. "Very well. I could not resist a little frivolity, knowing what I do. Your charming wife told me about the years of trying pills and thermometers and even artificial insemination. . . ."

I sat down heavily. My face must have shown what I was feeling, because the friendly little doctor reached over and patted my knee.

"Yes, Senator," he said, beaming. "After all these years you are going to be a papa."

Hiroshima—*August 10, Now*

Hiroshima is built on a group of small islands in the Ota River, near the edge of a large bay in the Seto Inland Sea. From the air the river's estuaries look like a spread-out six-fingered hand. Today the quiet city seemed much as it must have on that morning of August 6, 1945. Patches of clouds swept beneath the jet's wings as we circled for landing.

I thought of Celia back in Tokyo.

"The doctor told me," I had said, sitting beside her and taking both her hands in mine.

"It must have been that night in Boston," she said, snuggling up to me. "Lobsters and clam chowder, remember?" Then her hands clutched mine and she whispered, "Oh, Mouse, I'm scared! I feel like some kind of a fragile lamp globe. There's a tiny spark in me, and I'm afraid I'll do something stupid and snuff it out."

"You're as healthy as an ox," I said. "Or is the word cow?"

"That's flattering."

"Doctor Brandt's description, not mine. He says you're at least two months along. He's surprised you didn't notice anything before now."

"I missed last month, but that's happened before and—oh what the hell, I thought it was probably menopause, except I didn't have any hot flashes or weeping spells. What was I supposed to do—shout it from the rooftops?" Her eyes studied me anxiously. "Are you upset?"

"I'm delighted! I thought we'd just about had it." I gave her a ferocious glare. "But he'd better be born bald. Because if you've been making it with the iceman . . ."

She pulled me tighter. "Hugh, please don't joke about it. I'm still reeling. Me, a mama! My God, they'll do a *Time* cover on me. The Most Unlikely Mother of the Year."

"Ceil," I said, "do you feel well enough to go back to Washington?"

"Why?"

I told her about Professor Nakamura's invitation to visit Hiroshima. "And I don't know where the hell I might be going from there. What's more, in view of what the good doctor told us, you ought to be taking it easy instead of galumphing around the world with me."

"But I don't want to be away from you now," she said.

"It won't be for long, baby," I said. "I'll certainly be back in Washington by the beginning of the week. If Foster lets things go right down to that August 16 wire, my place is in the Senate."

"If he lets things get that far," she said firmly, "your place is with me in the deepest mine we can find in West Virginia."

"Look," I said, "I've crossed Brandt's palm with silver, and he's going to stick with you until you get on a JAL nonstop for the States. And when you get home, no running around. Rest and quiet. Understand?"

"All right," she said. "But you take it easy too. When do you leave for Hiroshima?"

"There's a three-thirty jet."

"Wham-bam, thank you ma'am."

"I'm sorry, hon. You know I've got to do this."

"Of course you do, Mouse. Don't pay any attention to me. I'll be in good hands with Brandt. I like him."

We held each other for a few moments, and then I rang for a bellboy who took my B-4 bag out to the taxi where Professor Nakamura was waiting. I kissed Celia again and closed the door gently.

The jet's wheels bumped against the runway and we were in Hiroshima.

The air terminal was like air terminals everywhere. We claimed our baggage, got a taxi, and Professor Nakamura said, "Senator, there is a small guest house in the hills where it is cooler and one has a view of the city."

"Fine," I said. Nakamura gave the driver instructions and we leaned back for the ten-minute ride.

There was no visible evidence of the massive damage the city had suffered. Nakamura saw me looking around, and said, "Part of the destroyed area has been preserved as a memorial, but it is some distance from here. You will be able to see it from the hills."

The people seemed cheerful and healthy; Hiroshima was just another bustling Japanese city. As we got into the outskirts, the houses were farther apart, with stone walls surrounding them. Children played in the streets, and birds perched on telephone wires, chirping at us as we passed.

The guest house was built in the old style, with huge wooden gates and winding pathways through the intricately constructed rock garden. Stone lamps and low benches lined the path. It was cool and peaceful there.

There was no formality of signing a register. I was introduced to the manager, who bowed politely. Two Japanese boys appeared, seized our bags, and vanished.

"Let us go up on the terrace and have some tea," suggested Nakamura.

I followed him outside. The terrace, which clung to the side of the hill was shaded by a stand of tall fines. Far below, I could see the city, golden and sleepy-looking in the late-afternoon sun.

Nakamura pointed. "There," he said. "Do you see that gray building? It is not possible to tell from here, but it is only a shell. That is the center of what we call our 'atomic park,' the memorial to all who died here."

Although the air was warm, I felt a chill.

So there it was. Out there more than a hundred thousand people died one terrible morning. Now I sat on a comfortable terrace and looked down at a peaceful city that had been, once upon a time, merely a target.

"Let me tell you about it," said Professor Nakamura.

Hiroshima—*August 6, 1945*

The air raid warning had sounded twice during that long-ago night. As always, the first alert came over the radio. Then, as flights of B-29s crossed the coast line, the sirens wailed.

High above the tense city, the motors of the *B-sans* grumbled as they passed. They almost always passed.

During the entire war, Hiroshima had been struck only a very few times by single bombers—in all likelihood jettisoning their bombs over the city to avoid wasting them in the ocean.

Professor Yoshije Nakamura, then in his late thirties, was doing research on supercharged radium at the National Institute for Cancer Research, which had been relocated in Hiroshima when it became evident that for some reason the city was being spared the ruinous bombing other nearby cities had suffered.

No one knew why the river city was so fortunate. Perhaps it was because of the huge prisoner of war camp that was rumored to be in the outskirts of town. Some said it was because President Truman's mother lived in the Genji Hotel, where she had been trapped as a tourist when the war began on December 7, 1941.

Even war becomes a routine. Because of the summer heat and the lack of air conditioning Nakamura developed a habit of going to work at six A.M. and working straight through to two in the afternoon, when he would take his bicycle and ride up to the cooler hills to amuse himself by painting miniature views of the city.

The morning weather plane was a regular visitor to Hiroshima. High in the stratosphere, white con trails streaming behind it, the American plane generally appeared around breakfast time. It would set off the First Warning alarm, but when

—as always—it was not followed by a flight of bombers, the All Clear would wail.

In 1945 Hiroshima had a population of around 250,000 people. No one will ever know for sure how many really lived there, or how many died, because there were no census records. In addition, during the early summer hordes of Japanese soldiers entered the city and began constructing fortifications against the anticipated Allied invasion.

Food was scarce. There was virtually no gasoline for civilians, and even bicycles were in short supply. Many children had been moved to the country because it was easier to feed them there than to transport food to the city.

On the morning of August 6 Professor Nakamura was attempting to measure the emission of a particle of radium encased in a glass capsule. He was experimenting with a radioactive bolus that a stomach cancer patient might swallow to apply radiation directly to the lesion. Shortly after seven A.M. he heard the First Warning alarm, and went to the window to look up.

High above, in the bright morning sky, a single *B-san* circled. After a few moments it vanished, and the All Clear sounded.

Nakamura went back to work. His assistant brought him *ocha*, the fragrant green tea, and he sipped it gratefully. With food growing ever scarcer, he knew he was drinking more tea than he should. But at least it warmed the stomach.

At eight another First Warning sounded. The Japanese radar had pinpointed an American bomber approaching the city. Its presence was not enough to warrant alarm, and the Take Cover signal was not used.

Looking out the window, Nakamura saw nothing. He returned to his work bench. Momentarily, he felt a slight trembling. Perhaps it was the passing of a heavy truck, although he had not heard one; perhaps it was the weakness in his legs, which had been growing more pronounced due to the poor diet on which he subsisted.

At exactly fifteen minutes past eight, as he turned toward

the radiation meter to check his figures, he was blinded by a searing flash of light. He threw himself to the floor, thinking a bomb had exploded just outside the window.

Few people even looked up from the streets of the city when the B-29 flew overhead. Those who did, and lived, would never see again.

Some saw a parachute floating down from the airplane. Parachutes meant that the Americans were in trouble, and that was cause for celebration. There were few victories to be celebrated any more.

Those looking at the parachute as it descended were permanently blinded by a sudden flash of light. Screaming, they threw themselves to the ground. While they were still dazed by the unexpected light in the sky, the ground began to tremble. Buildings crumbled. Modern "earthquake-proof" high rises settled, each floor pancaking the one beneath it, crushing people and office equipment impartially.

Water spurted in the streets. More than 60,000 water-main breaks occurred—dropping the water pressure to zero and making firemen helpless.

Confusion was everywhere. Electric lines shorted and started fires. Thousands of charcoal hibachis overturned, spilling red-hot coals onto straw mats.

What happened next is hopelessly mired in the conflicting memories of the survivors. Some say the fire storm began almost immediately. Others say it was an hour or more before the holocaust swept the city. Some reported flights of bombers over the stricken city; others assert the skies were empty.

But by ten that morning of August 6, 1945, Hiroshima was a dying city. As the fire storm rose into a ten-mile-high mushroom cloud, the hot air swept upward, pulling cooler air in from outside the city. The inrushing wind reached gale proportions, literally tumbling the screaming survivors into the heart of the blaze. At one point the rushing winds created a huge tornado, which whirled out to sea, where it became a waterspout that destroyed four small fishing boats.

As unhurt survivors from the outlying areas rushed into

the city to help, they met a staggering column of horror. Horribly burned, dressed in charred rags, refugees were pouring out of Hiroshima. Many were blind, led along by more fortunate, sighted victims.

"*Awaremi tamai! Itai! Itai!*" they called. "Have pity on us. Pain! Pain!"

And their horrified neighbors whispered, "*Gambare.*" "Be brave."

In the first hours of the morning, while the fires were still scattered among the wreckage, cries for help were heard from beneath the rubble, and the luckier survivors tore at the brick and stone with bare, bleeding hands. Many were rescued—but many more lay beneath the wreckage until the relentless flames arrived and stilled their screams.

As the flames rose higher, thousands crept into the water of the Kyo River, standing neck deep. Except for moans of pain, they were silent.

The wind began to blow harder.

Professor Nakamura, who had first been careful to replace his capsule of radium in its protective lead container, emerged from his laboratory to a scene of unimaginable horror.

A stream of moaning refugees passed him on the street. All were blind.

"*Mizu! Mizu!*" they screamed. "Water! Water!"

Nakamura shouted at them, caught at their arms, and recoiled with horror as the burned skin sloughed off in his hands. They were fleeing directly into the path of the fires. "*Choto mate!*" he called. "Just a minute!" Paying no attention, they staggered away.

The streets were full of rubble and fallen telephone poles and trees. Live electric wires spat angry sparks from the gutters. Nakamura picked his way carefully, avoiding the shorted cables. Past the river, filled with men and women standing passively in its water, some holding children's heads above the surface; past Asano Park, also filled with refugees; past what had been a ten-story office building—now only a few feet high, with each floor collapsed on the one beneath it;

past spectacles of horror and death that even after a quarter of a century made him tremble as he spoke of them, Yoshije Nakamura somehow found his way through the maze of danger to safety in the hills.

Behind him, a funeral pyre of smoke rose like an accusing finger pointed to heaven.

As more Allied planes appeared overhead, flames swept into Asano Park and drove its refugees into the river. Those who could not run perished.

Those in the river were no more fortunate. The tide was rising.

Out of the clouds a black, greasy rain began to fall. At first the victims rejoiced, holding their hands cupped to catch the water. But it was foul-tasting, and those who drank vomited soon after.

Nakamura lay exhausted on a mat twenty miles from Hiroshima as nightfall came. He could see the great fires consuming the city, and felt guilt because he had survived. Honor demanded that he return to help, but the farm family who had rescued him from the stream of refugees on the road refused to return his clothing. The farmer, his realism earned through decades of bone-grinding labor, knew how little one man could do.

In the outskirts of the city itself, in the absence of any word from their government, the Japanese survivors speculated. Because of a peculiar smell in the air, many thought poison gas had been used. Others theorized that a cloud of magnesium had been scattered over the city and ignited. Some blamed the catastrophe on a mist of gasoline which had been exploded by an incendiary bomb.

Nakamura, and perhaps a dozen others, considered the possibility of nuclear fission.

Later, although estimates varied, it was established that two-thirds of the buildings in the heart of Hiroshima had been destroyed. In addition to the more than 100,000 people who died, 40,000 more were injured severely.

In Tokyo, where efforts were being made to get Russia to

act as a peace intermediary between Japan and the Allies, an urgent message was sent to the Japanese ambassador in Moscow:

August 6, 1945
5:00 P.M.

It is reported that Stalin and Molotov returned to Moscow today. As we have various arrangements to make, please see Molotov immediately and demand his earliest possible reply.

The message was signed by General Hideki Tojo. There was no immediate answer from Ambassador Naosoke Sato. Meanwhile, reports of the destruction at Hiroshima poured in.

At six P.M. Radio Tokyo announced, "Several B-29s struck Hiroshima city at 8:20 A.M. and fled after dropping bombs and incendiaries. The amount of damage is now under investigation."

To Yoshije Nakamura, lying twenty miles from the devastated city, the words rang a death knell. "It was at that moment," he said later, "that I knew the war was lost."

That night, as the fires subsided, rescue crews began pulling thousands of bloated corpses out of the Kyo River, where people crouched in the water had suffocated from lack of oxygen. Shoulder to shoulder, jammed against the bridge pillars, hundreds still stood, dead, having waited patiently for rescue that came too late.

At that moment, back on Tinian, Tim Bond and I were quaffing free beer donated by the jubilant 20th Air Force fliers. In a few minutes we would take four warm cans of brew and go to the outdoor movie and see Rita Hayworth and Gene Kelly in *Cover Girl,* while out in the boondocks a Japanese sniper waited for us with his last clip of ammunition.

Hiroshima—*August 10, Now*

The sun had set over Hiroshima. The red clouds in the sky were mirrored in the placid river, and the quiet harbor far to the south was dark purple.

Nakamura and I had given up on the green tea and were drinking warm saki now. In the garden below, crickets chirped.

"We know now," Nakamura said, "that Russia had no intention of helping Japan negotiate a peace settlement. On August 8 Molotov called the Japanese Ambassador into his office and declared war on Japan. The next day Nagasaki was destroyed."

I sipped from the tiny porcelain saki cup. "Professor," I said slowly, "so far everything you've told me matched the official reports about the dropping of the atomic bomb here."

He nodded. "On the surface, yes. But in the morning I can show you many things. In the months after August 6 I found myself curiously unsatisfied by the official versions of the event. For example, as a nuclear physicist I know the sequence of events set into motion by a fissionable material reaching critical mass and going into chain reaction. At the very instant of explosion, the fissionable mass would throw off great quantities of neutrons, beta particles, and gamma rays. Yet—and it is this which first excited my suspicions—my own radiation meter, similar to what you would call a Geiger counter, showed only a normal background count once I had placed my radium capsule back in its lead safe."

"You mean right after the blast?"

"If there *was* a blast, Senator. Yes. I remember distinctly. One of the things I always determined after completing an experiment was if I had accidentally contaminated myself or my equipment."

"Perhaps your meter was broken."

"It recorded a high level of radiation until I placed the radium in its safe, then dropped to normal. At the time I paid it no heed. After all, a nuclear explosion was the farthest thing from my mind. It was only later that I remembered the detail."

"Did you check out your instrument?"

"It was destroyed in the fire. But three weeks later I returned with another instrument and made a careful survey of radioactive areas in Hiroshima."

"I thought you said there wasn't any radiation."

"Not at the beginning. But by the end of the first day, many people were suffering from what was obviously radiation sickness."

"Could it have been anything else?"

He shook his head. "The symptoms were classic. Headache, diarrhea, nausea. Then fever and lassitude. After this first period, for some, there was a remission. Many felt better for a week or ten days, unaware that they were doomed. But when the second stage began, with fever that went as high as 106 degrees, and the victim's hair began falling out, there was usually no hope. The white blood count began to drop. In those who were lucky, and who survived, it went down to around half of normal—say 3,500 instead of 6,000. If the count went below 2,000 the patient always died."

He sipped his saki. His face was impassive, but I could sense the pain behind his quiet voice.

"My wife and two sons both died of the radiation sickness. And, Senator McGavin, they were not even in Hiroshima that morning. They returned in the afternoon searching for me, and were caught in the black rain. It is my theory that there was no radiation whatsoever on the morning of August 6. I believe that whatever caused the sickness came later—perhaps with the black rain."

"How do you know?"

"Because when I did survey the city, there were unexplainable variations in radiation levels. If the radiation *had* come from an explosion, it would have followed certain straight-line patterns. But I discovered patches of extremely high radioactivity, directly alongside patches absolutely free of it. It was as if whatever had caused the contamination had been scattered over the city and blown here and there by the wind."

Scattered. Dispersed. The two words were very similar. I considered showing Nakamura the memo from Rosy Cooper about dispersing fissionable material at Hiroshima and Nagasaki, and decided against it. There would be time later, should it be necessary.

Of course, there is never enough time. I forgot that.

"What about the effect they called 'shadows in stone'?" I asked.

"Senator," he said fervently, "I have seen those 'shadows,' supposedly where a victim was vaporized, leaving his shadow burned into the wall of a building or a bridge. The most famous one is on the Kannon Bridge. But I swear to you, that morning, *after* the blast or whatever it was, there was no such shadow. I crossed that bridge twice, and I would have seen it. When the Allied Forces came into the city, they sealed off the Ground Zero area for several weeks and no one was permitted to enter. It was after that time that such artifacts as 'stone shadows' and the pages of an open book in which the paper was intact but the letters had been burned out were discovered. If they were there before, no one saw them."

"How do you account for the blast?"

"I do not know. Nor do I know what destroyed the city. At first I thought of an earthquake—the city rests near a fault. But when I examined the seismologists' records, there was no tremor recorded on August 6 or August 9."

He stood up and leaned over the rail, his slender hands gripping it tightly. Below, the lights of Hiroshima sparkled in the early evening.

"All I can say, sir," he said quietly, "is that for many years I have known that this city was not destroyed by an atomic bomb. And knowing this, the question that torments me is, Why does everyone *pretend* to have used a bomb?"

I joined him at the rail. Down in the garden the crickets stopped their singing.

"I am very grateful to you," Nakamura began as I turned to

get some more saki. My knee struck the low table, and the slender bottle started to upset. As I leaned forward to grab for it, something flared in the darkness of the garden beneath us and I heard the frantic slamming of a machine gun. I went on over the table and flattened against the terrace. The weapon fired again, and with its echoes still ringing in my ears I thought I heard a faint sigh from Nakamura, who was dangling over the wooden rail. I heard running feet in the garden, then silence, then the sighing sound again. I crawled over to Nakamura and pulled him off the railing by his pants leg. He fell heavily beside me and I heard the strange sighing sound a third time.

He would not make it again. A burst of bullets had half severed his neck.

Moscow—August 11, Now

The thing that struck me most about Moscow was its silence. The cars did not honk their horns; pedestrians spoke quietly or not at all.

As we drove along Leningrad Highway in the black Zim, its window curtains half drawn, the Russian beside me lit a long cigarette and exhaled contentedly.

"Have patience, Senator," he said. "We are almost there."

"There" would be the destination I had flown nineteen hours to reach. My pudgy companion's name was Grodin, and I had first seen him in the soft light of Japanese lanterns on the terrace of a guest house in Hiroshima.

I had started to crawl toward Professor Nakamura, and a voice hissed from the shadows, "Do not move!" I saw him creep to the edge of the terrace and peer cautiously over the railing. His right hand held a pistol.

In Russian he called down into the garden. A voice answered, and he stood up.

Extending his hand to help me, he said in heavily accented English, "It is safe now, Senator. They are gone."

I brushed off my trousers as if the dust were contaminated. "We'd better get a doctor."

"It is too late," he said.

"You're Russian."

"Yes. But I assure you, we are friends. We have been watching you since your arrival in Japan. I am sorry for this terrible occurrence. We were assigned to prevent such violence."

I looked at him incredulously. "*You* were assigned? Are you telling me the Kremlin has provided bodyguards for a United States senator?"

"Please come inside," he said nervously. "We are very conspicuous here." He nodded at Nakamura's body. "Do not worry about him. My men will arrange everything with the innkeeper. Your name will not be brought into it."

Dazed, I followed him through the door. A Japanese woman of middle years sat at a table crying and wringing her hands. The manager I had met just a few hours before stood near her, his face closed. The Russian spoke to him in Japanese, and the man nodded.

"We have placed your luggage in our car," he told me. "It would be better if you came with us."

"Where to? Am I being kidnapped?"

"Certainly not," he said. "If you insist, we will take you to the airport. Or to your consulate. It is simply that it would be better if you were not here when the police arrive. Someone will have reported the shots. We must hurry."

In the car, a blue Toyota, the Russian said, "I am Alexei Grodin. I am assistant to the vice-consul in Tokyo."

"The USSR vice-consul, of course," I said.

"Of course. When we heard of the attack on you in Jerusalem and of the murder of Mr. Hepburn, my government assigned me to prevent any further misfortunes from occurring. We failed, as you know. It is likely my next post will be in the African Interior."

I found myself liking this stocky Russian. "Why is the Soviet government so interested in my well-being?"

He shrugged. "I do as I am told. Once we are in a safe place, I must contact my superiors."

"Where do you suggest?"

"A few miles from here there is a spa. A hot spring. It is where tourists go. Also, it is near the airport. Is that satisfactory with you?"

"For the moment," I said. I needed time to think.

While Grodin was calling his boss, I sipped an Asahi beer and tried to figure out what was happening. A reaction to Nakamura's death had set in; I was embarrassed to see my fingers twitching.

Apparently the bomb attack in Israel had been a planned assault on me, and not by Jordanian guerrillas. Certainly if I had not bent at just the right moment this evening, I would be lying dead beside Nakamura, stitched with machine gun bullets.

My suspicions fastened on Howard Foster again. *Could* he be capable of ordering a political assassination? No matter how far-fetched it seemed, I had to consider the possibility.

Who else did I threaten? The Soviet Union? China? Our own defense industry?

My fingers twitched again.

"*Gospedin* McGavin," said Grodin, "my superior told me to convey an invitation of great urgency. Premier Nabov asks you to come to Moscow, at once and secretly."

"Why?"

"I do not know," he said. "But I am instructed to inform you that it is a matter of great urgency and that the future of world peace may be determined by your answer."

"I'll be go to hell," I said.

"I do not understand."

"Neither do I," I answered, mostly to myself. For a maverick senator bucking his Administration's policies, I was the most popular visitor in town. Everybody either wanted to shoot me or show me something. "Will I speak with the Premier himself?"

"I am told that you will."

"How does one go about getting to Moscow from here?"

"A courier plane will meet us at the airport in an hour," he said. "We fly from here to Vladivostok, where we board a jet for Moscow."

"We?"

"I am invited too," he said sadly. "It will be up to me to explain why you were almost killed."

"Alexei, my friend," I said, feeling lightheaded, "what do I have to lose? Let me make one phone call and we'll be on our way."

My slang mixed him up a bit, but he understood I had agreed to go, and relaxed slightly.

When I called the Imperial Hotel in Tokyo, I was told Celia had already left for the United States.

Well, that was one worry off my mind.

I don't know how Grodin arranged it, but we skipped customs and flew to Vladivostok, where we were spirited aboard an empty Aeroflot TU-144 supersonic jet. It was obviously a VIP plane; in addition to a section of regular airline seats, there was a spacious stateroom with a bed and reasonably complete bath. I made myself at home, took a shower, had a couple of nips with Grodin, who wondered if I played chess. I do not, and I left him staring gloomily out the window into the darkness of 45,000 feet. Taking a sleeping pill for the first time in many months, I slept my way over most of the Union of Soviet Socialist Republics.

It was afternoon in Moscow when the black Zim slowed at a corner.

"This is Gorki Street," said Grodin. "We are almost there."

"The Kremlin?"

"No," he said. "It was thought that might be awkward for you. We are going to a small apartment the Premier keeps near the Bolshoi Theatre."

"Ah, yes," I said.

So help me, my Russian companion *blushed.* "The Premier is sixty-seven years old," he said. "There are times when he wants to be alone, away from those who are constantly pressing for decisions."

"I know the feeling well," I said.

The car stopped. Grodin got out, and I followed him.

"Do not worry about your luggage," he said. "If you decide to remain in Moscow, it will be taken to your hotel. Otherwise, it will be put aboard your plane."

"Let's decide later."

I followed him inside the three-story building. A guard at the entrance examined Grodin's credentials and nodded us past. Inside, a second guard checked us again before we were admitted into the apartment.

I recognized Premier Mikhail Nabov immediately. He stood up and came to me, hand outstretched.

"Dorogoi gost i drug," he said.

"You are his dear guest and friend," Grodin translated.

"I am honored," I said.

Grodin spoke rapidly in Russian, and the Premier smiled and answered.

"The Premier invites you to join him in vodka and caviar sandwiches," said Grodin. "He recognizes that they have become a Russian cliché, but he says to tell you that he has been, I think the word is, 'hooked.'"

"It will do," I said. "You may inform the Premier that I too am hooked and that I accept with pleasure."

We socialized for half an hour, drinking the tiny glasses of vodka and eating the toast spread with Beluga caviar. I passed on ice cream, although Grodin assured me it was virtually the Russian national dish.

"Neither of us is a fool," Nabov said finally. Grodin's face stiffened as he translated. "I would be taking you for a fool, Senator, if I expected you to believe that many goals of the Soviet Union are not antagonistic to those of your own country. This is the way the world goes. But neither of our countries wants to destroy the other, and itself in the bargain. That is why I have watched, with great interest, your attempts to bring sanity to the nuclear race."

"I'm glad to hear that," I said. "As one of the two largest nuclear powers in the world, I'd think you would feel it is your responsibility to help decrease the tension."

"I agree," Nabov said. "But how do you know that I am not attempting to do just that? If you do not understand the motives of your own President, how can you presume to understand mine?"

"If you mean I don't know why the President resorted to a provocative action such as placing the ABMs in Japan, you're right, Mr. Premier."

Nabov smiled. "There is method in Mr. Foster's madness," he said. "I am betraying a confidence, but you might describe this so-called provocative act as what used to be termed a 'joint action.'"

"He hinted as much to me one time," I admitted. "I'm afraid I just don't understand what either of you hopes to gain from pushing Red China to the wall."

"Your country has its own reasons," he said. "As for me, the Sino-Soviet frontier abrasion has become almost intolerable. Perhaps the Chinese tiger does have sharp claws, perhaps not. If conditions were ever right for them to strike, that time is now. If they pass this opportunity, we will have learned something helpful of their resolve and their capability. You know, Senator, there is a joke in Moscow about a Sino-Soviet war. It goes, on the first day, we capture one million Chinese. On the second day, we capture five million. On the third day, we surrender. That tells you the temper of my people. Sober, realistic. The last thing any sane Russian wants is a war—with the United States, with China, with anyone."

"Is that why you're on Missile Standby? It looks to me as if you're playing both ends against the middle. You've got five hundred silos aimed directly at North America, and you're on a countdown hold."

"And China knows it. They will never have a better chance to show their claws. If they do not, we have all learned something vital to world peace."

"And if they *do* show their claws, the United States will have lost twenty million people."

"We believe the escalation will be stopped before missiles are actually fired."

"It seems to me you're pretty free with American lives,"

I said. "What would your attitude be if the Chinese were issuing ultimatums to you instead of us?"

"I would hope that your President would attempt to aid me in difficulty—just as I have attempted to help him."

"Would you mind explaining how aiming five hundred missiles at us *helps?*"

"Comrade Grodin," said the Premier, "please inform Senator McGavin that I am about to show him a film, and then leave the room until I ring for you."

Grodin passed the message and left. Nabov slid open a panel in one of the walls. Inside was a 16mm projector.

"I am afraid," he said in flawless English, "that one of my predecessors was somewhat underhanded in, whenever possible, having secret films made of supposedly private conversations. This one was photographed through a two-way mirror."

"Your English is very good, sir," I told him.

"Thank you." He motioned for me to draw the curtains. I did, and he started the projector. It threw a small picture on the wall.

The footage was grainy old-newsreel quality. At first there was no sound track. I saw men walking in what looked like a corridor. It was hard to tell; the lighting was dim.

Then the picture got brighter and I saw two men seated at a table. It was easy to recognize them.

One was Premier Josef Stalin.

The other was President Harry S Truman.

The sound came on, muffled but intelligible.

A third man in the room, uniformed, was speaking in Russian. Stalin nodded, then the translator turned to President Truman.

"The Chairman congratulates you on your success against the Japanese," he said. "He hopes that the entry of the U.S.S.R. into the war had some effect in diminishing the Japanese resolve, and that the decisions taken at Yalta and Potsdam concerning Soviet rights in the Far East will not be overlooked."

"Tell the Chairman," Truman said in his flat, twangy voice, "that the Soviet Union entered the war too late to be much of a factor. If President Roosevelt's plan to catch the Japanese in a pincers beween Okinawa and Manchuria had been carried out, it would be one thing. But the Chairman knows damned well that with the exception of a few minor skirmishes, the Japanese never even saw a Russian."

"You spoke differently, Mr. President," said Stalin, "when you described your new weapon to us at Potsdam. Then, you were anxious for us to aid you in your campaign against the Japanese Empire. It saddens me to see how power can corrupt a nation whom we were prepared to accept as an equal brother. With a super-weapon in your possession, you take on the arrogance of the imperialistic British. Perhaps you dream of a new empire, where the sun never sets on the American flag!"

"Mr. Chairman," said Truman, biting out the words, "the United States is not interested in territorial gain. Nor will we sit still and watch you engage in it in the Far East."

"May I remind the President," said Stalin, "that it was the permission the Soviet Union gave American scientists to take valuable uranium from our Ural mines that enabled you to produce your bomb in time to end the war with Japan? Under the circumstances, I think it is only fair that the United States share her nuclear arsenal with the U.S.S.R."

"I'm sorry," said Truman. "That can't be done."

Stalin stared at him, then said, "I expected such an answer."

"You see," said the President, "we don't *have* a nuclear arsenal. After all that work and money, the thing didn't work."

Stunned, Stalin shouted at the interpreter, who repeated the President's statement.

"How convenient," the Russian leader said finally. "You hypnotized the Japanese into believing you had destroyed two of their cities. What do you take me for?"

Truman stood up. "Mr. Chairman," he said, "I have tried to be fair and honest with you here. Instead you insult my office and my country. I don't have to listen to any more of it."

"By the time you move your troops up from Okinawa," said Stalin, "you will find our brave Russian soldiers waiting in Tokyo."

"I wouldn't do that, Mr. Chairman," Truman said calmly.

"What will you do to stop me?" shouted Stalin. "Your people are sick of war. Your officers would rebel—your troops would refuse to fight."

"Mr. Chairman," said Truman, "you put one foot in Japan and we'll drop an atom bomb right down the Kremlin's chimney."

The little man turned and strode from the room.

The film flickered and ended. I opened the drapes.

Pressing a buzzer, Nabov said, "Do not mention my English to Comrade Grodin, please. It is my little secret. I find it an advantage to know how accurately my translator is rendering my statements."

Grodin hurried in. The Premier spoke to him for a moment.

"Comrade Senator," Grodin began, "the Premier hastens to assure you that any opinions expressed by Chairman Stalin do not apply to conditions today."

"I understand," I said.

"He says that this motion picture was made secretly, through a two-way mirror in the conference room. There was no copy—this is the original film. It was found in Chairman Stalin's personal vault, along with dozens of similar films made at other conferences. Premier Khrushchev attempted to verify its authenticity, but learned that the technicians involved in filming and developing it were executed a few days later."

"When was the film made?"

"September 4, 1945—two days after the surrender ceremonies on your battleship *Missouri*."

"Where?"

"Lisbon."

"It ought to be easy enough to find out whether or not President Truman was in Lisbon on that date. Was Stalin?"

"We do not know. But all available data indicates that your President Truman was in Washington then. However, data can be falsified. I will speak in veiled terms, since I do not want our young friend here to know what Chairman Stalin and President Truman discussed. But ever since this film was discovered, the world has walked a knife edge. If it *was* Truman, and what he said at first was true, we have squandered billions of rubles to meet a threat that does not exist."

"Why did you show this to me?"

"If your President Truman—"

"*Or* his double," I put in.

"Or his double," he conceded, "was speaking the truth, then there has been a quarter of a century of needless terror."

"What about your own apparatus?" I asked.

"You know I cannot speak of that."

"And you know I can't talk about ours."

"True," he said. "Senator McGavin, it was more my purpose in bringing you here to seek information, rather than give it."

"I don't blame you," I said. "But I can't give you any."

He lifted both hands and dropped them. "What is a man to believe? I would never admit to you that my nation has engaged in propaganda based on theory instead of fact. You would never admit to me that your own has done so. We can neither trust the other. But if the truth were found, this artificial gulf between our countries might be bridged."

"So China's the guinea pig."

"Yes. If China hesitates at the crucial moment, if her actions bear out what your President Truman said in that film, perhaps then we can all begin speaking the truth to one another."

"It's a nice thought," I said. "But even as you tell me this, your Baltic Sea missiles are aimed at my country."

"They will not be fired."

"So you say. I want to believe you."

"But you cannot," he said sadly. "I do not blame you. We are all blind men in a room filled with serpents. Whether or not we tread upon one is a matter of arrant chance."

"Sir," I said, "I'm not the cleverest man in the world. But I'm smart enough to know when I'm in over my head. I'm going to go home and try to put this puzzle together. That's what you had in mind, isn't it? That I'd join this piece with the others I've got and come up with some kind of complete picture?"

"Exactly, my friend," he said.

"Well," I said, lighting my pipe, "here I thought I was some kind of crusader, barging around the world looking for the answer to our problems. But maybe you're right. Maybe I'm really just the guy who stands on the wall and reports the progress of the battle offstage."

"You are angry?"

"No," I said. "I'm just tired, and bewildered and homesick. What I said before goes. I'm going home and try to sort something out of these conflicting stories, all of which sound realistic and true. Perhaps none of them is true. But I've done all I can living on jet planes. So, with your permission, I'll get on one more and go home."

"You are tired," he said gently. "Be my guest for this evening."

"Thanks, but no," I said. "All of a sudden I want to see N Street so bad I can taste it."

"N?" asked the Premier of the Soviet Union.

"That's the capitalistic street where I live," I said.

Washington, D.C.—*August 12, Now*

The clock was ticking.

It had been ten days since the original ultimatum was delivered by North Korea. The position of the United States had been attacked by statesmen and the press of virtually every nation, including Great Britain and France. The United Nations was in almost continuous session.

In Japan Premier Ito was conducting a Japanese filibuster. He had taken the floor two days earlier, refusing to yield to other speakers or to allow a vote. Outside, in the streets of

Tokyo, students battled with black-uniformed police, and nine young men were clubbed to death. One policeman was thrown into the moat around the Emperor's palace and held under by three students until he drowned.

The Soviet countdown was still on a two-hour hold, but *Pravda* warned Russian citizens to prepare for the worst. Cities were being evacuated. All borders were closed, trapping over seven hundred American tourists behind the Iron Curtain.

There was no official word out of China. U.S. intelligence reported that Premier K'ang Na-Soong was still holding at Yellow, despite constant recommendations from his general staff to escalate. China's nine nuclear submarines, aided by decoys and conventional underwater vessels, had slipped away from American hunter-killer subs and now, for all anyone knew, might be sitting on the bottom off the California coastline.

Egyptian jets made an attack on Israel's nuclear plant near the Red Sea. Only one got through, and the 500-pound bomb it dropped destroyed the plant's lunch room. Eighteen Israeli scientists taking their morning coffee break were killed. Israel retaliated by bombing Cairo Airport.

The eleventh meeting of Howard Foster's Rat Pack broke up with Vice-President Arthur Rand openly accusing the President of risking the security of the nation for some unstated and unknown personal aim. He was supported by Attorney General Martin Kuhn. But General Oscar Burton, Chairman of the Joint Chiefs of Staff, pledged military support for the President's policies.

Jack Sherwood, released from custody by writ of *habeas corpus*, dropped out of sight.

Celia had a telephone call from a friend on *Life* and flew up to New York on the shuttle.

And, in the big double bedroom on N Street, I snored my way through the summer afternoon. Once I thought I heard a distant bell clanging and sat up, sweat running down my arms. But it was only a Good Humor truck selling ice cream to the kids outside.

I tracked Jack Sherwood down in a small apartment near National Airport. It was after midnight, and when he opened the door, I could tell he was drunk.

"Glory be!" he said. "It's the world traveler. Come in, boss."

"Hello, Jack," I said. "I'm sorry I wasn't around to help. But Harry got you out, I see."

"That he did," my assistant said, motioning me to a chair in the cluttered living room. The place had a college atmosphere to it—walls covered with posters, books piled everywhere. "My kid brother's joint," he said. "He's down here trying to do a Ralph Nader on the FCC. Up until yesterday, that is."

"What happened?"

"They fired him. It seems he's got a subversive as a brother."

"I'll straighten it out," I said. "You were only acting under my instructions."

He poured himself a drink, raised his eyebrows when I shook my head at the proffered bottle. "Tapering off in your old age, boss?"

"I'm still bushed," I said. "A stiff drink would knock me out."

He tossed down an ounce of scotch. "Thank you for your kind offer," he said, "but it won't wash. You can't take the rap."

"There's no rap to take," I said. "It's a misunderstanding."

He wagged his head back and forth. "No, it isn't. First, to keep it straight, you did not tell me to go forth and steal secret papers. You told me to find out what I could. Like all good lackeys, I exceeded my instructions." He laughed, repeated, "Exceeded my instructions. Can't be too drunk if I can say that."

"You didn't do anything worse than a hundred guys have done around this town."

"Did too," he said. "I broke the eleventh commandment, Senator. Thou shalt not get caught." He shook his head. "And they caught me good. I had almost thirty pages of memos including one ballbuster from John Kennedy to the AEC in which he told them to stop bugging him about wanting to test in the atmosphere, because he wasn't going to let them do it."

"Do you remember any of the others?"

"Didn't get a chance to look at them. The FBI zapped me as I was coming out of the building."

"What about the girl who gave them to you?"

"For all I know, they may have shot her." Then, seeing my reaction, he added hastily, "No, I'm joking, boss. She's out on bail, but they're charging her with violating the National Security Act. She's mad as a hornet at me, that's why I said what I did. Sorry. I know that stuff isn't funny any more, since Phil Hepburn."

"That's not all," I said. I told him about Hiroshima and Professor Nakamura, and he gave a long, low whistle. "Someone's taking this very seriously," he said. "Do you think it's our friend over on Pennsylvania Avenue?"

"I can't believe that," I said. "I know Foster's up to his ears in whatever this Third Gen deployment is, but he'd never go so far as assassination."

"I don't know where you've been since we lost touch," he said, "and maybe it would be smart if you didn't tell me. But if it does you any good, I'm pretty sure they lost track of you. That was one of the questions they kept putting to me, where you were and what were you doing." He grinned. "I gave them zilch."

"Good for you. Listen, Jack, you can say no and I'll understand. But there's something I want to find out. Maybe you know where to start asking."

"Might as well be hung for a sheep, right?"

"I want to know if there's any chance whatsoever that Harry Truman might have been in Lisbon on September 4, 1945."

"You *what?*"

I repeated myself. He spread his hands. "All right, and I won't even ask you why. But I presume you suspect the normal files and records have been cooked, otherwise you could get the answer with a phone call."

"Yes. But be careful, Jack. Don't go out on any limbs."

He shrugged. "What does it matter? They can wipe me out for what I've done already. I get the idea I'll be better off if you can prove whatever it is you're out to prove. Then at least I'll be on the side of the angels."

"Meanwhile," I said, "I'll talk to Foster about you."

"Thanks. I don't look too good in stripes."

As I left, he said, "Don't worry about the sauce, Senator. I'll be in fighting shape by morning. I've just been feeling sorry for myself and worrying about my kid brother. He went out of here this evening like a demon. I hope he's getting drunk somewhere, and that's all. But he might be feeding somebody a knuckle sandwich. Paul's a pretty physical guy when he gets mad."

"He'll be all right, Jack," I said. How did *I* know? But it was the thing to say. We shook hands and I left.

It was after two when I got back to the house. Celia's car was in the driveway. I rang the doorbell three times, and she was in my arms before I could close the front door.

"Oh, Mouse!" she said. "I've missed you."

"Me too," I said. "What were you doing up in New York? I thought you were supposed to be taking things easy."

"George Harris wanted to talk with me, and he couldn't get away to come down here. Oh, Hugh, wait till you hear it!"

We went into the living room. The stereo was on, sending soft piano chords into the night. Celia sat on the couch and pulled me down with both hands.

"George has it on very good authority," she began, "that even if Foster pushes Artie Rand at the convention, there's going to be one hell of a fight. California is going to yield to Ohio on the first ballot."

"Ohio? I'm a New Yorker these days. Is Ohio so desperate for favorite sons that they have to pick me?"

"No favorite sons involved. Ohio is also committed to going your way on the first ballot. And you'll get New York and—"

"And meanwhile, California is laying back to see which way the wind is blowing before they commit themselves."

"So what? Isn't that better than having them come right out for Rand?" She stared at me. "I thought you'd be pleased. I was. This means you've still got a chance."

"I'm sorry, Ceil. Sure, I'm pleased. I guess it's just that it all doesn't seem to matter much any more."

"Hugh, what *happened* in Japan?"

"I went to Hiroshima."

"I know that. What else?"

When I told her about Nakamura, she became very quiet. Then I mentioned my secret trip to Moscow. "I talked with Nabov. He as much as said he was in cahoots with Foster on this ABM thing."

"But why?"

"He hinted that they were testing China's resolve," I said carefully. "If K'ang doesn't push the button, we'll have learned something about how far we can go in the future."

"And if K'ang *pushes* the button, we'll have learned something too, but it'll be too late. No wonder they call it Russian roulette!"

I sighed and touched her hair. "Baby, my ass is dragging. Let's go to bed."

Her face softened. "That," she said, "is the first nice thing you've said to me all night."

But it wasn't any good. For the first time in years, we rolled away from each other unsatisfied and frustrated.

"I'm sorry," I said. "I must be more tired than I thought."

"It's my fault," she said. "I shouldn't shout at you when you're worn out."

We held each other and talked quietly.

"Do you want a boy?" she asked.

"I don't know. How about you?"

"I'll take anything," she said. "Oh, Mouse, it's like a miracle. After all these years."

Thoughtlessly, I said, "Preservation of the species. Down

below the conscious level, our bodies are always aware of approaching danger. Reproducing is one way of achieving immortality."

She stiffened. "You cynical bastard," she said, and there was no levity in her voice. "Is that all you can think of now that it's finally happened?"

I pulled her to me. "Don't be like that, Ceil. I'm not deliberately gloomy. It's just all the crap I've been through in the past week."

She kissed my neck several times, nuzzling up against me. "I know, I know," she whispered. "I wish you were out of it. I'm afraid it's *you* they're after, not the poor old professor or Phil Hepburn, or some Israeli girl soldier. That's why you make me so mad when you talk about preservation of the species. I don't care about preserving the species. I care about preserving you and me and our child, and the hell with everybody else in the world!"

The call from the White House came at six-thirty. Celia was sleeping, so I kept my voice low. Yes, I would be happy to have breakfast with the President. Seven-forty-five was quite convenient. No, I would drive my own car, a limousine was not necessary.

When I came out of my shower, Celia was brushing her hair.

"Foster?"

I nodded. "I'm just as glad," I said. "Otherwise I would have had to call him. Maybe I'll be able to pull some pieces together this morning."

"Don't mention what I said about Ohio and California," she warned.

"I won't," I said.

"Hugh," the President said bluntly, "what were you doing in Moscow?"

"Talking with Nabov."

He frowned. "That wasn't very smart."

262

"Maybe. But the Premier hinted that things aren't as bad between the two of you as his missile readiness might indicate."

"What did he tell you?"

"He as much as said that the whole reason behind this Third Gen deployment was to test Red China's nuclear capability."

"Did you believe him?"

"I didn't disbelieve him. I'll say this, Howard—he leveled with me a hell of a lot more than you've been doing."

"Dammit," he said, "what do you think my job consists of? Sharing my responsibilities and decisions with every senator who makes noises around convention time?"

I bit into a link sausage. "If that's what you think, I can't answer you."

He took a sip of his coffee, then shook his head slowly. "No," he said, "of course it's not. I think you're one of the best men on the Hill, and you know I do. But then you go out and spout off, after I've done everything but go down on my knees asking you to lay off the ABM program. I sent you my word that I'll pull them out this week if you'll just keep *quiet*. You know perfectly well you're in over your head—and still you keep on. What in hell does it take to stop you?"

"Bullying my assistant won't do it," I said. "Getting my wife fired won't either. And most of all, trying to soft-soap *me* won't. All it takes is for you to show me clearly how and why you're acting in the national interest, and you won't hear another peep out of me. I told you that ten days ago, but you wouldn't listen."

"Maybe I'll listen now," he said. "Will you tell me what you've discovered on your trip? Then I can make sense in what I tell you."

"We'll see," I said. "Sure, I'll tell you what I've learned— and what I've surmised. Let's start with England. Hawkins knows his nation has no use for atomic bombs. But they're a symbol, he tells me. Then he lets loose a doubt that if the bombs are ever needed they'll even work."

Foster leaned forward, his expression one of polite interest.

"France," I said. "The President makes a big thing out of France being the only non-aligned nuclear power, some kind of balance wheel. But he's very interested in whether or not I've ever seen an actual bomb explode."

Foster offered me another cup of coffee, but I shook my head. My nerves were tight enough as it was.

"Israel. Bernardi comes right out with it. He's tested three aerial bombs, he says, and not one has gone off. Now the tower shot that he sets up functions perfectly. Bernardi thinks —as I do—that something, probably the Jesus Factor, keeps aerial shots from exploding."

"Go on," said Foster.

"I went down to Guam, and Rosy Cooper gave me the whole routine. According to him, everything's kosher. But you can't turn an honest man into a liar and expect it not to affect him. Rosy did everything according to the book, and do you know what? I didn't believe him."

"I'm not sure I know what you mean," Foster said.

"Come off it, Mr. President! I mean giving me a song and dance about flying a mission to Nagasaki, when I know from the evidence of my own eyes that he was on Tinian the whole goddamned day. That's the trouble with starting to lie, Howard. You can't sustain it. One lie breeds another, and it's like a chain letter. For the lie to succeed, pretty soon everybody in the whole world has to be in on it, and that's just not possible."

I lowered my voice and went on. "In Japan a nice little Japanese scientist, who is dead now because of what he knew, took me to Hiroshima. His name was Professor Yoshije Nakamura, and he was there on August 6. He saw a bright flash in the sky, and he saw buildings topple, but as a nuclear scientist he had very good reason to doubt there ever having been a nuclear explosion. He told me about people who were within several hundred yards of Ground Zero who sustained no radiation burns or sickness whatsoever. He believes it was only later, when the clouds from the fire storm condensed and rained back onto the city, that people began picking up radiation. And that, Mr. President, is a fact that leads me to a word

Rosy Cooper used in a memo to the Manhattan District in 1945—he did not say that fissionable material had been *detonated* over Hiroshima, he said it had been *dispersed*."

The President swiveled his chair and stared out at the south lawn. "Why did you go to Moscow?"

"Somebody shot Nakamura down with a machine gun. I think they were after me, too. A Russian agent helped me get away. When he contacted his superiors, they passed along an invitation from Nabov to come to Moscow for a talk. So I went."

"I wish you hadn't."

"Nabov told me very little in actual words. But he hinted at a good deal. And most important, he showed me a motion picture supposed to have been made secretly on September 4, 1945."

Foster stiffened. "What kind of motion picture?"

"A meeting between Truman and Stalin. Stalin wanted his cut of the Far East, and particularly he wanted a couple of atom bombs. Truman said he could go whistle for the Far East, and as for the bomb, it didn't even work."

"He couldn't have!"

"I saw and heard it, Howard. Stalin said he didn't believe him, threatened to move troops into Japan. Truman changed his tune and threatened to A-bomb Moscow if the Russians set foot in Tokyo."

"What else?"

"That was it. But tied in with everything else I've dug up, it makes you wonder, doesn't it?"

"Apparently it sets *you* to dreaming," said Foster. "Just to take one thing, Truman was nowhere near Lisbon in 1945."

I took a moment to light my pipe before saying, "That's very interesting, Mr. President, because all I said was that a film had been made secretly. I didn't say where."

"I'm sure you did."

"Play back your tapes."

He stared at me, and I went on. "I assume you're taping this conversation. Play it back and see if I mentioned Lisbon."

He stood up and threw his napkin to his plate, still half filled with scrambled eggs and sausages. "McGavin," he said, "you've already tested my patience to the limit. When are you going to stop?"

"I'll stop when I *can* stop," I said. Then, "Jesus, Howard, sit down before you have a stroke. Why won't you level with me so we can stop shooting at each other?"

"I am the President," he said stiffly. "My authority and responsibility cannot be shared."

"Howard, I know all about your responsibility and your authority, and I'm not trying to usurp either of them." I looked at him until he relaxed a little and sat down again. "But how can you just look the other way when I came in here with the kind of information I've presented this morning and pretend it doesn't exist and I don't either?"

Subdued, he said, "Hugh, I just can't talk about it."

My pipe was out again. I tapped the ashes into a tray bearing the Great Seal. "All right, Howard. I don't know what's up, and obviously you aren't going to tell me. But believe me, I'm not out to create mischief. I am very much concerned with finding the truth, and even more concerned with the welfare of this country and of the world. Does that sound corny?"

He shook his head. "That sounds like Hugh McGavin," he said. "I wouldn't expect anything else from you. And *that*," he snapped out, his composure regained, "is a compliment."

"Noted and accepted," I said, and shook his hand. "By the way, Howard, can you do something with the Justice Department about Jack Sherwood? He was only acting for me."

"He stole secret documents."

"So does every junior congressman who takes work home for the weekend. Come on, Howard. He's no more a spy than your daughter."

He sighed. "I'll see what I can do. But you'll have to fire him."

"Agreed. I can get him a job in New York at twice the dough anyway." I tucked my pipe away. "Oh, and that girl who helped him. What's the point in nailing her to the cross? Let's keep this in the family."

Foster frowned. "All right," he said. "I'll call Marty Kuhn. There won't be any official retraction, mind you. It'll just fade away. And she'll have to get the hell out of government."

"I'll take care of her up in New York," I said. "Thanks, Howard."

The sun was already high when I left the White House. But somewhere, over the top of the world, it was night and missile silos purred in readiness—aimed at this absurd city on the Potomac where truth and falsehood share the same security designation and no one, not even the Right Honorable Hugh McGavin, can tell one from the other.

Washington, D.C.—*August 13, Now*

We had a secluded table, Jack Sherwood, Celia, and I, in the rear of the Diplomat's second-floor dining room. Jack arrived early, fidgety and anxious, and before he could speak, I laid down the law. "Not one damned word of business for the next two hours." He looked surprised, but shrugged and started working on a double gimlet. I stayed with scotch.

When Celia came in with a large manila folder, I gave her the no-business routine too. She hugged me and sat down in a fluid, graceful motion that drew the admiring attention of nearby tables.

We ate as if food were going to be outlawed at midnight. The table sprawled with stuffed clams, with jumbo shrimps and great wedges of iceberg lettuce buried under avalanches of roquefort dressing. The steaks were thick and rare, and the baked potatoes split to hold sour cream and chives and crumbled bits of bacon. I passed up the potatoes, and rewarded myself by ordering a second bottle of burgundy, slightly chilled. The wine steward gave me a look that said "barbarian," but he did as I said. When the dessert cart came around, Jack and

I attacked the cheese while Celia made a valiant assault on a towering strawberry-and-cream concoction.

With the coffee and brandy before us, with the mahogany humidor displayed for our choice of cigars, I restrained a most undignified belch and said, "All right, we've had our fun. Let's get back to work."

I lit Jack's Corona. "Foster's going to take off the heat," I told him. "But I have to fire you. No problem, I know that Methods Inc. in New York is dying to get you, and they'll double the money."

Jack seemed barely interested. "I hope his amnesty is all-inclusive," he said, "because I've been up to my old tricks."

"What have you got?"

"First," he said, "Truman was never so visible in his life as he was that first week in September, 1945. The little guy was everywhere, signing bills, jogging up and down Pennsylvania Avenue, speaking to the DAR."

"So he wasn't out of the country."

"I didn't say that. There've been rumors for years that Truman had a double. If so, the double could have put on the show here while good old Harry shot over to Lisbon on a certain B-29 which just happened to be making a flight to Portugal that week. The flight was top secret, but a guy I know who was working as an operations clerk remembers it because it was so unusual for B-29s to be heading for Europe."

"Do you buy the double theory?"

"Let me pass on that one for now. Anyway, boss, I started checking anything else unusual that happened around that time."

"Such as?"

"Such as, with the war over, why did the Los Angeles draft board raid the studios of over fifty men who had been exempt because making films was considered morale-building war work?"

"What kind of men?"

"Cameramen and special effects technicians. I got my lead from a complaint the union filed with the IATSE's lobby here, and traced it through. They hit everybody—MGM, Warner's, and Fox were screaming like wounded Indians. But it didn't do any good. Those guys vanished into the service. And here's the interesting part—up to now, not one of them has ever reappeared on the union rolls."

"Why not?"

"Most of them went to work for government agencies after they were mustered out. By now, only a couple of dozen are still alive—and they're either in retirement or working for outfits like the Space Center and the National Geodetic Society."

"Interesting," I said.

"Isn't it?" said Jack. He inhaled his cigar, choked. "Next, again in September, 1945, almost a third of the young Turks at Oak Ridge and Alamogordo pulled a vanishing act too. Most of them have since turned up holding down cushy jobs in one government project or another. I checked this one further, and it seems to be a pattern through the years. At any given time, you can't put your finger on a couple of hundred bright scientists who ought to be highly visible. Something out there in the hills is using up a lot of talent. I figure it might be Project JF."

"There's that name again," said Celia.

"Sorry," I said.

"In that case," she told me, "maybe I ought to take *my* little find and go home. You don't deserve me."

"Give me one more minute," said Jack Sherwood. "I didn't believe this one at first, so I checked it out again with the universities themselves, and it held up."

"What universities?"

"Six in this country," he said. "One in Canada, two in Asia, and one in Australia. The names don't matter, but what does is that they were all well advanced in seismology."

"Earthquakes?"

"Right. I got onto it because there were a lot of per diem and travel vouchers that somebody neglected to pay—the vouchers were locked up in the Q file, but the complaint letters about them were right out in the open. I traced them back to the vouchers and found out that in August, 1945, twelve of the best seismologists in the world were flown to Hawaii for a secret conference."

He put a folder on the table. "It's all in there, boss. Enough to lock us both up for a hundred years. The names of the seismologists who are still alive, ditto for the Hollywood guys and the nuclear whiz-kids."

"Wow," I said slowly. "Methods Inc. doesn't know what they're getting."

"I just hope it helps."

"It probably will. I'm not sure what it means, but we'll get right on it."

"Not me," he said. "I'm fired. Remember?"

"Right," I said, "and you should clean out your desk right away. But if you're not busy for the next couple of weeks, you might want to take on a free-lance thing for this lovely reporter lady, Celia Craig. I'm sure she wants some of these story leads checked out."

"And you'll find me a far fairer employer than the bureaucrat you used to work for," Celia said.

"You're both nuts," Jack said, "but I like you."

Celia opened the brown envelope in her lap and took out an 11x14-inch glossy photograph. "Take a look at this."

I did. "Manhattan," I said. "Taken from about 30,000 feet."

"Right. But look closer."

I studied it. There was something strange about the aerial photograph.

"It was taken at night," I said. "There's no traffic moving."

Celia nodded. "The United States Air Corps made this photo in June of 1945 with a new flash device they had developed for aerial reconnaissance. When I was up in George Harris' office yesterday, I mentioned that you were digging around the events of 1945. He told me he might have something interesting for you—and this arrived by messenger this afternoon. There's a note with it."

I read the message typed beneath a *Life* letterhead.

Senator McGavin:

In 1945 I was in the Signal Corps, and one of the assignments we had was to improve methods of taking aerial photographs. The flash unit with which I took this night photograph of Manhattan was one such improvement. Although I was transferred off the project in July, 1945, a buddy of mine who was then a sergeant remained with it until the end of the war. I know, although it has never been made public, that this flash was used at least once in the Far East. My friend's name is Howard Parker, and he lives in Lancaster, Pennsylvania, where he runs a photo studio. I have often wondered why the story of the flash was buried, and why the unit has not been used since World War II so far as I know. Celia told me you were examining those days with a microscope, and while it may have nothing to do with what you are looking for, this particular gadget was certainly unusual. Good luck,

George Harris, Senior Editor

I handed the note to Jack. "How long would it take you to get to Lancaster, Pennsylvania?"

"Hold on there," said Celia. "Jack works for me, remember?" She turned to him. "Jack, how long would it take for you to get to—"

"Couple of hours. It'll be pretty late."

"Can't be helped," I said. "Find out what happened with this flash gadget." I looked at the photograph again. "Anything that could take a picture this clear from 30,000 feet at night would be brighter than hell."

"Brighter than the sun," Jack said.

I froze. He looked at me, at Celia.

"What did I say?" he asked.

It was after midnight when Jack Sherwood drove slowly down Main Street, looking for Howard Parker's photography shop. The wide street was empty and quiet. He passed the square, with its four statues of Civil War heroes, turned left past the Hotel Douglas, and found the Parker Photo Shop just beyond.

The small window was filled with hand-colored photographs of brides, of boys and girls in graduation gowns, of smiling children. Jack tried the door. It was locked, but in the back of the store he saw a crack of light under the door. He tapped on the glass. The rear door opened and a middle-aged man came out, squinting in the darkness. He switched on the main light and opened the door.

"We're closed."

"I know," said Jack. "I'm a friend of George Harris. Can I come in? It's important."

"George Harris from the Signal Corps? He's with *Life* magazine now."

"Yes sir."

"Come on in," said the man. "I'm Howard Parker."

They went into the back room, which smelled of photo solutions. There were a small cot and a table, and, piled around on shelves and bookcases, thousands of photographs.

"It's a mess, I know," said Parker. "I've been batching it here since my daughter got married. Somehow it seems too much trouble to go out to the farm by the time I get finished." He put on a pair of hornrimmed glasses. "So you know George? Funny, I was just talking about him the other day. We had a lot of good times together, George and me. He always was a lucky bastard. He got transferred out of the Signal Corps

272

just in time, and spent the rest of the war in New York. Me, I got sent to the Pacific."

"Where was that?"

"One of those islands. Tinian. I can't really complain. I got my Air Medal for going on a couple of missions over Japan."

He went over to a hot plate and turned it off. "I was just getting ready for some coffee," he said. "Instant, but it's that freeze-dried stuff. Not too bad. Want some?"

"Thanks. George mentioned you and he were working on some kind of magnesium flash for aerial photographs."

"The Volcano," Parker said, measuring a spoonful of coffee into each cup. "That's what we called it. The official designation was Aerial Reconnaissance Terrain Fill Light, or some such nonsense. I always wondered what happened to the Volcano. That was sure some gadget."

"George had a picture of the whole island of Manhattan taken at night from 30,000 feet," Jack said.

Howard Parker handed him a steaming cup and nodded his head. "Yeah, I remember that." He wagged his head slowly. "That was a close one. We nearly got the whole outfit court-martialed over that trick."

"Court-martialed?"

"That was the first operational test of the Volcano," said Parker. "We'd never fired up the whole device before. As it was, only one of the four tubes went off, and that's what saved our asses. If all four had fired, we'd still be in Leavenworth. You see, we didn't have authorization to try the gadget over populated areas."

"Why would you want to take flash pictures anyway?"

"Oh, maybe you might want to pull a surprise mission at night, to see if you could catch vehicles on the road, troop movements, things like that," the photographer said. "But that's not what they built the Volcano for. Look, do you know anything about aerial photography?"

"Not much."

"Well, the best time to take shots is in the early morning

or the late afternoon. That's when the sun is low and objects cast shadows. If you know what time the photo was taken, you can figure out how tall a building or a smokestack is by the shadow it casts."

"So?"

"Well, the disadvantage—especially back then, when we had to use slow films like Panatomic X, with an ASA rating of only around twelve—was that we'd get good detail in the highlight and middle-range areas, but the shadows would go absolutely clear on the negative. No detail at all. So you could see what was in the light, but there could be a thousand small antiaircraft guns in those shadows and you wouldn't know it. Follow?"

Jack nodded.

"Well, that was the idea of the Volcano. What it was, actually, was four great big rings of plastic tubing filled with magnesium. They were hinged together, so we could fold them into a bomb bay, and when they opened up outside the plane, the outer ring was around forty feet around. The one inside was a little smaller, and so on down to the smallest. We'd release them, and then set off the flash by radio signal."

"I still don't see *why*."

"Well, the idea was that once the gadget had floated down to twenty thousand feet or so, the photo plane would have turned and come back over the recon point. We had a battery of six cameras, all interconnected. We had an automatic sequence that took less than a tenth of a second to complete. First, all the cameras would take a picture of the terrain normally—I mean, with the shadows thrown by the low sun. A fraction of a second later the film would have been advanced, and as the shutter clicked again a radio signal would set off the Volcano. What we got were two different photographs— one with side lighting so we could estimate heights, the other lit from above, with the light bombing straight down into those shadow areas. By superimposing one picture over the other, we had the best of both techniques. We could still see enough shadow to make our measurements—but the flash would have acted as if the sun were directly overhead, so we had detail down in the shadow areas too. We only used it a couple of times, but it really worked."

The photographer finished his coffee and rinsed the cup. "That is," he added, "it worked except over Manhattan. Only the inner ring ignited there. Which is all that saved our asses."

"That's the second time you've said that," Jack prodded. "I saw the photo. It looked fine."

"Sure it looked fine," Parker said. "But you should have seen the negative. It was so dense I could hardly print it. So overexposed that I had to yank it out of the soup after three minutes."

"So what? Why would they court-martial you for a photo that didn't come out?"

"Look," said Parker, "we were at 30,000 feet. The Volcano went off at 25,000. Only one ring out of four, mind you. And it made a flash so bright that anyone looking straight at it without protective goggles could have been blinded for life. The army hushed the whole thing up—and we were lucky too. At that time of night it was just our dumb luck that nobody was looking up. Like I said, that one ring was bright enough to blind you. Can you imagine what four would have done? In fact, in Japan, we deliberately *tried* to blind people. What the hell, it was no worse than dropping thermite on them."

"Where was that?"

"I'm not allowed to talk about those missions. The other guy wanted to know about them too, and I told him the same thing."

"What other guy?"

"I told you I was talking about George just the other day. It was another friend of his, a Mr. Norris from San Diego. He said he met George on an assignment and they got to talking about different kinds of hardware. It's funny . . . now they can get pictures from the satellites that we used to bust our asses taking flak and fighters for. Anyway, he was a real nice man, in photography himself, he said. But I drew the line right where I did for you. I'm sorry, but that's classified information."

Jack took out his credentials. "I work for Senator Hugh McGavin. You've heard of him."

"Sure. Who hasn't? I tell you this, he's got my vote. We've got to get rid of those bombs."

"And here's a letter George Harris sent him. Now, I'm cleared for Top Secret. You can talk to me."

Parker hesitated. "I don't know."

"Would you like to call the Senator and speak directly to him? Mr. Parker, what you know could be very important to the work the Senator is doing. We need your help."

"Well," said the photographer, "if you can't talk to a senator, who can you talk to? He is the government, you might say."

"Want me to call him?"

"No," said Parker. "I believe you. And besides, I never did see what all the fuss was about. I don't know why they think it's such a top secret affair about where we first used the Volcano."

"Where was that?" asked Jack Sherwood.

Howard Parker bit at his lip, then answered:

"Hiroshima."

Tinian, Marianas Islands—*August 6, 1945*

For Sergeant Howard Parker, United States Signal Corps, then on TDY with the 20th Air Force, Tinian was one big bore. He spent his days tinkering with the flash device and his nights drinking warm beer, bought two cans at a time after standing in a line that stretched twice around the EM club.

The short circuit in the firing mechanism that had caused the Volcano to misfire over Manhattan had been traced and located, and theoretically the Aerial Reconnaissance Terrain Fill Light was in operating condition. A static test on the uninhabited end of the island burned the bark off palm trees a hundred yards away, and the flash was seen above the horizon as far away as Guam.

"Great!" said Parker. "We'll be able to shoot at f-32 and at five-thousandths of a second."

The photo recon officer, Captain Morris Meredith, said gleefully, "This baby'll melt the eyeballs right out of those Japs' heads!"

Despite constant attempts to maintain security, it was impossible to keep secrets on the small island. When *The Busted Flush* returned from its nuclear mission to Tokyo on August 4, it was only a matter of minutes before the entire base knew something had gone wrong. No one knew just what, but most of the 20th Air Force fliers enjoyed seeing the 509th stub its toe.

The same thing happened on August 5, when a second B-29, *Diamond Lil*, limped home, failure written over the faces of her crew. Later that afternoon, Parker's ship, *Candid Camera*, was scheduled for a mission the following morning.

At breakfast, served in the darkness of one A.M., *Candid Camera*'s flight engineer, Steve Bennis, asked Parker if he knew Rosy Cooper.

"Who?"

"A major in the 509th. He's flying right seat with Captain Meredith."

"Why?"

"Getting in his flight time, I guess."

Parker shrugged. "If he's nuts enough to want to fly over Japan for the lousy flight pay, that's his problem. Me, I'd opt for Air-Sea Rescue. But this one's a milk run anyway. We come over at 30,000, drop the Volcano, take our photos, and get the hell out."

"What's so special about Hiroshima?"

"Nothing. It hasn't been hit much, so I guess they figured it's a good place to burn a few eyeballs."

"I know the captain keeps saying that. Will that flash thing really blind people?"

"If it's low enough. We're going to set it off at 2,000 feet. That's low enough."

"Are all photographers as mean as you?" asked the flight engineer.

"Nope," Parker said cheerfully. "Just the ones from Pennsylvania."

Candid Camera appeared over Hiroshima at eight in the morning. Major Rosy Cooper flew co-pilot, while, happy to have a day off, the regular co-pilot put in sack time back on Tinian.

Far below, the city crawled beneath the B-29's nose.

"We'll show those yellow bastards," Captain Meredith said. Cooper said nothing.

"All set back there?" Meredith asked on the intercom.

"Everything's ready," Parker answered. "All cameras hooked into automatic."

"Drop the TFL," ordered Meredith.

The plastic rings fell away from the plane's bomb bay, slowed by a drogue chute that pulled out the main canopy. The folded rings opened, and the cumbersome apparatus floated down toward Hiroshima, 30,000 feet below.

Candid Camera continued straight and level for six minutes more, then the pilot turned the ship around and headed back over the city.

"Parker," he said, "are you ready?"

"Ready, sir."

"Why are you letting the device get so low?" asked Cooper.

"The way I see it, Major," said the pilot, "we're going to get our pictures anyway. So let's see if we can't leave these gooks something to remember us by. If they're looking up when the TFL goes off, it'll be just like looking into a flame thrower."

"Do you have authorization for this?" asked Cooper.

"Do I need authorization to injure the enemy if it doesn't interfere with my primary mission?"

278

Cooper did not answer.

"Coming up on drop point," called the navigator.

"Okay, Parker," said Meredith, "it's all yours."

"Photo sequence started," reported the navigator.

In the specially constructed bomb bay of the B-29, a series of cameras clicked automatically.

"Watch your eyes," warned Parker. "Don't look down."

A radio signal shot out from the plane. Far below, the four plastic rings filled with magnesium ignited.

To the men in the B-29, it was as if the sun had exploded beneath them.

The flash burned through the corneas of those on the ground, looking up at the distant bomber, with a bright, greenish explosion of light that was the last thing many of them would ever see again.

The intense brightness faded, and once again the city looked peaceful and quiet.

"Cameras all clear," said Parker.

"Okay," said the pilot. "Let's go home."

Parker relaxed in his position near the central fire control gunner. The mission was over. He was therefore surprised to hear Major Cooper's voice say urgently, "Wait a minute. Navigator, take a look through your drift meter. Something's happening down there."

"Yes sir," said the navigator. There was a pause, then: "Holy shit!"

"What is it?" Cooper's voice.

"I don't know, sir. Looks like the whole city's falling down."

"Radio," said Cooper, "get me Base Ops on Tinian. Fast!"

"Yes sir," said the radio operator.

"Captain," said Major Roseman Cooper, "switch off the master intercom. I don't want the crew listening in on this."

"Yes sir," said Meredith.

The earphones on Parker's head went dead. *Candid Camera* circled for a few minutes while Major Cooper transmitted a message to Tinian; then the plane straightened out and headed south at full speed. The intercom came on again and Captain

Meredith said, "This is for everybody. Not a word of what happened here today. Am I clear? Anyone who even mentions this mission gets a General Court-martial."

Parker looked up at the central fire control gunner. "Mention *what?*" he asked. "I wouldn't know what to mention if somebody asked me."

"Beats me," said the gunner. "Hey, look at that."

Parker looked.

Streaming in toward Hiroshima, a flight of B-29s blackened the sky.

Washington, D.C.—August 14, Now

General Oscar Burton stood up and started to say something. President Howard Foster raised a hand and stilled him.

"Go on, Hugh," he told me. "What else did Jack tell you?"

"That from Hiroshima on, there were always at least three planes equipped with the Volcano orbiting Japan, just outside flak range."

"I'd like to talk with him personally," the President said.

"You can't," I said. "On his way back from Lancaster, somebody forced him into a bridge abutment over the Susquehanna. He was killed instantly."

"Hugh, I'm sorry," said the President. "I didn't know."

"We'd better get this Parker fellow up here right away," said General Oscar Burton.

"Forget it," I said. "I called the local FBI office in Lancaster. By the time they got to Parker's photo shop, somebody had blown it up with half a pound of plastic explosives. They didn't find enough of him to bury."

The President spread both hands on his desk. "What do you want from me, Hugh?"

"Howard," I said, "I don't think I've got time to fool around.

280

Suddenly everybody who gets close to me winds up dead. Hepburn, in London. That bomb in Jerusalem was probably meant for me. The same goes for the machine-gunning in Hiroshima. Now Jack is dead. I can't risk carrying what I know around in my head any longer. Once it's out in the open, there won't be any reason to put me out of the way. Me—or Celia."

Foster pressed a button on his desk intercom. "Gardner? Put a detail on guard at Senator McGavin's home. Check to see that Mrs. McGavin's all right, then stay put. Nobody goes in, and if she wants to go somewhere, give her protection."

He looked at me. "Anyway, that's one worry off your mind," he said. "Hugh, I have to give you credit. You've kept at it, piece by piece, until you worked your way right into the heart of what we've been concealing all these years."

"The bomb," I said. "It doesn't work. It never did."

Instead of answering, he went to the window and looked out at the early morning sunlight. "Hugh," he said, "on the other side of the world, K'ang Na-Soong is asking himself, 'What are the Americans up to? Are they really willing to go to war over an unimportant missile installation in Japan? Are they willing to risk a nuclear exchange just to assert themselves?' And that is what K'ang *must* believe. Why do you think I authorized the ABM deployment in Japan? We absolutely *must* face China down, we must convince her that we are willing to go to war over this thing. And in so doing, we must force her to the crucial moment of decision—will she or won't she fire her bombs?"

"What if she does?"

"Then we've lost everything. What we're banking on is that she will draw back at the last moment—as, indeed, she appears to be doing this morning."

"How?"

"K'ang has sent word to North Korea that he expects them to act with restraint in case the August 16 pull-out does not occur."

"He's leaving them out there on the limb?"

"Apparently. And that tells us that, for one reason or another,

China is not willing to commit herself to a nuclear first strike."

"Mr. President," said Burton, "do you plan to tell the Senator any more? Because you're getting very close to disclosure of the entire JF Project."

"Yes," Foster said slowly. "I'm afraid we have to let the Senator into our little club." He turned to me. "Hugh, people are always talking about the loneliness of this office. Well, they don't know *how* lonely. Not just for me but for every President since 1945. Each of us has held a secret that had to be maintained for the good of the nation and the world. It began with Truman—that's why I was so upset when you told me about the film the Russians had made in Lisbon. None of us had ever considered such a possibility. But obviously, from the secrecy in which they've held it and from their own actions in recent years, the Soviets find themselves in the same uncomfortable position we're in." He smiled wryly. "That was Harry's biggest problem. He always was too damned honest."

"So what he said was true? The bomb didn't work? Not the one I dropped, not any of the others?"

"None of ours did," he said. "But how could we be sure about the Russians? Oh, by now we're convinced they've been playing the same game. But there were several years during which we had to maintain our own fictional nuclear posture to hedge against the possibility that the Soviet bomb *was* functional and would be used against us at the first sign of weakness. Then Great Britain and France entered the club and the game started all over again. No sooner were we approaching some kind of mutual accommodation with them than China got into the act. And now there's Israel."

"We know that Israel's bomb doesn't work," I said.

"No," he said. "We know that Bernardi wants you to *think* Israel's bomb doesn't work. But maybe it does. Maybe his scientists have figured out a way to overcome the Jesus Factor." He hit his fist on his thigh slowly, methodically. "There's no end to the damned thing," he said. "I've just about concluded that China's bluffing, that their bomb doesn't work any better than ours. So what happens? Now we have to figure Israel out.

Do you see what I mean, Hugh? I play one continuous game of paper-scissors-rock."

"What?"

"It's a kid's game, you must have played it. You put your hands behind your back, and on a count of three throw one out in front. A fist is a rock. It breaks two fingers, which are scissors. Scissors cut paper, a hand held out flat. But paper covers rock, a fist, and the whole damned thing starts over again."

"I understand, Mr. President. But you can't say we haven't offered you help. You didn't have to carry it all alone."

"I think I did," he answered. "Truman thought so, when he started Project Jesus Factor back in 1945. Eisenhower didn't know a thing about it until the day he was inaugurated. And he chose to carry the knowledge alone too. That's the way it's always been."

"What if something happens to you?"

"There's precedent," Foster said. "When Kennedy was killed in Dallas, Johnson learned about the project minutes before he took the oath of office in Air Force One. Oscar, will you ask the bag man to come in?"

General Burton left the room.

"How much do you know about atomic theory, Hugh?" asked the President.

"A lot more than I did a few weeks ago."

"Well, that's where it all went wrong. With theory. We tested the first device on a tower in New Mexico, it blew right on schedule, and we thought we had it knocked. But then you dropped one over Tokyo, and instead of exploding it just turned white-hot and melted down.

"Hugh, we've had to keep the project secret even from the AEC. There are fewer than ten men in this country who know the truth. Even the scientists on the project do their work in little isolated pieces. It's the Manhattan Project all over again."

"So that's where all those scientists have been disappearing to?"

He nodded. "We keep them tied up for three or four years

283

and then give them a profitable research project somewhere."

Burton reentered. With him was an army warrant officer.

"May I have the bag?" asked the President.

The officer handed him a black attaché case. Foster took a key from his pocket, unlocked the case, and opened it.

"You will note," he told the warrant officer, "that I am removing Official Document 14-B, addressed to and to be delivered to the Vice-President in case of my death or incapacitation."

"Yes sir," said the warrant officer.

"Thank you," said Foster. The warrant officer turned smartly and left. Foster handed me the envelope.

"Go ahead," he said. "This will explain everything. When you're finished, I want you to talk with Rosy Cooper again."

"Cooper? I thought he was on Guam."

"I had him brought home when I heard about your trip to Moscow. He was going back to his command tonight, but I think I'll have him stay around for a while. There's a lot about this that he can tell you."

The two men left. I sat down in the President's chair, behind the oak desk made from the timbers of the *Constitution*. It felt like any other chair behind any other desk.

The envelope was sealed with a blue strip of ribbon and red wax. I slipped a paper knife under the seal and lifted it. Inside were several sheets of heavy bond paper. I glanced through them. Most were names and addresses. The first sheets, however, were in the form of a letter.

Dear Arthur,

If you are reading this, I am either dead or incapacitated to the point where you must assume my Presidential duties.

Enclosed are the names of the only other men and women in this country who know the truth about a secret we have held since 1945: the secret of our apparent nuclear posture.

Arthur, this nation does not possess a workable

atomic bomb. We have *never* possessed one. Our entire defense system is based on this lie—that we have a huge supply of workable atomic warheads. We have expended billions of dollars to maintain our illusion —all the while working desperately to solve the problem that prevents our nuclear devices from working as bombs.

If this seems confusing, I do not blame you. The scientists are working to overcome what they refer to as the J Factor, or Jesus Factor. This effect prevents a nuclear device from detonating *when it is in motion.* Devices mounted on towers or anchored anywhere on land, above or below the surface of the earth, explode as planned. But the same device, in motion, will not go into chain reaction. Instead of exploding, it melts down into white-hot slag. The prevalent theory is that changing magnetic and gravitational forces exert an effect on a moving object that somehow alters the course of the high-speed neutrons that would ordinarily bombard uranium or plutonium, and prevents them from splitting the atom.

In 1945, when the existence of this Jesus Factor was learned, President Truman established a secret project named after the effect. In the intervening years, each President has overseen this project personally, as our scientists attempted to produce a workable bomb. At this writing, our efforts have been unsuccessful.

Our course is hampered by the constant danger that one or more of the other so-called nuclear powers have either bypassed the Jesus Factor, or have managed to solve it. However, I feel certain that the Soviet Union's bombs are unworkable, as are those of Great Britain and France. The Soviet Premier and I have had certain oblique conversations which may lead, in the near future, to our testing the resolve of the Red Chinese in a maneuver to learn, once and for all, whether *their* bombs are operational.

Meanwhile, although the cost is huge, our delivery systems and such defensive plans as the Safeguard ABMs must continue just as if we, and our enemies, did indeed possess workable atomic warheads. For if our estimate of any potential enemy proves wrong and we reveal our own nuclear weakness, the response might well be instant and total annihilation.

My personal belief is that even if the Jesus Factor is never overcome, the secret of our nonexistent nuclear arsenal must be maintained. That has been the opinion of every President since Truman. Naturally, you must make your own decision. But as I see it, the threat of nuclear destruction has functioned as a deterrent against major wars thus far, and if we have been able to avoid a world conflict because of the imagined existence of atomic weapons, their cost has been well spent.

At a time that must be very trying for you, I am sorry to burden you even further. But I have every confidence that you will meet the challenge and exert every effort to maintain peace and security for our nation.

With all best regards, your friend—

HOWARD FOSTER

The World—*August 14, Now*

President Howard Foster's televised press conference that morning in Washington was beamed, via satellite, to every major city in the world.

"After consultation with the government of Japan," he announced, "the United States of America has decided to accede to the wishes of the world community and remove the defensive Safeguard Missiles from the Japanese island of Honshu. As we have stated repeatedly, these missiles, intended for defensive purposes, were placed on Honshu to protect major Japanese cities against offensive attack.

"However, Premier Ito has informed me that it is the opinion of his government that this protection is no longer required. I have therefore ordered that the missile sites be dismantled and the missiles themselves removed from Japanese soil.

"Premier Ito also informs me that United Nations observer teams are invited to inspect the former missile sites, to ascertain that the dismantlement is proceeding as I have stated.

"It is my personal opinion that this incident has only heightened the vital necessity for world leaders to find some effective way of communicating with each other before misunderstandings and miscalculations lead to another, more serious world crisis.

"It is easy for the strong to threaten; it is less easy for the strong to show forebearance. I am sure no member of this audience believes that today's gesture toward world peace was forced by the threats of the People's Republic of North Korea. It is the responsibility of the powerful nations to overlook provocative statements and actions from those less powerful, since—because they have less to lose—such nations are able to gamble more.

"Finally, let me assure our friends everywhere that this withdrawal of defensive missiles from Japan does not in any way weaken the resolve of this nation to defend the peace on whatever field it is threatened. The Safeguard missiles were placed in Japan on request from the Japanese government. They are being withdrawn for the same reason.

"I thank you."

In London Prime Minister John Phillip Hawkins turned to his wife and said, "I suspect Hugh McGavin's fine hand behind the scenes somewhere, Ida."

"Does this mean things will be calm for a while?" asked his wife.

"Let's hope so. But of course, now that the Jews have a bomb, the Arabs will be demanding one next. And the Chinese might be happy to oblige."

"Wouldn't it be nice . . ." his wife began, then stopped.

"What?"

"Nice if something you once said were true. Something about, it would be funny if we all got mad enough to press the buttons—and when we did, nothing happened."

"A beautiful thought," he said. "But a bit Alice in Wonderland, don't you know?"

In Tel Aviv Prime Minister Levi Bernardi watched the television set with pleasure.

"Sanity!" he said explosively. "Sarah, this weary old planet may make a few more turns after all!"

"Arab!" she said. "Your Senator friend delivered the message just as you planned."

"Oh?"

"You," she said. "I know you, Levi. You are as smug as a Bedouin rug merchant. You feel you have achieved a coup."

"Perhaps I have," he said. "At a cost of some two billion pounds, I may have purchased freedom from the mushroom-shaped cloud."

In Moscow Premier Mikhail Nabov sat quietly sipping a vodka. Near his right hand was a telephone.

"My little voice is stilled," he said to the young ballerina who leaned against his knee. "There will be no war."

She did not answer. In the four months during which she had shared occasional moments with him in this private apartment, she had learned when to speak and when to listen.

He picked up the telephone. "General Beloussov? Yes. Yes, I know. Give the order to discontinue the countdown."

In Peking Chairman K'ang Na-Soong watched the lazy goldfish sliding silently through the green water of the small pool.

The wind has ceased, he thought, and the kite floats earthward.

288

The young boys, who watch, will be angry.

This was not the time for our kite to reach for the clouds. The string was too weak and would have broken. But there is time, K'ang thought. For us, there is always time to wait.

In a motel room near Hagerstown, Maryland, a stocky man who had registered as Harry Norris of San Diego returned an authoritative knock on the door with a series of revolver shots. Tear gas canisters were thrown through the window, and in a moment a muffled shot was heard inside. When FBI agents entered cautiously they found the man dead, a still-hot pistol clutched in one hand. Later it was learned that he was an unsuccessful racketeer from San Francisco, being blackmailed by Chinese communist agents. A small amount of plastic explosive was found in his luggage, and the crumpled right-front fender of his green Cadillac bore traces of paint that matched a damaged area on Jack Sherwood's Volvo. After further investigation, the murders of Howard Parker and Jack Sherwood were marked CLOSED.

In the penthouse suite of the Hotel Brigham Young in Salt Lake City four men argued heatedly.

"He can take it on the first ballot," said one. "But he's got to get out here and make some show of being available."

"You're drunk," said another. "If Foster comes forward for Arthur Rand, that's all she wrote for Hugh McGavin."

"Don't be too sure," said a third. "A lot of delegates think Foster went too far with this Japanese missile thing. And he's a lame duck. They won't be as scared of him as they would if he had another term to serve."

"Listen," said the first man, "we're just wasting time, second-guessing. I don't know what will happen if the President names Rand, and neither does anybody else. But I *do* know what'll happen if our boy doesn't get his tail out here and make some gesture toward the delegates. This aloof, don't-give-a-damn routine went out with Adlai Stevenson. Now, we know California is going to pass to Ohio on the nominations, and they'll pass their vote, too. If McGavin moderates his stand just enough to convince the industrial states that they aren't going to lose all their military contracts, he might just make it. But we've got to get him out here."

The fourth man, who had not spoken until now, picked up a telephone.

"Operator," he said, "I want to speak with Senator Hugh McGavin in Washington, D.C. Yes, I'll wait."

He bit off the end of a cigar and spat the tobacco onto the rug. "Did any of you smoothies think of *asking* him to come out?"

"He knows he's needed here," said the first man.

"Have you told him that in so many words?"

"No, but—"

"Goddamn amateur politicians," growled the fourth man. "Lesson number one—never take anything for granted. The hell with subtlety. The direct approach, that's what people understand."

He straightened. "Hello? Howdy, ma'am. Is this Mrs. Mc-Gavin? . . . Good morning, how's the weather? . . . Well, this is Henry King, out in Salt Lake City, and it's hotter'n Hades here too. Is the Senator there? . . . No . . . no, I reckon I better not disturb him there. I tell you what, ma'am, suppose I leave a message for him? . . . What? No, no, I don't mind if you record it." Covering the mouthpiece with his hand, he mumbled, "Crazy female, she says she's going to tape-record me." Then, back into the phone, "Yes'm, I'm ready. . . . Sure, I'll talk straight to him. Now?"

He cleared his throat. "Senator, this here is Henry King, out in Salt Lake City. Some of the boys and me were sittin' down this morning, and . . ."

"It's nice to take off the mask," said General Oscar Burton.

"What's that?" I asked.

"My public image, the saber-rattling, victory-at-all-costs, take-the-high-ground *military* posture. Part of that posture over the years has been to pretend it's only the determined and constant supervision by civilian authorities that keeps the military from plunging the nation into nuclear war. Every time a guy like you calls for de-escalation, I'm supposed to stand up and yell, 'More bombs! More missiles!' It gets to be a pain after a while. You can't—"

The President interrupted him. "Hugh," he said, "there's no doubt in my mind that it was the Chinese who perpetrated the attacks on you. We'll stay on guard a little longer, although now that K'ang's backed down, the danger is gone."

"Jack Sherwood will be glad to know that," I said. Foster started to speak, and I cut him off. "I hope you're not going to give me the bit about expecting casualties. That poor girl in Jerusalem didn't even know she was in a war."

"We were slow to react," admitted the President. "Look, where do we go now? I've given you what you said you wanted, the truth. What are you going to do with it? I hope you've abandoned any idea of presenting your suspicions to the Senate. Now that you know what we've done and why we did it, the need for secrecy must be obvious to you."

"I'm not being evasive, Howard," I said, "but I haven't made up my mind yet."

"All right," he said. "I've asked General Cooper to get in touch with you to brief you even further. You see I'm being completely open with you. But, Hugh, don't make any statements without speaking to me first."

"That's fair," I said. "Where's Rosy now?"

"Driving in from Dulles International. We caught him at the loading ramp. He's mad as a hornet."

"Look," I said, "Celia's upset over Jack. Why don't you ask the General to come out to my place?"

"I'll do that," said the President.

"After you've finished with the General," said Oscar Burton, "you and I might talk for a while. I'd like to show you some of the weapons we *do* have, in case you're beginning to think this nation is defenseless."

"Okay," I said. And, to Foster, "Thanks."

"You had a call from a man in Salt Lake City," said Celia. "A Henry King. He sounded like Chill Wills."

"He's pretty high up in the National Committee. What did he say?"

"I recorded it. Come on inside and I'll play it back."

I sat on the couch and stuffed my pipe while she warmed up the tape recorder. She pushed the PLAY button:

"Senator, this here is Henry King out in Salt Lake City. Some of the boys and me were sittin' down this morning, and we came to the decision that the success of your bid for this nomination is out of our hands now. To put it right on the table, you got a good shot at it if you do two things. First, come on out here and let the delegates see you're available and interested. Second, those industrial states need some kind of assurance that you wouldn't pull the plug on all their military contracts if you got in the White House."

There was a pause, and muffled voices as if King were speaking to others in the room, then he went on: "Now I can't make this too plain, Senator. If you come out here in the next couple of days—and if you make some conciliatory statement to reassure the industrial boys, I think you've got a real good chance to be this party's candidate in November." He paused again, said, "Thank you very much, Mrs. McGavin. I reckon that's all."

"I'll be sure the Senator listens to it," said my wife's voice. She pushed the STOP button, and then the doorbell rang.

"There's your friend from Guam," she said.

I got up.

"I suppose I'm out of *this* conversation, too," she said.

"I'm afraid so."

I opened the door and let Rosy Cooper in. He was in full uniform, the fruit salad almost covering his left breast pocket.

He took off his service cap. "Well," he said, "here I am. The meanest man in town."

"Come in, General," said Celia.

"I want to apologize first for Guam," he said. "I was acting under direct orders."

"I think I've heard that excuse before," said Celia. "I'll leave you two alone. Have fun." She left without a backward look.

"You've got an angry wife there," said Rosy Cooper. "Maybe I'd better come back later."

"No, just sit down," I said. "Celia gets protective when she thinks anybody's got the knives out for me."

We sat in the living room. Although the August sun was heating up the outdoors, the central air conditioning was doing its job.

"Coffee or anything?" I asked.

"No," he said. Let's get right to it, Mac. The President told me to give you the straight poop. Frankly, I'm glad. You don't know the strain involved in living a perpetual lie."

"I'm beginning to find out," I said. "Okay, Rosy, tell it any way you want to."

"It all started," he began, "when we got Tex Ritter's message about the failure of your Tokyo mission."

"Something's gone wrong," said the C.O.

Rosy Cooper looked at the radio message.

"Little Boy didn't work?" he asked incredulously.

'That's what Ritter says."

"Why?"

"Maybe they armed it wrong. Even though Rogers practiced on the ground, it's different up there. Maybe a component malfunctioned. Or . . ."

"Sabotage?"

"It's happened before."

Cooper shook his head, still stunned. "What became of the bomb?" he asked. "Was it destroyed?"

"We don't know. If it wasn't the Japanese have it now."

"My God," said Cooper. "We'd better get on the horn with Washington."

"I've already got a scrambled circuit set up," said the C.O. "The question is, do we risk another bomb tomorrow without knowing what went wrong with the first one?"

"We can schedule a mission," said Rosy Cooper. "We can even send the plane off on it. If we discover what went wrong before they reach the target, we can make adjustments."

"All right," said the C.O. "I'll talk with General Groves and Doctor Oppenheimer. Maybe there's something they can do back in the States. You take charge of debriefing the crew. Who worked on the fusing?"

"Captain Rogers, the weaponeer. His assistant, Lieutenant Randolph. And Lieutenant McGavin, the bombardier."

"McGavin?" the C.O. sighed. "He's so young. I don't understand these kids. Is it possible that he had some kind of moral qualm about using the bomb? Could he have caused it to malfunction?"

"I doubt it," said Cooper. "We had Kobe set up for Little Boy Number Two. Shall I go ahead with the mission?"

"Yes," said the C.O. "We've got that Little Boy, and two plutonium Fat Men. But that's it, for the rest of the month. Groves has already told me he can't provide any more fissionable material until September."

"We'll find out what the trouble is," Cooper said confidently.

But, of course, he was wrong. The crew of *The Busted Flush* was interrogated unmercifully without result.

"It was a Christmas tree," Captain Rogers insisted. "All green. Every circuit was operating when we dropped."

"But it malfunctioned," the interrogator repeated wearily.

"I can't help it. We did our job."

"Is there any chance Lieutenant McGavin tampered with the circuits?"

"Why would he do that?"

"I don't know. Answer the question."

"He couldn't have. He never touched the circuits. I only wanted him to observe the arming procedure in case there was a malfunction and something had happened to me."

"But there *was* a malfunction."

"Not while the bomb was in the bay. It must have happened after the release."

"Did Lieutenant McGavin ever make any comment that indicated he was opposed to the use of the bomb over populated centers?"

"Not that I know of. Even if he had, there wasn't any way he could have affected the bomb's functions."

"Could he have disrupted its power supply?"

"No. Once we buttoned up the bay, the bomb was on batteries, completely self-contained."

"Perhaps he deliberately chose the wrong aim point."

"Forgive me, Major, but have you ever dropped a bomb?"

"A few."

"Then you know that even if you release at the wrong aim point, the bomb still explodes. It hits the wrong target, that's all."

"All right, Captain," said the interrogator, "let's start over again."

In Washington, President Harry S Truman listened quietly as each of his advisors spoke.

"It will be at least a week before we can assemble another test at Alamogordo," said General Leslie Groves.

"Why so long?" asked the President.

"We simply don't have the plutonium," said the General. "By cannibalizing small supplies we've been using for other tests, we should be able to get enough, but it has to be shaped into lenses for the implosion—"

"Hold on, hold on," said the President. "I'll leave the technical jargon to the scientists. All I want to know is when you can test."

"August 10," said the General. "Maybe the day before, with luck."

Truman turned to the Secretary of War.

"What about that, Henry?"

"No," said Stimson, shaking his head. "Mr. President, we're coming into the rainy season. Before we know it, winter will be here, and that'll mean another five months of an expensive holding action. If we're going on those beaches, we *must* do it in September. If this atomic bomb isn't going to work, we have to know immediately."

Truman said to Groves, "I understand you have three more bombs ready to use."

"Yes sir."

"Then you'll have to make your test with one of them." The President leaned forward. "What's your next scheduled target?"

"Kobe," said Groves. "Of course, we could go back to Tokyo."

"No," said Truman. "If the first bomb fell into their hands they'll be waiting for you. Make it Kobe. Meanwhile, go ahead and plan for your own controlled test next week. Is that acceptable to everybody?"

There was a mumbled chorus of assent.

"All right, gentlemen," said Truman, "that's it for today."

Diamond Lil had taken off for Japan. The humid, mosquito-swarmed night of Tinian sweltered the interrogators and crewmen.

Two months of commanding B-29s in the Pacific had convinced High Command that daylight bombing, as pioneered in Europe, was not going to succeed against Japan. Bombers en route to Japan were buffeted by jet streams that reached two hundred miles an hour. During the first sixty days of the year there were only three opportunities to bomb visually. On every other day heavy clouds covered the Japanese mainland. Bombs directed by radar from 30,000 feet were tumbled by the wind.

The bombers themselves began to break down from the constant strain of flying in the rarefied air of the lower stratosphere. Each day dozens of B-29s aborted their missions, unable to reach the target.

Frustrated by their inability to hurt the enemy, the 20th Air Force threw the book away. Choosing a target area in urban Tokyo, designated Meetinghouse, they decided on a desperate gamble.

All guns were stripped from three hundred B-29s. They were loaded to overflowing with fire bombs. Instead of an altitude of 30,000 feet, their flight plan specified 5,000 to 10,000 feet.

At that time Tokyo was defended by approximately 650 heavy-caliber antiaircraft guns and more than five hundred interceptor planes. The thought of attacking the heavy defended city without guns terrified the bomber crews. But the weaknesses of the Japanese defenses would be used to protect the fliers.

Instead of the usual daylight attack, it was decided to hit Tokyo at night. The Japanese aircraft industry had not been able to produce an effective night fighter, and the 20th did not fear the conventional aircraft protecting the city. As for the antiaircraft guns, they had not been converted to radar control, and this low-level attack promised to confuse the crews attempting to operate the guns manually.

On March 9, 1945, three bomber wings—the 73rd, the 313th and the 314th—left Tinian at twilight. 325 B-29s lifted heavily into the humid air and flew toward Japan, rising slowly to their assigned altitude.

Twelve bombers of each group were pathfinders. As they made landfall by radar, the local Japanese time was nearly midnight. Over Tokyo, the pathfinders dropped a series of E-46 bombs, which burst at 2,000 feet, scattering hundreds of two-foot canisters down onto the city. The pattern was planned to sow a huge, fiery X across the target.

The following planes salvoed their bombs into the marked area. While the fire raged below, tornado-like thermals rose from the holocaust, tumbling the big bombers like scraps of paper in a windstorm. Thousands of M-69 and M-47 fire bombs rained from the attackers.

As the fire storm built, air was sucked from the lungs of the terrified victims. In one theater, bodies were stacked nine feet high. Those who stood in the Stumida River to escape from the flames choked and died as the conflagration consumed all the oxygen in the air, suffocating them.

It took almost three hours to destroy the Meetinghouse target. In the last flight of bombers, tossed violently by the turbulence over the blaze, crewmen vomited at the ghastly smell of burning flesh.

The single attack flattened sixteen square miles of Tokyo. More than 125,000 died between midnight and dawn. A quarter of a million buildings ceased to exist, scorched and melted by heat that reached 2,000 degrees.

The answer to effective use of the B-29 had been found. In the following months, the *B-san's* revisited Tokyo three times, and the Japanese people knew the terror of helplessness.

When he was informed of the atomic bomb Douglas Mac-Arthur shrugged and made plans to use it. If one plane could do the work of three hundred, it was all the same.

But now it looked as if the promise of the atomic bomb was false.

Calmly, the 20th reviewed their resources. If Japan could not be collapsed rapidly by a super-weapon, it would be toppled slowly by fire bombs.

Hiroshima—August 6, 1945

After the failure of *Diamond Lil*'s mission against Kobe, Major Rosy Cooper got drunk at the officers' club and, looking for something to do, signed himself aboard a photo-recon plane, *Candid Camera,* as co-pilot. Had he known of it, the C.O. would have stopped Cooper, but by the time anyone learned of his executive officer's action, the B-29 was airborne.

Suffering from a throbbing hangover, Cooper sat glumly in the right seat of the bomber and listened to Captain Morris Meredith's nonstop ravings against the Japanese. Meredith, Cooper gathered, was resentful that he was flying noncombatant missions.

"I put in a full tour in the ETO," said Meredith. "We showed those Nazi bastards no mercy, I tell you."

The beat of the engines echoed through Cooper's bourbon-soaked headache. He tried not to listen to the pilot.

At eight A.M. they were over the recon area.

"We're carrying a new kind of flash," Meredith said. "Four plastic rings filled with magnesium. They call it a TFL."

"A what?"

"Terrain Fill Light. We'll show those yellow bastards."

"With a flash? Good luck, Captain."

Candid Camera made its run over the drowsy city below.

"Drop the TFL," ordered Meredith.

Cooper, who had not attended the briefing, mumbled, "What's that city down there?"

"Hiroshima."

In a few moments, a voice on the intercom warned, "Watch your eyes!"

The magnesium-filled rings ignited. The sky lit up with a greenish explosion of light.

"Okay," said Meredith, "let's go home."

As the B-29 turned south, Cooper saw, to his amazement, hundreds of small fires breaking out within the city.

"Wait a minute," he said. "Navigator, take a look through your drift meter. Something's happening down there."

"Yes sir." A pause, then: "Holy shit!"

"What is it?"

"It looks like the whole city's falling down."

Cooper hurried back to the navigator's compartment and pressed his eye to the telescope-like drift meter projecting down through the bottom of the bomber. He turned a knob and increased the magnification.

Below him he saw buildings sprawled in the streets like a child's casually thrown blocks.

"Earthquake," he said.

"What was that?" asked the navigator.

"Give me your intercom," Cooper demanded. Startled, the navigator stripped off his headset and microphone, handed them to the executive officer.

"Radio Operator," said Cooper, "get me Base Ops on Tinian. Fast."

While he waited for the connection, he added, "Captain Meredith, switch off the master intercom. I don't want the crew listening in on this." To the navigator: "Lieutenant, this is confidential. How about waiting in the tube?"

"Yes sir," said the puzzled flier. He crawled back into the padded tube connecting the fore and aft sections of the bomber.

"Base Ops, this is Major Cooper aboard *Candid Camera*. Do you read me? Over."

"Base Ops replying, we read you five by five. Why are you broadcasting in the clear?"

"Top priority," said Cooper. "Get me Top Hat."

"Sir, he's not on the base."

Another voice came on the circuit. "*Candid Camera*, this is Top Hat. What the hell do you think you're doing?"

"Emergency, sir. Where are you?"

"Airborne on a check ride. Dammit, man, use code."

"I don't know any code," Cooper said desperately. "Listen, I'm over our recon target—"

Base Ops cut in, frantically. "Code name for that target is Delta, Top Hat."

"Thanks," Cooper said.

"Delta," said Top Hat. "All right. I know where you are, *Candid Camera*. What's happening?"

"Top Hat," said Cooper, picking his words carefully, "if you'd send your firemen over here we might be able to make this place look like Trinity. Do you read me?"

"Trinity's struck out twice," said Top Hat calmly.

"If we played a Meetinghouse here," Cooper pleaded, "the out-of-town team might think we'd delivered a Little Boy after all."

There was a pause, filled with static. The voice, when it came back on, was expressionless.

"Commander, Sunflower, do you read me? Have you been listening?"

A third voice, louder, said, "Top Hat, this is Sunflower. I read you loud and clear. Yes, I've been listening."

"Can you divert to Delta? Over."

A pause. "Yes sir."

"Scrub Laramie. Concentrate on Delta. Over."

"Roger, Top Hat. Sunflower over and out."

"*Candid Camera?* Get that?"

"Yes sir. Thank you, sir."

"Don't thank me, Major. Just be *right*. Top Hat out."

The reconnaissance plane circled the burning city until a gunner's voice said, "Hey, look at that!"

Rosy Cooper looked out the right window of the B-29.

The sky was full of planes.

"All the way back to Tinian," Rosy Cooper told me, "I kept the radio hot. Pretty soon we had a five-way command conference call going on. There was always a chance the Japs were monitoring us, but we kept switching channels and using code and doubletalk. History indicates we got away with it."

Still stunned from what I had heard, I repeated, "An earthquake? That's what wiped out Hiroshima?"

"An earthquake started it," he said. "A hundred B-29s loaded with fire bombs finished it. Our experience with fire storms in Tokyo led us to hope that we might be able to convince the Japs that we'd hit them with an atomic bomb provided we played it strong."

"Why didn't anyone report so many B-29s?"

"They did. It all depends on which report you read. We suppressed those that specifically mentioned the bombers. Most of the survivors were terribly confused, of course. Some reported bombers, some claimed to have seen parachutes. The only thing consistent in their stories was that there had been a tremendous flash of light, and then buildings began to fall down. Thousands of fires were started at that instant. The fire bombs merely helped them along."

"But I was told the seismograph tracings didn't indicate an earthquake."

"Once our guys got through doctoring them, they didn't."

"And the movies?"

"Special effects. We raided every trick photographer in Hollywood. They should have won a dozen Oscars. No one will ever know how good their work was."

I shook my head. It was so simple.

"There was one more thing we had to do," Cooper said. "And that's what all the conversation over the radio was about."

"What?"

"We instructed the scientists to remove the plutonium from the two Fat Men bombs, put it through a primitive breeder reactor, then take the radioactive waste and grind it up into tiny particles."

"Which," I put in, "you 'dispersed' over Hiroshima."

He nodded. "Its dispersal wasn't uniform, of course, so some areas got an extra-heavy dose while others received none at all. This was the part the scientists were against. They argued that the city was already destroyed, why did we have to poison the survivors? I still have nightmares myself about that decision. But we had to do it. It was our only chance to convince the Japs we really had hit them with an atomic bomb."

"What about Nagasaki?"

"Dr. Oppenheimer, back in New Mexico, suggested that there might be an aftershock to the quake. By the night of August 7, a gang of seismologists had been gathered together in Hawaii. They shacked up in the Royal Hawaiian Hotel and began analyzing the facts."

Honolulu—*August 7, 1945*

"The fault line definitely runs along this curve," said Professor Allan Brewster of the University of Melbourne. "It was this same fault that caused the Tokyo quake of 1923. The pressure has undoubtedly been building since that time."

"What are the chances of an aftershock? A serious one?" asked Major Rosy Cooper, who had flown back to Hawaii that day.

"Who knows? My personal opinion is that the pressure was not completely released yesterday. If there *is* another shock, it should be in a matter of days. Hours, perhaps."

The room filled with the voices of men arguing. Some of the scientists admitted candidly that seismology was anything but an exact science, that trying to predict whether or not there would be another earthquake in Japan was like throwing dice. And as for foretelling its location . . . !

Others were more optimistic. Assuming the pressure along the fault still existed, there was a better-than-even chance that a second shock would occur—and if it did, its location could be predicted, at least to the point of saying it would occur along the known boundaries of the earth fault.

"There are three cities in its path," Professor Brewster pointed out, on a large map of the Japanese islands. "See? The fault curves down from Honshu, across the strait to Kyushu. It passes within a mile of Kitakyushu, down the coast through Sasebo, curves inland for a few miles, then back out to sea right through the middle of Nagasaki."

"And," queried Cooper, "if there is another shock, it'll be along that line?"

"In all probability."

There was another period of discussion, in which considerable pessimism about Brewster's prediction was expressed, but when no one offered an alternative suggestion, Cooper thanked the scientists for their assistance and left a dozen bewildered seismologists to the mercies of a high-ranking security man who demanded their signatures on pledges not to reveal where they had been or what they had discussed.

On a scrambled circuit, Cooper spoke with his assistant on Tinian.

"I'll get to High Command too," Cooper said, "but meanwhile, start the wheels moving. According to the seismologists, there's a fair chance there will be a second quake along a line from Hiroshima, down across the strait to Kyushu. The cities to cover are Nagasaki, Sasebo and Kitakyushu. Have you got that?"

"Got it," said the assistant.

In a matter of hours, B-29s carrying Terrain Fill Lights were orbiting the Japanese homeland. Flights of sixty B-29s carrying fire bombs flew to a point just out of Japanese radar range and circled until their fuel was low, then turned back to Tinian, passing their replacements who took up the boring standby duty. Rather than land with full bomb loads, the B-29s jettisoned their incendiaries into the sea.

August 8 came and went without sign of earthquake activity below the orbiting B-29s. Several times fighters rose from the airfields beneath, struggled into the thin air, gave up, and spiraled down without ever having reached the 35,000-foot altitude of the B-29s.

A jeep aircraft carrier had moved within sixty miles of the Japanese coast. Aboard it were stripped-down P-38s with special wing pods to carry the pulverized radioactive wastes.

As night fell, the vigil continued.

Back on Tinian, High Command waited nervously. So far Japan had not responded to the ultimatum given after Hiroshima. Leaflets had been printed and scattered over a dozen Japanese cities, warning them that they might be next on the atomic list. Among the cities were Sasebo, Kitakyushu, and Nagasaki.

Time was running out. The original plan to follow the first atomic bomb with another in quick succession was meant to convince the Japanese that the United States had an unlimited arsenal of the new weapons. That plan was dangerously near collapse.

The air crackled with radio messages: propaganda directed at the Japanese citizens urging them to prevail upon Japan's military leaders to surrender and prevent further destruction.

On the morning of August 9, 200,000 people went about their daily business in Nagasaki. Once, at 8:30 A.M., when a B-29 passed high overhead, the sirens wailed and the more cautious crowded into the caves that were used for air raid shelters.

A troubled man, Prefectural Governor Negano looked up at the departing airplane. The previous day he had conferred with the publisher of Nagasaki's newspaper, *Minyu*, Takejiro Nishioka, who had just returned from a visit to Hiroshima. Nishioka, still deeply troubled by what he had seen in the ruined city, urged that Nagasaki's entire population should take shelter at the approach of even a single bomber. This was the first confirmation Governor Negano had received indicating the truth of the American claims about their "atomic bomb." He felt a sense of relief as the distant B-29 flew away.

At 10:55 A.M. sirens blared again. Another B-29 was approaching. Some civilians went to the shelters; others, inured to danger, ignored the warning.

In a few minutes, when the bomber showed no signs of attacking, the city began to relax.

Then, at 10:58 A.M., a mighty shock struck Nagasaki.

To those in the shelters, it was as if they had been picked up and thrown against the cave walls. One survivor, Yoshida Koga, remembered only thinking, "Atomic bomb!"

The roof of a Catholic cathedral fell in and crushed more than a hundred worshipers at mass.

A waiting train was lifted from its tracks and hurled against a concrete abutment. Electric wires fell from above and sent thousands of volts through the metal cars. No one survived.

Fire was everywhere. Screaming people ran down the cluttered streets.

The B-29 passed overhead again. Now parachutes fell from it.

Terrified, thousands watched with horrid fascination as the parachutes drifted closer.

Suddenly there was a flash of light that seared through the valley like the explosion of a sun. Those looking directly at the parachutes saw only the beginning of a greenish-white brilliance and then, their optic nerves destroyed, never saw again.

Radio messages reached the flight of B-29s circling at sea, using the code name for Nagasaki, ordering, "Strike Daffodil."

The words sent sixty B-29s laden with fire bombs speeding toward Nagasaki. Aboard the jeep carrier, the pilot of a P-38 Lightning revved up the engines of his twin-fuselaged plane and prepared to take off.

By the time the bombers arrived over Nagasaki, the city was already dying. Those buildings that had not been destroyed by the earthquake were in flames. Thousands of refugees streamed toward the hills, many blinded by the TFL burst.

Other thousands were trapped under fallen wreckage. Their pleas for help assailed the ears of the fleeing refugees. Few were rescued; as the relentless flames crept over the tumbled buildings, countless voices rose in a frantic chorus of despair, then fell silent.

The B-29s came in at low level and salvoed their bomb loads into the flames below. Just as at Meetinghouse in Tokyo, where the technique had been perfected, the hundreds of small fires blended rapidly into one gigantic blaze, and within minutes the entire Urakami Valley was a furnace.

Shortly after noon, a black rain began falling on the city. A few moments before, a single P-38 had flown over Nagasaki, circling briefly before turning out to sea again.

The fire storm had created a pillar of smoke that rose ten miles above the city. It could be seen as far away as Sasebo.

By now Japanese intelligence experts in Tokyo had intercepted a radio message, supposedly from *Bock's Car*, the B-29 designated as the "bomb" ship:

> *Bombed Nagasaki 090158Z visually with no fighter opposition and no flak. Results technically successful but other factors involved make conference necessary before taking further steps. Visible effects about equal to Hiroshima. Trouble in airplane following delivery requires us to proceed to Okinawa. Fuel only to get to Okinawa.*

With trainloads of wounded arriving at Omura Naval Hospital, thirty miles north of Nagasaki, the Japanese high command was convinced that the atomic bomb had struck again.

Back on Tinian, *New York Times* reporter Bill Laurence was at his typewriter, composing a story of the Nagasaki raid given to him by crew members. It would win him the Pulitzer Prize. At no time was he aware the crew's report was false.

Collier's reporter Charles Kern also filed a story. Filled with details taken from his own mission to Tokyo, it revealed too much about the truth of the malfunctioning bomb and was killed by the censor.

In a Tokyo air raid shelter, well after midnight, members of the Japanese military and political leadership gathered and waited for Emperor Hirohito to appear. When he did, the Emperor listened to arguments for and against continuing the war.

General Yoshijiro Umezu, Chief of Staff of the Imperial Army, argued, "We can prevent the Americans from delivering the atomic bomb if we take proper antiaircraft measures."

Hirohito listened as another officer asked, "Can you promise that not a single *B-san* will get through the antiaircraft defenses? It would only take one bomber to destroy Tokyo."

Umezu equivocated, and finally admitted that he could not make such a promise.

When a vote was taken, the results were divided, and the meeting's moderator, Kantaro Suzuki, turned to the Emperor and said, "This group has been unable to agree. Your Imperial decision is requested."

Hirohito stood quietly. He looked around the silent bomb shelter before speaking.

The 124th Emperor of Japan said, "I have concluded that continuing the war will only result in the destruction of our nation. Those who wish to continue the struggle promised that new forces and weapons would be ready at Kujukurihama by June. It will soon be September, and even then we will not be ready for an American invasion. I cannot watch my innocent people suffer any longer. Ending the war is the only way to restore peace."

Held rigid and silent by discipline, the military men in the room nevertheless managed to show their despair.

"I feel tremendous grief," the Emperor went on, "thinking of those who have served so honorably. I see the faces of the soldiers and sailors who have died or been wounded in far-off lands. I see their families, who have lost their homes and often their lives in the bombing raids. It is painful for me to consider disarming our brave warriors. But it is more painful to consider allowing our nation to be destroyed. The time has come for us to bear the unbearable. I must swallow my tears and instruct the Foreign Minister to accept the Allied Proclamation as issued at Potsdam."

The Emperor turned and left the shelter without another word.

World War II was over.

Washington, D.C.—*August 14, Now*

"So that's it," I said.

"Mac," said General Rosy Cooper, "I've lived with this since 1945. And during all those years I've asked myself constantly —were we right? Not in tricking the Japanese to surrender. That saved millions of lives on both sides. But was it right to maintain the hoax?"

"Was it?"

He spread his hands. "We had to be sure some other nation wouldn't take advantage of our weakness to use their own bombs that *did* work."

"*If* they had such bombs."

"Would you take the risk of assuming they didn't?"

I looked away.

"Mac," Rosy said, "before you wrap this thing up, General Burton thinks you ought to go out to Swasey Proving Grounds and look around. Any chance of you flying to Utah?"

"I'm supposed to go out for the convention anyway. I guess I could take a look."

"Good," he said. "I hope you find what you're looking for."

I didn't answer. I was no longer sure I wanted to.

"Hugh," Celia said, packing, "how would you like it if I got out of the newspaper business for a while?"

Startled, I just kidded her. "How could we afford your tape recorders?"

309

"I'm serious."

"What would you do?"

"You forget Hugh Junior," she said. "While he's little, he's going to need a full-time mama. Besides, if I start going bananas I can always go back to work." Before I had quite taken all this in, she went on, "Anyway, it wouldn't be kosher to have a working wife in the White House, especially a writer type, would it?"

"Eleanor Roosevelt didn't do too bad," I said absentmindedly. "Listen, if we're going to make that three o'clock plane, we'd better get moving."

"I'm all set. Knowing you has been fun, Senator. We've lived out of some of the nicest suitcases."

"Still nervous about flying?"

"Flying doesn't bother me," she said. "It's *crashing* I'm afraid of." She held my arm. "Kiss?"

I turned to her. "Kiss."

Swasey Proving Grounds, Utah—*August 15, Now*

Brigadier General Maxwell Newton looked like something right out of the recruiting posters. He was tall and slender, ramrod-straight, with steel-gray hair along his temples.

Newton was CO of Swasey. Although President Nixon had cancelled bacteriological and toxin weapons research just a few years before, we were now obviously back in the germ business bigger than ever.

"The place is yours," said the General. "What do you want to see first?"

"What do you suggest?"

He picked up a small metal canister from his desk. "How about this?"

"It looks like one of the spray cans my wife uses on the rugs."

"Basically, that's what it is."

"What's in it?"

"This one's a dummy. The real thing holds 350 cc's of pure bacterial culture. One of our more successful is a mutation of pneumonic plague. Designated PP-9. It's airborne, of course, and this one canister could cover fifty or sixty square miles. Then, since human beings and animal life are carriers for some days before they show symptoms, they accelerate the spread of the disease."

"What's the recovery rate?"

"Negligible. Six to eight percent."

I was horrified.

"Not bad," he said.

"Very efficient."

Newton took it as a compliment. "Thank you. Now, as for delivery, we don't need ICBMs or expensive bombers. In fact, a single modified U-4 can penetrate enemy air space well above the range of their SAMs and scatter enough of these canisters to destroy a small nation such as Cuba. By taking advantage of the prevailing winds, ten such planes could knock out the Soviet Union." He picked up a slide rule. "And listen to this: even assuming a cost of around six thousand dollars for the culture, canister, parachute system, and delivery—and taking a minimum estimated kill of 200,000 per canister—our figures come out to less than three-tenths of a penny per kill."

He put down the slide rule. "That's hardly in a class with the cost of a nuclear missile, is it, Senator?"

In quick succession Newton took me through the laboratories testing nerve gas and various toxins, and one heavily sealed building which specialized in viruses that do not exist in nature. "We're leery about these," he admitted. "If they got loose, they might work *too* well. There's no guarantee they'd stop at the enemy's borders."

I looked through a window at what appeared to be a babies' nursery. Dozens of cribs filled the room. In each a tiny form huddled under the sheets. Looking closer, I saw that they were baby monkeys.

"We use monkeys because their nervous system is so similar to our own," Newton explained.

One of them raised up in its crib, stared straight at me, and, waving its tiny arms, began to scream.

"Don't let that bother you," said General Newton. "These animals suffer from a form of culture shock. They've never seen their parents, so they undergo transference. Happens all the time. Some of the ward technicians get real shook up by it."

"By what?" I asked numbly.

"What that little fella's doing," Newton said, a kind of paternal pride in his voice. "He knows something's wrong, he hurts, and he's crying to you for help."

"Why me?"

"Because he thinks you're his mama."

I called Washington from the officers' club. I don't even remember everything I said. President Foster told me to have a couple of drinks, said, "I know it's tough when you finally realize what we're up against. I'll send Jake Dobsen out to talk with you."

That was nice. The man I had been defying for two weeks was now patting my shoulder. I took his advice, had three drinks and no lunch, and at sunset was back in Salt Lake City, walking alone and wondering why I didn't want to go back to the hotel and face Celia.

The drinks had hit me hard. My legs felt trembly, and it was as if my feet were sinking into pillows. I had a sensation of falling backward whenever I stopped moving. Something had to be wrong besides the liquor, but I seemed unable to cope with it.

I found a cocktail lounge and went in.

"Scotch," I said.

"Sorry, mister. You've had enough."

I stood, weaving slightly. "I think you're right."

Outside, night had come. How had I gotten so drunk on only three drinks? As I walked my feet sank deeper into those pillows. Then I sat down in a doorway to rest.

Rough hands pulled me up. I knew from the coldness in the air and the quietness of the night that I had lost several hours.

"Come on, buddy," said a man's voice. "Move it."

"Use your bombs," I said. "Use your gas. Kill everybody. But you can't make *me* do it."

"Let's take him in," said the voice.

"Wait a minute," said another. "It's Senator McGavin."

There was more talk, a blurred ride in a car, a confusion of sight and sounds that must have been an elevator, and then a door opened and I saw Celia's frightened eyes looking down at me.

"Hi," I said, stuttering a little. "Sorry I'm late."

Salt Lake City, Utah—*August 16, Now*

"What's that?" I asked.

"Vodka and tomato juice. Get up, Hugh. Jake Dobsen's been calling every ten minutes."

I went into the shower, sipping at the drink. "Sorry. I must have had one too many. But it never hit me like that before."

"Use the cold water," she said, turning it on.

I yelped. "You're being strangely unsympathetic."

"You deserve it. I hate to hit a man when he's hung over, but this time I'm really mad. What's happening to you? You're falling apart, and every time I try to get close and help out, you shove me away. When you get through with Jake, I want some answers."

Remembering the little monkey, I said, "No you don't, baby."

313

"Don't patronize me, you son of a bitch!"

"What?"

"Oh, the hell with you," she said. She turned away, but not before I saw that she was crying. I reached for her, but she twisted away. I followed her, drying off.

"Ceil, I'm sorry."

"You don't trust me."

(You chew in your sleep!)

When I touched her shoulder, she pulled back. "Sorry," I said again, and went in to dress.

Twenty minutes later, in one of the Salt Palace's small offices, I shook hands with the Senate Majority Leader.

"I'm sorry I kept you waiting, Jake. I'm not feeling too well."

He nodded. "It's got you by the horns, hasn't it?"

"My God, why does Foster let that crazy bastard keep his command? He's Doctor Death. He *enjoys* it. Do you know he's got the cost per kill figured down to three-tenths of a cent?"

"All right. But he's precisely the kind of officer we need to run a place like Swasey. Any ordinary man would cave in under the moral responsibility. But all Newton understands is taking orders. He's programmed to react when the button is pressed."

"Do we have such a button, Jake? I know Foster reactivated the CBW program, but I never realized it was that close to being operational."

"We've got the button," he said. Then, "I tried to warn you off." He paused, and when his voice came again it was filled with an incredible sadness and anger. "Ah, Hugh, why couldn't you leave it alone?"

"Jake, that stuff I saw out at Swasey is ten times worse than any atomic bomb. So why are we spending half of our defense budget on delivery systems for something that doesn't exist?"

"Do you *want* us to open the Swasey arsenal?"

I shut my eyes. "My God, no!"

"Then we have to keep on trying to solve the Jesus Factor.

And until we do, we've got to keep on pretending our bomb *does* work. Otherwise, how would you sleep at night, knowing that Cuba, or the U.A.R., or Peru, for Christ's sake, were doing the same kind of arithmetic General Newton does, figuring out the cost per kill with the United States as the target? Can't you see that the only thing preventing certain two-bit dictatorships from threatening the world with extinction is their own fear of nuclear retaliation? Take that away and we're at the mercy of anyone who can sneak an airplane past our radar."

His words hit me with the simple, unreserved conviction that only truth carries. Jake was right. We were all still animals in the cave, straining at the leash. Released, we would fling ourselves at each other, rending and tearing until only the strongest survived. Civilization, morality, justice, love? Words used by the weak to convince themselves they are sheltered from the wrath of the strong.

Had I come so far to find only this?

"What are you going to do?" Jake asked.

There was a distant ringing in my ears. I felt dizzy.

"Hugh? Don't you hear me?"

What's happening? Why is the world getting so far away? Who are all those faces? Is it you, Jack?

"Hugh, what's the matter?"

And Barbara, whose hair will never be long now? Your face is before me too.

"Dammit, Hugh, snap out of it!"

Phil Hepburn. And a small Japanese man named Nakamura.

"Get a doctor!"

And Tim . . . I can see you the clearest.

"Senator, can you hear me?"

The bomb bay alarm! It's ringing!

Celia. Help me.

Please.

The doctor was closing his black leather bag. "You've been under considerable strain lately, haven't you?"

"Quite a bit."

"Luckily, the human organism is smarter than we give it credit for. When you overload the circuits, a fuse gives way. Better than burning out the wiring, wouldn't you say?"

"I guess so."

Jake Dobsen, looking worried, said, "How're you feeling?"

"Tired."

"Get as much rest as you can," said the doctor. I thanked him and he left.

"Sorry, Jake," I said.

"The doc gave you a shot of something."

"I want a press conference," I said. He stared at me. "Don't worry. I'm on your side now. But I've got to go on record before the convention."

He picked up the telephone, spoke quietly. When he hung up, he said, "We can go down to Conference Room A right now. The cameras are all set up for Artie Rand."

The reporters were waiting. I didn't waste any time.

"Gentlemen of the press," I said, "and fellow Americans everywhere. You all know my commitment to an immediate de-escalation of the arms race. I do not apologize for that position, but I am here now to tell you that I now believe it was based more on idealism than reality; more on hope than good sense; more on ignorance than careful appraisal of the facts. I am here today to admit that I have been wrong."

Several photographers pushed in closer.

"I was wrong," I reported. "Perhaps one day this nation will be safe without the nuclear deterrence that has been our first line of defense. I hope so. But such a day has not yet arrived. And until it does, we must remain strong, ready to protect ourselves whenever—and however—it becomes necessary. Thank you."

As I stepped down, the reporters mobbed me.

"Did you and the President make some kind of deal?"

"Senator, are you trying to soothe the industrial states?"

"Does this mean you're changing your stand on the ABMs?"

"No comment," I said.

"Senator," said an attendent at a desk in the rear of the room, "your wife is on the phone."

"Hello?" I said. "Ceil? I can't talk now, but—"

"You don't have to talk," she said. "Just listen."

"I've got reporters all around."

"I just bet you have. Well, hang on, this won't take long, and then you can go back to your adoring public. I never completely agreed with your position on the bomb, but at least I thought you were honest about it."

"Wait until I get there," I said. "I'll explain—"

"Explain to Foster," she cried. "Don't worry, I won't jeopardize your shot at the White House. I know that means more to you than anything in the world, including your own self-respect. But don't look for me when you get home."

"Ceil, listen—"

"You sold yourself out and you sold me out. You sold out Junior, or whoever the hell it is growing in there. Goddamn you, McGavin, why did you pick this particular year to knock me up?"

Before I could answer, she had hung up.

The suite was empty when I got there. She had packed rapidly, leaving tissues and a torn stocking on the thick rug. In one corner lay the little velvet mouse.

I sat down on the bed. The room seemed very large and empty.

"Hugh?"

I looked up. It was the Vice-President.

"Come in, Art. Forgive the mess. Ceil had to leave suddenly."

I offered him a drink and he declined. "Hugh, it's all yours," he told me. "The President's going to nominate you personally and ask for a vote of acclamation."

"Because I backed off?"

"That wouldn't swing him, you know that. No, I don't know just what it was but he told me he's finally sure of you."

"All right," I sighed, "I know what he meant. But he's wasting his time."

"Why?"

"Because I won't be here. Listen, I can't explain, but tell

317

Foster I said there are some men who are able to press the button and some who aren't. I finally figured out which one I am. You're the one for the job. You can tell him I said that, too."

"I don't want it," said the Vice-President.

"Maybe not," I said. "But you'll take it. Because you see, you *are* the right man. Not me. I never was. I just didn't know it before." I stood up. "I'll campaign for you, you know that, but right now I've got to go."

"I'm going to the Salt Palace," he offered.

"I'm not," I said, heading for the door.

"Where can we reach you?"

"I'll let you know. Right now I've got to catch a plane before it gets away."

Puzzled, he said, "It must be important."

"It is," I said softly.

"Then I hope you make it."

I looked back at him. Already, he seemed more sure of himself. Had he always really wanted the job after all, been afraid to reach for it because he imagined himself surrounded by giants?

The door closed behind me. "Good luck, you poor bastard," I said. "You'll need it."

Afterword

Although I, as the author, take full responsibility for the fictional story of THE JESUS FACTOR, I owe a great deal to help given to me directly and indirectly by many.

Of course, there really *was* a 509th Composite Group, assigned to the real 20th Air Force, and that group *did* carry out the atomic bomb mission. But the characters and events in *my* version of the 509th never existed—there was no such airplane as *The Busted Flush;* her crew is drawn entirely from my imagination; the air strikes over Tokyo and Kobe, and the other events in the book (including those in which actual historic figures are made to appear) relating to those air strikes, are my invention.

Thus I have had to eliminate, for purposes of this story, the real commander of the 509th—Colonel Paul Tibbets—and the real commander of the 20th Air Force, General Curtis LeMay. Both were kind enough to read portions of the manuscript and offer their suggestions, for which I thank them. I thank, also, the dozens of other Air Force personnel, the scientists and reporters who helped me in the extensive research for this book.